DEDICATION

This book is dedicated to my mother, Mary Lampert,
who lived just long enough….

Disclaimer

* * *

Credits

Cover design by Damon Za.
Cover photo by Brian Schade/Restless Wings Photography.

Chapter 1

IT SHOULD HAVE BEEN IMPOSSIBLE. All of it.

Dr. Janet Hogan pushed her virtual reality goggles onto the top of her head and rubbed her tired eyes. She'd been standing so long her back and feet ached. The weeks and weeks of long days, longer nights, and weekend work in the VR lab nine stories up at the University of Texas Southwestern Medical Center were taking their toll. Under other circumstances, she wouldn't have minded. She and her team were discovering hundreds of new nucleic acids, proteins, and enzymes. That was exciting. But they were showing up in people's cells without explanation. They violated so much of what was known about human genetics and biology.

They simply couldn't be.

But they were.

"Sometimes cancers go into spontaneous remission and we don't know why," she'd said during a team meeting six weeks earlier. "But not all of them, not all at once, not all around the country. Not to mention that

AIDS, diabetes, and so many other diseases are disappearing too."

They'd gotten their samples from patients at the hospitals on the campus near downtown Dallas. The people had been seriously ill; some were terminal. Then they'd recovered. Their doctors couldn't explain what had happened: their treatments hadn't changed.

Janet's mother back in Raleigh, North Carolina, was one of the surprise survivors. A month ago, she'd had end-stage, metastatic lung cancer. Tumors throughout her body. Even her targeted, personalized therapies were no longer slowing the disease in its haste to kill her. She was taking morphine to control her pain and make her final days comfortable—physically, anyway.

She should have been dead by now.

Instead, she was not just getting better, she was cured, no tumors anywhere. She was at home, putting on the weight she'd lost to the disease and the treatments.

She called it a miracle.

Janet kept waiting for the other shoe to drop—for the word to come that her mother had relapsed or gotten a bad test result—despite everything she was seeing in her own lab. It was stress she didn't want and didn't need, but couldn't avoid.

There were thousands of reported cases just like that. The numbers were growing every day.

Janet had to understand what was happening. And why. And how.

She needed to understand soon, too, before teams at other research centers figured it out. They were getting similar results. She'd seen the lab notes and data they'd posted on the cloud.

Now a new impossibility was floating in the VR space in front of her. She scrubbed her face with her silver mesh VR gloves, then rubbed her eyes again.

Dr. Ellanna Barnes put a hand on Janet's shoulder. "You okay?" asked the lab's post-doctoral researcher. She had also been Janet's best friend since medical school.

"You bet," Janet replied in a voice too bright and chipper. "Never better!" She scowled and stuck out her tongue. "Bleeah."

"Me too," Ellanna said, rubbing Janet's arm. "The sim's right, though. I've checked every step. The individual reactions are all right—"

"But the results are all wrong."

"You don't believe me?"

"I believe *you*." Janet waved at the VR space. "I don't believe *that*."

She sighed and pulled the goggles down onto her nose. A simulated telomere, the end-cap of a chromosome, rose out of the floor in front of her. The narrow ladder of little red, yellow, green, and blue balls connected by gray bars rose almost to the ceiling in a tight spiral. Before she'd stopped the simulation, it had been growing before her eyes.

"Telomeres sometimes grow in sperm cells," Janet said, "even get rebuilt to their initial lengths. I get that, but—"

"Not like this, in kidney cells." Ellanna waved her hand around the lab. "Or liver, bone, or blood. They ought to get shorter every time the cell divides. Once they get too short, the cell stops dividing and eventually dies. That's Chromosomes 101."

Janet walked up to the telomere to touch spots here and there along its length and read the data blocks that popped into view. "But instead they build back to full length and stay there when the cell divides."

"I don't get it, either." Ellanna adjusted her VR goggles. "I mean, I get the mechanics, but not the reason. It's crazy."

Janet rattled her thumb and fingers against the leg of her slacks. "The cells could become immortal." She turned to her friend. "That could mean all sorts of trouble. Cells have to die for the body to stay healthy."

"Unless they don't need to divide so often."

"Maybe, but that would create other problems. If cells live longer, do people live longer too? What would that mean?" The lab seemed to have gotten colder.

"They're already living longer. Your mother for one."

Janet grimaced, then looked away. "Oh, good."

"Janet!"

"Sorry." She shrugged. "You're *sure* the sim's right?"

Ellanna slid a finger across her virtual control panel and ninety percent of the telomere disappeared. "This is where the regrowth started. When you're ready, I'll walk you through it."

Janet closed her eyes for a moment, took a deep breath, then said, "Go ahead."

* * *

The next afternoon, Janet twisted the top of the VR joystick in her right hand and pushed the other one forward to virtually fly down into the reaction site of a simulated ribosome. Satya Pramanasudh, her lab manager, flew along with her. Janet glanced back to make sure they were staying ahead of an approaching messenger RNA molecule. The surface model they were running magnified both molecules to millions of times their actual size. The massive ribosome looked like a Technicolor Texas thunderhead. It seethed and shuddered, towering above their heads and disappearing far below their feet.

The nucleic acid, a long splatter of color suspended in the air, arrowed in, bringing the recipe for a protein that had been unknown just days ago. By themselves, the protein and mRNA would have been major discoveries, but they were just two entries on the lab's ever-growing list.

The ribosome uncurled to widen the cleft between its two subunits, and the nucleic acid's leading tip slid in. Janet twisted the top of her left joystick to spin around so she and Satya could back in ahead of the mRNA. She laughed, surprising herself.

"What?" Satya asked. "You're blushing."

"It looks sexual."

"It does." Satya chuckled. "Tab A goes into Slot B, there's a lot of grinding and thrusting, then out pops Baby C. Only it doesn't take nine months to get results."

"We've been spending way too much time in the lab, haven't we?"

"So true."

As she had been for weeks, she was using these simulations to map new reaction pathways and their results while Gerardo Santangelo, her graduate student, finished cataloging the changes in the samples. Ellanna stayed focused on the telomere regrowth she'd discovered. Satya helped wherever she was needed.

"There's so much going on," Satya said. "The more we look, the more we find. It could take forever to figure it all out."

Yeah, Janet thought, *but we don't have forever*. She slid them sideways to let the front of the mRNA pass, then followed it into the reaction site to watch the amino acids in the coding region, each as big as a basketball, play their roles in creating the new protein.

The nucleic acid chugged through the cleft like a cog railway train climbing a hill. All around it, the blue and red fields of negative and positive electrostatic potentials shone like Northern Lights. They crackled and hissed in the scientists' earbuds as they neutralized or reinforced each other, driving or blocking individual reactions.

Beyond the mRNA but still inside the cleft, free amino acid molecules answering the siren call of the electric fields, flowed in from the simulated cellular fluid, jostled for position, and settled into the proper sequence in the chain that would become the new protein.

The previous week, they'd gone to the office of Dr. Mohamed Sayid, the Egyptian-born chairman of the genetics department. During the meeting, Ellanna had asked, "Who's going to believe this? What if… no."

"What?" he said.

Ellanna's silver hoop earrings glittered against her dark skin. She turned her tablet computer around and around in her lap as she worked up her courage. "What if this is happening in normal cells too? Or… whole organisms? What then?"

"Don't worry about that now," Sayid said. "If you can prove these results, they'll make your careers."

"Yeah, if," Janet said. "What if it just looks like we're right? We've only seen this *in silico*, not *in vitro* or *in vivo*."

"That's all right."

"Until someone finds that one little detail we got wrong, or shows that the sim messed up the reactions. Maybe there's a mistake in the databases. We haven't even gotten to the cellular level."

"*We* haven't," Satya said, "but the real world has. That's the in vivo you're looking for and the reason we're studying it."

Janet took a pen from Sayid's desk and tapped it against her hand. "So if our data generalize, the implications are huge: the end of disease, the end of aging? El's right: who's going to believe that?"

"We have to be sure of our results then," Satya said.

Janet glanced at her and tossed the pen back onto her boss's desk. "You bet. Nothing to it." *Better listen*, she thought. *Satya's been doing this for ten years. No, fifteen: since 2020. El and I don't have ten between us. It's G's first year. We could make a mistake and never know it.*

"Satya's right," Sayid said. "Results *and* conclusions, which you're not getting while you're in here. Back to work."

Back in the lab, Satya asked, "Did you catch that?"

Janet dragged her attention back to the simulation. "What? Sorry, I was daydreaming." She looked around and discovered she'd missed at least a dozen mutations on the new protein, each marked by a yellow glow.

"We have many more samples to go through, but if you need a break...." She put her hand on Janet's arm.

"I'm all right." *Have to keep going.* "Just give me a minute." She closed her eyes, bowed her head, and crossed her hands in front of her. She concentrated on her breathing and let her mind clear so she could draw up the energy.

Satya took notes and checked references while she waited. When Janet opened her eyes again, the older woman asked, "Ready?" At Janet's nod, she tapped a button on her control panel to restart the simulation. They let the small changes pass by, just marking them as they went. When the most important mutation appeared, the yellow differential glow brightened.

Janet asked the VR system for a projection of the mutations' effects. Her shoulders slumped when it displayed the message, "Insufficient data." *Should've known. Too early to ask.*

Twenty minutes later, they were done. Janet pulled down her goggles, draped them around her neck, leaving the earbuds in place, and sank into an office chair by the wall while Satya took care of the last details. She ran her fingers through her curly brown hair to fluff away the goggle-head caused by the head strap.

For the first time in months, she noticed the lab's dim lighting, gray walls and black ceiling, the faint hiss of the air conditioning, and the whine of the computers' cooling fans. *It's like a cave,* she thought, *or a—* She smothered that comparison. Watching her lab partners lightened her mood. They looked like mimes, wearing ski goggles and puffy gloves rather than face-paint, berets, and striped shirts as they bent and stretched, pushed, pulled, and poked at thin air, or strode around the room holding bundles of nothing. *I shouldn't laugh,* she thought. *I look the same way.*

Gerardo, standing at the workstation across the room, reached up to pull a simulated molecule into the analysis system's virtual input port. He gripped the air, then brought his hand down toward the desk, stopped, and let go. A chime tone sounded in Janet's ears.

"There's another one," he said.

"What is it this time?" Satya asked, standing near the center of the VR space.

"Pancreatic."

"Black female, age 60," Ellanna said, leaning over his shoulder to read the display. "Family history positive, mutation sequence was 6A, rated Stage III when the reference sample was taken. She's clean now."

Satya took a winding path across the room to join them. "Any more to do?"

Gerardo touched his controls, then let out a relieved sigh. "That was the last one."

With a sigh of her own, Janet put her goggles back on. She stood and walked across the room, weaving as Satya had among the simulacra that hung in the open space. "Let's see the summary." *How many more impossibilities are there this time? Are we ready for this? Am I?*

CHAPTER 2

JANET SQUINTED AGAINST THE GLARE of the spotlight that pinned her at the podium on the auditorium stage of the Simmons Research Building. Her mouth was dry and her palms wet. She wished they were the other way around. During their rehearsals, Dr. Sayid's critiques had felt like surgery without anesthesia, but in the end they had given her some confidence that she could get through the press conference announcing the team's discoveries without fainting. Her shoulders were still tight, but she'd eased her death grip on the podium's wood sides.

The small stage was the focus of an arc that formed a third of a circle; the gray-green seats rose in steep rows. Sayid, Ellanna, and Dr. Michael Farinelli, Janet's boyfriend and an epidemiologist at UT-Southwestern, sat at a table at the center of the stage. A white cloth with the medical center's logo covered it. The reporters occupied less than a quarter of the seats but that was a big in-person crowd for a scientific announcement. By far the larger group was following it online.

So far, the reporters in the room and on the web had gone easy on Janet. They watched the 3D simulations and videos and typed notes, even when her technical material was going far over their heads.

"Wait a minute, wait a minute," a reporter called from the audience.

Janet looked up from the display mounted in the podium to find the man who'd spoken.

"Antonio Corolli, Total Web News," he announced as he stood up. His wavy black hair and thick moustache glittered against his olive complexion. "Where did these bugs, these viruses, come from, Dr. Hogan? Who created them? What government lab did they escape from? What aren't you telling us?"

He pointed his phone at Janet to record her answer, even though his network's camera, like all the others, was connected to the microphone on the podium, and the announcement was being streamed live.

What? Janet thought. *Is he serious? Wait: breathe, take your time.* She picked up a glass of water from the table, took a sip, then set it down and looked at him again. She kept her voice level. "I don't have any idea where they came from or who might have created them. In fact, their interactive pathways are so complex, I don't see how anyone could have designed them."

"But they spread around the world and nobody noticed?" Corolli said. "How do you expect us to believe that?"

"We were shocked too," Janet said. "The viruses are mutated forms of ones that had infected insects, birds, and plants. When Dr. Barnes identified the first one and told us it used to infect an insect called a European corn borer, we were just as surprised as you are. As far as we can tell, though, each virus is benign by itself, so no one would have noticed. It takes all five of them working together to produce these results."

"Let me interject something here," Sayid said. He waited as the cameras swung over to him. "I've worked in viral research for over 30 years. Nobody I know could have done this, not even the Nobel laureate I worked for. I've never seen anything like it."

"But you can't prove they didn't get out of some secret rogue lab somewhere," Corolli said. "Or that they were a failed bioterror attack."

"You've been watching too many bad sci-fi movies," Sayid shot back. "If you think that happened, I'll leave it to you to prove it. We have enough to do."

A rustle of amused conversations swept the room.

"So as far as you're concerned, there's no chance this pandemic is the result of some experiment gone wrong."

"I didn't say that. Dr. Hogan, please go on."

After Janet finished and answered a few technical questions from the science reporters, a woman with collar-length red hair sitting near the front of the auditorium raised her hand. "Lisa Lange, Global News," she said when Janet pointed to her. "Let me see if I can boil this down to the basics. You're saying that, one, these viruses are curing a lot of diseases that have plagued us for… well, forever. Two, we're immune to those diseases now: we can't catch them at all. And three, the viruses stop aging. So, have we become immortal?"

Watch it, Janet thought. *Sayid said they'd try to put words in your mouth.* She stroked the rim of the podium with her hands. "Just from a genetic point of view, with so many mutations being reversed or repaired and telomeres being rebuilt, our cells might be immortalized." She heard Sayid grunt and glanced to her left in time to see him shake his head. She hurried to add, "We don't know how these results will translate to the whole body but being immune to cancer doesn't mean you're immune to drowning or dying in a traffic accident."

Lisa said, "But if we don't have to worry about disease anymore, can't we live forever, if we're careful?"

"Maybe if you hid in some kind of cocoon."

"But then you'd probably die of boredom," Ellanna said.

The reporters laughed.

"Or reruns," Janet added.

The reporters laughed again, harder.

"Seriously, can you be that careful that long?" Ellanna said. "Forever's a really long time."

Janet said, "Look, these are initial results. There's a lot more research to do, but so far there's no evidence that these viruses are a panacea."

"Just one more thing," Lisa said. "I've been reporting from a refugee camp in Somalia. I just got back. The conditions were awful, as you can imagine. If those refugees got just enough food and water, are you saying they could survive in that kind of environment for hundreds of years?" Memories of what she and her videographer Oriel Salvador had experienced—the heat that sucked away strength, the stench of the latrines and the unwashed bodies, the children's bellies distended from near-starvation, the diseases the camp doctors struggled to treat, the desperation, the death—flickered through her mind and she begged silently for some hint of hope.

"I don't know," Janet replied. "We've been researching genetic and cellular processes, not adaptation to extreme conditions or nutritional restriction. I don't even know whether these viruses have spread to Somalia."

"Where *have* they spread to?" Corolli called.

"I'll take that one," Michael said. "We know they're in most of the northern hemisphere, and Australia and New Zealand. Reports are coming in from the rest of the world but they're still too spotty for us to have a clear picture."

Janet flashed him a grateful smile.

"So given what you've just told Miss Lange," Corolli said, "and what she's reported, could these bugs be giving whites some kind of genetic advantage, some fountain of youth, while the rest of the world suffers?"

Janet gaped at him. *Haven't we gotten over that?* She glanced at Ellanna, whose expression showed she was as shocked as Janet.

Lisa scowled at the other reporter, who smirked. Returning her attention to the stage, she asked, "Didn't you say earlier that you've found the viruses in people of all races?"

"That's right," Janet said.

"So then," Lisa continued, smiling sweetly, "this white supremacist idea is nothing but, um, hot air."

"There's no evidence to support a racial hypothesis," Michael said. "That data's unequivocal. No doubts at all."

* * *

As they rode the elevator back to their fifth floor lab after the press conference, Ellanna said, "Can you believe that one guy's questions?"

"Total Web News," Sayid said, shaking his head. "He was a piece of work. Total Web Distortion would be more like it."

"Totally Whacked Nutso, if you ask me," Ellanna said. "Rogue government lab? Shit. There's something going on between him and that red-haired chick too. I thought she was going to call him an asshole right in front of everybody. *That* would have made total web news."

Sayid chuckled. "Oh, she did but I don't think it was news to anyone but us."

Ellanna nudged Janet. "Reruns. That was good."

Grinning, Janet put her arm around Michael's waist and hugged him. "Thanks for helping."

"Of course," he said and leaned down to give her a quick kiss.

"Anyway, that's done," Sayid said as the elevator doors opened. "You lovebirds will be back to work tomorrow instead of messing with this media stuff. Next week at the latest."

* * *

Lisa and Oriel had been in Dallas less than a day after their flights from Africa. Hung over, dehydrated, and jetlagged, Lisa ached all over. Her head throbbed. She'd whined all the way from the hotel about how much makeup she had to use to hide the bags under her eyes, what the humidity was doing to her hair, how she hadn't had time to get it cut.

Oriel had let her bitch. It was her way of fighting off how bad she felt so that when they shot the stand-up, she'd be the perky but professional reporter her audience and fans admired.

A huge yawn caught her by surprise as she stood next to her seat in the auditorium. She blushed when some of the reporters around her laughed. To her right, Corolli called out, "What's the matter? Someone keep you up last night?" For a moment, her face darkened; then, without looking in his direction, she stretched, holding her arms straight out from her sides, the middle finger of her right hand extended. She held the pose, her eyes fixed on the stage, then dropped her arms and casually turned her back. Whispered conversations scuttled around them.

"Welcome back to civilization," Oriel said through her earpiece.

"Why didn't you tell me that son of a bitch was here?" she asked through her microphone.

"I didn't see him 'til he farted—I mean, asked his first question. Sorry."

She turned to face him where he was standing above her on the aisle running across the middle of the auditorium. "At least he managed to show the world what a jackass he is. Again."

"Don't get too smug." Oriel detached the camera from its tripod. "He has his fans. Where do you want to do the stand-up?"

Lisa looked around the room. Other reporters were using the stage as a backdrop. "Outside." She hooked her thumb over her shoulder. "That garden we saw when we came in."

When they walked out onto the second-floor courtyard, Lisa picked one of the round, dark gray marble patio tables. Oriel set up his tablet and scrolled through the recorded video, marking the sequences she would want. After working with her for ten years, he knew her preferences, at least when it came to her reporting. He allowed himself a wry smile. *She even stayed awake, so I won't have to show her what she missed.*

He glanced up when he realized he wasn't hearing her rehearsing her lines. The scent of her perfume drifted down over his right shoulder as she watched him work.

"Don't you dare show our favorite asshole," she said. Years earlier, with a few lucky guesses, Corolli had scooped her on a story she'd been struggling to put together for months about corruption in a multi-state mental health program. He'd never let her forget it.

Oriel chuckled. "I can make it look like they were answering you instead of him."

"No," she said, "I've got something better. Let's shoot the lede before I start to sweat."

By the time she'd finished refreshing her make-up, he was waiting at the camera. She took her place at just the right spot on the sidewalk, glanced up at the sun, checking its angle toward her face, and turned left a little.

"Immortality," she said to the camera. "It's been humanity's dream for thousands of years. Today at the University of Texas Southwestern Medical Center in Dallas, scientists announced it may be within reach.

"According to Dr. Janet Hogan and her colleagues, five new viruses have spread around the world. By themselves, she claims, each one is harmless. But when a person is infected with all five, the viruses end aging, cure AIDS, cancer, and other serious diseases—even the flu and the common cold. They fix deadly mutations in our genes. In short, they make immortality possible.

"The implications are breathtaking, the possibilities endless. If other scientists confirm these early results, they will change human society more than any other discovery ever has.

"Have you wondered what life will be like a hundred years from now? Or five hundred? Get ready—you might be on your way to finding out."

CHAPTER 3

SARAH GREEN-DALE BURST FROM THE ELEVATOR into the reception area of the seventh story office suite of Save America From Every Threat, Inc., in Washington, D.C. She ignored the LED spotlights, color-balanced to match natural sunlight, which brightened to improve visibility across the threshold, and the recorded voice that warned her to be careful as she crossed the gap between the elevator car and the floor. Long, angry strides carried her, fists clenched, arms rigid against her sides, across the hypoallergenic organic cotton carpet.

Her afternoon meeting with the new National Institutes of Health Director, Dr. Roland Graves, had been a disaster. After years of effort, she thought SAFE-T had finally gotten the NIH to put in place the disease surveillance system they'd been demanding. And then.... *The nerve!* she fumed. *How could he possibly say, in the office—in the face—of the senator who chairs the committee that funds him, that he still didn't have enough money and people? Fool! Charlene will kill him for that.*

"There you are," Gayle Forrester said. SAFE-T's chief statistician rose from the overstuffed chair in the lobby to intercept her boss.

Sarah glared at Gayle. *Bet she's been there for an hour, waiting to pounce.* "Not now," she said as she skirted the padded edges of the receptionist's desk.

The hallway door beeped as it swung open. Gayle hustled to follow on stumpy legs. The thirty extra pounds she'd never been able to get rid of, despite Sarah's nagging, made her pant.

"I've found something that's probably concerning," she said, brushing a thick hand through her collar-length white hair. "It could be very important."

"'*Probably* concerning? *Could* be?' Do you have percentage values for that?"

Gayle ignored the remark and plunged on, holding out her tablet as she hurried to keep up. "It relates to the death and injury data I've been tracking. Dr. Bowersox agreed you should see it."

Sarah heaved a melodramatic sigh. *What part of "not now" didn't you understand?* "Summarize it for me." *And then go away.*

"Geneticists in Texas," Gayle puffed. "They were studying causes of unexplained remission in morbid cancer patients and—"

"Tell me the time, don't build me a watch."

Gayle tried to keep her composure. "They think we might have become immortal."

Sarah stopped so suddenly Gayle bounced off the wall as she dodged her boss. When she recovered her balance and turned around, she took an involuntary step backward.

Sarah planted her fists on her hips. "Since when did the *National Enquirer* become a reliable source?"

"This... this is real. It was just published in *Science* magazine and they had a press conference." Gayle held out her tablet again. "Just watch the report. It won't take long."

Sarah refused to take the computer. She wanted to see whether the statistician would hold her ground, knowing she'd back down if her position was weak. More to the point, Sarah didn't want to deal with something so outlandish.

Gayle didn't budge.

Sarah took the tablet. "Tell me how this relates to us."

"It's all there. Just run the video." Gayle clasped her hands in front of her, trying not to wring them.

Sarah pinned the woman to the wall with her eyes, then turned her attention to the screen. The video clip was from Global News. Her frown deepened: they hadn't been SAFE-T's friend, sometimes questioning its motives and methods. The caption said the reporter was Lisa Lange.

When the report ended, Gayle asked, "What do you think?"

"What do *you* think?"

"Well, if this is right...." She gestured at the computer. "I mean, if she didn't distort what the scientists said too much. For starters, how are we going to feed everyone?"

"That's not our issue. We've got food and farm safety mostly under control." *Mostly.*

"Where's everyone going to live?"

"Okay, construction safety needs more work—"

"And how will they get around?"

"Yes, yes, I know. Traffic safety, airlines, all that. This is old news. You're wasting my time, Dr. Forrester. What does this mean to me?"

"You're missing the big picture, Sarah. What I'm... ah...." Gayle sneezed into the sleeve of her blouse. "I'm trying...." She sneezed again.

"Bless you," someone said in a tenor voice from behind Sarah.

She turned. "Hello, Kenneth."

"Are you abusing Gayle again?" Ken Bowersox was Sarah's deputy. She forgave him his daily fashion *faux pas*, a striped shirt conflicting with twill trousers today, and twenty years out of date, round, wire-rimmed glasses. He'd co-founded SAFE-T with her and ran the organization day-to-day while she did the outside work.

Gayle sniffled. "It's just allergies."

Bowersox's expression told both women he knew better.

"Maybe *you* can explain why this is so important," Sarah said.

He took her arm, turned her toward her office, and nodded for Gayle to follow them. "As Dr. Forrester said, think big picture. If the reports are right—and more important, if the scientists are right—what they've found makes everything we do more vital."

Sarah waved the tablet in front of her. "You don't believe this immortality stuff, do you?"

"No, but if you listen carefully, that's not what the scientists said. The reporter hedged too."

"They said their viruses correct genetic damage." Sarah turned and handed the computer back to Gayle. "All kinds? Can they prove that?"

Gayle said, "I read their report and watched part of the announcement while I was waiting. I didn't understand the genetics but the data they provided were strong... statistically, anyway."

"But have you talked to a real scientist about it?" Sarah asked as she strode through the door into her office. *Maybe that'll make her go away. I don't have time for this.*

Gayle sneezed again.

"Sarah," Bowersox warned quietly.

Sarah crossed the room and sat on the front edge of her desk, arms crossed.

Gayle stopped just inside the door. "I did, and—"

"So it's been published in a big-time magazine. So what?" Sarah asked. "Scientists have been fooled by clever frauds before. And reporters going to a news conference doesn't mean anything. They're always suckers for a pretty face and a splashy story. Isn't anyone saying this is too good to be true?"

Gayle dug the toe of one shoe into the carpet. "There was one guy who claimed it was all a government experiment gone wrong."

Bowersox, settled into a comfortable slouch on the sofa with one foot on the coffee table, snorted. "Sounds like our buddy Corolli again."

Gayle nodded.

Sarah stood and walked around the desk, its Spartan top bare as usual. She sat in her posture-control chair and let it guide itself into place. "So you think we ought to take this report at face value." She rested her arms on the desktop, hands clasped.

Bowersox pointed a finger at her. "As I said, our work will be even more important if it's right."

"*If* it's right. Immortality, or something like it, just because of five viruses? Sure. We're going to look stupid if we run with this and six months from now they come out and say, 'Oops, we made a mistake.'"

Gayle said, "But—"

"There are lots of folks in this town who would love to see us take that fall." *I just met with one.* Sarah leaned back in her chair. "No. I won't risk SAFE-T's reputation on this."

* * *

An hour after filing her report, Lisa and Oriel were standing in line at Dallas/Fort Worth airport to check their bags.

"Ooh, I'm beat, partner." She sagged against him and he squeezed her shoulders. They'd been together for years. She was from Boston and could trace her roots back generations to County Galway in Ireland. He was born in Bogotá, Colombia, and counted the Chibcha tribes and their Spanish conquerors as his ancestors. Besides being her videographer, he was her first-cut editor, best friend, and occasional lover.

Now she was praying their flight to Los Angeles would be delayed. Before they'd left Africa, her assignments editor, Stan Wells, had hinted he had something new for her, but he insisted she come to LA to discuss it. Despite the assurances she'd dragged out of him, it felt like a setup and she didn't want to fight for her job while she was still so tired.

"And you had an early night too," Oriel said. "Get too much sleep?"

"Impossible." She stretched the word across a yawn.

Oriel studied the people standing around them. "Then it's jetlag. You must be getting old or something."

Lisa half-heartedly swatted his butt.

A forty-something woman in jeans and a pink sleeveless top, standing in the next line, was eyeing the two of them. As a reporter, Lisa was used to the awkward stares when she was recognized, but it had been a while since she'd had to face them.

The woman finally worked up the courage to ask, "Are you Lisa Lange?" When Lisa nodded, the woman ducked under the retractable nylon band to grab her hand. "That was the most wonderful news!" she gushed. "I just can't believe it. Is it really true that we're immortal?"

"That's not—"

"I just had to tell all my friends. And they've been telling their friends and we've watched your report over and over and we're so excited! And everyone will be healthy forever and…." She paused, eyes shining. She was about to go on when her phone rang. "Hi! Oh, I know. You wouldn't *believe* who I'm talking to!... It's Lisa, Lisa Lange, the reporter!... Yes, really! She's here at the airport. Can you believe it?... I'll let you talk to her." She held out her phone.

"Sorry," Oriel said, pushing Lisa toward the counter. "We need to check our bags now. Sorry." He bent over and slid his equipment cases to her.

As soon as they were done they hurried down the line of check-in counters.

The woman called after them, "'Bye, Lisa! Thank you so much! I love you!"

Stares and a rustle of conversation followed them.

"Do you have a bag I can put over my head?" Lisa asked.

They hustled through the pre-cleared security line, then down the corridor to the airline's lounge. Lisa couldn't help noticing that her face was on every video screen. Every bit of conversation she heard had something to do with the viruses. Her phone chirped, buzzed, and chimed with incoming messages and calls. She ignored them but her hand kept straying to the clip holding the phone. Once inside the club, she led Oriel to the upper level and plopped into the first chair that had an open one beside it. Oriel perched on its arm.

"You have *got* to be kidding me," she whispered.

Oriel grinned. "Didn't get that kind of attention in Somalia, did you?"

"But I only said 'maybe.'" She stared out the club's windows at the airplanes on the ramp below them. "What if they're wrong? What are people going to think then?"

Oriel didn't reply.

As she sat there, the adrenaline rush from the encounter at the bag check line and the flood of exposure on the concourse faded. She gave in to the draw of her phone and watched the messages scroll down the screen faster than she could read them. Lost in thought, she put it back on its belt clip and didn't notice as her partner stood guard, keeping people from approaching. She yawned, then yawned again.

Oriel checked his watch. "Got time for a cat-nap."

"Wonderful idea," she said, already dozing off. Her phone warbled. "Ohh," she moaned. "Go 'way."

Oriel recognized the ring tone. "Isn't that Stan?"

"Huh?" The phone warbled again. Lisa realized he was right. She was alert in an instant, fumbling to pull the phone out while brushing at her hair with her free hand. "Hi, Stan," she said, holding the phone's camera in front of her face. "What's up?"

"You still in Dallas?"

"Yeah. Why?"

"Cancel your tickets. Your report lit us up like a bomb. You should see the numbers. We need you to stay and follow up."

"That's… great. Hang on a second." She looked up at Oriel, who nodded and walked away. Lisa turned her attention back to Stan. "Oriel's taking care of it. So it's not just me getting lots of traffic."

"A new record every second. The IT guys are going crazy trying to keep us from crashing. The marketing guys are ecstatic."

Lisa's worries about what the network had planned for her vanished like water into the Somali sand. "How long do you want us to stay?"

"As long as there's a story. We're going to send Dr. Monte too. He broke his leg skiing last week but it wasn't as bad as we thought."

Lisa made a face. *It's my story, goddammit! I don't want that dweeb horning in on it.* "I can cover it."

"We're going to hit it from two sides. You do the human interest, he'll do the hard science."

"What was wrong with my report? It's all over." She tried to keep the hand holding the phone from shaking as a cold knot grew in her stomach. "You can't take this away from me. You said it's breaking records." She glanced around the room, realizing people were watching her. *Don't get shrill.*

"Your report was perfect," Stan said, his hands making calm-down gestures on the little screen. "You got the key angle but the story's too big for one team now. You're the lead, Lisa, you're the star, but we can't spread you too thin. Monte's science stuff will be important but your reports mean more to our viewers."

Lisa sighed. *Yeah, he would say that.* "Can you send another camera guy with him? Oriel won't be able to shoot both of us." *That way I won't have to have anything to do with dear Dr. Monte.*

"Sure, sure."

Okay. He's not just bullshitting me. "You'll want something quick."

"The story's hot and so are you."

Oriel caught Lisa's attention after she hung up. "So?"

"We done good." She stood up and smoothed the front of her slacks. "And the reward for good work is more work. Nothing changes, huh?"

Oriel pointed his phone at hers. "They sent you a receipt for the ticket."

"Stan's sending your best buddy, Dr. Monte, *and* someone to work with him."

"There is a God," Oriel said, looking up at the ceiling.

Lisa chuckled and gently backhanded him on the stomach. "God*dess*. You can thank me for that later."

"No problem. You ready to face your hordes of admirers?"

Lisa shrugged. "Part of the job."

"Still tired?"

"Not anymore—there's work to do." She did a little hip-wiggling dance. "'I'm taking what they're giving 'cause I'm working for a living.'" She hip-bumped him. "Hunh."

Oriel snorted. "So who did that?"

"Phil Vassar," she said, picking up her purse. "With Huey Lewis. Ever heard of them?"

"I've never heard of any of those old singers you know." He stepped aside to let her pass. "You're going to fall asleep in the car."

"Wanna bet? Dinner?"

"You're on. At that steakhouse you heard was so good."

"Can you afford it?" Lisa grinned. "I'm getting hungry already."

Oriel grinned back at her. "You're dreaming. And you will be before we leave the rental lot." He licked his lips. "*Filet mignon* with horseradish sauce, big baked potato…."

* * *

Reverend William Baxter's mind wandered as he drove his old Lincoln away from Magnolia Manor, the North Carolina nursing home Dr. Maureen Sams, his close friend owned. The building had always been a place of very mixed emotions for the Senior Pastor of the Christian Covenant Church in Raleigh, just as it was for the staff, the residents, and their families. Every time he walked in, the smells—cleansers, old bodies, medication—reminded him of his grandmother dying in her bed. *How scared I was… thought I was going to die then too. Seven years old, what did I know? Put my feet on this path, though.*

Nearly all of Maureen's original patients had left. She'd managed to stay open by merging with a couple of other facilities.

The halls have always been quiet but today they were like a tomb.

A gap opened in the afternoon traffic on New Hope Road. The car engaged its self-drive system and eased into the flow.

No, that's not right. An angel rolled away the stone that sealed Christ's tomb. Some angel must have done that for the folks who've gone home too. I should be happy for them but….

Deep in thought, he almost missed the warning signal when the active cruise control failed. He slammed on his brakes and managed to stop inches from the bumper of a battered old pickup truck. While he waited for the light to change, he hummed "Roll Away the Stone," drumming his fingers on the steering wheel. Two lines from the chorus kept repeating themselves: "It's so dark I cannot see / Roll away the stone and set me free."

But free from what? There weren't as many miracle cures as there had been a few months ago but something was itching at the back of his mind and deepening the lines on his wide, dark brown face. *Not everyone's gotten better. And some who have… Joella Gaines, so angry the last time I saw her. Now she's been home with her son for months, healthy, and still—no, Will, trust the Lord. He has a plan for her too.*

To get his mind out of the maze it was stuck in, he turned on the radio to listen to "Revealing the Word," a Christian news and commentary program.

At first he could listen with only half an ear as he guided his car through the busy intersection and the traffic around the strip malls on either side, but he knew the commentator's voice instantly. *What are you up to now, Brother?* When he could pay more attention, Brother Elijah was saying, "That's the news, or what this web site is calling news, anyway. My commentary is this, and I'll bet you can see it coming. There is one way to eternal life and *we* know what it is: salvation through our Lord Jesus Christ. Once again, scientists are invading God's territory. They tried—and failed—to prove that man is the result of blind evolution, of random chance. *We* know the truth about *that*."

Baxter frowned. *What's this about?*

"They made the technologies to kill innocent babies—God's creations—while they were still in the womb and said it was for the good of the mother. We know the truth about that too."

"Amen," Baxter said. Another hint of something tickled his brain but he couldn't spare the concentration to follow it.

"They're cloning animals. Love your little poochie too much to let it go? No problem! You can have another one just like it. An identical twin built in a factory years after the original, the *natural*, dog was born. No mother, no father, just chemicals and test tubes.

"They say they'll be able to grow new organs for our bodies soon. Ruin your liver with alcohol? No problem! We'll make you a new one. Don't worry about the cost: alcoholism is a 'disease,' so Medicare will pay to treat it. My tax dollars are paying for your new liver, sinner! Rather than let Jesus into your life to heal your soul, let society pay for a new organ for you to poison. Go on down to the Walmart Neighborhood Market and pick it off the shelf. 'I'll have a new liver, please. Extra large. Charge it.'"

Baxter chuckled, a wry grin crinkling new lines on his face. *He's always had that way with words… sometimes with* the *Word too.* He pulled into the turn lane for Poole Road, toward downtown and his church.

"And now, deep in the heart of Texas, on the so-called buckle of the Bible Belt, we have this new blasphemy. Scientists have declared that we're immortal! They aren't claiming that the Rapture came and we were left behind, not that they believe in the Rapture. No, they're saying we've all been infected with some kind of virus and now we're going to live forever."

"Forever?" Baxter exclaimed. The preacher's words so stunned him, he nearly forgot to straighten the car out of the turn. Just beyond the convenience store on the corner was a shopping center entrance. He pulled in and parked in the first space.

"Sinners, just keep on sinning," Brother Elijah continued. "You don't need Jesus Christ to save you, you're immortal already! No need to come into the Light and the Truth of the Word. No need to walk in the path of righteousness. 'This is the way, walk ye in it?' Why should I? I've *got* eternal life. Come on, Satan, we're gonna have us a *party*.

"Brothers and sisters, this isn't right. It *can't* be right. We have to pray that it isn't correct, either. This has the mark of the Devil on it, the way disease and deprivation and sin do."

Disease? Baxter thought. *Disease? But people are being healed.* Brother Elijah kept talking, but Baxter was no longer listening. *Can there be a "disease" that cures? An anti-disease? Is that what happened at Maureen's place?*

He sat in the car, staring at the buildings while he thought. Two recent conversations made sense now. He understood why his good friend Laval Reece was conducting so few funerals at his mortuary. And why his seminary classmate, Isaiah Soames, was spending more of his hospital-visit time with wounded gang-bangers from his East LA district than with the sick.

Something miraculous is going on. My dear Brother's wrong: this isn't the work of the Devil. Only God could do this. Only God would do this. But how can I prove it?

He called Maureen to tell her what he'd just learned. She pinched her lips with her fingers and looked away on his phone's screen. "That must be what Darci meant a few minutes ago," she said, referring to her head nurse. She squinted her eyes as she thought. "I don't know, Will. Did Brother Elijah offer any proof?"

"He didn't, but the program had the links. Wait." He tapped at the screen. "Here they are."

Maureen nodded as they appeared on her tablet. "I'll call you as soon as I know something I trust."

* * *

Janet stormed into Sayid's office and slammed the door. "I hope you're man enough to admit you were wrong!" she snarled. She stopped right at the front of his desk, hands on her hips, and glared at him. His brown skin had taken on a new shade of gray in the hours since the press conference, but she didn't see it.

From Sayid's perspective, the view wasn't any better. His young researcher's oval face was blotchy and pinched, her cheeks sunken, her eyes red and swollen. Her hair was limp, smashed down, instead of being puffed up as usual. "I—"

Janet waved him to silence. She'd pulled out her phone and was stabbing at the screen. "Please," she whispered, then rushed through controls on the display. Staring at the screen, she fidgeted for several seconds, then said, "Good." She tossed the phone to him. "I just got this. There's no video. Listen."

"This is the Mother Earth Brigades," the voice mail began. "Murderer Hogan! How dare you infect Mother Earth with such a malignancy? Not even Mother Earth herself is immortal. To claim immortality for mere humans is the ultimate insult to the Mother who gave us all life.

"Do not lie to hide your crimes. Mother Earth knows how humanity is poisoning her day after day with its pollution and waste. The fever of her human infection rises.

"Humanity is a cancer on the body of the earth. Anyone who would dare immortalize such tumors must be excised before they cause more harm.

"Your plans will fail. You and your team of Mengeles will not be safe anywhere: not in your homes, your cars, or your laboratories of immortality. Your police, your FBI, not even your pustulent infection can protect you from Mother Earth's wrath.

"We, the true doctors and healers of Mother Earth, will see to it that her skin is wiped clean of your syphilitic pox. Prepare to be sanitized.

"The Mother Earth Brigades have spoken."

Sayid took the phone from his ear and handed it back to Janet. She had remained standing, hands on her hips, while he listened. She turned it off.

"They're… mmmph." He swept his gaze over the clutter of papers and data chips on his desk, landing on the one clear spot near the front, around the framed pictures of his wife, three children, and new granddaughter. He whispered, "I never thought…." After a moment, he looked up. "Have you told the police about it?"

"I can't!" she shouted, waving the phone around as if she wanted to throw it away or slam it down on Sayid's desk. "We can't call out. You wouldn't *believe* the calls we were getting. We're blocking the lab's phones now. You're lucky I could get through to my voice mail. Every time I turn the damn phone on it starts ringing." It flew out of her hand, thumped off a pile of magazines stuffed into a high shelf of the bookcase behind the desk, then tumbled to the floor. Janet stared at where it had fallen. "What if my mother calls? She's in a panic, I know she is."

"At least you can turn it off." Sayid reached down and picked up the phone. "When I was your age—"

"Can't you even say you're sorry? Why are these… these crazy people calling me? Why are they saying these things? Why do they want to kill me? *I* didn't create this! *I* didn't say the viruses make you immortal! I… why…?" She wiped at the tears now streaming down her face, then rubbed her hand on her slacks, leaving a black mascara stain there. "What about Ellanna and Satya and G? This is happening to them too, and nobody gives a shit and we don't know what to do and nobody's helping! Don't you even *care*?"

"Dr. Hogan," Sayid said, his voice low and tight, "that's enough." He met and held her stare. "Sit down."

Janet was shaking, her breath coming in ragged gasps. After a long moment, she sat.

"Now, look at me. Do you think this is happening just to you and your team?"

For the first time, Janet actually looked at her boss and saw how drawn his face was. "Oh."

"That's right," Sayid said, "I'm getting the same calls you are. Everything else too." He rubbed his face with his hands. "So is the Center Director. Did you know that our servers crashed?"

Janet nodded, took a tissue from her purse, and wiped her eyes.

"IT says it's from all the traffic. That hasn't happened in years. This caught everybody by surprise. We haven't talked with you because we've been dealing with our own problems. We left you to fend for yourselves. That was a mistake and I apologize."

Janet watched her hands still trembling as they lay in her lap. "I do too," she said, sniffled, and wiped her nose. "I wasn't being very professional. It's just that I—I mean we—we've never had to deal with anything like this."

Sayid pushed some of the data chips into a pile. "None of us have. Now we do."

* * *

David Wade turned right as he left the office from which his staff was running the twentieth annual Earth Action Forum at EXPOrtland, the city's gleaming and environmentally superb convention center next to the Willamette River. Trina Gonsalves, following him, stopped in the doorway.

"Hey," she called, "workshop's the other way."

"I know," Wade said without slowing down.

Trina ran after him. "But you're supposed to introduce—"

"You can do it," he said as she caught up to him. "Staff's got the bio and his gift."

"David! The Forum is kicking ass, the Greenpeaceniks are six shades of Kelly with envy as usual, and you're acting like you've just been force-fed a turd sandwich." She popped the remainder of a miniature taco into her mouth. "One made with white bread, processed sugar, and cheese food to boot." She swallowed. "Which I know you didn't, 'cause I snuck into the staff room and everyone back there is just giddy at how things are going. What are you doing?"

"Taking a walk."

She stopped, hands on her hips. "David Wade, I swear sometimes you have your head so far up your ass the brown you're seeing isn't dirt."

Wade turned to face her, scowling. "Don't you ever miss the days right after we graduated, Trina? We were done with classes at Western Washington, out in the real world, getting our hands dirty, making a difference. God, I miss that."

A group of attendees in the hall behind him laughed at something. Surprised, he glanced at them, then at Trina.

She shook her head. "Do you have to practice at being stupid, or does it just come naturally? Never mind, I know the answer. Yes, I miss it, but look at what you're doing—"

"Not doing, you mean. When you get down to it, this conference doesn't mean shit."

"And so you're going to take a walk."

Wade turned and waved over his shoulder. "Yes I am. *Bye*, Trina." He opened a door into the service hall and let it shut on her exasperated, "Oh." In minutes he was walking onto a loading dock that would let him slip past anyone, reporters in particular, who might wonder why he wasn't upstairs, basking in the Forum's success.

The riverside park had more people in it than he expected, so he stayed across Naito Parkway until he was closer to downtown. A big, excited crowd had gathered around a public information screen near the Salmon Springs fountain. He was going to avoid the gathering but the flashing banner headline caught his eye: Breaking News Alert: Viruses Grant Immortality? May Have Escaped Gov Lab.

Yeah, right, Wade thought, then noticed who the reporter was. *This ought to be good for a laugh.*

"This is Antonio Corolli, reporting from Dallas," the reporter announced. Wade watched him tell how government sources were denying that rogue viruses had escaped from any of their labs despite the fact that a Texas researcher had revealed the outbreak. Worse for the feds, he said, the viruses had spread around the world, doubtless infecting billions of people. The epidemic was out of control, with no hope of being contained.

Wade snorted and turned away. *That's the same shit he always pulls. No proof, just wild claims. To think we used to trust him.* He was about to walk off when Lisa's report came on. In spite of himself, he stayed to watch. He noticed the differences between her report and Corolli's right away, and the excited way the people around him responded to it. When the next report began, he headed for the benches by the path along the river. A work crew was repairing the solar panel arrays on the Hawthorne Bridge a couple hundred yards away. On any other day, the noise of the traffic, the workers, and the news screen would have annoyed him, but this time he was lost in thought.

He settled onto a bench and pulled out his phone, which let him search the data cloud and scroll through other reports on the viruses. He was surprised at first by how few gave the immortality angle much attention, then thought, *No, they're right to be skeptical.* He called up a search program and told it, "Find any material, published before today, that corroborates the immortality aspect of the reports on these viruses."

"Searching," the synthesized voice said, then, "Here's what I found." The first two articles it displayed were "Unexplained Decline in Mortality Across the United States" from *Morbidity and Mortality Weekly Report* and "Surviving a Rapidly Changing Environment" from *American Funeral Director* magazine. Wade chuckled at the irony in the second title, but a chill ran through him as he read the article.

Morticians are worried, he thought. People aren't dying like they did a year ago, even six months ago. Business is down and they're laying people off.

He opened and scanned the *Morbidity* article. The name of the magazine was almost too bizarre for him to believe, but the article was scholarly, the data clear and well documented, showing monthly numbers for the last year. The trends between the articles matched. *What if those viruses are real?* He gazed out at the water, ignoring the tourist boat that floated by. *I need an independent opinion.*

"Call Lew in Research," he told the phone.

Lew Crandall answered seconds later. "Yeah, boss?"

"I need you to look into something."

"Bet I'm already on it."

Wade frowned at the image on the screen. There was sunlight on Lew's bushy brown beard. He was outside somewhere.

"Look to your right," the young man said, grinning. "A hundred yards."

"I can't hide from you, can I?" Wade said a short time later when his wiry young assistant sat down.

"Tried to call you, got voice mail. Called the office at the Forum, they told me you'd gone walkabout. Figured I'd find you down here somewhere and it was too nice a day for an outdoors guy like me to be stuck in the office." He pushed up the sleeves of his plaid flannel shirt. "Easy."

"So what do I want to know?"

"The truth about those viruses?"

Wade grunted. "Is it that obvious?"

Lew took a deep breath. "If you're not interested, you shouldn't be in charge of EARTH."

"Tell me."

Lew reviewed what he and the research department had learned.

Wade rubbed his hands together. "So, if death rates collapse, population growth goes crazy. We're three years away from hitting eight billion already. Imagine what will happen: Energy use will go way up, pollution, overfishing, and factory farming all get worse too." He stood and walked across the path to the cast-iron railing above the river.

Lew followed.

"Clean water's scarce in too many places now." Wade ran his hands back and forth along the top rail as he thought about the conference he'd just left. "The news is probably just hitting the Forum. It'll make what we've been doing trivial. There are too many people already. If these reports are right—"

"That's still a pretty big if."

Wade turned to look at him. "I thought you said—"

"The science is solid—so far—but the peer review was rushed. Genetics is as complex as the environment. They could have gotten something wrong and nobody caught it."

Wade stared out over the water again, thinking. "All right. But assume the worst case. Malthus' predictions wouldn't be the half of it. Overcrowding, mass starvation, resource wars—my God." He squeezed the rail but the rest of his body shifted and twitched. "Ever hear the saying, 'That scares me and I'm fearless?'"

Lew chuckled. "Mountain bikers *never* say that."

"No, you wouldn't, but I'm a fool if I don't. Ideas?"

"Somebody needs to be punished." Lew leaned on the railing. "We—"

"Forget punishment." Wade noticed his researcher's disappointed expression. "That's what our so-called friends at the Mother Earth Brigades will want to do, but—" He squinted as he considered his options. "Even if one of those conspiracy theories turns out to be true, trying to punish someone will be a waste of time."

"You don't think—"

"I don't *know*," Wade said. He poked Lew in the chest with his finger. "Do the analysis. Who could have done this? Whom would you target? The lab in Texas? That'd be just pointless and stupid. What *credible* source has any proof the viruses were released on purpose or got away?"

Lew shrugged. "So—"

"Even if the viruses did get loose and have spread around the world, the biggest lawsuit ever filed wouldn't mean shit." He looked up the river toward the workers on the bridge. "This is bigger than you can imagine, Lew. If it is worldwide, we don't have much time to act. Remember how hard it was to get everyone to agree to reduce CO2 emissions?"

Lew looked embarrassed. "Not really. I was pretty young."

Wade peered at him, then chuckled. "So you were. Okay, consider this: if those reports are right, now we have to tell everyone to stop having kids. In fact, we have to make them stop. Today. What do you think the chances of *that* are?"

Lew shoved his hands into his pants pockets and whistled. "No more sex? Won't happen."

"Sex is okay," Wade said, "kids aren't. That's a huge cultural problem before it's an environmental one. Cultural, religious." He kicked at a clump of grass at the base of the fence post. "Political. We have to think bigger than ever… no, different first, then bigger."

"'Think globally, act locally.'"

Wade grimaced. "Sure. How are we going to reach seven and a half billion localities?"

"Seven and a half? Oh, the people. You don't need to get to the little kids."

"Maybe not today, but what if they're going to live forever too?" He glanced at Lew, then meandered along the path. "See? Whatever we think of first, it'll be too inside-the-box, too ordinary… and too small."

The young man followed, his eyes fixed on the gravel at his feet. "There's got to be something, boss."

* * *

Oriel scanned the cloud as their car drove itself toward Dallas on the Airport Freeway. Talking heads were chattering about the discoveries, their speculations competing with their hype for top billing.

Lisa mumbled in her sleep. He let her rest. There'd be plenty of time to tease her later. And enjoy that steak dinner at her expense. She'd been this way as long as he'd known her: fully "on" when it was time to work or play, but fully "off" when work or play was done. For now, she was off, and had been since just after they'd gotten onto the highway. When they got back to the lab complex, she'd be on again, wide awake and ready to go full bore.

He woke her up after he'd parked at an office complex north of the labs.

Lisa wasn't surprised her call was forwarded to voice mail when she called Janet and Ellanna for follow-up interviews; she was surprised that their mail boxes were full. *That never happens.* She and Oriel had no luck with the others who worked in the lab either. Every electronic medium they tried was blocked, shut down, or being ignored. Even the Public Relations department stiff-armed them.

The persistence Lisa had discovered while she was a new reporter at the smallest TV station in Des Moines was coming back. It had started with her determination to air a child prostitution story the station manager didn't want to broadcast. His arrest a week after it did revealed why—and ended the harassment she and the other female reporters had endured for months. That intense focus had lost her a husband but ignited her career. She realized she hadn't felt that focus for a very long time.

"This isn't working," she said, slapping her phone onto her thigh. "Something's wrong." She looked sideways at Oriel, gauging his reaction.

"Took you long enough," he said.

"You shouldn't have let me sleep." She glanced at the research buildings down the hill ."We're wasting time. Let's do what we should have done in the first place."

Before they could get to the portico of the Simmons Building, they had to work their way through a crowd milling around at the foot of the driveway. Guards and a deep, concrete-lined flood channel kept everyone away from the building. Oriel was a pro at getting through security checkpoints and the one beyond the bridge over the channel from Harry Hines Boulevard was no different, but there were guards at the entrance too, and they wouldn't let him park. They wouldn't let Lisa walk in, either, or wait outside while Oriel took the car to the garage.

"What now?" he asked as they drove back toward the street.

Lisa's frustration was turning into a burning need to get inside. She twisted in her seat to look back at the complex. "That's not just one building. There's got to be another way in." She straightened around as Oriel waited for the traffic light to change. "Go left."

To their surprise, there were no guards at the south entrance but there weren't any parking places along the narrow drive, either. The east entrance was also unprotected and it had an open visitor's garage next to it. Within minutes they were parked and inside the research tower. Lisa had learned in journalism school that if she walked through someplace as if she belonged there, most of the time she wouldn't be stopped or questioned. Oriel's camera and their ID badges normally helped too, but now the mood in the building was different, tense. No one wanted to talk with them. Everyone was camera-shy.

Still, after a couple of wrong turns and one stop to ask for directions, they were back in the Simmons Building but on the third floor. The directory screen by the elevators didn't list Janet's lab, even though every other one seemed to be there.

Lisa decided to just get into the elevator. She held the door open while she scanned the department listing posted inside, then stabbed the button for the sixth floor.

"Genetics is on five," Oriel said, a quizzical look on his face.

Lisa winked at him. "Bet there'll be guards. We'll go up one more, come down the stairs."

Oriel grinned. "See? That nap did you good. You're being sneaky and devious again."

"Just doin' my job," she said as they walked out of the elevator. She picked a stairwell at random and they trotted down. When they stepped into the fifth floor corridor she was delighted: no guards were in sight and her target's name was on the placard next to the second door on her right. "Bingo," she whispered.

They paused just long enough to make sure their equipment was turned on and for Lisa to smooth her hair, then walked into the lab. A woman with dark brown skin and wavy, jet-black hair was working at the end of a lab bench near the door. She looked up as they entered. "Can I—" she said, then saw Oriel's camera. "How did you get in here?"

"Is Dr. Hogan available?" Lisa asked, putting on her best pleading-for-help face. "Or Dr. Barnes? I haven't been able to reach them. Can you help me? I'd really appreciate it."

The woman studied Lisa for a moment. "Stay right there," she said. "Don't touch anything. I'll see." She turned, strode through a side hall, and disappeared around a corner. A door opened, then thumped shut. Oriel panned the camera around the lab and took close-up shots of the equipment on the benches and the displays on the walls.

"That's odd," Lisa whispered. "There's no one else here." She had expected the lab to be busy. Instead, the room was silent except for the hum of the fluorescent lights overhead and the whirring and clicking of a machine they couldn't see. Lisa nudged Oriel and pointed: the phone icon at each workstation was pulsing red. "That's why we couldn't get through."

He zoomed the camera in to capture a few seconds of video of the display.

A man entered the lab with the raven-haired woman. Lisa recognized him as Janet's boss.

"How did you get in here?" Sayid asked. "We've said all we can say to the press right now. I hope you have some idea what—"

Lisa pointed a microphone at him. "Dr. Sayid, what can you tell me about what's happened since the press conference?" Oriel had the camera up to his eye and was recording.

"You're the one who asked about immortality, aren't you?" Sayid said. "Yes, you are. Do you realize what you've done? The trouble you've created?"

"Why don't you tell me?" Lisa said. "We were surprised there was a crowd outside and so much security. Has something gone wrong? Where is everyone? Is there some kind of danger?"

"Danger?" Wrinkles creased Sayid's forehead as he frowned. "Who knows, with all the crackpots you stirred up, telling everyone we're immortal. You and that… that other guy and his conspiracy theories. The whole Center's in an uproar because of how you distorted the facts."

"What *are* the facts, Dr. Sayid?"

"The facts are," he put his hand on Lisa's shoulder and turned her toward the door out of the lab, "that I don't know how you got in here but I do know how you're getting out. Come with me." He shifted his hand to Lisa's elbow and pulled her along. Oriel backed up, keeping his camera aimed at Lisa and Sayid.

"If there's a problem, Sir," Lisa pressed, "you're not going to be able to hide it forever."

Sayid refused to say anything more. A pair of security guards had reached the lab as the three entered the hall. The guards escorted Lisa and Oriel to their car and made sure they drove off the UT-Southwestern campus.

"Now we know a little more," Oriel said.

"Not much. Find anything while I was sleeping?"

"Nothing useful. You haven't checked your own sites, have you?"

"When have I had the time?" Lisa rubbed her face, then ran her fingers through her hair. The thrill of getting into the lab had drained out of her, replaced again by exhaustion and by the frustration of being blocked by Sayid. She sighed and reclined the back of her seat. *Stan wants another report but I don't have crap,* she thought. *What did Sayid mean, "crackpots?" I can't think. God, I don't want to be in front of the camera again. I'm so tired. Makeup can't hide it. But goddammit, there's something… something….*

Oriel drove to the top level of a parking garage across the boulevard from the complex. The lowering sun was starting to turn the white sides of the research buildings yellow, heading toward gold. The green frames around the neat rows of square windows and the round air conditioning vents were glowing. It would be a dramatic background if they could pull a report together.

After he parked, he fished his tablet from the bag behind his seat and slipped the chip on which he'd recorded the encounter with Sayid into a slot. He checked Global News' site first, then scanned the video. "You'd better look at this." He held the computer out to Lisa.

"Not now." She was slumped in her seat, head back, eyes closed.

"Look at it, Lisa. You need to file soon. You don't want Corolli stealing this story."

Lisa opened her eyes and glared at him, then took the tablet. She sat up, scrolled the recording back and forth, sometimes listening to the audio, sometimes not. After a few minutes, she stopped, minimized the video window, and lay back in her seat again. "I don't know," she said. "There's something there but I can't get it."

"Yes you can. You have to." He took the small computer from her, brought up her website, and explored it. "Look."

Grumbling, she sat up again. He'd left the display at her "Talk to Me" page. At first, she didn't recognize what she was seeing. The traffic analysis software gave her a summary:

"How can I become immortal?": 256,739
Protest messages: 47,385
Death threats: 23
Marriage proposals: 118
Miscellaneous:....

The words and numbers sank in. She turned to her partner, who had slid his seat backward so he could read the screen over her shoulder. "That's just since we filed the first report. I don't get that much traffic in a month. Two months."

"Not even marriage proposals?"

Lisa was too puzzled to react to the joke. There were new threads on the viruses. She read through some of the postings. There were thousands. Already. Pleading, hopeful, angry, excited, fearful. She looked up at the glowing buildings in front of her and focused on two of the windows on the west side. On the fifth floor. "I've got it."

Half an hour later, Lisa was standing at the edge of the parking garage, the research buildings shining over her right shoulder in the setting sun. She'd put dark contact lenses in her eyes so the sun shining in her eyes wouldn't make her squint. Her hair was glowing crimson and gold. Oriel made a last adjustment to the camera, then cued her.

"The hours since researchers here in Dallas announced their discovery," she said, "have revealed millions of Americans' hopes and dreams… and fears. But while America longs for more legitimate information, a physical and electronic shell has gone up around the scientists who uncovered the viruses, silencing them."

In the report as it appeared on Global News, the video switched to the empty lab, the pulsing phone symbols, and an e-mail rejection message Oriel had shot earlier, then returned to Lisa.

"Even if true immortality doesn't come to pass, this should be a day of celebration. Instead, I'm receiving death threats—dozens. Is that happening to Dr. Hogan and her team? Why would the very people who proclaimed the end of so many terrible, incurable diseases be in danger?

"Tonight, key mysteries—where the viruses came from, how they work, why they've come now—have yet to be solved. But the hopes for a future as shining and golden as the research labs behind me are already under attack." The video did a slow pan-and-zoom past Lisa's shoulder to focus on the buildings, then dissolved into a time-lapse shot showing the sunset sweeping across them, turning them from gold to pink to gray as Lisa finished in voice-over. "As the cloak of darkness descends on Dallas, a cloak of silence has descended on the UT-Southwestern Medical Center. Will these mysteries go unsolved, their answers hidden in the shadow of ignorance? Will the hopes of millions of people die at birth, smothered by unreasoning fear?

"One thing is certain: we won't have to wait forever to find out.

"I'm Lisa Lange."

CHAPTER 4

JANET SAT ALONE AT THE DINETTE TABLE in her condo, trying to finish her take-out Indian dinner. She was so tired she could barely eat. The day's events had left her drained, numb. State police officers had driven her home and Texas Rangers were guarding her building. One of her escorts had suggested she try the Tandoori chicken. Now it was a churning ball of heat in her stomach. *Why did I let him talk me into this? Never had it before. Stupid.*

She jumped when her phone rang. She'd set up a white list that permitted some callers and blocked all the others but in her foggy state of mind, she wondered who it might be. Then she knew.

She hurried around the end of the breakfast bar and snatched the phone from the charging station as it finished playing her father's ring tone for the second time. A shiver ran through her. She squeezed the phone too hard and it almost squirted out of her sweaty hand, the way it used to every time he called when her mother was so sick.

The phone rang for the third time. She had to answer, not let it click off to voice mail. She gasped, "Accept," and held it in front of her so she could see the screen.

"Daddy?" As hard as she tried, she couldn't quite keep the quaver out of her voice.

"Oh, you're all right." There was palpable relief in his tenor voice and on his face.

Janet closed her eyes and tried to relax. "I guess."

Robert Hogan frowned. "Are you sure? Momma's so worried she can't even talk. We saw those reports, tried to call, got your voice mail, then…." He peered at her from the phone's screen. "Are you sure you're okay?"

She fumbled for a chair behind her, found it, and sat down. "It's been a crazy day."

"How crazy? They said on the news—"

"Really busy," Janet interrupted. *Maybe they don't know.* "Don't believe everything you hear." She rested her forearms on the bar. "Tell Momma not to worry. I'm all right."

"Janet…."

She wanted to scream at him to stop prying but didn't have the strength. "Daddy, please… I'm just tired, okay?" *Department store managers don't have days like this, do they, Daddy?*

He frowned and looked away.

Tears of exhaustion welled in Janet's eyes. In the months before the discoveries she'd buried herself in her work so she wouldn't have to think about the cancer destroying her mother in that North Carolina nursing home. She'd felt guilty about being a thousand miles away in Dallas.

Janice Hogan had played the noble martyr, even talking like she'd accepted her fate. She'd said, "When it's time for me to go to my reward, I promise I'll wait long enough so you can come and say good-bye. Until then, no moping, hear?"

Then she'd recovered.

Janet hadn't known what to think then. Now.... "Daddy?" she called. "Where are you?" Her father's face had left the screen, replaced by part of her parents' living room wall. The corner of a sofa-size painting they'd bought years ago—a small church in a mountain meadow—hung above a faux parchment lamp shade.

"Right here." He picked up the phone again as he sat on the couch. "I went to tell Momma you're okay. She's lying down. Said she's too upset to come to the phone but wants you to know she loves you."

Yeah, sure. "I love her too."

"Maybe we should come out—"

"No, Daddy."

"But...."

Janet hung her head, shook it. When she looked up again, he was watching her, worry lines creasing his forehead and arcing around his brown eyes.

"All right," he said, knowing he wasn't going to get a better explanation.

After they hung up, Janet needed someone to talk to even more. She couldn't put that burden on Ellanna—not tonight—and she'd never been able to talk with her kid sister, Chris. She tried Michael, got his "I'm driving, can't talk now" message and wished again that he'd get his car fixed so he could let the computer drive it.

She wandered into the bedroom and picked up a family picture from the dresser, the one of the five of them taken at their cabin before "Little E," her brother Eric, was killed in a traffic accident when he was 12. Another photo stood next to it, taken when she was 18, before she left for college. *There's always an empty spot since Eric.... What's going to happen to me?*

The doorbell rang and Michael called from the entry, "Hey, Squeak."

She rushed out of the bedroom and nearly tackled him as he closed the door. For a few minutes she just held him as tightly as she could. She was shaking but couldn't cry. He just stroked her back with his free hand and crooned, "It's all right, Sweetie. It's all right."

"No it isn't," she said into his shoulder. "It won't ever be."

* * *

Sarah mingled with the U.S. senators, representatives, and their staffers in a private upstairs room of an exclusive restaurant a few blocks from Capitol Hill. She had set up the reception so SAFE-T could lobby the legislators but everyone was talking about the viruses.

Dressed in a sea-green silk kimono that clung to her slender body and was slit far enough up the sides to let her walk easily, she sipped a glass of Chardonnay as she moved from one conversation to the next. The wine was drier than she liked but it gave her something to do with her hands while she waited for Charlene Hamilton to arrive.

Thirty minutes late, Hamilton walked in with her chief of staff, Roger Dale. Sarah hurried to greet her and the two women exchanged hugs and pecks on the cheek; then she welcomed Roger the same way.

Hamilton was known around Washington as "the old gray mare" thanks to her long, wide-jawed face and dull gray hair combed in a simple, collar-length style. She'd turned that nickname to her advantage in the last campaign, making the song her theme, and Vermont's voters had re-elected her in a landslide.

"Sarah, you look positively stunning," the senator exclaimed. She stepped back, holding Sarah's hands. "That green complements your eyes so well. Don't you think so, Roger?" Her own suit was unornamented black, severe rather than business-like.

Roger's gaze met Sarah's eyes, then drifted to her dress. He stroked the brocaded sleeve. "Sarah's always had particularly good taste," he said. "In clothes." Their divorce ten years ago had left its scars, but because appearances counted for so much, they remained cordial in public.

"Oh, that's not all," Hamilton replied. "She married you." She squeezed Sarah's hands.

"That was a long time ago," Sarah said. A shadow flickered across her face and an uncomfortable warmth spread under her salt-and-pepper hair. She glanced at Roger, then couldn't lift her gaze from the floor.

Realizing what she'd just said, Hamilton bit her lip and glanced around the room.

Roger broke the awkward silence. "What would you like to drink, Senator?"

"Vodka-Seven."

He looked at Sarah's glass, asking if she wanted a refill. When she shook her head, excused himself to weave through the crowd to the bar at the far side of the room.

Hamilton leaned close to Sarah. "Sorry," she whispered.

By the time Roger returned with the drink, the women were discussing the viruses. Sarah had tried to avoid the subject but Hamilton wouldn't let her. "What's SAFE-T's position?"

"We're still developing it," Sarah said. "Kenneth thinks we should get involved—"

"And he's right." Hamilton took a sip of her drink and said to Roger, "Perfect. Thanks."

"I'm not so sure," Sarah said. "It's too big, too outlandish, too...." She waved her free hand around as she struggled for the right word. "There's too much chance they're wrong."

Hamilton took a bacon-wrapped scallop from a passing tray. "Doesn't matter if the science is right. This is all about emotions: life and death, social justice, health." She paused to emphasize the next word. "Safety. You should understand that better than most."

"Those emotions will turn against us if we're wrong. Emotion's a big part of our opposition anyway. I'm not going to risk shooting myself in the foot over something so voodoo. It's wishful thinking, not science."

Hamilton put her hand on Sarah's arm and guided her behind a screen that hid the coffee bar and the doors to the kitchen. She took another sip from her drink. "The world changed this afternoon. The Hill's buzzing about the viruses and look at what happened tonight: they hijacked everything, didn't they?"

Sarah nodded.

"You've never let risk hold you back before. There's going to be big money involved, to say nothing of power and influence. You need to decide right now if you're a player or not."

"But—"

"You're not listening, Sarah." She put the glass on the counter, then reached up to touch the lobbyist's earrings. "By the way, I meant to ask you where you found jade that complements your dress so... and your eyes." She caressed Sarah's earlobes and jawline with her fingertips.

Sarah looked up at the Senator. "Oh... well... I—"

"And this silk," Hamilton slid her fingers down Sarah's neck, past the mandarin collar and onto her chest until her fingertips surrounded Sarah's breasts. "So soft, so sensual."

"Leenie...."

"So luscious." Hamilton caressed the sides of Sarah's breasts while her thumbs slid back and forth across her nipples. She leaned in to kiss her lover.

Sarah gave in to the kiss for a moment then forced herself to pull away, anger and delight swirling and eddying through her. "Leenie, we shouldn't... not here."

Hamilton straightened up and sighed. "You're right. What if we got caught? Such a scandal." She winked. "But the alcohol and your perfume...." She grinned. "It's all their fault... and that dress." She slid her hands down to Sarah's waist. "Truly, it is gorgeous. There's only one thing wrong with it."

Shocked, Sarah glanced down. "What?"

"Silly," Hamilton said, her eyes twinkling. "You're still wearing it."

Sarah shoved her hands away.

The senator grabbed Sarah's hands. "Am I going to have to take you home and spank you to make you do what you're supposed to?"

"About...?"

"About everything."

Sarah's lips pursed and she looked away, as if she were thinking. "You know better ways to talk with your hands."

* * *

The Sunday after the viruses were announced, Baxter's sermon was titled God Has Blessed Us Every One. His strong stand in favor of the viruses, that they were in fact a gift from God, was a stark contrast to the position of other ministers. As a result, the rest of the day was hardly a day of rest. Lisa was one of the few reporters to get a live interview with him.

With the help of Baxter's media staff, Oriel set up the scene so it appeared that Lisa was in the sanctuary with the minister, even though she was in a studio in Dallas. Her pad was linked to Baxter's so she could share videos and other feeds with him.

"Reverend Baxter, you called the viruses a gift while other members of the clergy are calling them a curse, or worse. Why did you take such a controversial stand?"

Baxter smiled and laced his fingers in front of his chin. "I do not fear speaking the truth, Miss Lange."

"Doesn't it worry you, though, that so many of your colleagues think the arrival and effects of the viruses are not God's work?"

"Truth is not determined by majority vote," Baxter said, leaning forward in the high-backed chair he used during services, "nor by who speaks the loudest. I have seen slow-motion miracles with my own eyes, miracles I can only attribute to the viruses as agents of God. The Psalmist urged us to bless the Lord, who heals all diseases and redeems our lives from destruction. I have seen that, Miss Lange. I have seen the Lord's work."

Lisa tapped her lips with a fingertip. "Where, Reverend? What did you see?"

"I have a dear friend who owns a nursing home. Many of her former patients—dozens of them, many of whom were terminally ill—have been cured and walked out of the facility."

"So they took up their beds and walked, you might say."

Baxter chuckled. "Actually, I did say that, but all of them have been kind enough to leave their beds behind."

Lisa smiled, then grew serious. "But because of the viruses, Reverend?"

Baxter glanced to his right at the sound of a sanctuary door opening, then closing. "Perhaps there are two kinds of miracles happening here: the cures themselves being one, the second that we get to see the mechanism of God's action."

"That's never happened before," Lisa said, cocking her head.

"Who are we to say what the Lord can or cannot do?"

"Some of your opponents—"

"They're not my enemies, Miss Lange. We just see things differently."

Lisa scrolled through the notes on her tablet and selected a link. "What about this?"

A video of Brother Elijah standing before a few rows of his followers played on Baxter's tablet and the webcast. "*Of course* these so-called experts deny this new scourge is the work of man!" he proclaimed. "*Of course* they deny this scourge is targeted at the poor, the weak, the downtrodden! We've heard these lies before. We've believed them before. No longer!"

The people behind him nodded vigorously.

"No longer. These lies have no power over us. They will not overcome us, *we* will overcome *them*. We *shall* overcome!"

Baxter shook his head. "I pray for him. Today, as we do every Sunday in my church, we recite the Lord's Prayer, asking God for forgiveness for our trespasses while we seek to forgive those who have trespassed against us. Surely others—and let's be clear, he means whites—have done sinful things to we Blacks and others in the past. But there must come a day when we lay down that burden of anger and forgive those trespasses."

Lisa checked her tablet. "Many of our viewers, like Donna from Kansas City, are saying the viruses are the Devil's work."

"She's not alone, but evil is not the only force at work in this world."

"There's no indication the viruses have distinguished between good people, or at least those who might be considered worthy of more years of life, and those who aren't so good."

Baxter thought of Joella Gaines, then pushed the memory aside. *That's unworthy of you, William.* "Jesus Christ warned us of the consequences of passing judgment on each other, Miss Lange. Who are we to usurp the powers of the Lord and sit in judgment?"

"And if, say, a murderer might also have received this gift, as you call it?"

"God is infinite in His wisdom and mercy. Even in these sinful days, He has given us sinners more time to realize our sins and repent. He is challenging us, through this worldwide miracle, to use these means and motivations to mend our ways."

"Casey writes from San Francisco that these are the early days, that there are many unknowns about where all this will lead."

Baxter pinched his lips with his fingers for a moment. "That's a fair point."

"There's also this." Lisa selected another clip.

David Wade appeared on the screen. "Earth Action: Return To Harmony is deeply concerned about the implications of these viruses. Assuming Dr. Hogan is correct about the viruses' effects, our calculations leave no doubt that the earth will experience massive overpopulation, out-of-control pollution, and a return to the global warming we are barely averting today. Shortages of clean water and food will lead to famine and resource wars. All of this will happen within ten years. The word 'catastrophe' does not even begin to describe what we are facing."

"Aren't you being naïve if you ignore those certainties?" Lisa asked.

"Moses told the Hebrews, 'The Lord thy God is a merciful God; He will not forsake thee, neither destroy thee.' I believe that same merciful God will prevent the horrible things this gentleman predicts. If that makes you think I'm naïve, so be it."

"So you reject his fears?"

"Must we always assume the worst? I've dedicated my life to spreading the Good News of salvation through Jesus Christ. News doesn't have to be bad all the time."

"But what would you say if all those people who have been 'cured' suddenly relapsed?"

Lisa had hugged Oriel when he'd suggested that question while they were setting up. "That's the elephant in the room," she said, grinning as she typed it into her tablet. "Bet he dodges it."

Baxter said, "Salvation is always available to those who accept Jesus as their Savior."

"I meant, will you insist that those suddenly false cures, those viruses, were still good news, the gift of a merciful God?"

"Let's not get ahead of the story, Miss Lange."

* * *

As soon as Antonio Corolli heard what Baxter had said in his sermon, he began hunting for someone who would disagree. Religious leaders were obvious choices, so he left them for other, less imaginative, reporters. He wanted a big hit, a big name, an opinion leader whose words he could turn into something with big impact.

He crossed the politicians he knew off his list. *Too much bullshit, too little credibility,* he thought, *except Levine, and he won't talk to me. Sucks that my source lied that time. Wasn't anything personal.*

He was eating lunch at the little sandwich shop near his apartment, watching one of the staff empty a recycling bin, when he realized his answer was right in front of him. *Who's going to feed all those people who should have died? What about all their crap? David Wade. He's the one I want. Even if he has been stiff-arming me for years. Food... pollution... environment. He'll want to tell everyone what deep shit we're in.*

Wade wasn't eager to talk to Corolli but he agreed to a brief remote interview. That had gotten Lisa the quote she'd played for Baxter—without her acknowledging the source.

Corolli convinced Wade to do an in-person interview the following afternoon at the International Rose Test Garden in Washington Park, overlooking downtown Portland.

When they met, Wade insisted on standing at the top of the amphitheater so Corolli's camera would point down Tanner Creek Canyon to the urban sprawl of the city's east side and Mount Hood in the distance. The reporter didn't care: he had a supply of other image and video files he planned to use.

The finished report opened with Corolli saying, "The world is heading for calamity and no one is willing to face it. Leading environmentalist David Wade made that clear in an interview with me today. Rather than a new age of immortality, these new viruses spell doom for humanity, and the entire planet, if someone doesn't take drastic action immediately."

"We have to act now," Wade said. "Poor countries will feel the effects first—" The video jumped to a different piece of the interview the reporter had spliced in. "But the developed world won't be spared."

"Worldwide famine," Corolli declared, "caused by a nuclear war, could result from something as simple as a water shortage in Mongolia."

"The world is totally interconnected," Wade said. "A nuclear winter would cause a widespread famine. Say there wasn't enough water in Mongolia because the Khangai Mountains' glaciers' melt water was being diverted to a more powerful country. If there was no other source, the people would become refugees."

"That could lead to a war," Corolli said as a mushroom cloud from a nuclear explosion rose above an image of fleeing Korean War refugees, "if the neighboring countries already couldn't feed their own people."

"Russia, India, and China still have nukes," Wade said.

Over a clip of the President stabbing his finger at someone, Corolli said, "This environmental leader predicted that governments would deny the possibility of a war until it happened, giving them no time to stockpile food. The resulting famine would kill millions of Americans in just months. Even if nuclear wars don't happen, Wade predicts the earth will choke on human-caused pollution." A montage of images played as the reporter spoke: piles of garbage on city streets, belching smoke stacks, and dead, oil-soaked pelicans.

Wade said, "We remain a throwaway society, despite the progress we've made in recycling over the last forty years."

"The idea of recycling everything was Utopian to start with, wasn't it?" Corolli asked.

"With more people living, and living longer, recycling won't be enough," Wade said as video showed a front-end loader digging into a towering pile of aluminum cans. "Living more simply, with less stuff, will help, but as long as the population continues to grow unchecked, we won't be able to avoid using more of everything."

With the verdant park as his background, Corolli said, "Population control is everyone's greatest concern. Beautiful spaces like this could be sacrificed just to house the new billions." The video switched to the inside of a tiny home as he continued in voice-over. "One hundred square foot micro-homes like this one could become not just a come-and-go fad, but mandatory for anyone greedy enough to want to own their own home." The video switched to a man in his pajamas, scrambling through the open glass door at the end of a coffin-like box. It sat on the top row of an array of identical containers—two high and twenty long—resembling a bank of dryers at a laundromat. "Or perhaps something like this Japanese 'capsule hotel' could be all you get if you're single. Each slot is barely tall enough to sit up in. There's a bed, minimal storage, and an info-center inside, and a communal bath and kitchen down the hall."

"Look how much Portland has grown," Wade said, gesturing across the garden toward the city and the mountains. "But it's small compared to places like Los Angeles, Mexico City, or Karachi. There are thirty cities around the world with populations over thirty million. With the death rate near zero now, Earth Action: Return

To Harmony predicts there will be a hundred such cities in twenty years."

Over a background of a city sidewalk full of people, Corolli said, "Amazingly, despite his doomsday predictions, Wade had no idea how to keep this population bomb from exploding."

"Everyone has to pitch in to come up with creative solutions," Wade said. "We can't hide our heads in the sand and hope the problem goes away. We're all in this together."

Corolli closed the report with the rose beds behind him. "Experts still refuse to admit the new viruses are human creations. The roses here are just as artificial—human manipulations of nature—but nowhere near as dangerous. They may have a new role soon: grave decorations for a dead future, the stillborn victim of humanity's excesses and bad judgment."

Back in his office, Wade pounded the arms of his chair. "I knew I shouldn't have talked with him! I *knew*!"

CHAPTER 5

WITH DR. MONTE NARASINGHAR, Global News' health reporter, in Dallas to cover the medical details, and since UT-Southwestern continued to keep the press away from Janet and her team, Lisa shifted her attention. Janet's comment at the press conference that the viruses weren't a panacea gave her the angle she wanted. She and Oriel filmed her next report at a nursing home in Prosper, Texas, on the north side of the Dallas Metroplex.

"The Mount Hope Center of North Dallas," Lisa said as she walked down the hallway, "tries hard to be a cheerful place for its remaining residents." She ran her hand along the colorful wallpaper, past the framed photographs and artwork and the vases of artificial flowers. "Most of the patients have been discharged: returned to their former homes or their families, or moved into new apartments."

A member of the staff dressed in teal blue scrubs hurried by holding a stainless steel tray. He apologized as he cut between Lisa and the camera, then resumed whistling once he was past her.

"For those who live here, though, there's a deep sense of despair. Some have conditions the viruses haven't cured. Others are too frail to live anywhere else."

The scene shifted to one of the rooms, where a black woman, her face wrinkled and hair pewter grey from more than eighty hard years, was sitting in a simple brown chair next to a bed. She was holding the hand of an Asian woman who lay propped up on pillows. The head of her bed was raised so she could look out the window. Her white hair was pulled back and tied in a neat braid that draped across her left shoulder, but there was no particular expression on her face and her dark brown eyes were unfocused.

Lisa sat in a chair borrowed from another room. "Ngai Nguyen's senile dementia," she whispered, as if she didn't want to disturb them, "is no longer progressing, her doctors say, but she can't live alone. Her family died tragically in a traffic accident six months ago. Bessie Monroe is her only friend. She used to be a resident here too. Now she lives a few blocks away in a small apartment, making do on Social Security." She turned to the woman. "Bessie, what's your life like, now that the viruses have healed you?"

"Oh, it ain't no bed of roses, no, but I ain't complainin', neither. I ain't dyin' now. Year ago, I was." She smiled. "Then Jesus sent the viruses. Ain't that funny? Folk used to catch a virus and maybe they'd die, didn't they? Yes, Lord, I thank Jesus every day."

"So you're happy now?"

In the bed, Ngai started singing, her voice quavering and weak. Her words and the tune were unrecognizable but had the rhythm of a children's song. Oriel panned the camera shooting over Lisa's shoulder from Bessie to focus on Ngai.

Bessie let go of Ngai's hand and reached up to caress her hair. "Hush, Sweetie," she said. "Hush now. It's all right." She looked back at Lisa. "Every time she hears that h-word, she sings the Barney song." After a moment, Ngai's voice faded to silence but she turned to look at Bessie and smiled.

"You've still got arthritis," Lisa pressed. "It wore you out just walking over here."

"Yes, that's right, but I do, I come," Bessie said, meeting Ngai's gaze. "Jesus, he lookin' out for me. I go to church, say my prayers." She nodded toward Ngai. "Pray for her."

Ngai brought her hands up in front of her face, her lips moving, as if she was praying.

"I'll be all right," Bessie said.

"How long can you keep visiting Ngai?" Lisa asked. "If she isn't getting any better—"

"Long as I have to, Honey." Bessie sat back in her chair, facing Lisa again. "It make me sad, sometimes, but I can't just leave her. The nurses, they fine but they just doin' they jobs. She don't have no friends 'cept me.

"I guess I'm blessed." She glanced at Ngai. "I'm all right but I worry about her. I could be like her. She such a sweet little thing 'fore the 'mentia took her mind away. She better now but she ain't better, if you know what I mean. Why didn't the viruses cure her like they did me?"

* * *

Even after talking with Charlene long into the night after the reception, Sarah thought the news reports about the viruses were just the latest media frenzy. There was too much about the whole story that felt wrong. And she could see how the people who had come out in favor of the "new immortality"—they called themselves "Pro-Life"—and those who feared or opposed what the viruses were doing were manipulating the press. She knew the techniques: she'd used them all herself. As the week went on, her doubts deepened.

On Tuesday, Ken Bowersox stormed into her office with Gayle Forrester at his heels. "Six months ago, what you said last week about protecting our reputation would have been wise. Today, every poll, including our own, not to mention all the credible reporting out there, says you're wrong."

"I'm right," Sarah said through clenched teeth.

Bowersox walked up to the edge of her desk, put his hands on it and leaned toward his boss. "One word, Sarah: immortality. No matter what you think, most people believe the viruses have given them immortality. They don't want to hear anything else. They're angry that people are still dying from accidents and gunshots. The bandwagon's leaving the station and we're not on board."

Sarah stood, forcing him to straighten up as well. "But it's not real. They can't have what isn't real." She looked back and forth between her visitors. "We can't just follow the herd on a train to nowhere."

"Sarah? Kenneth?" Gayle said from her usual seat at the far end of the sofa, as close as she could get to the office door. "You're both right."

They looked at her with puzzled expressions.

"It's not just accidents," she explained. "The scientists never said anything about the other kinds of diseases: bacterial, fungal, parasitic. My contact at Johns Hopkins didn't, either. All they ever talked about, all that's in the article, are genetic and viral diseases. If that's right—"

"Then the poll numbers are even more important," Bowersox said. "Joe and Jane Sixpack won't get the distinction between bacterial and viral diseases but they'll be pissed when Aunt Tillie dies from a staph infection after she went to the doctor for another facelift."

Sarah stared across the room, thinking. She flicked her gaze to a painting that hung on the wall opposite the sofa, then jerked away. *Charlie.* She wrenched her mind back to the present but a surge of excitement bloomed inside her. "Of course! People will demand protection from those diseases, and accidents and… there's so much more… to ensure their immortality, whether it's real or not." *How could I have missed that?*

The statistician nodded. "A lot of those things are deadly too."

"And what's more unsafe than dying from something that's preventable?" Sarah asked, smiling at Gayle, although there was more calculation than delight in her eyes. "Okay, you're right. This does fit with our mission. Fits perfectly. I'm just a little slow. Now that I see it, it's an opportunity SAFE-T doesn't dare miss." She cupped her hands in front of her, then spread her fingers up and out, "It's like a flower opening up."

Gayle exchanged a "not that again" look with Bowersox. It was one of Sarah's favorite images. They knew the risks of her sudden enthusiasms: they were the ones who had to clean up the mess every time she went too far. This time, though, was different.

Sarah reined in her emotions with a big shrug. "Still, it depends on whether the scientists are right. They could be wrong. In fact, we'd better assume they *are* wrong, no matter what the reporters and the polls are saying." She walked into the middle of the room, forcing Bowersox to turn to face her. "But, you know what luck is, don't you?" she asked Gayle.

"Well… I… sure."

"It's when preparation meets opportunity. This is the beginning of a great opportunity; we need to prepare to take it." Sarah grinned at her staffers. "Thank you for changing my mind. You've made my day!" She hugged her deputy, then strode over to Gayle, who stood as she approached. The height difference between them left the older woman's head on Sarah's chest when they hugged. Gayle pulled back from the embrace as soon as she dared.

"Really, you did," Sarah said, her arm still around Gayle's shoulder. "Start planning our response, Kenneth. Remember, preparation meets opportunity!"

* * *

The scene in the report shifted to Lisa standing in front of another light-brown wood door. "Besides the elderly," she said, "most of the other patients here are accident victims, like 16-year-old Leo Francis of nearby Krugerville." She turned and opened the door.

Inside the room, Leo was propped up by the elevated head of the bed. A translucent corrugated plastic tube ran across the light-blue institutional blanket to his throat. In the background, a mechanical ventilator was pushing air through the tube into his lungs. Oriel had turned up the recording volume on Leo's microphone to catch the intermittent whishing as the machine helped the boy breathe. Leo's parents were standing on either side of the bed, his mother stroking his shoulder-length, curly blond hair. His narrow face still held some of its baby fat but his blue eyes had a hardness that Oriel kept zooming in on.

Lisa said, "Leo, tell us what happened."

The boy waited for the machine to inhale for him. After the rush of air filled his lungs, he spoke, his voice tight with the effort to control his breathing. "Me and my buddies, we was out four-wheelin' in the woods. Hit a stump or something. Threw me off. Broke my neck."

"But you survived," Lisa said, as if she was surprised.

The ventilator hissed. "Yeah. My friend Rickey called 9-1-1."

When Leo didn't continue, his father picked up the story and Oriel panned the camera left to him. "Fire department called for the helicopter an' they took him down to Plano."

"First time I got to fly in a chopper," Leo said with a grin. "Didn't see much, though."

"Didn't your son have the immortality viruses in him?" Lisa asked. "Why didn't they help?"

"His doctors said they wouldn't help," his mother said. "The viruses, I mean. They tried some medicines on him but his neck's still broke. They say maybe in a few years they might could fix a broken neck." She started to cry. Oriel zoomed in the video to a tight close-up of her face. "But they think… they say…."

"They say his spine is healed, sort of," his father said, "and maybe they won't be able to grow it back together right… something like that."

"So your son may be like this for a very long time," Lisa said.

His parents gave the smallest of nods, as if that was a possibility they couldn't yet face.

"Leo, what do you think about that?"

Leo waited for the machine to breathe for him. "I don't think it's right," he said. "It ain't fair that I should be like this for… forever."

* * *

After Gayle and Bowersox left, Sarah was about to return to her desk when the painting caught her attention again. It showed a sailboat racing across the water, its mainsail and jib inflated. A woman was sitting at the tiller but her face was painted without details. A man and another woman were leaning out from the near rail, which was so high above the water the boat seemed ready to tip over. A bright red triangle, out of place against the muted colors of the rest of the painting, poked out ahead of the jib.

SAFE-T's staff and visitors wondered about the painting. It was out of place with the room's other decorations, awards and pictures of Sarah with various dignitaries. The director never said anything about boating except in the context of safety, but every so often she would make it clear that as long as she ran the agency, the picture would hang in her office.

"Clarissa," Sarah called to her computer as she eased herself onto the sofa. "Close the door. No interruptions."

"Yes, Sarah," it replied. The office door beeped as it swung shut.

As Sarah gazed at the painting, her insides collapsed and tears she never let anyone else see formed at the corners of her eyes.

She had been twenty-five that sunny summer day, comfortable at last with her bisexuality, still single, still just Sarah Green, although Roger Dale, whom she'd been dating since college, had a good chance of changing that. Charlie Garvey, her friend since their sophomore year at Boston College, had been after her to come sailing with him almost from the day they'd met, but she never had. With the Congressional August recess under way and her boss, a veteran congressman from Boston, back in his district, she'd wangled a weekend off.

She was going sailing for the first time in her life, on the Chesapeake Bay, in a tiny boat. Charlie kept saying the most outrageous things. His wife, Carol Stahl, insisted they weren't true but Sarah wasn't entirely convinced he was teasing.

Once they were out on the bay, Sarah relaxed. Instead of being the non-stop green roller coaster she'd feared, the water was smooth. The boat's hull sliced through it with just the slightest hiss, the bass rumble from the sails in counterpoint. Soon Sarah was grinning with delight, doubly so because Carol had insisted she leave her phone on shore.

In the afternoon, as they headed back to the marina, Charlie set the mainsail on the port side with the jib and Sarah shrieked in surprise as the boat heeled over. Carol grabbed her and dragged her up to sit on the starboard rail. "Lean back," she shouted over the rising rush of air and water. "Hang on. Hook your heels on the bench. Don't worry, you won't fall out."

"Why are we doing this?" Sarah asked.

"We can go really fast. Hiking out like this balances the boat."

"Isn't it dangerous?"

As Carol shook her head, the bow dug into the crest of a wave, sending a spray of salt water over the women. Caught by surprise, Sarah squawked and sputtered as she wiped her face.

"Male driver," Carol said, grabbing Sarah's arm. "Has to splash in the puddles."

The idyllic day was destroyed a few minutes later when a red, fifty foot long cigarette boat roared out into the bay, its four inboard engines at full throttle. The young man at the wheel saw the sailboat but the tequila he'd been drinking all day kept him from realizing he was on a collision course until it was too late. Then he turned the wrong way.

Sarah never saw the red boat or felt the impact. Charlie and everyone on the cigarette boat were killed. Carol and Sarah were badly injured and spent weeks recovering.

The accident had been preventable. Seven people, including a six year old girl, had died that day, and the course of Sarah's life had changed.

Thirty years later, Sarah gazed at the painting. "I promised I'd never let it happen again, Charlie," she whispered. "I'm trying."

* * *

As they drove back to their hotel, Lisa reached over from the passenger seat to stroke Oriel's arm. "The way you spliced together those bits with the kid was wonderful," she said. "I didn't think he was ever going to admit he might be paralyzed forever."

"Thanks. I know a few tricks. Getting the old lady to sing, now, that was—"

"Luck," Lisa said. "Pure luck."

* * *

Arnie Steen managed a small 'Trons Town electronics chain store in Round Rock, Texas, under the name Larry Lavaliere. The store was empty this afternoon except for Arnie and one employee. Business wouldn't pick up in the strip mall until later.

The job was a cover for what Arnie considered his calling, being the master bomb maker for the Mother Earth Brigades. The Mothers considered themselves the true defenders of the planet's ecosystems. The people they considered Earth's rapists and pillagers, and the sheep who just went along, called them ecoterrorists.

The Mothers were organized in small, isolated cells. Few members knew each other and they rarely met in person. All used code names, distorted voices, and video avatars in their electronic communications to keep their real identities hidden. Arnie went by "Weasel," as in "pop goes the weasel," because it fit his way of working: sneak like a weasel into some place and make something go "pop" that wasn't supposed to. Like a dam. Or a ski resort.

His phone chirped when an encrypted text message came in. *SVTC now*, it read, followed by a phone number. "Hey, Toby," he called from his stool by the cash register. The University of Texas engineering student was playing one of the latest video games. "I need to do something in the office. Cover for a few minutes, will you?"

Toby straightened from his usual slouch, which added a couple of inches to his gangly frame, and ran a hand through his short red hair. "Uh, sure, yeah!"

"If you need me, leave the curtain open and knock on the door."

"Okay." Toby had wondered about the calls and messages that made his boss run back to his office. Larry trusted him to run the store, though, so he figured if he needed his privacy, that was his business.

Arnie heaved himself off the stool and hustled through the red curtain that hid the back of the store from the retail space. As he closed the office door, he turned on a small white-noise generator that sat on a filing cabinet. Months ago he'd forgotten to turn it off after a call. When Toby had asked about it, he'd claimed it helped him think by keeping out distractions. He was pleased when the young man took the hint and stopped bothering him when the door was closed.

He activated the special video teleconferencing software on his phone as he sat down. The Mothers' computer experts claimed its security algorithm was unbreakable. He dialed the number from the message. The phones exchanged information and synchronized their internal clocks.

* * *

In a quiet room full of computers in an ordinary-looking office building near Washington, D.C., a data recorder opened a new channel.

* * *

Arnie's phone displayed a series of messages, then asked for his thumb print on the touch screen, iris and retina scans via the camera, and a voice print, for which he said, "Green earth." When the software was satisfied, the display reported TOP SECRET CODE WORD: MOTHERS in a red banner across the top.

The face looking back at him from the screen was approximately human: eyes, a nose, and a mouth molded into the rough bark of an old tree. It was Treebeard the Ent, an old movie character. The person behind the image was Arnie's channel to "Mom," the Mother Earth Brigades' leader, but he knew nothing else about him… or her. Arnie's own representation was a skinny cartoon weasel with bulging eyes and a bulbous black nose at the end of a pointed snout. It looked nothing like him: overweight, baby-faced, with short, tousled brown hair, the stereotypical image of the geeky store manager he cultivated.

"You've heard about the viruses," Treebeard said in a raspy voice.

"Who hasn't? Mom's worried, right?"

"Nutso. I showed him some numbers… coming your way now."

Arnie's phone chimed as the file arrived. "Got 'em," he said.

"He doesn't know whether to shit or go blind. We've kicked some ideas around but they all suck." The Ent's tree trunk head twisted back and forth. "Mother Earth's going to be crawling with human locusts before long, eating everything in their path and leaving nothing but shit and piss behind. We've got to stop it."

Arnie opened the file and scanned through it, then whistled. "So what do you want me to do, build an insecticide bomb?"

The Ent pointed a gnarled-branch finger at him. "Give me some credit. We don't need to kill everybody. The scientists said the last virus was the key in the lock. We pull out the key."

"Right," Arnie said sarcastically. "What the fuck do I know about biology?"

"You don't have to. Lots of labs are working on the viruses. Maybe one of them—"

"Don't make me laugh," Arnie said. "Who's got a Level IV containment lab we can use without being detected? How long would it take to figure out what we'd need? Or how much? How do we spread it? How can we be sure it'll work? Bombs don't work for everything, you know." He scowled at the phone. "Too fucking many questions you don't have answers to."

The avatar watched him, holding its moss-covered chin in its hand. "But if we could make it, you could spread it, couldn't you?"

"Jesus, you're stupid," Arnie said. "This thing is worldwide. Do the Mothers have the resources for a worldwide strike? I can bomb one place, easy. This… I don't do impossible shit."

Both were quiet for a long moment. Finally, the other person said, "You could hit the lab in Dallas while we try to come up with something better. The press is still buzzing around down there. It'll get plenty of attention. It's all about psychology, right? We need to do something quick, that's the thing."

Arnie didn't like the constricted feeling he was getting in his chest. The chance to take action usually gave him excited tingles, but not this time. He needed to slow this down. "You think so, huh? You are so freaking wrong. Bombing that lab will blow up in our faces bigger than shit. That doctor's a hero to the sheep right now and you want me to kill her. It's psychology, all right, and you need to learn some."

As he shut down the VTC software after the call, Arnie thought, *Jesus, what a stupid idea. Mom should kill it. Needs to. But if he doesn't….* He shivered. *I don't like it. Can't let them rush me. Rush, and you take stupid risks, make stupid mistakes.*

He slipped the phone back into its holster, then turned off the noise generator as he opened the office door. His short walk back into the storefront was filled with dark thoughts.

* * *

In another quiet room in that nondescript office building, a message window popped up at one of the workstations. The man sitting at the computer read the message, and then forwarded it. He checked a calendar, stood up, stretched, and headed for the door. "I'm going to see the boss," he said to the woman sitting in the cubicle nearest the exit.

"Okay," she said, without looking up.

CHAPTER 6

IMAM VOSHON LELAND, the leader of the Islamic Council of North Texas and Baxter's host for the Black Ministers' Convocation's annual convention in Fort Worth, escorted him through security and into the conference center ballroom. The side doors were blocked.

The delegates were hungry for reliable information about the viruses, so at Baxter's request, the host committee had arranged a Saturday afternoon session with a special speaker. A young black woman was standing near the front of the huge room, guarded by two muscular men wearing bulky but tailored suits and close-cropped hair. She was fidgeting, clasping and unclasping her hands as she looked around. One of her guards spotted Baxter, leaned over, and spoke to her.

"Ah, that's Dr. Barnes," Imam Leland said.

"Why couldn't Dr. Hogan come?"

"They said she was unavailable." Leland grimaced. "They've been threatened. That's the reason for all the security."

Baxter sighed. "Even after they announced a miracle."

"Not everyone sees it that way."

"Surely God would not do wickedly," Baxter said, paraphrasing Job.

"Allah, never. Man? That's another story."

Leland made introductions when they reached Ellanna. Baxter put his hand on her upper arm, trying to reassure her. She was trembling. "I'm sure the audience will be very interested in what you have to say," he said.

They mounted the stage and Baxter strode to the podium while Ellanna and Leland took their seats. The guards moved to positions in front of the stage. A video screen dominated the center of the wall behind the lectern. Other screens hung from the ceiling so the people in the back of the room could see.

As the room quieted and late-comers straggled to the vacant chairs in the front rows, the webcast director signaled Baxter that they were live on the Internet.

"Brothers and sisters," the minister said, "we are blessed that our convention is here in Fort Worth, because the scientists who've been doing the research we've gathered to learn about work just across town in Dallas. Well, for you Texans, that's just across town. For me, it seems like halfway back to home." He paused for the chuckles that rippled through the audience.

He led the assembly in a prayer, then introduced Ellanna, who walked to the lectern as the audience applauded politely. He reached out to shake her hand, then pulled her close to kiss her cheek and whisper in her ear, "You'll do fine."

As he released her and stepped away, she took her place and adjusted the microphone.

"Reverend Baxter, Imam Leland, thank you for inviting me to speak today." She looked up and was dazzled by the spotlights pointed at her. "I'm not used to speaking before such a big audience. In fact, I haven't been this nervous since I defended my dissertation at Stanford." She paused while the audience laughed and clapped.

"You're all right," a woman called, which generated more applause.

Ellanna grinned. "You're making me blush, now, but thank you. The last few weeks have been very difficult for Janet—Dr. Janet Hogan, that is—and for the rest of our team. I've worked in the lab for the last few years. A lot of people have jumped to conclusions about what we know and what it means."

She described what genes and chromosomes were and how they worked, then went over the team's initial discoveries and what they had learned since.

"It's important that you understand that real people from all walks of life, all social classes, and all races have been infected by the viruses. We don't know everything the viruses do yet, and it will be a long time before we do. Yes, there are reports of cancers going into remission with the viruses seeming to be the only common factor, but anecdotal reports are not conclusive. Even when we see changes in a patient's genome, that doesn't establish a causal link to the viruses."

She paused to scan the audience. "We've never said these viruses will make people immortal. Never. They won't stop a bullet or keep you from drowning. As far as we're concerned, all this talk about immortality is premature at best, dishonest at worst."

She smiled with surprise when the audience broke into applause. As it died down, she glanced back at Baxter. "That's all I had prepared. Shall we let people ask questions?"

A man in a black, silver, and gold dashiki robe and round kofia hat was striding toward the front microphone.

"You'll find this group isn't shy about asking questions," Baxter said as he joined her at the podium. *Especially Brother Elijah,* he thought. *Have to put him off.* "I'm going to exercise a point of privilege and ask the first question. Dr. Barnes, let's say this thing, this effect, whatever it is you've discovered, is real and that we can all live for a very long time, even if not forever. Don't you think that presents a tremendous opportunity for spiritual enlightenment and growth, a chance for every one of us to come closer to our Creator?"

"I'd like to think so," Ellanna said. "To be honest, our focus has been on the science. We talk about what all this might mean, but there's so much we don't know yet. The biology is hard enough. We have to leave the deep thinking about the religious implications to all of you."

A rustle of uneasy conversation swept through the audience. The man in the robe made a big show of coughing to announce his impatience.

"You're not saying those other implications aren't important?" Baxter asked, turning to her.

"Oh, no. We've had to think about them a lot more in the last few weeks." She shrugged. "But there are only so many hours in a day."

Baxter recognized a woman standing at a microphone at the side of the hall.

"Am I going to get a chance to speak?" the man in the dashiki demanded.

"You will, Brother Elijah," Baxter said. "I won't forget you." *Much as I wish I could.*

"Thank you, Mr. President," the woman said. "Dr. Barnes, is it too much to hope that only the righteous have received these viruses?"

"I'm afraid it is," Ellanna said with a sad smile. "Viruses are just biological machines. They don't know the difference between a sinner and a saint."

"I believe it is my turn now, Mister President," Brother Elijah announced.

Even with people standing at other microphones around the hall, Baxter knew he couldn't put the preacher off any longer. "All right, Brother Elijah, go ahead with your question."

"Thank you, President Baxter," he said, his voice full of scorn. "Now, let me get this straight, *Doctor* Barnes. First you claimed we've all become immortal."

"No we—"

"Then I saw your white mistress give another interview where she denied she'd ever said any such thing. Now you come here and tell us that A—" He held one finger high above his head. "You don't think about the moral consequences of your work, that Almighty God never enters into your thought processes, if they can be called that, and B—" He held up a second finger. "That you know next to nothing about these things you've discovered."

A murmur grew in the hall.

"My first question… my first question to you, Dr. Barnes, is this: are you taking any money from the government for your studies?"

Ellanna gasped and jerked backwards at the preacher's allegations and his sudden change of direction. "We've applied for a grant, sure. Most of the support for this kind of research comes from the NIH or one of the other federal agencies but—"

"So since you're taking Caesar's gold, we should expect that Caesar is telling you what you can and cannot study, and what you can and cannot say about your findings. Isn't that true?"

"No! That's not true at all!" *This is crazy!* Ellanna glanced at Baxter for help.

Before he could step in, Brother Elijah was speaking again, pointing an accusing finger at her. "Did not some servant of Caesar at the National Institutes of Health for White Folks condescend to give you money to do what he approved of—I mean, approve your grant application?"

"I... but... that's not the way grants work," Ellanna protested. *National Institutes of Health for White Folks? What planet is he from?* "If you're turned down the first time, you find out why, fix it, and send it back in. Even then, you might not get funded."

The rumble of conversation in the hall was growing louder.

"So until that servant of Caesar is satisfied that you're going to do the work he wants, you don't get his gold, do you?"

The nervous shaking that had gone away during her presentation was back now. *Stay calm,* she thought. *He's setting a trap, wants you to say something stupid.* "I wouldn't characterize the process that way at all," she said, trying to be professional and keep her voice level. "Give and take is normal but we've never, ever, been told what to study or what not to study. That's just wrong."

The noise in the ballroom fell away a bit. Ellanna dared to hope she was regaining control.

"Well, I didn't expect you to admit that you're one of Caesar's minions," Brother Elijah continued. "So I guess I should also not expect you to admit that those same servants of our oppressors are refusing to let you to tell us the truth about what you know. But I'm going to demand that, anyway. Is it not true, Dr. Barnes, that this is just another way for this nation's government to keep the African-American down?"

Around the hall the noise grew louder again. A man to Ellanna's left shouted, "That's right! That's right!"

Brother Elijah thundered, "Is this not just another way to keep the nigger down? To deny the black man and black woman their rightful dignity, their place at the table? And how can you, as an African-American woman, how can you be a part of this?

"Tell us the truth, Dr. Barnes, if you have the courage. Did not the government in fact create these viruses, just as they did the AIDS virus? And did they not release these viruses just in white communities? Weren't these viruses designed only to be effective in whites, to ensure that the black man and the brown man and the red man and the yellow man would be kept subservient to the master race, the Aryan race?"

"That is *not* what I said," Ellanna said, trying to be heard over the rising din.

"Oh, yes," a woman called. "Speak the truth, Brother Elijah."

The preacher paused, letting the noise reach its peak, then fade. "You're among friends, here, Sister Ellanna," he said, nearly whispering. "Look around. You're among your brothers and sisters. Why don't you, right here, right now, throw off that white lab coat of twenty-first century slavery, tell Caesar you're not going to do his bidding, not going to lie for him, not going to cover up the truth anymore?" His voice was rising now. "Are you going to serve your people, Sister Ellanna, or are you going to serve Caesar? Are you—in front of this assembled congregation—are you going to repent and serve Almighty God—as we do—and tell the truth? Or are you going to continue to lie for Caesar's gold? What are you going to do, Sister Ellanna?"

"Tell it, Sister!" another woman called out.

"Yes, Jesus!" cried someone else. "The truth! The truth!"

Ellanna stared at the preacher in silver and black. She gripped the lectern so hard that the skin over her trembling knuckles faded from its normal dark brown to near tan. She muttered, "That's so twisted." In a louder voice, she said, "I haven't lied, and I won't now. You're the one who's—"

"What was that?" Brother Elijah shouted. "What was that? Let the hall be quiet so we can hear her answer."

Ellanna looked at Baxter, pleading for him to intervene.

"Brother Elijah," Baxter said, "why don't we let someone else have a chance to ask Dr. Barnes a question?"

"First let her answer mine, President Baxter. I thought I saw her say something, but I couldn't hear her. She should answer my question first, before she answers someone else's. And don't let her hide the truth."

"Let's hear it!" a man shouted. "Let her speak!"

"Of course I'll let her speak," Baxter said, "but with no more interruptions. Give her a chance to answer your questions. You say you want to hear the truth from her. If *you're* telling the truth, then give her the chance to speak." Without waiting for the preacher to agree, he said, "Dr. Barnes?"

Brother Elijah remained at the microphone, his feet apart, head and shoulders back, arms crossed over his chest, eyes boring into Ellanna. The room grew so quiet the only sound was the rush of the air flowing from the air conditioning system.

There was a glass of water on a small table next to the podium. Ellanna picked it up, hoping that a sip would unstick her mouth. The glass shook as she raised it to her lips. She managed to drink without spilling any water and put the glass back in its place. "I hope," she said. The room that had been so large before was squeezing her from all sides. "When Reverend Baxter prayed for open minds and understanding, and we all said Amen, I believed you meant it… that you were seeking knowledge and understanding. Instead, some of you have turned this Q and A into an inquisition based on distortions and plain old lies. Some of you have demanded the truth while refusing to acknowledge the truth that is right in front of you. Understanding doesn't happen when the answer is decided beforehand.

"Put yourselves in our shoes for a minute." She took a deep breath and focused on Brother Elijah. "Imagine what this is like: we've been called every name in the book by people who don't know us and don't know anything about our work. A few, clearly unbalanced people have even threatened to kill us. Until now, that's been done on voice mail or e-mail or something, not to our faces. Imagine how terrifying that is.

"Maybe it's different when you know that what you're doing is right. Maybe Dr. King felt that way, I don't know—that was long before I was born—but it hurts, and it's wrong when what you know—when what *little* you know—is so twisted and distorted that you can't recognize it. And by one of your own."

She gazed around the room as best she could against the spotlight. "I know—I *know*—that no one has ever told our team what to say or what not to say. I also know we're a long way from fully understanding what we've discovered. That's normal in science. What I *don't* know is where these viruses came from, and for me, for now, it doesn't matter. I know they've infected me. I'm certain they've infected all of you too. Whatever they've bestowed, blessings or curses, they've bestowed on all of us. *All*… of… us."

The silence in the hall was a blanket, absorbing and stifling Ellanna's words. The audience had slipped away. "What I've told you today is all the truth I know as clearly as I can tell you in layman's terms. If you can't or won't believe that… well, I don't know what else to say. I'm sorry. The truth is all I have."

"Well, *I'm* not satisfied," Brother Elijah declared. "You have disappointed me, Sister Ellanna." He turned and strode out of the hall, to scattered applause and shouts of support.

Baxter asked for more questions but those who might have wanted to express other opinions in public were afraid to do so. He wrapped up the session, and as the delegates filed out, he asked Ellanna to come up to his suite.

She hesitated, then agreed.

Once they were seated in the living room, Baxter said, "I want to apologize for Brother Elijah's behavior. He doesn't represent the majority opinion of the Convocation, I assure you. I know people who have been healed by your viruses… black people."

"You didn't say that," Ellanna murmured. The glass of water she was holding provided no comfort.

"But as you saw, there's a portion of our community that shares his views. You have to understand that."

She looked up for the first time. "I just wish people wouldn't jump to conclusions. I wish powerful people would act responsibly and give us time to do our work instead of prejudging it." She stared hard at Baxter for a moment. "And I wish they'd give us a fair chance to explain it."

She set her glass on a coaster on the coffee table and stood. Baxter, Leland, and her guards stood too. "I don't blame you for what happened downstairs, Reverend Baxter. Maybe you didn't see it coming." She stopped, her jaw muscles twitching. "But now it's gone viral." She grimaced at the bitter pun. "I hope you understand that it just got a lot harder for us to do our work… or explain what it means and be believed. That wasn't what I expected."

Baxter said, "I understand, and again, I apologize." He reached into the inner pocket of his suit coat and pulled out his phone. "May I pass you my business card? If I can help get the truth about your findings out, I'd like to try."

Ellanna hesitated, then took her phone from her purse and let it accept the card. She glanced at it, then put the phone away. "I think I'd better be going."

Baxter held out his hand and she took it. "Imam Leland will see you out."

After the four had left, Baxter returned to his chair with a deep sigh. The suite was silent except for the sound of a vacuum cleaner somewhere down the hall. *The first test of my leadership and I failed.* His Bible lay on the coffee table. Verses scrolled through his mind but none offered the guidance and consolation he needed.

He bowed his head to pray.

* * *

"I appreciate your taking the time to see me, Dr. Hogan," Wade said as he followed Janet into her lab. Her perfume was causing the inside of his head to tingle.

"I'm surprised they let you in," she replied. "The Center's been screening everyone with a one-micron filter. Your chances would have been better on line."

"They wouldn't let me contact you that way, either. I think they were just stalling until they could make a decision. I've been a public figure for a long time."

Janet swept a hand across the room. "Here or in my office?"

Wade surveyed the lab. It was similar to hundreds of others he'd visited, including the ones in EARTH's headquarters building. Ahead and to his left, three work benches were set in parallel, coming toward him from the outside wall. Glass-fronted storage cabinets stood above gray work surfaces cluttered with microscopes, centrifuges, plastic arrays of test wells, glassware, and other equipment. Behind him, a row of freezers stood against the wall on the right. A datawall was on the left, diagrams and data windows scattered across it.

Janet watched Wade look around. She cocked her head to one side. "Ever been in a lab?"

She's a lot better looking in person than in her bio, Wade thought. "What? Oh, sure, lots of times." *And she's half your age.* "I just… I guess I expected something more dramatic." He grinned. "It's silly, I know." *God, what a stupid thing to say. Trina'd be laughing her ass off.*

Puzzled, Janet said, "I'm sorry you're disappointed."

Wade laughed, embarrassed. "Don't be. I'm being foolish. Here is fine. I'd like to meet the rest of your team, if they're available."

Janet introduced him to Ellanna and Satya. "Gerardo, my grad student, is upstairs."

She and Wade pulled up stools in one of the aisles between the benches, so they could talk with Ellanna through the space under the cabinets while she worked. Wade scanned Janet's left hand. *No ring… what am I thinking?*

"You're concerned about a population explosion," Janet said.

Gets right to the point, doesn't she? Wade thought. "We've run a lot of projections and—"

"You're getting ahead of the science, Mr. Wade."

"Aren't you concerned about—"

"No, I'm not," Janet said, her lips a thin, flat line.

Startled, Wade met her eyes, noticed the gold flecks in the brown irises, and found he couldn't look away. "This is a very serious problem. It's—"

"Just like everyone else's," Janet said. "And they all want me—*us*—to solve it, yesterday, if not sooner."

Wade glanced at Ellanna, who was making sure she looked busy filling the sample wells in the tray in front of her. He caught her peeking at them and she quickly looked down at her work.

"Your bio says you've got a science degree," Janet said. "You should know better than to jump to conclusions from data that's as incomplete as ours."

"Okay, Professor," Wade said with a grin. "Message received. We didn't realize you felt that way about your conclusions. May the humble student ask a question?"

"I'm sorry," Janet said. "It's not *our* conclusions we're having trouble with. What would you like to know?"

Wade cleared a space on the lab bench for his tablet. "Mind if I link this to the datawall?"

"I'll do it." Janet's fingers brushed his as he passed the tablet to her. She missed his smile at the touch but when she gave it back, there was no chance for another one. He slid his stool around next to hers so they were both looking at the big screen. Ellanna shifted a bit so she could see better. Satya joined her from beyond the second bench.

Wade called up a graph that showed lines arcing up from left to right. "You're right to think we made some assumptions."

"A lot of—" Janet said, then blushed and looked away. "I'm sorry. I'll be quiet."

She's so cute when she looks that way. He patted her on the shoulder. "That's all right."

He pulled himself back to his topic. "Our assumptions are based on factual data. The CDC is seeing signs of a significant drop in the death rate. We used their data to project how low it might go—not all the way to zero, though." He smiled at her.

She frowned and he looked back at the datawall. She checked to see whether Ellanna was watching them, but couldn't catch her eye.

Sensing her distraction, Wade nudged her arm with his elbow. She shifted away from him on her stool. "The lines on the chart show Earth's population over time for the different growth rates. As you can see, they—"

"All blow through the carrying capacity line," Janet said. "I can read the chart."

Delighted, Wade thought, *She gets it!*

"According to you."

He frowned, worried by her flat tone.

Janet took a pipetting tool from the top of the work bench and played with it while she thought.

"Those rates are very low," Satya said.

Wade leaned back so he could see past Janet, steadying himself by holding the backrest of her stool. "A fraction of a percent of the current rate. That's the black line on the chart."

Ellanna whistled. "That's bad."

Wade called up another chart. "These are the growth and birth rates we have to get down to, in order to stay under the ceiling by certain dates." He glanced at Janet. She wasn't looking at the display.

"Good luck with that," Ellanna said.

Janet slapped the pipetter onto the work bench, launched herself off the stool, and stalked into the open space between the benches and the datawall. "So what do you expect us to do about all this, Mr. Wade?" she said, her back still toward him.

Despite her angry, rigid posture, Wade found himself admiring her figure. "I was… I was hoping you had some idea how we could keep this from happening. Maybe partner…." *That sounds so weak.*

"We happen to be very busy right now, Mr. Wade."

"EARTH has its own research teams who could—"

"Add to our already excessive workload," Janet said.

Ellanna and Satya exchanged worried glances.

"There's also the small matter of funding," Janet added.

"I'm prepared to authorize up to a million dollars for this work," Wade said.

Janet stood still for a moment, then looked over her shoulder at Ellanna. "That sound familiar?"

Ellanna nodded.

Not understanding her comment, Wade plunged on, slipping off his stool to take a step toward her. "The health of the planet, of all humanity, could be hanging in the balance, Jan—Dr. Hogan. We're facing a terrible problem. If we could just—"

Janet spun toward him, her face red. "See what I mean? See what I *mean? No!* No, I don't know how to solve your problem, Mr. Wade. I have no goddamn idea. I don't know if there's anything to worry about, if this immortality effect everyone's so goddamn wrapped around the axle about will last, if it's even real. All those folks who got well all of a sudden, like my mother? Maybe they'll all keel over dead tomorrow." She waved at the chart on the wall. "*Then* what will your projections mean? They'll be crap, won't they? Maybe you can use them as organic fertilizer." She marched across the lab and stopped at the entry to the anteroom outside her office.

"Good luck with your problem, Mr. Wade," she said. "I hope you find someone who can help you with it. In the meantime, if you happen to come across someone who can help us figure out the fundamental problems of what these viruses really do, and how, and why, please don't hesitate to give Dr. Sayid a call. We could sure use the help." She disappeared around the corner. Seconds later, a door slammed shut.

Gerardo walked into the awkward silence in the lab, holding up his tablet. "I've got the—" He looked around. "What?"

Satya slid off her stool. "Come," she said. "Show me."

He flashed a perplexed look at Ellanna as he walked past.

"Tell you later." She stood, walked around the end of the bench, and took Wade's arm. "Let's go down to security."

As they waited for the elevator, he said, "I put my foot in it, didn't I?"

Ellanna favored him with a long, appraising look, then gestured for him to enter as the door opened. "Welcome to our world," she said, pushing the button for the ground floor. "Everybody wants something impossible from us, but no matter what we do, or don't do, somebody else thinks it's wrong."

Wade scanned the elevator's control screen for a moment, then turned to face her. "I respect Dr. Hogan's work—yours, the team's—very much. I didn't realize things were so difficult for you. Please accept my apologies."

The elevator door opened. "This way, please," she said.

* * *

Ellanna tapped on Janet's office door. "It's me," she called.

Janet was sitting at her desk, her elbows on the surface of the ell, chin in her hands. When Ellanna sat down across from her, she looked up. "Screwed that one up royally, didn't I?"

"He meant well. Apologized on the way down."

Janet sighed. "Guess I should too."

"He really likes you."

"*What?*" Janet gaped at her friend.

"I was watching him. He's sweet on you. He *wants* you," she teased.

Janet threw a pencil at her. "Stop it."

Laughing, Ellanna said, "It's true. I swear. He wants to live with you *forever*."

"He didn't say that."

"You were too mad to notice his expression when you dumped on him, then walked out."

"I don't need this," Janet moaned.

In mock exasperation Ellanna said, "What *I* want to know is why you get the come-ons and I get shit on. It's not fair."

Janet leaned way back in her chair, the heels of her hands over her eyes. "Oh, God," she said. "Oh, God."

* * *

Lisa began the next in her series of reports, "Immortality in America: Winners and Losers," standing in front of a dark red brick, five story Gothic Revival building. Its tall, pointed windows outlined in contrasting white trim filled the frame over her left shoulder. "Nashville," she said. "The Music City. Music Row, Division Street, the West End, dozens of recording companies and studios. That's Ryman Auditorium behind me, the Mother Church of Country Music and long-time home of the Grand Ole Opry." The scene shifted to a music club, a band on stage, some patrons dancing, others sitting in their seats, moving and clapping with the music. In voice-over she said, "If you're a country or bluegrass lover, this is your heaven. If you're a country or bluegrass musician, it's your Mecca. You have to come here to have a chance to be somebody."

The picture returned to Lisa, now picking her way through a cluttered and dirty alley behind a run-down building. A gusting wind from a distant thunderstorm ruffled her hair. "The music industry has always been tough to break into. It's hard to make it to the national stage, to be famous." She knelt to pick up a piece of paper she'd placed there ahead of time, held down with a rock that Oriel kept out of view. The band advertisement had once been posted somewhere, on a street light or utility pole. She held it up for the camera and continued walking. "But for every singer who makes it to the big time, hundreds end up like this group, scuffling to get gigs, and eventually—" She crumpled the paper and threw it toward a dumpster. "Tossed aside.

"The immortality viruses haven't made things any easier."

The scene shifted again. Lisa was sitting on the worn wooden steps of the front porch of a house that was at least a hundred years old and needed a fresh coat of paint. Across from her, leaning against one of the heavy wood columns supporting the porch roof, sat a brown-haired man who might have been in his thirties, forties, or even fifties. Carlisle Boone's face held traces of youth, but the lines around his mouth and on his forehead suggested he wasn't young anymore, no matter what the calendar might say. An acoustic guitar rested on his jeans in front of a bright red shirt with the name and logo of a music festival on it. When Oriel was setting up the two-shot, Boone had protested that he played bass, but he'd given in, made one more compromise.

In the front yard, more dirt than grass, one camera faced Lisa, the other the musician. Behind Oriel, outside the chain-link fence, neighborhood kids had gaped, awed for a moment to be watching a real live interview. After a few minutes, though, when all Carl and the lady did was talk, they'd wandered away, disappointed and bored.

"How long have you been coming to Nashville?" Lisa asked.

"Twenty years, off and on," Boone replied. "Just a kid, the first time. Just a dumb kid from Natchez. Thought I was the greatest bass guitar player ever."

"And?"

"Oh, ever'one was real polite. Told me I was good, just not quite good enough, yet." He looked at the guitar as if he were seeing it for the first time. "But if I kept working, I'd sure be a good session player soon." He set the instrument beside him on the porch.

"And now, twenty years later?"

"I'm still not quite good enough. Not yet."

"But you keep coming back...." Lisa looked concerned, even a little puzzled.

"It's all I do, Ma'am... all I do half-decent, anyway." Boone shifted, looked straight at Lisa for a moment, then down at his arms crossed over his stomach.

"Didn't the new immortality give you some hope, then? You've got more time...."

Boone made a hissing noise between his teeth, as if he'd started to say "shit" then thought better of it.

"No?" Lisa asked, as if surprised.

"Just made it harder. More kids comin' to town, desperate to be rich and famous, just like I was." He rubbed his hands on his pants legs. "It's funny. They got all the time in the world now but... seems like they're in a bigger rush than before."

"Do you still want it?" Lisa's voice was gentle.

Oriel's video zoomed in on Boone's face, his eyes, exposing the pain they revealed as the question went straight to his heart. He looked down and away. "I'm just tryin' to survive."

* * *

Arnie Steen was running down the street as fast as he could, his augmented legs letting him keep pace with the fleeing police car ahead of him. The grenade launcher mounted on his back lobbed rounds at the zigzagging vehicle while he fired at it with both hand-held Gatling guns. Bullets and shrapnel pinged and sparked off the car's armor. A lone gunner shot back from one of the back seat windows. Around them, the city blazed, sirens wailed, and explosions boomed.

Ammunition's running low. Have to kill them before it runs out or they'll get help. Be in deep shit then. He was alone.

There was still a chance, though. His enhanced vision told him the car's armor was weakening. There were soft spots. And he'd picked up a pattern in the driver's evasive maneuvers.

Two grenades left. The driver was about to fake right, weave left, then veer far right. Over to there. He made a quick estimate of the grenade's time of flight.

Aim.. launch… now! The weapon burped as the round left the tube.

The car jinked, wove, veered, and….

CRITICAL PRIORITY CALL flashed in huge, gold-shadowed red letters in front of him, blocking his view. Everything else went silent.

"The fuck?" Arnie shouted.

"Treebeard the Ent has placed a Critical Priority call," a resonant male voice announced. "Do you wish to answer?"

"No!"

"The game is frozen," the voice replied. "You may resume after the call. Treebeard the Ent—"

"All right, all right," Arnie growled. "Answer. Jesus!"

The game's imagery and sounds disappeared from Arnie's virtual reality goggles and earbuds, replaced by a dark, dismal forest. The Ent avatar creaked into view. "Greetings, Weasel."

"What?" Arnie demanded. "I was in the middle of something."

"Better some*thing* than some*one*," the Ent said. Its bark skin crinkled around its eyes and lips as it chuckled.

"Yeah, yeah. *What?*"

"Message from Mom: get the lab."

"Didn't you tell—" Arnie found himself staring into an empty forest. The Ent had vanished. Then that scene dissolved back to the frozen game. RESUMING, flashed in front of him, IN 5… 4… 3… 2… 1.

The car yanked to the left. The grenade dropped into the spot Arnie had aimed for and exploded without effect. Standing in the middle of the street, Arnie could only watch.

A burst of gunfire caught him square in the chest. Little pistons on the inside of his game vest thumped him in the ribs and sternum. He fell backwards, caught the edge of the living room coffee table, and flopped onto the floor. His vision turned red, then black as jeers and laughter echoed in his ears.

"Shit," he said.

"Play again?" the game asked.

Arnie sat up, rubbing his shoulder, then his butt. "No, goddammit," he said. "Got stupid work to do. *Stupid.*"

* * *

The eight-foot-tall guitar outside the downtown headquarters of America's Music Video towered over Lisa in the low-angle shot that opened the second part of her report. The camera panned up until the company's logo at the top of the skyscraper appeared above her head. Lisa said, "While individual musicians struggle to survive, Nashville's music industry is doing anything but struggling."

In a lavish office, glowing oak paneling gave way to tall windows that looked out on the Nashville skyline and the black roof of the Ryman Auditorium far below. The female executive sitting across from Lisa was wearing a silk suit that cost thousands of dollars. Modest but flattering, its bronze and gold tones complemented her deep brown skin and black eyes and hair. Oriel's lighting defeated the glare from the windows and made the suit shimmer. The caption at the bottom of the screen read, *Susan Gallarie, Director, Nashville Music Group.*

Lisa opened the interview with a friendly lead. "Country music has never been stronger."

The woman smiled. "That's right. Our market is growing and so is our talent base. We've expanded our pool of new musicians quite a bit in the past year or so."

"Can you attribute that to the viruses?"

Gallarie hesitated. "That's hard to say. Of course you're aware of the miracle of Colby Freed: the viruses cured her cancer and she's resumed her career... very successfully, I might add. We'll be releasing her new album, Second Chance, next week." A small ad slid up into the lower left corner of the screen, offering a link to free samples from the album. "But we haven't noticed an unusual influx of musicians to the Music City. Things are always very vibrant here."

"I spoke with a musician yesterday who hasn't made it in twenty years of trying," Lisa said, stalking her victim.

Gallarie's expression softened to show her concern while she maintained her perfect posture. "It's always been a very competitive business. But she's still here, still trying, isn't she?"

"*He,*" Lisa said, "thinks it's just going to get worse."

"But he'll have the advantage of more years of experience in the business, more time to hone his talent," the executive parried. "Now that he doesn't have to worry about growing old, he can take as much time as he needs to find his niche."

Lisa leaned forward into the video frame. "So as far as you're concerned, he should see his glass as half-full."

"A winning attitude has always been a key to success."

"Just like yours."

Gallarie's smile was under tight control. "We have a winning attitude, Miss Lange."

"No matter how many people get chewed up in the process."

"Talk to any musician," Gallarie replied, folding her hands in her lap. "Their greatest reward is playing the music they love. Whether it's in a little honky-tonk in Laramie or a stadium in Los Angeles, the music matters most."

"And you think they'll be happy playing that little dive forever?"

Gallarie shrugged. "Times change, fortunes change. Ask Colby Freed. Who knows who'll be the next big star? Maybe your friend. All it takes is one lucky break."

CHAPTER 7

A WEEK AFTER WADE'S VISIT, Ellanna's computer chimed when it picked up a news story. "Oh, great," she said, "wonder what this one is." She tapped the screen.

Janet glanced at the clock on the datawall. "Bet I know."

"This is a Global News NewsPulse," an off-screen announcer said, "brought to you by—" Ellanna muted the audio, then transferred the video to the wall display so everyone could see it.

"Whenever she's in town," Janet said. "My stalker."

Lisa appeared, standing in the garden courtyard behind the Simmons Building. Ellanna unmuted the audio. "The new immortality—its causes and consequences—continue to haunt scientists here in Dallas," she said. "In an exclusive interview with Global News, Dr. Janet Hogan, the lead researcher, confessed that her lab and others around the world know little more today than they did when they discovered the miracle viruses over a month ago. Here's what she said."

The video showed Janet in the lab. "There are hundreds of people studying this now but there's so much to learn that we don't understand." The image jumped. "Anything. People… have gotten well because of the viruses. They should be happy that cancer and AIDS and so many other diseases are gone—"

"Forever?" Lisa asked.

"I can't say that… but… yes… maybe." Again the video jumped across the edits. "I don't know if cancer will come back."

In the lab, Janet fumed. "That's *not* what I said," she exclaimed. "I said the press was saying yes, not us!"

"So this immortality could go away tomorrow?" Lisa asked.

"We don't know. We don't know how long it took for the viruses to mutate into the right forms. They could change again. We do know the mutations are real, they're worldwide… stable in people."

"She makes me so mad," Janet growled. "I said they *seemed to be* stable, not that they are."

The video showed an image of a cluster of viruses. It split into half a dozen copies, which spread out, then dissolved into photographs of people in native costumes from around the world.

"Isn't that clever," Ellanna said.

Lisa continued in voice-over. "So despite Hogan's continued denials that people are immortal, experts say the viruses will keep on protecting us from disease and death, perhaps forever."

The video returned to the lab. "Meanwhile," Lisa said to Janet, "you keep getting threats."

On the screen, Janet looked down, dejected. "Every day."

Sayid hurried into the lab and glanced back at the datawall when he saw the team all looking that way. "Oh, good… you're watching it." He grabbed a stool and sat down.

The video returned to Lisa's stand-up location. "This firestorm of protest has affected other members of her team too."

"It's been so awful," the video showed Satya saying. "Everyone is so frightened. Why do people want to kill us? We haven't done anything to them."

Lisa said, "All of the lab personnel we spoke with confirmed they had received death threats. The Dallas Police, FBI, and Homeland Security have been unable to stop them, even though they've made arrests.

"Hogan wouldn't discuss her future research priorities, but one of her staff did."

The caption at the bottom of the screen read, *Gerardo Santangelo, graduate student.*

"Wait," Janet said.

Ellanna paused the video.

"When did she get you?"

"In the parking garage this morning," Gerardo said. "I meant to tell you but we got busy." He shrugged. "Sorry."

Janet ran her fingers through her hair, then gestured for Ellanna to restart the report.

"We've got to learn all we can about the viruses and the mutations," Gerardo said on the screen. "The more we know, the more good outcomes there'll be."

"Even to the diseases you say the viruses don't protect against?"

"Who knows? It's all chemistry."

The video switched to a replay of one of the simulations Janet had shown during the press conference. In voice-over, Lisa said, "So for all their high-tech wizardry, today's scientists are just as baffled by Mother Nature as they have ever been. The truth remains elusive.

"Millions of people around the world are alive today thanks to these mystery viruses, but serious moral and ethical questions have been raised by religious leaders." The report flashed a picture of Brother Elijah—Ellanna groaned—then images of David Wade, smokestacks, and sand dunes as Lisa said, "Experts warn the world's population will pass ten billion in less than ten years, maybe less than five. Will the surging population wipe out all the gains we've made against greenhouse gas emissions and global warming? Will the continents and oceans be stripped bare to feed the hungry? And if so, what then? These scientists have no answers."

"You never asked me about that!" Janet shouted, pounding her fists on the work surface of the lab bench. "Don't blame me!"

Lisa's face returned to the screen. "Once again, science and technology leave us wondering about our future. Reporting from the University of Texas Southwestern Medical Center in Dallas, I'm Lisa Lange."

Ellanna stopped the video. "That's just what I told Wade," she said into the silence. "If we keep working, we're wrong. If we stop, we're still wrong. We'll never know enough to satisfy her, either." She threw her hands in the air. "I give up."

"We can't give up," Sayid said.

Satya slapped the counter top. "Yes, we can!"

"No, we can't." He pointed at one of the lab's computers. "If we quit, the people who're threatening us will think they've won. They'll move on to other labs, try to shut them down too. Do we want to do that to our friends?"

Ellanna put her fists on her hips. "So we should just be good little martyrs, huh? And after we're dead, then what?" She stalked away from her desk to pace in the space between the benches and the door into the hall.

"We're not going to die," Sayid said. "You don't know how many—"

"No, and it doesn't matter," Ellanna shot back. "My mother calls every day. She's afraid every call will be the last. I keep telling her we've got more protection than the president but she's terrified anyway." She shot an angry glance at Janet. "I haven't told her we're still getting threats. I'm a scientist, not a soldier. I didn't sign up for this."

"Neither did I," Sayid said, shoving his hands into his pockets. He stared at his shoes for a moment, then looked up. "I sent my wife and youngest son to live with my brother in New York on Monday. They left in the middle of the night. We didn't tell the boy until the last second. He's only weeks away from graduating from high school. You can imagine how he felt."

"So what does that do for us?" Ellanna demanded. Sayid's hurt and angry expression made her add, "You know what I mean… for all of us. You too."

Sayid struggled to keep his temper. "What it says," he said slowly, "and what it shows, is that we have to think beyond ourselves."

Janet shook her head. "I've got quite enough to think about right now, thank you. I'm glad you've got the time."

"It's time for you to do some growing up, Dr. Hogan," Sayid snapped. "You too, Dr. Barnes." He met and held each woman's gaze in turn. "As you might have noticed, this affects a hell of a lot more people than you, but you're the ones riding the tiger. Are you going to quit just because some know-nothing," he turned to Ellanna, "like that phony preacher criticizes you? You haven't before."

"There's a big difference between criticism and death threats," Janet exclaimed. "This isn't some conference at a fancy hotel."

Ellanna winced and sucked in a breath between her teeth. "You weren't there."

"Okay," Sayid said, "that's fair. That's right. But if we stop, someone could be tricked into doing something wrong. We have to prevent that."

Janet picked up a single-tip pipetting tool that lay on the work bench and clicked the tip-release button with her thumb. "We can't control what other labs do."

"We influence them," Sayid said. "We know more than anyone else about these things, and like it or not, we're the most visible. They're watching us. We have to get on top of the public relations situation, even sound like we've been listening to the critics. How much time have you been spending on your social media?" He held up his hands to stave off their protests. "I know, you're tired and that's where the threats are, but telling the story our way is a part of our work too. If we quit telling our story, someone else will do it for us." He waved at the datawall. "Just like that. We can't let that happen."

"And that's how we're going to make the threats stop and the reporters go away," Ellanna said.

Sayid shrugged. "We know we'll do what's right. We can control the scientific outcome."

Janet kept clicking the pipetter, refusing to look up. "That's what you said after the press conference." She knew they were watching her, waiting for her decision. "It's not fair," she whispered.

Sayid said, "Who said… no." He walked over to her and put his arm around her shoulders. "You're right, it's not fair."

Janet looked up at him, surprised.

"It's not fair for the poor and weak to be forced to live the way they do now for who knows how long. It's not fair for the wealthy and powerful to live even longer and get even richer and more powerful. It's not fair that some sick people have recovered while others have died. Nothing the viruses have done is fair.

"But fair or not, you have to decide whether to quit or go on. Either way, there are risks. It's not fair to ask someone your age to make such big decisions from so little information. It's not a damn bit fair. But these are your decisions to make, not mine."

A timer chimed. Gerardo walked along the workbench to a centrifuge that was spinning to a stop. He pushed a couple of control panel buttons. The beeps the machine made were loud in the otherwise silent lab.

"Face it," Sayid said as Gerardo kept working. "This is the most fascinating and challenging science you've ever done. It may be the most important work you'll ever do. It's the biggest thing I've ever been a part of and hard as it is, I can't walk away from it. Can any of you?" He met the gazes of the other three scientists, then looked down at Janet. She hesitated, then shook her head. After a long moment, he patted her shoulder and walked out of the lab.

* * *

Working at night from his apartment, Arnie pulled together a lot of information in the weeks after he and

Treebeard first talked. Getting the architectural plans for the lab building was a snap.

He took some vacation days from his job to drive from Austin to Dallas to look around. The security and the terrain around the building made him reconsider a direct attack: there were too many ways it could be stopped. He drove to the top level of a parking garage—the same one where Lisa had filmed her sunset report the day the viruses were announced—and watched the traffic around the North Campus. Not long after he arrived, three unmarked vans pulled up to the Simmons Building's covered entrance. Arnie pulled out a camera with a powerful zoom lens and studied the vehicles. He caught a brief glimpse of an assault rifle as a young man wearing a bulky brown vest got out of the first van and hustled into the building, accompanied by two people in business suits.

"So…," he said. After the vans drove away, he wrote a few notes on a paper pad.

He found locations where he could watch trios of vans cycle through the east and south sides of the campus as well. As he expected, there was no obvious pattern to when the vehicles came and went.

By the time he got back to Austin, he had a plan, a list of things he needed to make it work, and a rental contract under a false name for an apartment near the research center. A week later, everything on the list was checked off. He didn't need a checklist for the steps that remained. He shredded and burned the list and notes, crushed the ashes, and washed them down the drain.

He sent Treebeard an encrypted message consisting of a picture of an eye, colored red: "red eye," a pun on "ready."

His contact called back a few minutes later. "What's the plan?"

Arnie glanced at his apartment windows to confirm the blinds were closed. "You should know better than to ask."

The avatar's eyes narrowed. "And you should know that Mom won't approve a plan he doesn't know about."

"Ever heard of plausible deniability?" Arnie asked. "Bet Mom has, and likes it. Besides, I can't sit on this. The longer we wait, the more dangerous it gets: people start connecting dots. I've got a week, maybe less, before I have to abort. I'll need a couple days to get the last pieces in place."

The Ent sighed. "Give me 72 hours—no, wait, I just thought of something." He turned away from the phone. From the figure's posture, Arnie suspected he was checking another phone or a computer. He chuckled at the image of a giant tree typing. When Treebeard turned back, he said, "Problem. Mom's traveling all week. I don't know when I'll be able to get to him in private."

"That's your problem," Arnie said. "If I don't hear from you in five days, max, I'm pulling the plug and we won't be able to try again for a long time, if ever."

Treebeard's trunk bent in a ponderous nod. "I'll get back to you."

* * *

Will Baxter eased his Lincoln down the street. It was nearly two a.m. but the bars were still open, as were the pool hall and the liquor and convenience stores—open but enclosed in burglar bars, security systems, and bulletproof-glass cashier's cages.

He'd grown up not far from here and the neighborhood had been rough even then. He'd learned about its nightlife when he was a boy, sneaking out of the house to meet his friends. Tonight, like so many nights before, he was here to minister to the people of the street: the homeless, drunks, prostitutes, and addicts. *Is it my imagination or are there more of them now?* With the car windows rolled down, the cacophony of blaring music, too-loud conversations, revving engines, and screeching tires surrounded him. Once in a while he caught a whiff of tobacco or marijuana smoke. *Sweet Lord Jesus, bring Your grace to these sinners. Jerusalem, wash your heart from wickedness, that you may be saved.*

Ahead of him, three women sashayed down the sidewalk like high-fashion runway models, feet crossing in front of each other to make their hips sway, shoulders back so their breasts would bounce and jiggle and draw men's eyes. Two were black and the other was either black or Latina. Even in the cool night air, one wore short, tight pants, the others skirts that emphasized the curves of their hips and buttocks and the lengths of their skinny legs. Their tops were scant and revealing, too.

He spotted an opening among the parked cars beyond the women and pulled in. The three exchanged glances; then, as the other two positioned themselves to keep watch, the one closest to the curb sauntered up to the car and leaned over to rest her forearms on the window frame.

"Hi, handsome," she cooed. "Lookin' for a little party?" She arched her back to push her breasts forward and rolled her shoulders back and forth. The unbuttoned white top, tied at her solar plexus, revealed plenty of cleavage and the scant brassiere underneath didn't quite cover her areolas. No matter how many trips he'd made to this part of Raleigh, no matter the strength of his faith, Baxter was still a man, and the woman's display made his pulse quicken and his penis stiffen. He was ashamed, knowing how hurt Maureen would be if she knew he couldn't control his reactions. He cherished her trust. She slept fitfully during his nights on the street.

He held his voice steady. "Why don't we go for a little drive, Sister?"

The prostitute gave him a quick appraising look, then glanced around the car, checking for danger signs. "All right," she said, flashing her best smile. As she straightened to open the door, she looked back over her shoulder. "See you later, girls."

While she settled into the passenger's seat, Baxter checked his mirrors, then pulled into traffic. This wasn't the way he preferred to minister to the people he met here. His first choice was to park and walk along, witnessing to whomever he met, but if he sensed a particularly lost soul, he would try to set up some kind of one-on-one ministry.

The woman leaned over and stroked his arm. "I'm CeCe," she said. "What's your favorite party?"

"I'm Reverend Will—"

"Ooh," CeCe exclaimed. "A *man* of the *cloth*! I'm a holy roller, y'know." Laughing, she leaned back, pulled up her short skirt, spread her legs, and pulled the crotch of her panties to one side. "See? Holey." She rolled her hips. "And I'm a roller."

Angry at himself for being caught off guard, Baxter stared straight ahead.

Since she didn't get the reaction she expected, CeCe slid across the bench seat, snuggled up to him, and whispered, "Dressed like this, I get pretty cold. I bet you could warm me up real quick."

An all-night gas station was ahead on the right. Baxter pulled in and parked next to the curbing, within the glow of the bright lights above the pumps.

"Mmm, lots of cameras here. Is that what you like?" She stroked his ear and jaw line with her finger.

He turned on the bench seat to face her. Looking straight into her eyes, he put his hands on her hips and gently pushed her back toward her side of the car. When she tried to bring his hands up to her breasts, he instead took her hands and held them away from her body. Her eyes were dilated, more than they needed to be for the relative darkness of the street and far more than they should have been under the station's lights. He wasn't surprised.

"Sister, when I said I was a minister, I spoke the truth. Can I speak a greater Truth to you now?" He didn't wait for her to respond. "This is no life for you. It's no life for anyone. Jesus doesn't want you to lead this life of sin. And you don't have to. In Hosea, God said whoredom takes away the heart. I can feel the hurt in your heart. I can see it in your eyes. Give up this life and let Jesus into your heart. He can heal you. He *wants* to heal you. The Lord has seen your adulteries and still asks, 'Will you not be made clean?'"

CeCe tried to pull her hands free. "You really are a preacher man, aren't you?"

"Yes, I am."

"I heard this before." She straightened up in the seat, pulled her hands from his grasp and tugged the hem of her skirt down. "Man come along, talkin' like a preacher, then when I say amen, he want to play. An' then he don' want to pay, neither. I ain't got time for that. You here to pray, pray by yourself. I got work to do, gotta make my money."

"Money for what, Sister?"

"I got childrens to feed."

"What else do you have to feed?"

CeCe didn't answer.

"*I* know," Baxter pressed. "I can see it in your eyes. 'She that lives in pleasure is dead while she lives.' You can't go on like this forever."

"Sure I can." CeCe looked straight out the windshield. "Sure I can. I ain't gotta die. Why should I die when I can already live forever? Shit." She turned away from Baxter and pushed the door open. As she got out, she said, "I ain't got time for talk." After thumping the door closed, she turned to lean on the window sill. "But next time? You want to play? CeCe do more than show you what she got." She straightened up and strode toward the intersection and the darkened street beyond.

Baxter sat in the idling car, watching her. He'd gotten this response so many times before but he still ached at the loss. *Well, a loss for tonight. Lord Jesus, did I at least plant a seed of hope?* He prayed for a moment more, then drove around to one of the parking spaces next to the convenience store that was part of the station. Even though there was nothing in the car to steal, he raised the windows and locked the doors after he got out. As he headed for the shop to buy a cup of coffee he heard the *pop-pop-pop* of gunfire behind him. Two sets of screeching sounds followed, the first receding as a car raced away, the other ending in a crunch as the second car ran into something he couldn't see. Fumbling in his pocket for his phone, he ran toward the crash scene, ready to comfort another dying gang member or drug dealer but praying he wouldn't have to.

* * *

Lisa's third report began in the cluttered office of Reginald Traylor McHenry III, Esquire, attorney at law, criminal defense lawyer, the flamboyant and controversial senior partner of his large Mobile, Alabama, firm. His trademark Mark Twain-style white suit, with its wide lapels and long-tailed bow tie, contrasted with his ebony skin. His shoulder-length dreadlocks were more white than black, accentuating the difference. The walls of the office were covered with framed photos, newspaper and magazine clippings, and a large wall screen separated into smaller display windows showing web pages in which he figured. He'd never met a camera he didn't like or a criminal who didn't need defending, and the more heinous the alleged crime, the better. He escorted Lisa around the office, graciously but pointedly telling her the stories behind the pictures and publications while Oriel set up his equipment. When it was time to put on his microphone, he slipped it on with the ease of long practice.

Lisa opened the report with an easy question to get McHenry rolling. "Why have you filed a motion for a new sentencing hearing for Tremaine Sovrel?"

"Times have changed," the lawyer replied, leaning across his desk toward Lisa. "The life sentence my client received may have been fair and appropriate before the immortality came—at least, so the courts of this state have ruled—but today it is unconstitutionally cruel. No judge or jury on this earth can lock a man up for the rest of time."

Lisa said, "But Sovrel was charged with more than two dozen rapes over ten years, and was convicted of twenty. He wasn't tried on the others because the victims were afraid to testify. He's suggested there were more assaults he hasn't been charged with. He's a dangerous man."

"A man can change," McHenry said, spreading his hands. "We are not asking that he be released right away. In light of the changes the viruses have brought about, we feel a hundred years is sufficient time for the Department of Corrections to provide him with the counseling and ministering he needs to be healed. All we're asking for is the chance for him to prove he can become a trustworthy member of society."

The scene shifted to a small living room in a modest house elsewhere in Mobile. Over a dozen men and women of various races and ages sat crowded together in two rows in front of Lisa. One of the men in the back row was holding up a framed picture of his teenage daughter. Gray ovals on the screen covered the faces of several women. Many held tissues Lisa had given them before the interview.

Oriel zoomed in on a black woman in her middle thirties who was sitting on the left end of the sofa as Lisa asked her first question. "Aisha, you were just a teenager when you became the first victim in Sovrel's ten-year crime spree. You've heard what his lawyer says, that keeping him in prison for more than a hundred years is cruel. How do you feel about that?"

"How do you think I feel?" the woman replied, her hands trembling in her lap. "I've been afraid for the past twenty years."

"Afraid he'd get out?"

"At first I was afraid he'd come after me again, maybe kill me. After he went to jail, I was afraid some judge would let him free because of some little rule the police didn't follow. Now that man wants him to get out in ninety years. What's he going to do then? *We* know."

The people around her nodded.

"His lawyer says he can be healed in that time."

"That's bullcrap," a white woman said, her voice electronically distorted, her face hidden behind one of the gray masks. "Pardon my French but that's bull. He ain't gonna heal." She pointed toward Aisha. "She ain't healed in twenty years. None of the rest of us have neither, since we was attacked."

"We thought we'd get better over time," an Asian woman in the back row said. "I thought I'd put it behind me, after years of counseling. Now that lawyer has torn the wound open again and it's not going to close. If his sentence is reduced, we'll just get more frightened every day."

The scene shifted back to McHenry's office. Lisa said, "Sovrel's victims say they'll live in fear of him every day if his sentence is commuted."

"There's no need for them to be frightened," McHenry replied. "A hundred years is a long time, enough, I'm sure, for medical science to repair whatever caused my client to act out the way he did. The viruses cured cancer and AIDS. What can't be cured now? It's unfortunate those good people don't have any more confidence in our doctors than that."

"You make it sound as if the viruses were created…."

"I don't know if they were created or not." McHenry leaned back into his tall leather chair. "What I do know is that we have time to heal my client. After that, keeping him in a maximum security prison is more than punishment; it's torture. We Americans don't condone torture."

Back in the living room, Oriel caught the shocked expressions on the group's faces as Lisa replayed McHenry's comments. The woman sitting next to Aisha exploded, tears streaming down her face. "Torture? I'll tell you what torture is! It's being dragged out of your house at two in the morning, made to drive out into the woods with a knife at your throat, being raped for hours, praying to die so it would be over, being tied to a tree with your clothes and raped again, then left with a promise he was coming back for more. That's torture."

Oriel panned across the group as everyone tried to talk at once. Aisha put her arm around her sobbing neighbor.

"That lawyer's a man," Aisha said when the room had grown quiet. "He can't understand what we're going through. Even if Sovrel stays in jail, what happened will be part of us for the rest of eternity. We'll never be free."

Lisa gave McHenry the last word.

"I know it's hard for those people," he said, "and I'm sorry for them. I don't want them to suffer. But the Constitution and justice demand that my client not be punished more than he deserves. I intend to see that he is treated fairly by the criminal justice system."

* * *

A couple of days after his encounter with CeCe, Baxter went to the home of a member of his congregation. As he pulled into the driveway of the older brick home on a busy street, Jerrold Hammersmith, dressed in jeans and a Duke Blue Devils football jersey, struggled down the steps to meet him.

"Let's go for a walk, Reverend," Hammersmith said after they'd exchanged greetings.

"Are you sure?" Baxter asked.

"Sure." He looked like he was in his early sixties but his skin was an unhealthy gray. His face was sagging and there were deep bags under his eyes.

Baxter turned with him to walk down the drive. "How can I help you?"

"I hurt all the time. All over. My doctors can't explain it and they can't fix it." The men turned onto the sidewalk with Hammersmith closest to the curb. "They've got all sorts of names for it: fibro-something, chronic pain disorder, something-or-other pain syndrome. You know. I think they make up a new name every time I go in just so they'll have something to talk about." He laughed, but without humor. "I don't care what they call it. I just want it to stop."

"What have they tried?"

"What haven't they tried? They gave me drugs, morphine, even the new gene drugs. Some helped for a little while, some never did. The viruses haven't done me any good, either. I tried a chiropractor, acupuncture." He paused while a heavy truck rumbled by. "Even went to a lady who does herbal remedies. She gave me this tea and capsules full of some powder she mixed up. They didn't do anything."

"And now?"

Hammersmith stopped in the shade of an elm tree. Baxter turned to face him.

"I can't go on like this, Reverend Baxter. I can't." He ran his hand through his thin white hair, then scratched behind one ear. "I try not to complain but Sally knows. I can't sleep much, so I'm always tired. I can't work, so she has to work for both of us." He looked down, scuffed at a small pile of sand on the sidewalk with his shoe. "I haven't treated her the way a man should—you know—the pain won't let me. I'm not a man anymore." He turned to watch grass clippings swirl in the air as cars sped by.

"I know I'm depressed. The doctors sent me to a psychologist—no, psychiatrist—well, one of them, anyway. She tried to get me to do things to keep my mind off the pain, but I can't do it long enough. The pain always wins. Tried praying too. Man can't pray twenty-four hours a day."

Baxter searched back through what he'd learned in divinity school and since. "Paul wrote to the Corinthians that partakers of suffering would also partake of consolation. Jesus suffered for us and was risen up into glory. If God allowed his only Son to suffer, it was because He had a plan for Him. He has a plan for you too."

The man stood in the shade for a moment, not meeting Baxter's gaze. On the street behind him, traffic kept rushing by. Finally, he said, "But Jesus suffered for two days, not even that. The Romans killed Him and then He was done suffering. I'm just a man and it's been ten years. If God has a plan for me, I need to know what it is. Now."

Baxter put his hand on Hammersmith's arm. "It's hard to be patient. Even Jesus lost hope on the cross, yet today He's our hope and relieves our pain."

The man looked up, meeting and holding Baxter's gaze. "You don't get it, Reverend. Nobody does." The intensity of his anger frightened the minister. "I was a Marine. Went to Iraq, Afghanistan. We'd joke that we knew we were going to heaven when we died 'cause we'd already been to hell." He laughed bitterly. "We didn't know what hell was. Now I do and I'm not afraid of it. I can't hurt burning in hell any more than I do now. I can't let my Sally hurt for me for all eternity." He glanced to his right. Behind an opening in traffic, a large dump truck was rumbling toward them. "Pray for me, Reverend."

"Brother Jer—," Baxter shouted. He grabbed for the man's arm but wasn't quick enough.

Hammersmith dashed in front of the truck. The driver hadn't even touched his brakes when the grille and bumper slammed into the man, hurling him down the street. The driver locked up the truck's brakes and it howled to a stop, straddling the dead man.

Moaning, the minister ran to help a man whose life he knew he hadn't saved.

CHAPTER 8

"SATYA, YOU READY TO GO?" Janet called from the space in front of her office.

"Almost," her lab manager replied. "Just checking off the last few things. There." She set her tablet on her desk and turned it off.

Janet walked into the lab, grunting as she pulled on her armored vest. She shifted it around to get the weight balanced. "I can't believe they call these things lightweight," she said as she overlapped the tan front panels and pressed the Velcro strips together. "It's so heavy my legs are getting fat."

"I don't know why you're putting it on so soon," Satya said, "we're leaving from the east side, remember?"

"You're right." Janet shrugged under the shoulder pads. "Well, it's on."

Satya picked up her own vest, followed Janet to the door, and turned off the lab lights.

"Don't do that," Janet said. "We're not supposed to reveal when we're leaving."

"Aah, I keep forgetting. I must be getting old. It's such a habit, you know." She flipped the lights back on.

As they stepped into the hall, Texas Ranger Coral Ayers, one of their escorts, asked, "Ready?"

Janet yawned. "More than, I guess," she said with a laugh.

Ayers tipped her head to the side. "Two step." A second Ranger fell in behind them as they walked to the elevator.

* * *

Sitting in a second-floor apartment across Forest Park Road from the North Campus complex, Arnie watched three vans pull in at the covered doorway of the building closest to him. A minute earlier, he'd heard from the radio scanner and decrypter sitting on the table in front of him the code announcing someone was leaving the lab. The Texas Rangers were using country and western dance terms for code words today. He didn't know yet whether any of his targets would use the east exit this time—they didn't always—but he would know soon enough.

He slid from the recliner onto the floor so he could see under the awning where the vans had parked. He set a pair of binoculars next to him, then pulled over a computer and activated the wireless links to three tiny video cameras. Depending on what happened next, he might have a second or less to decide to act.

The tension he'd been feeling since he put the plan together rose. His whole body was tingling. *It's like this every time,* he thought. *No, this is different—the wrong action, the wrong time.* He tried to will his body back to the state of focused calm he needed. *It's too late for second thoughts. Relax… just do the job.*

Nevertheless, his mind wandered as he watched and waited. For one thing, he'd never been this close to one of his devices when it was to go off. The old pickup truck with a camper shell over the bed was parked on the street less than 100 feet away. For another, he still wasn't convinced Treebeard had talked with Mom and gotten his approval. Something hadn't been right about that last phone call. *Who really made the decision? They don't want me to know.* He thought about the scientists, then crushed the thought. *They're targets. That's all.*

* * *

Three identical silver vans were idling, their right side doors open, as Janet, Satya, and their escorts reached the exit. The Rangers stopped short and Ayers spoke into her mike again. "Boot scoot," she said, then cocked her head to listen to the information coming back in her earpiece. "Okay. Dr. Hogan, first van. Miss Pramanasudh, last one. Ready? Let's go."

Janet and Satya hurried to their vans and climbed into wraparound seats that looked like open cocoons, installed where the middle and back rows of regular seats would have been. Another cocoon was mounted behind theirs in each vehicle, facing rearward. Once the passengers were seated and strapped into their five-point harnesses, the doors on all three trucks closed.

Decoy teams of guards and other vans performed the same actions at the other entrances around the complex.

In Janet's vehicle, Ayers took the front passenger seat. The man who'd come with them from the lab clambered back to take the rear-facing cocoon seat. Ayers pulled an automatic rifle from its mount and checked the bolt. She said something Janet couldn't make out, waited a moment, then looked at the driver. "Go."

He released the brakes and accelerated up the driveway.

* * *

In the darkened apartment, Arnie put down his binoculars. He'd seen what he needed: an extra person, a woman, had gotten into the first van. *This is it.* He switched his attention to the video feeds. The cameras were mounted in the side mirror of the pickup. One pointed up the hill toward the research campus while the other two showed views of the street. He started recording and used a joystick connected to the computer to zoom in a little on the portico.

For a few seconds, he drummed his fingers on the case of the machine. *Stay calm,* he reminded himself. *Focus.*

The vans pulled out and came toward him. The first one passed a tree he'd picked as a reference point. He waited, counting seconds in his head. With his right hand he twisted the top of the joystick clockwise and pulled the shaft back. The image from the camera eased to the left and widened as the vans approached. Arnie's left hand hovered over the keyboard. *Five… four….*

* * *

The Ranger facing the rear in Satya's van tried to get comfortable in his cocoon. The air conditioning wasn't doing much to overcome the late afternoon June heat and humidity. The tight quarters, seats, and protective gear he was wearing made it that much less comfortable. Behind him, he heard his protectee undoing the straps on her vest. "Ma'am," he called.

* * *

One... now. Arnie stabbed the Enter key.

The pickup exploded. The middle van was hurled sideways between the trees along the road, its left side crushed by the blast. It twisted and spun in the air, landing at the head of the creek bed that crossed the campus.

Satya's van shuddered as if it had hit something solid. The airbags in her cocoon seat thumped into place. They could not protect her from shrapnel, however. One of the bags collapsed when debris penetrated the shielding inside the vehicle's walls. A metal shard slammed through her ribcage, deflating her right lung. She screamed and tried to double over but her shoulder belts held her upright.

The van slewed to the right but its weight and momentum kept it going forward. The injured driver struggled for control as the truck careened through the debris cloud. He wrestled the steering wheel to the left, trying to keep the van from rolling over. The armor-protected engine kept running and the run-flat tires held long enough for him to catch the vehicle before it could topple. It caught the edge of the crater and shot left, ramming what had been the rear of the pickup before sliding onto the sidewalk and smashing into the fence around the apartment complex.

Janet's van, meanwhile, yawed and slid to the right and bounced over the curb. It slammed into the end of a retaining wall, and ricocheted back into the street. The left rear tire had been shredded by the explosion. The armored fuel tank stayed intact but the force of the blast split the welds holding the fuel line to it. Fuel gushed out and was ignited by sparks from the sliding wheel. The van spun back to the left and tumbled onto its side when the wheel caught in the pavement. It slid down the hill, trailing sparks and flames.

The airbags for both Janet and the Ranger behind her inflated the moment the blast hit but they didn't protect him from the shrapnel or the wall being crushed inward by the shockwave. While the back of Janet's seat protected her, and the airbags and five-point harness held her body in place as the truck thrashed and tumbled, her head thudded against the sides of the cocoon.

The van scraped to a stop against the curb. Janet heard someone screaming. The screams continued for some time before they faded into a hiccupping moan, then stopped.

The airbags deflated. She lay in the seat, her ears ringing. She tried to open her eyes. She thought she was back in the lab but the room seemed to be spinning six different ways at once. It was dark. *I* told *Satya not to turn off the lights.*

* * *

"*That's* right!" Arnie shouted, his ears ringing from the blast. "Praise the Mother!" He had no way to know whether the scientists had been killed. *Hope not,* he thought. *Let 'em tell their stories. Press'll be all over it. I've done my part. Now Mom can do his.*

Even though the explosives in the pickup were shaped to direct their force toward the vans and away from the apartment building, the window facing the street had shattered and the wall had buckled inward. Smoke was blowing in through the window, setting the smoke alarms shrieking. People were screaming and running in the hallway.

Arnie stopped the recording, put the computer and other equipment into a backpack, and stood up. He'd post the video files later. He was calm now, peaceful. It would be easy to vanish into the chaos and head for Austin. There was no need to rush, but he needed to look panicked like the rest of the building's residents until he was away. And if the building burned down, that was even better: there'd be no biological samples to connect him to it.

This is like cocaine, he thought. *Quick hit of satisfaction, then it's over and you want more.* Need *more. A month from now Mom will want more. Count on it. Maybe then he'll believe bombs aren't enough.*

The smoke made him cough. Under all the other noises, he could hear sirens. He opened the door of the apartment.

* * *

Someone was shouting, "Doc, you okay? Doc!"

Who's 'doc?' Sayid's gone home. Janet tried opening just one eye. That was better… a little. It was hard to see. She coughed. There was a haze of some kind beside her. *How can smoke make a wall?* A woman came out of the smoke but she was floating in the air at an impossible angle, parallel to the floor. *Is she an angel?* The woman grabbed at Janet's belly. Janet tried to push her hands away.

The woman slapped Janet's hands aside. "Stop it. Got to get you out of here. Van's on fire."

Van? I'm in my lab… and the lights are out.

A pressure on Janet's left side released and her body shifted. That didn't make sense, either. Her left arm hurt. Something was pressing against it just above the wrist. She whimpered.

The floating woman grabbed for Janet's chest. *What's she trying to do?* Janet wondered. She felt a pressure against her chest, then heard a loud ripping noise. The woman was touching her all over, fast. She wasn't being very friendly. *Will she rape me? She looks like a soldier. Angels don't look like soldiers.*

"C'mon, Doc," the woman said. She twisted her head at a crazy angle and shouted, "Jackson, you okay?" She waited a moment, then shouted, "Jackson!" again.

Jackson didn't answer.

Who's she talking to? Nobody in the department's named Jackson.

The woman twisted her head at another crazy angle. "Hey," she called. "Check on Jackson."

A man appeared next to the floating woman. He was carrying something round, like the gas cylinders they used in the lab but smaller. "Got him," he said, then tried to crawl on his side under Janet's seat.

Jackson's in a CO2 can? No wonder he can't talk. What's he… what's it…? Nothing made sense. A moment later, Janet heard a whooshing sound.

The man said, "Jackson. Come on, buddy. Let's get you out of here."

Jackson's empty now. Janet giggled. *Had an orgasm. Needs a nap, just like my Michael.*

While she'd been distracted, the floating woman had put her arms around Janet's ribs and was trying to pull her out of the seat. Janet grabbed the sides and held on. "Gonna fall." *Fall? Can't fall down... I'm not up.*

"No, you won't, Honey," the woman said. "I won't let you. Just slide forward… that's it… now swing your legs down toward me."

Janet stopped. "Can't fly, like you," she said. "Not an angel." Besides, she felt so heavy, like she was wearing a lead coat. She rolled her shoulders and the weight fell to her elbows.

The flying woman helped Janet free her arms, then put one hand on her thigh and eased her legs around. With her other hand, she held Janet's upper arm. "Just roll to the left, onto your tummy… that's it."

Janet's toes touched something hard, then her heels did the same.

"Good," the woman said. She put both hands on Janet's hips and pulled her up and around. "Slide your butt to the right, now."

What's she doing? "Don't touch me like that."

The hands kept pulling. "Keep sliding. You're all right."

Janet felt weight coming onto her feet. *How can I be flying if I'm standing up? Maybe I have magic shoes, like Dorothy. Play* Wizard of Oz *again, Momma.*

"You need any help in there?" a man shouted from above Janet. Or maybe he was behind her. Or beside her.

"Yeah," another man called. "Can you open the back door?"

"Dude, no way. What'cha got in there?"

"Burns, shrapnel wounds, broken legs, unconscious."

"Let's get the doc out first," the floating woman said from beside Janet. "Get her out of the way, then cut Jackson out. She's pretty much okay. Concussion, probably.

"Okay, Doc, watch your head. Can you twist around to your left and stand up?"

Janet did. "Am I flying now?"

"Not yet," the woman said, with a chuckle. "Does anything hurt?"

Janet's left forearm was throbbing. "Here," she said, holding the arm out. She coughed. There was a sharp smell of smoke around her. *Have to get the vent hood fixed.*

The woman caressed her arm. "Does that hurt?"

Janet shook her head. "Just sore."

"Okay, look up."

Janet felt the woman's hands on her hips again. She looked up. Two men were floating above her. Outside the window. Standing on the side of the building. *How can they do that? Must be angels too.* Then they crouched down, reaching through the glass to her. *Am I dead?*

Before she could process that thought, the woman said from behind her, "Put your arms above your head."

"Why?"

"Just do it. Now!"

Janet raised her arms. The men each grabbed one arm, between the elbow and the shoulder.

The woman's hands gripped her very hard. "On three," she said. "One... two... *three.*"

And Janet was flying, right through the window. As she lifted off, she pulled her knees up toward her chest. The men swung her out and then down. She caught sight of the North Campus buildings and her world lurched. She looked around at the welter of flashing lights, cars, fire trucks, and smoke. Someone was holding her ribs again, a man. *Nice cologne... good hugger... warm. Holds me tight.*

"Put your legs down, please, Miss," he said.

She looked down. Her legs were wrapped around his waist. Horrified, she lowered them but the ground was wobbly, like she was standing on an air mattress.

"Lie down right here, Miss," the man said, his arm tight around her waist as he guided her onto a little bed.

What's that doing here? was her last conscious thought for a while.

CHAPTER 9

LISA'S REPORT FROM THE BOMBING SCENE opened with her weaving around the construction workers and equipment getting ready to fill in the crater left by the exploded pickup truck. "It will be days," she said, "maybe even weeks, before all of the damage caused by yesterday's fatal blast is repaired."

The video panned up and left to the apartment building beyond the street, focusing on a particular second story window. "A few facts are already known. All of the residents of this building have been accounted for, except one. While Dallas Police aren't saying anything publicly for fear of compromising their investigation, sources tell me it appears the missing person rented an apartment under a false name.

"The truck used in the attack, a battered 2010 Toyota Tundra," the screen split to show the truck before and after it blew up, "was sold for cash last week but hadn't been registered by the new owner. The previous owner is being treated as a person of interest."

In footage shot the night before, ambulances pulled up to the emergency entrance of a hospital and gurneys were wheeled inside. "In addition to the three Texas Rangers killed in the blast," Lisa said in voice-over, "several others are still hospitalized, some with life-threatening injuries. One of the targets of the attack, Ms. Satya Pramanasudh, Dr. Janet Hogan's lab manager, remains in serious but stable condition. Dr. Hogan herself was held overnight for observation but has since been released to an undisclosed location."

The research buildings appeared to Lisa's left and she gestured toward them. "UT-Southwestern officials say this was the first successful attack to be carried out. Dozens, they say, have been thwarted.

"I've been reporting on the winners and losers in the new world the viruses have created. This attack, with its dead and wounded, adds to the list of losers. A shadowy group calling itself the Mother Earth Brigades claimed responsibility in a message last night." Lisa read from her tablet. "They said, 'This will be the first of many attacks against those who would seek to destroy Mother Earth. If no one else will defend her, we will.'

"*Is* the earth the ultimate loser to these mysterious viruses? Who can say with any certainty? We've known about the viruses for just a few short months. Experts insist we're asking for more than science can deliver in such a short time."

Video of the wreckage superimposed over a picture of the research complex replaced Lisa's image as she said, "Adding to the uncertainty is the unknown. What will win out in the end: science or fear, humanity or catastrophe? Reporting from Dallas, I'm Lisa Lange."

* * *

Janet stared in confused disbelief at the woman standing at the door outside the Richardson, Texas, apartment she and Ellanna had been put up in. Her brain was foggy from the pain medicine. She knew she should recognize the woman but the memory just wasn't coming.

"I'm *so* glad you're okay, Dr. Hogan," the woman said. "I was so worried when I heard you'd been attacked."

"Do I… do I know you?" Janet asked.

"Janet!" Ellanna exclaimed from the living room. "Don't stand there!" She hurried to the door. "Who are you?"

"Dr. Barnes," Sarah said, "you know me. Sarah Green-Dale, President of SAFE-T—Save America From Every Threat." She thrust out her hand. "I'm one of your biggest supporters."

"How did you…?" Janet asked.

Ellanna tugged on her sweater. "Don't stand in the doorway like that. Someone will see you." She turned to Sarah. "I'm sorry, she can't talk with you." She put her arm around Janet's waist to guide her back into the apartment, hooking the door with her heel to swing it closed.

Sarah caught the door before it shut. "Please, I have a very important offer for Dr. Hogan."

Janet tottered toward the sofa. "No, not now." She slumped onto the cushions.

"I can help you with your security," Sarah said.

"I know what we can do about security," Ellanna said. She opened the door, pushed Sarah aside, and looked up and down the hall. "Hey," she called to the Texas Ranger standing halfway to the stairs at the end. She jerked her thumb at Sarah. "How the hell did she get here?"

"She's not armed," the Ranger said, then held up his phone. "Command post said she was okay."

"Jesus Christ," Ellanna muttered. "You could have brought her here yourself." She turned to Sarah. "All right. You've got five minutes, maybe less. I decide when you're done. You can see what condition she's in."

"Thank you so much," Sarah said. She hurried around the coffee table to sit at Janet's side, while Ellanna perched next to her friend on the arm of the sofa.

Sarah squeezed Janet's hand. "I'm so glad you're going to be okay. How's Miss Prama… Prana… I'm sorry, I can't say her name. The other lady who was hurt?"

"Time's a-wastin'," Ellanna said as Janet tried to form an answer. "Get to the point."

Sarah shot Ellanna a hurt look. "I just want you both to know how much I care. But since you're going to be that way, I came all the way from Washington to tell you that SAFE-T's board has authorized me to offer you up to one million dollars to use as you wish: for more security, more staff, whatever. In addition, we're ready to start a fund-raising campaign to make sure you have all the money you need to finish your work."

Janet blinked at Sarah. "Why…?"

"SAFE-T knows how important it is," Sarah said. "But we know too, that the viruses don't cure or protect against everything, like the horrible things you've just been through."

Ellanna shifted and glanced at the wall clock, making sure Sarah noticed.

"I'm sure you know there's a lot of worry about antibiotic resistance returning. The viruses won't protect against it. We saw what happened back in the teens when it got out of control. We want to help you make sure that doesn't happen again."

"But we're not—" Janet said.

"That's a whole different field," Ellanna said. "It's not our specialty."

"You're a microbiologist, Dr. Barnes," Sarah said. "You could lead that effort while—"

"We're not splitting the team," Ellanna said. "What else?"

"You can do whatever you wish," Sarah said, backtracking. "We just want to make sure you have what you need to protect us, humanity. A million dollars to start, guaranteed, with more support as soon as we can get it. All I need to know is where to send it."

Janet looked up at Ellanna. "That's a lot more than we have now."

"Strings?" Ellanna asked. "What do you want from us?"

Sarah sat back, her eyes wide. "Why, nothing, except that—"

"Uh-huh," Ellanna said. "Except what?"

"Except that you finish your work… so humanity can be protected from all diseases, not just some of them. So we can live for—" She changed direction at Ellanna's glare. "So we can reach our fullest potential as a species."

Ellanna said nothing for a moment but clenched her jaw, working it back and forth.

Janet watched her.

"You have something in writing?" Ellanna asked. "Janet's not in any condition to be making those decisions now."

"Of course," Sarah said, pulling a memory chip from her purse. "It's all right here where no one else can see it." She pressed the chip into Janet's hand. "Just our little secret. Look at it when you're ready." She leaned in to give Janet a gentle hug. "Hope you're all better soon," she whispered.

Ellanna stood and held out her hand. Janet looked at it, puzzled, then put the chip in it.

Sarah stood, inched around the coffee table, and gave Ellanna a hug too. "Thank you for letting me see Dr. Hogan," she said. "I know she'll do—you'll all do—so much good for us."

Ellanna looked down at Janet, who was staring blankly across the room at the far wall, then took Sarah's arm and led her to the door. "She needs to rest."

Once they were in the hall outside the apartment, Ellanna pulled Sarah up short. "You've got a hell of a lot of nerve!"

Sarah held up her hands as if to ward off an attack. "I'm only trying to help you," she said. "Your work *is* that important to me, to us. All of us."

"So how *did* you find us?" Ellanna said. "No one's supposed to even know she's here."

Sarah drew herself up to her full height. "You shouldn't be surprised. My staff knows how to data-mine public records. We knew she wouldn't be at home. Make a few guesses, structure the query right, and the answer pops out. I'm amazed the press hasn't found you already."

Ellanna scowled, thinking hard. "We need to protect her," she said to herself.

"Yes, we do," Sarah said, "but let me tell you something. Even with SAFE-T's money, you'll never be able to do enough. That attack was going to happen sooner or later. I found you here. Others will too. Soon. Then what?" Her eyes locked hard with Ellanna's. "The sooner you finish your work, the better. For all of you.

Something to consider." She turned and walked down the hall.

A hot ball of anger in Ellanna's chest warred with an iceberg of fear in the pit of her stomach. "Science doesn't work like that," she whispered as Sarah disappeared down the stairwell.

* * *

The day after Sarah's visit, Sayid strode up to the Texas Ranger guarding the back entrance to the apartment building Ellanna and Janet were staying in, Wade at his heels. "I'm Dr. Sayid," he said as he handed his ID badge to the Ranger.

The man took it, placed its end in a special slot in his phone, and watched the display. After a moment, he returned the card and held the back of the phone up to Sayid's right eye. "Look straight into the lens," he said. Seconds later, the phone beeped.

"Who's this gentleman?" the Ranger asked.

"David Wade. I added him to the visitor list before I left the campus."

The Ranger eyed Wade, who was bouncing on the balls of his feet as he stood next to the scientist. "ID, please, sir." Once he was satisfied, he said, "You can go in, gentlemen."

"I'll stay here," Sayid said as he escorted Wade to the door. "This is between you and Dr. Hogan."

"It's more than just personal," Wade said. "The whole world—"

"I know your position, Mr. Wade. I'm not sure bringing you here was the right thing to do. I don't want to make things worse by giving Janet the impression *I* want her to do what you want." Sayid pressed his thumb against the print-reader on the lock. "And I don't need to be there for the personal stuff. She has a boyfriend, by the way." The door clicked as it unlocked. He pulled it open. "Second floor. There's another Ranger at the landing. He'll escort you."

Wade looked at Sayid for a minute. *I should be grateful for getting this far*. "Thanks," he said as he stepped inside. "I won't be long."

Ellanna was standing in the doorway, waiting for Wade, her arms crossed over her chest. "You didn't bring Lisa Lange with you, by chance?" she asked, scowling.

"Uh, no… why?"

She pushed herself off the door frame. "Ground rules: think of me as a momma bear protecting her cub. Janet's pretty fragile, so what I say goes. When I say you're done, you're done. No second chances, no arguing. Got it?"

How badly was she hurt? Wade thought. *Was it a mistake to come so soon?* A wry smile crinkled his cheeks. "I'm no bull grizzly, momma bear. I'll be good."

Ellanna didn't return the smile. "Yes, you will." She glanced at the Ranger. "Thanks."

As they walked into the apartment, she called out, "Loverboy's here."

Surprised, Wade flushed.

"Michael?" Janet said, looking up eagerly from the recliner where she'd been watching TV. Her expression changed to puzzled disappointment when she spotted Wade. "Who's he?"

"Jan—Dr. Hogan, I'm—"

Ellanna stopped him with a hand on his arm. "David Wade, the environmentalist guy. Do you remember? He came to see us a few weeks ago?"

Janet's brows knit as she tried to recall the visit. "I… no, I'm sorry. Why'd you call him loverboy?"

"He tried to make nice to you, *real* nice, and you got mad and went off at him."

Janet frowned and shook her head. "Was I having a bad day?"

Wade said, "Dr. Hogan, I—"

"Wants you to save the world," Ellanna said.

"May I speak for myself, please?" *Bitch. Momma bear, my ass.* He left Ellanna's side before she could answer and pulled an arm chair around to a 90 degree angle next to Janet's. *She looks great. Concussion must have been pretty bad, though.*

"If you're an environmentalist, why do you want to see me?" Janet asked.

"Janet—may I call you that?"

"Okay." She rubbed her left arm, which still hurt.

"Dr. Barnes was... well, I do care about you... personally, I mean. I've been very impressed with your work and, when I met you last time, with you. Even though you did get mad at me." He grinned a little. "I want you to know that."

Janet smiled, then frowned when Ellanna cleared her throat. "Thank you, but I've—"

"I know," Wade said, "but I'm glad you're... still with us. We need you."

"We?" Janet looked at Ellanna. "Didn't that lady say that too?"

"Which lady?" Wade asked.

"Your nemesis," Ellanna said. "Sarah Green-Dale. She was here yesterday."

Wade's eyes narrowed and his jaw tightened. *Shit!* "I see. Thanks for telling me." He turned back to Janet. "I take it she wants you to cure everything the viruses don't."

"I...." Janet turned to Ellanna, now seated on the sofa, for help. "Short term memory," she said, shrugging.

"She offered us megabucks," Ellanna said. "A mil now, more later. When and how much TBD."

"To doom humanity and the earth," Wade said. "Not as she sees it, of course. Did you accept?"

"We're not making any decisions right now."

"That's wise." *Please don't choose her way, Jan.* He leaned forward. "Whatever she can offer you, EARTH can match, and more. Last time I offered you a safer place to work if you needed it. That offer's still open." He glanced at Ellanna. "For the whole team, and your families or... friends."

"That's very... generous," Janet said. "But why?"

"It's more than just personal, Jan."

Ellanna coughed discretely and smirked at Wade's annoyed glance.

"What you've learned so far," he continued, "and what you're going to learn, hold the keys to our survival. Or our destruction, at our own hands."

"And you want her to...," Ellanna said.

"When you know enough, block what the viruses do. At least... at least don't let things get worse. Immortality is immoral, not just unrealistic or impractical. We don't have places enough or food enough or water enough for an ever-growing population of immortals to live. Not on earth and not on anywhere we think we can reach. Anything close to immortality will lead to violence, destruction, and genocide. We can't let it happen."

Ellanna sighed. "I guess you didn't learn much last time, when Janet jumped in your stuff. We can't just swirl things around in a test tube and make magic happen."

"That's why I said, 'when you know enough.' But I have to be impatient too. We don't have the luxury of time. I'm ready to help any way I can, any way EARTH can. We have to—*you* have to—solve this, Janet. We need you." *I know you can. Please say you will.*

Janet moaned, leaned back in the recliner, and put the heels of her hands over her eyes.

Ellanna stood. "Time to go."

"I…." Wade watched Janet slide her hands down to cover her face. As he stood he reached out to touch her forearm. "Hope you're better soon."

When Ellanna returned from seeing Wade out, Janet asked, "What did I do to deserve this?"

"Got me, Wonder Woman." She sat in the chair Wade had used and took Janet's hand. "But we're in it together. Plus one. Michael's coming down the hall."

Janet snorted. "Wonder Woman. You got that right. All I do anymore is wonder."

* * *

A few days later, Janet walked back into the lab. Her physician had set her pain meds dosage higher than she wanted, so she'd cut it in half and lived with the discomfort. This was the first day her muscles didn't feel like they'd been beaten with a meat tenderizer. Her headache had gone away too.

Returning to work was a big step. She wished she could go home to her own condo too, but the security people wouldn't let her, telling her they had more work to do before it would be safe. She didn't have the energy to argue.

She stopped just inside the door. At first, she didn't know why she was crying. Then she realized she had crossed the room and was stroking the sweater Satya had left hanging on the back of her chair. Her lab manager was going to live but Janet was sure it was her fault she'd been so badly hurt. *If she didn't work here....*

As she thought about Satya, she felt a warm, comforting presence around her. She looked down and saw Ellanna's dark hands on top of her own.

"Oh!"

Ellanna hugged her friend tighter. "How're you doing?"

"Okay." Janet tried to smile. "I guess."

Ellanna released her and picked up a box of tissues from the desk. "Here," she said, "before I need one too."

Janet wiped her eyes and blew her nose.

Ellanna asked, "You call Satya this morning?"

"I don't understand how she got hurt," Janet said. "She had her vest on."

"Not completely," Ellanna said. "She told me yesterday she opened the front when she got into the van. She was hot. Thought it was safe in there."

"Oh, my God." Tears came again. Janet sagged against the desk and Ellanna reached out to hold her. When she finished, she pulled back and dried her eyes with another tissue, then dabbed at her friend's shoulder.

"Hey?"

Janet sniffled. "Made a mess on your lab coat."

"Lesson learned, huh?"

Puzzled, Janet looked up.

Ellanna grinned. "Never take off your protective gear," she said, waggling her finger.

Janet nodded.

"Don't worry, it'll wash." She rubbed Janet's upper arms. "So, has your noodle stopped ringing enough to do some hard thinking?"

Janet made a face. "I don't know. Why?"

"G and your Mikey found something going back through their notes. They told me about it and I bounced it off Sayid. He wants your take on it. Could be important."

Janet shrugged. "All right. When?"

"Whenever you're ready."

Janet looked around, then raised her hands, palms up. "Might as well."

"Go put your stuff away. I'll call them."

As soon as their boss arrived at the lab, the three scientists sat down with Janet's graduate student at his desk at the end of one of the work benches.

While his computer booted up, Gerardo said, "A couple of weeks after we discovered the viruses, Dr. Farinelli said, just off the cuff, that it was weird how they had spread so fast."

"We've all thought that," Ellanna said.

Michael hurried through the door from the hall. He pulled a chair into the huddle next to Janet's, put his arm around her shoulders, and kissed her on the temple.

She winced but didn't pull away.

Turning to the rest of the group, he picked up the conversation. "G's right. Even back then, I wondered whether there was only one new virus. If the others had been around for a while, not doing anything we'd notice, the new one could be the key to starting the reaction cascade."

"Dr. Hogan suggested as much at the press conference," Sayid said, "but how would you identify the right one? There are so many cascades."

"It wasn't as hard as we thought," Gerardo said. "At first we tried to trace the DNA mutations—which ones came from which viruses."

"You followed the patterns of healing?" Janet asked.

"That's what I started on, with a lot of help from Dr. Farinelli, but it didn't work. The diseases all went away differently, and like Dr. Sayid said, there were too many paths to follow."

"So things stalled," Michael said. "That was the day after Janet and Satya were attacked. But that night, after I went home from the hospital, I woke up thinking that we needed to know where and when the mutated viruses first showed up."

"Could you?" Janet asked. "I mean, we have no idea when—"

"That's right," Gerardo said, "but remember, we needed just one. I posted questions asking whether anybody had samples of the viruses from before all this began, especially a long time ago. Bingo! And the labs that had them were all willing to sequence their genomes for me. I got sequences and dates going back to 1940. All of them except the corn borer virus had already mutated by 1985. There's the key in the lock."

"But they hardly grow any corn in China," Sayid said.

"Which would explain why East Asia was the last place to be affected. I got a lot more data than I expected on the corn borer. Here's an example." Gerardo set up two world maps side by side on the screen. "Watch the virus' spread on the left, compared to the disappearance of AIDS." He activated the simulations. The insect virus' distribution advanced across the map in distinct hops of color, while the syndrome's data changed more smoothly, but the AIDS plot tracked the virus' spread. When the virus fanned out into East Asia, the changes on both maps slowed, then accelerated.

Janet stared at the final pair of maps. "That doesn't make any sense." Her head was starting to ache. Trying to think about what she was watching made it worse.

"Airborne vector?" Ellanna asked.

"But how would it be transmitted to humans?" Gerardo said.

Sayid broke in. "Okay, that's a problem for later. The important question right now is what we're going to do with this. We can't let anyone else be attacked the way Janet and Satya were. Maybe we can stop this pandemic after all."

Janet said, "But it's a good pandemic, isn't it?"

"Is it?" Ellanna asked. "After what happened to you two? Girl, your head's still a mess."

Janet rubbed her forehead. "I'm sorry." She needed to take something for the pain. "It's just… Michael, can you get my purse and some water?"

No one spoke until he returned.

"It's just that people are recovering. My mother did."

"That's the problem," Michael said.

Janet shot him a hurt look.

"I didn't say that right," he said.

"How's that shoe leather taste?" Ellanna asked, poking him in the ribs.

"What I *meant* was, with the death rate down and aging stopped—"

"That Wade guy's pretty much got it right, doesn't he?" Gerardo asked.

"Except for fighting all the ways to improve crop yields and make more fresh water," Sayid growled. "Him and that Green-Dale woman."

"Who wants me to cure everything else anyway." Janet swallowed the pills she'd taken from her purse, then put her elbows on her knees and her head in her hands.

Gerardo slumped in his chair. "This is nuts."

After a long silence, Sayid said, "You could try to counteract something."

"Oh, sure, bring back cancer," Ellanna said with a snort. "I'd just *love* to have another chat with Brother Elijah."

Janet grunted in agreement.

Sayid held up his hands, as if warding off a physical attack. "No, no… I meant something like bringing back aging. Reactivate the telomere-shortening process but make it slower. Maybe people don't want to live for a million years, or a thousand, but just a little longer. That would buy us some time, anyway."

"Yeah," Ellanna said, framing a video screen in front of her face with her hands. "I can see it now: 'Scientists make plans to kill us slowly. Is immortality just for the rich? It's our Top Story.' *That*'ll make us popular."

Janet turned her chair so she could lay her throbbing head on Michael's shoulder.

Sayid laced his fingers together behind his head and stared at the computer screen. After a moment, he said, "All right, point taken. *But*." He looked at each of them in turn. "Even after what's just happened, the public wants more than science. No, they want something other than science. They don't want explanations."

Gerardo said, "But—"

"No buts. They want to know what's going to happen to them." He held out his hand to stop Ellanna's protest. "I *know* you don't know. I know you *can't* know." He stood and looked out the lab window, then turned so he could lean back against the counter in front of the computer. "This isn't about genetics anymore, if it ever was. It's about psychology. Those people out there need to hear something that isn't pie in the sky or the end of the world. You're the best people in the world to give them that."

"We can't just make something up," Janet said, her head still resting on Michael's shoulder.

Sayid shoved his hands into his pockets. "Of course you can't, and I'm not asking you to. But I think it's time for you to change the direction of your work. There are plenty of labs digging into the details of how the viruses work. Let them keep doing that. You have the credibility and authority to provide a scientifically valid definition of what's next, what we're going to do in response to the viruses." He stood up straight. "Maybe bringing back aging isn't the best idea but I believe in you. I know you'll figure something out."

He stepped away from the lab bench so he could lean down and put a hand on Janet's shoulder. "I'm so glad you're still with us," he said softly. "I don't know what we'd do without you." He squeezed her shoulder and then walked out of the room.

* * *

"This is such a beautiful neighborhood," Lisa said to Oriel as their car glided down the winding Raleigh street. "I'll bet it's gorgeous when the leaves turn." Large homes, most dating back to the 1970s, sat well back behind trimmed lawns. Pines, maples, and hickories towered sixty feet and more above the houses but were so far apart that the neighborhood felt both open and enclosed.

"Sure didn't see anything like this in Somalia," Oriel said with a chuckle. "There must be more trees on this block than there were in the whole country."

"There: 6120." She pointed to a split-level house on their right with cream siding.

Oriel eased the car into the long driveway that led past the house to a detached garage, stopping at the brick walk to the front door. "Hey, look at that!" He pointed at a bright green car parked in the garage. "Old Dodge Charger. Bet it's an '09."

"Mph," Lisa said, unimpressed.

"Thought you liked old songs. Wasn't there one called 427, or something like that?"

"Four what?" Lisa said as she got out of the car. "There was a Beach Boys song called '409,' but that's from the 1960s."

"That's what I meant, I guess," Oriel said.

As they were gathering their equipment from the trunk, a man in his late fifties, with worry lines on his face and graying hair, walked down the path to meet them. "You must be Miss Lange and Mr. Salvador," he said.

Her arms full of equipment, she managed to free one hand enough so they could shake. "It's a pleasure to meet you, Mr. Hogan."

Oriel set the camera down on the drive and also shook hands.

"Don't rush," Robert Hogan said. "Janice is still primping. I don't know why you want to talk with us. We've done so many interviews since—"

"How is Janet?" the reporter asked. "I covered the attack for my network. It was so awful."

"Don't you know?" Hogan had been raised to be polite, even to someone he didn't like, so he didn't say anything about how he felt Lisa had treated his daughter in her earlier interviews.

Lisa glanced up from the equipment case she was holding, an apologetic look on her face. "I'm sorry. Everyone in Dallas is being so tight-lipped." She set the container into the trunk of the rental car and opened it. "That's understandable, I guess, but so many people are concerned." She pulled out a plastic box.

Hogan watched her detach a small microphone from the box. "She's all right," he said. "She went back to work yesterday… I guess it's okay to say that."

Ah-ha! Lisa thought. *We need to go back.*

"But she feels so guilty about what happened to her lab manager."

"I'm sure she does," Lisa said. "Since you're here, why don't we get you miked up? We can do some shots outside, then go in."

As Oriel helped him put on the microphone, he pointed toward the garage. "Saw your old car. She's a beauty."

Hogan smiled. "Thanks. My one hobby." He gazed up the driveway. "I taught Janet to drive in that car." He took a moment to gather himself. "I… well, we'll see."

Lisa checked her phone. *Experience pays off again,* she thought. She'd put her own mike on and plugged it into her phone before getting out of the car. The recorder software was on when Janet's father had appeared and had captured the entire conversation. *We'll fix the audio if we have to. Oriel will get some back-side video and it'll look like Hogan's talking to me. Perfect.*

When they walked in, Janice Hogan was bustling around the living room, straightening photos that were a degree out of alignment, flicking away invisible dust, smoothing microscopic creases in the fabric of the sofa. Mr. Hogan wrestled an overstuffed chair into place for Lisa while Oriel set up the cameras and lights. Lisa placed the couple on the couch so the pictures of Janet and her siblings on the end table would be in the video frame.

Once everything was in place, Lisa asked the couple about themselves and their children to put them at ease and set them up to divulge more as the interview went on.

When Janice told how she'd had terminal cancer and been cured by the viruses, Lisa asked, "Do you think your daughter had anything to do with that?"

"We're so proud of her," Mrs. Hogan said, her husband nodding his agreement. "But I don't think so. That sounds so awful but I was taken back to Wake Med—"

"That's the hospital?" Lisa asked.

"Yes, Wake Forest Medical. And then they sent me home. That was a long time before Janet made her announcement. We're very faithful people. I don't know what to make of this talk of viruses and all. What I do know is that I was blessed with a miracle. I give thanks to Jesus every day for what He did for me."

"So you're cured now?"

"Oh, yes."

"Never felt better," Mr. Hogan said. He took his wife's hand.

She leaned against him and smiled.

"Janet's a good daughter," he said. "She loves her mother and wanted to help but… it just broke her heart. She was so far away and couldn't do anything. She tried not to pester Mother's doctors too much." He grinned at the memory.

"She wanted to come home so bad," Janice said, "but once I accepted what was going to happen—"

"That you were going to die," Lisa said.

Mrs. Hogan swallowed hard. "That's right. I put my trust in the Lord and put my foot down to Janet and said no. She needed to stay in Texas and do her work."

"What do you think of her work now?"

Hogan exchanged a glance with his wife. "Proud, but worried too."

"Scared to death would be more like it," Janice said.

"Don't say that, Dear. Please don't."

Oriel zoomed in on the couple as they looked into each other's eyes.

Janice broke the gaze and looked at her lap. A tear formed. "I can't help it. I'm frightened for my baby, that's all." She sniffled. "Now I—I mean, we—we have a chance to live forever and it's a wonderful gift and she—" She took a shaky deep breath. "I'm sorry."

"Those crazies," Hogan said, his face becoming red with anger. "What they did to her, it's not right. If anything bad comes from those viruses, it's not her fault."

* * *

Janet watched Sayid's back as he left.

After the lab door closed, Ellanna stood and leaned down to grasp her friend's elbow. "C'mon," she whispered. She helped Janet to her feet then maneuvered her toward her office. Once there, she pulled the door closed while Janet sat down at the desk. "You sure let Sayid walk you into that decision." Ellanna's voice was quiet but her eyes revealed her worry.

Janet didn't answer right away. She picked up a pencil and tapped it against her other hand, her eyes fixed on that motion. "He pushed all the right buttons. Back when this whole thing was starting, he told me how my advisor at Stanford had called me a little bulldog. She was right, and he knows how I am when I run into a hard problem: I don't want to quit. I can't quit."

"Even after what just happened to you?"

"*Because* of it." She flipped the pencil onto some papers on the desk. For the first time, she met her friend's gaze. "I don't know. One part of me is scared to death for you and the rest of the team… even more than it was before. But another part of me has set its teeth, locked its little legs, and is growling and growling and won't let go. Doesn't know how to let go. If it gets knocked off the bull, it'll just charge back in again until it wins or the bull wins." She poked her finger at the edge of the desk. "Sayid knows that and he keeps pushing that button."

"When did we start talking about bulls?" Ellanna pulled Janet's guest chair over so she could sit facing her friend across the ell that stuck out into the room.

"You know what an English bulldog looks like, don't you?"

"Sure: squat, ugly, bad underbite."

"Know why it's called a bulldog?"

"Unh-uh."

Janet put her hands a foot apart on the desk top, curled as if forming the sides of a bowl. "The Brits used to put a bunch of them in a pit with a bull, then bet on who was going to win. The dogs were trained to attack the bull, grab hold of anything they could—legs, tail, testicles. They'd just bite down and hang on. The bull would kick at 'em and try to hook 'em with its horns. He'd gore them, stomp on them, but if there were too many dogs, they'd wear him down and he'd drop to his knees. Then they'd go for his throat and rip out the jugular. End of bull."

"Ugh," Ellanna said, shuddering. "Didn't that kill a lot of the dogs?"

"Sure." Janet shuffled the papers on the ell, as if she was looking for something. "They just bred more. No problem."

"And Sayid called you a bulldog?" Ellanna sat back in her chair, eyes wide. "Girl, that's no compliment!"

Janet scratched at the side of her head. "There's lots more geneticists where I came from."

"Janet!" Ellanna jumped to her feet and slammed her hands onto the desk. She leaned forward until she was nose to nose with her friend. "What exactly the hell are you saying?"

At first, Janet didn't move, her eyes locked with Ellanna's. Then she slumped back in her chair and rubbed her forehead with her fingertips. "That Sayid's right. That I'm too stupid or too stubborn to know when to quit. I know it's dangerous but my jaws are locked and I won't let go."

"Even if it kills you."

Janet shrugged. "Yup." She looked down at her lap.

Ellanna barked a short laugh. She pushed herself upright and stared down at her lab partner. "You're one messed-up chick."

Janet shrugged again. "Yup. They made me the monster I am today." After a minute, she looked up. "You don't have to stay. If you're smart, you won't."

Ellanna snorted and put her hands on her hips. "Do you think it matters now? Those crazies already know who I am, where I live, all that. You think they'd listen if I said, 'King's X, please don't shoot me. I'm not playing anymore'?"

Janet didn't respond.

"Fat chance, huh? Fat… freakin'… chance. We're screwed now, you and me, just plain screwed. Dead women walking." She turned and took a step toward the door, trying to pace in the little room.

"You *don't* have to stay," Janet said. "I mean it. Get away from Dallas, work for some other lab. You know your stuff. Lots of labs would take you in a heartbeat…

and keep it quiet. Sayid would put in a good word for you. He's got connections everywhere."

Ellanna walked around to Janet's side of the ell and sat down on it. She folded her arms across her chest and watched Janet watch her. "And what suicidal maniac is going to take my place here?" She shook her head. "You don't know me as well as you think you do. I'm stupid too: stupid-loyal to my friends. And I'm a bulldog, just like you." She pulled down on her cheeks, trying to make jowls, and stuck out her lower jaw. "Woof woof."

* * *

"Didn't get much out of that interview," Oriel said as they waited at the traffic light where the Hogans' street crossed Six Forks Road.

Lisa shoved his shoulder. "Thanks! After all the time we've worked together?"

"You're looking for something new, aren't you? Not the same old thing, parents worried about a kid in danger."

"Yeah," Lisa admitted.

"So it's a wasted trip."

"Not entirely...." She slumped in her seat. "Mrs. Hogan's a winner but they were almost losers too. Maybe I could...."

The light turned green. As the car eased into the intersection, she exclaimed, "Wait!"

The car stopped and rolled back, beeping a needless warning since no other vehicles or people were behind it.

"Navigation," Lisa said. "New destination: Wake Forest Medical."

"Wake Forest Medical Center," the system confirmed and turned the car right onto Six Forks Road.

"I've got it," she said. During the drive across town to the hospital, Lisa described her idea to Oriel, then typed notes into her phone. He built a library of images and videos to fit. Once they arrived, she stood in the grass in the traffic island in front of the main entrance, going over the notes, turning them into a script in her mind, then practicing the lines out loud to get the right tone and pace.

When she was ready, he returned to the camera he'd set up, made a few adjustments, then cued her. The late afternoon sun was turning the light yellow bricks above the entrance the color of butter behind her.

"The viruses that brought immortality to America—and the rest of the world—don't care about winners and losers, but that's what they've created," Lisa said. "Some businesses prosper, others collapse. Concepts like justice and just punishment need new definitions. Some people find new meaning in their lives. Others sink deeper and deeper into despair. Still others, like Janice and Robert Hogan—the parents of Dr. Janet Hogan, who discovered the viruses—find both."

The finished report would show the Hogan's pride, fear, and anger.

"Medical experts call the way the viruses have spread a pandemic—a worldwide epidemic—like the Spanish flu of 1918 and the Black Plagues of the Middle Ages. Those pandemics killed millions. This one is different. Instead of spreading nearly unavoidable death, the immortality viruses are spreading unavoidable life. The daily wins and losses that once added up to a lifetime have taken on new meaning, maybe bigger, maybe smaller than before. No success will last a lifetime. Perhaps no failure, either. But there's no guarantee that the successes will balance the failures, even over an eternity. Eternal human life could become a plague. Some advocates claim it already has. For some ordinary people—losers already—there is no doubt.

"There are many questions but the most important one is this: how will we, as individuals and as a society, deal with this eternity plague? Today we have no answers but it won't take all eternity to find them. Or for them to find us.

"In Raleigh, North Carolina, I'm Lisa Lange."

CHAPTER 10

SARAH TRIED TO LIE STILL. The upstairs back bedroom of the A Street Northeast townhouse in Washington, D.C., was quiet now. She was physically spent and emotionally satisfied but her mind refused to settle down. Next to her in the antique four-poster bed, Charlene Hamilton had turned away from Sarah and was snoring. Hamilton shared the townhouse with another senator, a common practice among legislators. She wasn't the only one who had occasional overnight guests.

What's happened to Leenie and me? Sarah thought, brooding. *Since the viruses came, everything's changed—well, almost everything. Do we know who we are anymore?*

Hamilton shifted a little and mumbled something as a dream started.

We've been fighting so much… about everything. Political or personal, we fight about it, deceive each other, betray each other. But here we are, desperate for each other, even while we serve our own mistresses. She snorted. That *has two meanings. At least two.*

She rolled onto her side and pushed at her pillow to fluff it up, trying not to disturb her lover. *Making love is so much safer. Not completely safe, but we don't have to use those nasty dental dams anymore. Leenie tastes so much better than plastic ever could, even the flavored kind.* She smiled.

She'd seen news reports during the week. Gay and lesbian groups were becoming much more aggressive. One of their new slogans—"Make love, not babies"—wasn't new, but "Sodomy means never having to say, 'I'm pregnant,'" horrified conservatives. Sarah sighed. *They're correct but they're not* right. *We need to bring people together, not piss them off.*

Then there was abortion. No one was saying anything new but the shouting was worse than ever. *Roger fought so hard to keep me from having mine. We thought we wanted children but the time wasn't right. I thought my affairs with women were over, that I was committed to him. I was so sure I knew what I was doing. There'd be time later... but there never was. Then we divorced. What if I'd listened to him?*

She'd never known the fetus' gender. She tried to do the math in her head, then pulled her hands from under the comforter to count the years on her fingers. *My God, is it that long ago?*

She wanted to cry. Everything had seemed so hopeful at first, so wonderful. *But there's a new reality now. It took, what, three months, not even that, for our hopes and dreams to crash.* She ran her hand back and forth along the edge of the mattress, as if she was trying to comfort it. The little round spots on the front of the bird's-eye maple dresser stared back at her.

Faint orange light from the next street over filtered through the curtains. A dog bayed at a siren warbling through the night. The bits and pieces of Sarah's frustration crystallized into jagged shards in her soul. So long as she didn't do anything, they didn't hurt, just glistened where they stuck out. They cut deeper only when she tried to act. *But I have to act. I've spent my adult life trying to stop people's pain. Our hopes weren't wrong; still aren't.*

The viruses are not a plague, and they aren't causing one, no matter what that Lange woman said yesterday. The problems they've caused are hard. Of course they are; they're complicated. She pressed her lips together and clenched her fists. *Hard problems have never stopped you, Sarah. You made a promise: no more innocent victims. So many people still need help. They have to be protected. If Hogan won't do it, I'll find someone who will. I don't know who, I don't know how, but I will.*

Hamilton moaned, said something that sounded like "Sarah."

Sarah rolled over and spooned against her lover, slipping her arms around her waist. "I'm here," she whispered, and kissed the back of her head. "It's all right. I'm here for you. You're here for me too, aren't you?"

* * *

The women got up early after their night together. The senator had a breakfast meeting with constituents and Sarah needed to go home to change before returning to SAFE-T's offices. Charlene had been encouraging but not helpful. Sarah hoped the walk past the Senate office buildings and down the hill to Union Station would clear her head.

The hazy pink dawn gave way to brilliant morning heat as she reached the escalator that took her down into the chilly Metro station. She was halfway to the bottom when the escalator jerked as if it was going to stop, then continued. Sarah stumbled down a few steps before she could grab the handrail and regain her balance. Ahead of her, a man in a suit wasn't so lucky and fell hard at the foot of the escalator. Sarah ran down the last few steps and helped him get up. His jacket was torn and dirty but other than being shaken up, he assured her he was all right and hurried off. *They told us that wouldn't happen anymore,* she thought, making a mental note to have someone call and complain.

As she reached the lowest level, an inbound Red Line train hummed to a stop at the platform. Riders rushed out, heading to their jobs. She watched them surge toward the escalators and stairs leading to the exits, ignoring the flashing warning signs and recorded audio messages SAFE-T had forced the Metro to install. *They're not paying attention!*

She sank onto a cement bench to wait for her train. The cavernous station's dim lighting and high, arched ceiling of rows of gray, hollowed-out concrete squares compressed her, amplifying her exhaustion from the sleepless night. The huge vault sucked up the last sounds of the departing commuters, leaving her smothered by silence. *It's all for nothing,* she thought. *They're doing what they've always done, not what's good for them.* The advertising screens mounted on the wall across the tracks cycled through ads for shoes, apartments, hair-loss treatments, and a reminder to be careful when boarding the trains. She saw them but didn't see them. *They call me a do-gooder, a super-nanny, a—what's the latest one? A smother-mother.* She rocked back and forth on the seat, trying to quiet the cackling inside her head, to think.

A sudden realization made her want to smack herself on the forehead. *How could I have been so stupid? The answer's all around me. We assumed everyone would eat right, be safe, stop fighting because the benefits were so obvious but they kept on doing the same old things. Then the fear-mongers stepped in, told everyone how awful the future was going to be.* She sat up straighter and ran her hands through her hair. *We were right about a few things, important things. Medical researchers are out of work and there's lots of money that can't be spent as planned. People still want to live forever, even if it isn't as automatic as we thought it would be. We have to take control, get to work, solve problems, make a better future, and make people believe it's possible. I can do that.*

The station's walls seemed to get brighter. She heard people around her talking. The subtle tang of ozone and the mixed odors of the thousands of people who passed through the station each day tickled her nostrils. She absorbed the energy of the people, the lights, the trains. She pulled out her phone and called her staff, catching them at home, stuck in traffic, on the subway.

An hour later, after a quick change of clothes and a quicker, all-organic breakfast, she was marching back to the Metro on the way to her office. With a twinge of guilt and two checks to make sure no one saw her, she snuck around the barriers SAFE-T had made the city install at the crosswalk and dashed across the street.

* * *

Just before noon, the phone belonging to a woman whom some people knew as Treebeard the Ent chimed as its news-tracker picked up a feed. The link in the pop-up window read, *Eco-terror: Dallas Bombing Linked to Terror Group*. She frowned, checked her calendar, saw that she had a few minutes, and clicked on the link.

A window opened on the screen and a voice announced, "This is a Total Web News Real-Time News Bulletin. Total Web News: your source for news in real time."

"This is Antonio Corolli, reporting from Dallas. The investigation into the car bomb attack on Dr. Janet Hogan, discoverer of the immortality viruses, has kept

Dallas Police, Texas Rangers, FBI, and the Department of Homeland Security busy around the clock. Total Web News has learned they now have a break in the case."

The video switched to the wreckage left by the exploded pickup. "This bomb-laden truck," Corolli continued in voice-over, "was purchased a few days before the blast by a man using the alias Steve Porter. DNA recovered from the wreckage does not match anyone by that name. It does match samples taken from an apartment rented about the same time by someone calling himself Irvin Semmelman, age 24, from nearby Plano." The screen showed the young man's picture, provided, the caption said, by the apartment management. "Semmelman remains unaccounted for, but his apartment had a clear view of Hogan's convoy when it was attacked."

The woman didn't know the face but she knew the plan. *Oh, shit.*

"Law enforcement sources believe Semmelman was a member of an underground ecoterrorist group, possibly the Earth Liberation Front, or E-L-F, which has been implicated in dozens of attacks on businesses, research laboratories, and ski resorts since the 1980s." The video showed a series of burned-out buildings, including one on a mountaintop. "If true, this bombing represents an important upsurge in the level of violence employed by E-L-F."

She didn't wait for the rest of the report. It didn't matter that Corolli had the details wrong. Weasel needed to use his emergency escape plan. She opened a desk drawer, pulled out a phone she used only on certain occasions, and turned it on. Working as fast as she could, she retrieved an animated image of a flying angel. The angel flashed three times, then flew off the screen. The sequence repeated three times. She selected Arnie Steen's number and hit the Send button. There was nothing more she could do. If his plan worked, he'd contact her.

* * *

Mid-week afternoons like this one were slow times at the 'Trons Town electronics store in a strip mall near the University of Texas campus in Austin. Arnie and Toby Cagle, a UT engineering student who worked there part time, had spent the early afternoon puttering around the shop, making sure the shelves were stocked, dusting and cleaning, and waiting on the occasional customer. By two o'clock, they'd exhausted their list of little jobs. They were sitting behind the counter, chatting about the trip Arnie claimed he'd taken into the Texas Hill Country when a striking young blonde walked in. Neither man paid much attention to the thick, tight curls that framed her face. They focused on her body, drawn by the tight, scoop-necked white blouse and blue jeans that looked like they'd been sprayed on. Arnie nudged Toby hard enough to break the young man's trance. Falling back on his company training, Toby called out, "Hi, can I help you?" and strolled across the store to meet her.

The woman appeared to be in her early twenties, perhaps a student at the university or a waitress at a restaurant that catered to the students. She looked around a bit blankly, then said, "Oh, hi. I'm looking for a video camera for my boyfriend? It's for his birthday." She flashed a dreamy smile. "Can you help me?"

Smitten, Toby guided her to the camera display and started telling her about the various models. In minutes, he had overwhelmed her with technical data. Arnie smiled to himself and wandered over to rescue the damsel in distress. "Maybe I can help."

"There are so many choices," the woman said with a disarming pout.

"What will your boyfriend do with the camera?"

"We like to go camping, y'know? And he likes to go into the woods and get video of the animals in their natural, y'know, environment? He's, like, a hunter? But with a video camera, not a gun." She wrinkled her nose. "But he likes to get close, y'know? To really get 'em. Good pictures, I mean."

I'll bet he does, Arnie thought, working hard to keep his eyes above the woman's shoulders.

* * *

Will Baxter eased the door of the funeral home run by his long-time friend Laval Reece closed behind him and crossed the lobby. He wrinkled his nose at the heavy clove-cinnamon perfume that hung in the air. The undertaker's secretary greeted him with a smile as he walked in. He leaned to his right to peer into Reece's office. "Where's the old man?"

"In the embalming room," the woman replied, her smile fading. "He was asked to take care of one himself."

In the back of the building's basement, Baxter knocked on the door just below the sign reading Staff ONLY, then opened it and slipped inside. The tangy smell of embalming fluid always made him a little uneasy but this time there were odors from the inside of a human body too. Water was gurgling into a drain and a wall-mounted fan was humming.

Reece looked over his shoulder as the minister entered. The mortician was wearing green scrubs, a white vinyl apron, and a clear plastic face shield as he bent over the middle of three stainless steel tables. His body blocked the view of the upper portion of a corpse. "You might want to stay over there, Will," he said without straightening up. "This one's pretty bad."

"I was there when he died," Baxter said as he crossed the short space to stand beside Reece at the head of the table. Still, he was shocked when he looked at what was left of the dead man's face. He'd been shot by a large caliber handgun at close range. The bullets had torn away much of the left side of his head as they exited. When Baxter had reached him that night, there was so much blood he hadn't been able to see much else. Now, with the exit wounds cleaned out, ruined bones, brain, and flesh lay exposed.

Baxter tried to keep his focus on the side of the young man's face where the bullets had entered but his stomach twisted and he looked away to find some place to sit or stand where he wouldn't have to see what Reece was doing. There was a steel stool at the foot of the table on his left, behind the mortician. He turned to hang his suit coat on a rack on the wall, then hurried around the far side of the table and straddled the stool.

Reece finished smoothing a bit of heavy wax over the packing material he had used to fill an entry wound, then straightened up and looked at his friend, whose eyes were closed. "Told you. You all right?"

Baxter held up one hand. After a moment, he opened his eyes and brought his hand down into his lap. "Praying for him." *And for all the others, especially Shawn.* He'd been at seminary when his youngest brother had died the same way.

"Hmm," Reece said. "And praying that you wouldn't make a mess you'd have to clean up." He winked. "You understand why I can't stop to shake hands."

"Of course. Please don't let me interfere."

* * *

A battered white delivery truck, its old FedEx logo visible through a thin coat of cheap paint, sat in the strip mall's parking lot. The driver was wearing an old phone earpiece, his feet up on the dash. "Go," he said.

Two men got out of the cab of a semi-tractor they had backed up to the loading dock of the grocery store that anchored one end of the mall. They trotted down the alley to the electronics store's light gray steel security door. FBI Special Agent Lee Foraker pulled a black rectangular box from his jacket and set it against the door. He knelt so he could tell when the box was aligned with the lock, then set magnets to hold the box in place. A red LED illuminated when he pressed a small button on the front. The box hummed for a few moments, then whirred, and the LED turned green. He pulled on the box and the door swung open.

As Special Agent Steve Miskevich slipped into the storage room, Foraker released the magnets and put the box back in his pocket. He closed the door behind him with care so it would make no sound. Miskevich led his partner into the small office just ahead on his right and stood next to the wood veneer desk. The other agent took his place behind the door. "Ready," Miskevich said into his mike.

The van driver tapped at his phone. "Send it."

* * *

Reece turned back to his work, scooping a blob of dark brown wax from a small canister and spreading it around and over the covered wound. "So what brings you here?"

"I just spent some time with the young man's family. They asked me to come by and see that he was being well taken care of. I knew that's what you'd do."

"And you're keeping your promise." Reece finished spreading and smoothing the paste.

From where Baxter was sitting, the face looked almost normal, except for the nose, which seemed to collapse away from him. "Laval, you know I—"

Reece shook his head. "You're a man of your word. I wouldn't expect anything less." He pointed to a framed photograph on the counter beyond the head of the embalming table Baxter was sitting by. "There's a better look at him."

Baxter took the picture and returned to his seat.

Reece picked up a piece of stiff, tight silver wire mesh the size of his hand. The surface was a jumble of ridges and dents.

"What's that?"

Reece walked over to his friend and held the object next to the picture frame. "Face mold. I'm ready to anchor it into what's left of his skull." He circled the left side of the face in the photo with a purple safety-gloved finger. "Then I'll build up a replica of this side with a special putty and cover it with synthetic skin. Match the color, add eyelashes and eyebrows, and he'll be ready for the funeral." He turned the mold over in his hands, a thoughtful look on his face.

Small metal pegs were sticking down from the edges of the mesh. There were speckles and splatters on Reece's apron.

"When I went to mortician's school, I never thought I'd learn to be a sculptor. It's one of the most rewarding things I do."

Baxter winced, his stomach clenching. "Won't the family know? If they bend over to kiss him goodbye—"

"He'll smell like a baby. The syn-skin smells the way little girls' dolls and babies do."

"You never told me that," Baxter said, glancing at the body.

"If I told you everything, I'd have to put you on staff," Reece said, grinning. "But seriously, it's calming, and at a funeral, that's important." He watched his friend for a moment, then returned to his work, aligning the edges of the mask against the dead man's face.

* * *

Arnie, Toby, and the woman had settled on a Hitachi camera and the men were busy showing her how to use it when Arnie's phone buzzed. It took him a moment to realize that the vibration pattern was the Mothers' urgent-message signal.

"Can you excuse me?" he asked. "My boss is calling."

"Sure, okay," the woman said. She turned back to Toby. "So why do we need this manual zoom if there's, like, a digital one?"

Arnie stepped away from them, pulled the phone out of its holster, flipped it open, and called up the message. He knew there was trouble as soon as he saw the angel.

He hurried to the back of the store, trying not to run. All he had to do was ditch his company vest and grab his briefcase. He was already in the small room, reaching for the briefcase, when he realized there was a man in a blue jacket standing next to it.

"Mr. Steen?" Miskevich said.

Arnie froze for a second, then grabbed the briefcase and turned to escape.

Foraker swung the door shut. "FBI. Don't move."

Realizing he was trapped, Arnie swung the briefcase up with both hands, trying to hit Foraker in the face. The agent deflected the blow with his left arm, stumbled across the doorway and into a filing cabinet.

* * *

Baxter looked at the picture he was holding. He'd seen frames like this one at Walmart. The frame wasn't what mattered. What mattered was the life, now lost, that it held, trapped in time, a good-looking young man, smiling at the camera. The background looked like a party scene. "Why did he have to die?" he whispered, not even aware that he'd spoken out loud.

"Why do any of these kids have to die?" Reece responded, his work making small squishing and clicking sounds, then a pop as he anchored the mask in place.

"Aaahhhhhh!" Baxter couldn't hold back. He vomited onto the embalming table, the picture frame slipping out of his hands and falling to the floor. It landed almost flat but the crack of the glass breaking sounded through the wet misery of Baxter's emptying stomach.

Without a word, Reece strode down the aisle between the tables. He peeled off his gloves, dropped them into the red biohazard waste can, then turned a knob. The sound of the exhaust fan rose to a roar. He crossed the room to another counter behind the door and pulled a few paper towels from the dispenser roll. From the cabinets above the counter, he took a drinking glass and filled it with water.

The blobby yellow fluid from Baxter's stomach was flowing back toward him on the table, heading for the drain near the foot end.

"You all right now?" Reece asked.

Baxter said, "I think so. I—" He retched.

Holding the glass and towels in one hand, Reece unclipped a heavy clear plastic hose from the side of the table and washed the vomit toward the drain. When Baxter's spasms were over, he returned the hose to its clip and handed him the towels and water glass. The minister wiped his face and rinsed out his mouth.

Reece turned down the fan. "I told you not to come too close."

* * *

In the front of the store, Toby turned away from the blonde and the camera when he heard a muffled boom from the back.

"Hey!" the woman objected. "Like, what?"

Toby looked back at her. "Didn't you hear that?"

The woman smiled at him.

For the first time he noticed that she had dimples—really cute dimples.

"Oh," she said, "maybe somebody was just emptying a dumpster or something." She took his arm and pulled him back toward her. A delicious scent hung in the air around her. Toby forgot about the noise. "Now, how are we going to recharge the battery if we're out in the woods for, like, a week?"

* * *

Baxter patted at the sweat beading up on his forehead. "That's not it." He stared at the raised lip of the table, then pounded it. "Damn it, damn it, damn it to Hell, Laval! Why? Why is this happening?"

"Why do gang-bangers kill each other?"

Baxter waved his hand. "Not just that. A few days before that young man was killed, I was ministering to a young woman. She was a prostitute… and a mother… and an addict. There were more of them up and down the street. Yesterday I went to visit with a man who was in constant pain. His doctors couldn't stop it." Baxter hunched over on the stool and gazed at the off-white vinyl tile floor. "He committed suicide right in front of me."

"I saw that report." Reece took off his apron and face shield, hung them on a coat hook on the wall, then walked across the room, pushing another stool. The faint odor of vomit hung in the air. He put his arm over his friend's shoulder. "Must have been horrible."

Baxter barely nodded. After a moment, he said, "The viruses gave them a chance to turn their lives around, even if they didn't come back to Jesus right away. And what did they do?" He pointed at the dead man. "That. Or what Mister Hammersmith did."

Reece stood and paced between the table and the storage racks that lined the wall, his hands in the pockets of his scrubs. "This Eternity Plague has sure thrown us a curve ball." He turned to face his friend. "You've heard that's what people are calling it now?"

"Yeah."

When the minister didn't say anything else, Reece turned and resumed pacing. The only sounds in the room were the humming fan and the gurgling water on the table that held the corpse. Finally, he said, "You've been saying this plague was a blessing, a gift. What do you think now? Your friend Brother Elijah is acting like he had it right all along."

Baxter grunted and took a sip from the water glass, then set it on the embalming table.

The mortician frowned but said nothing.

"I've never told anyone this…."

Reece waited.

"Brother Elijah really is my brother. Jeffrey, our prodigal."

"Well, well, well," Reece said, his eyes wide. "That explains a few things."

"Here's a fine irony for you. One of the first things the original Elijah did was to intercede with God to bring a dead boy back to life. Forgive me for saying this, but the one thing my dear brother is good at is raising a ruckus. Middle child, always fighting for attention. He knows how to get his face in front of the cameras but he doesn't have any more answers than the rest of us."

Chuckling, Reece perched on his stool and leaned forward to rest his forearms on his legs. "You heard about the march he's going to lead from Atlanta to DC?"

Baxter snorted. "All the way up, they're going to be chanting things like, 'No justice, no peace.'" He looked up. "Does 'justice' mean anything now?"

Reece sat up straight and gaped at his friend. "I don't believe you just said that. You've worked so hard for social justice and now you're saying it's meaningless?"

"Oh, no, but social justice wasn't what that prostitute, or that young man," he pointed at the corpse, "or brother Hammersmith needed when I was with them. None of them had any hope. No hope for the future, not even hope for salvation through Christ."

"Not even Hammersmith?" Reece asked. "He found a way to run to Christ, even if it's a way you reject." He paused, hand on his chin. "Maybe that's it. Maybe he's discovered a new truth… that we can't just run to Jesus in our hearts, we have to find another way."

Baxter leaned back and stared at the ceiling. "Suicide's a sin."

"Terrific," Reece replied. "What does that leave us with? The stuff that's all over the news: overpopulation, famine, war." He gestured toward the corpse. "Violence? See any good choices there? I sure don't."

"There are still people trying to do good in the world."

Reece crossed his arms across his chest. "How much of *that* have you seen lately?"

"That's not a fair question. I have to go where the troubled souls are."

"And sometimes I end up taking care of the ones you couldn't save. I'm not criticizing you," Reece added when the minister bristled. "People like this kid have always been a part of my business. Since the Plague came, they're at least two-thirds of what I have left. If it wasn't for them, I'd have to cut my staff or even shut down. Other things equal, I'd rather do that than hold funerals for so many like him." He turned to his right. The silver mesh filling the space in the young man's skull glittered under the room's work lights. "Maybe then I could go learn how to sculpt a whole body for once, not just pieces."

Baxter stood and put his hand on Reece's shoulder. "Laval—"

"You were wrong, Will. The Lord wouldn't make the world go crazy like this."

The minister lowered his arm. "Do you think this is a slow-motion version of the destruction of Sodom and Gomorrah? Or did my hopes blind me to the Devil's hand?"

"Maybe they did… but in a way, that isn't what matters."

Puzzled, Baxter peered at Reece. "What are you saying?"

"Just what you've taught me ever since you became a minister. Before that even." Reece stood from his seat. "We can spend our time fighting the Devil and risk losing, or we can turn to God, who can't lose. Jesus and the disciples told us over and over that eternal life can only follow the death that ends earthly life. No matter what else happens, that's part of God's plan for every one of us. We *have* to die—somehow."

* * *

The impact of the briefcase with Foraker's arm left Arnie off balance. Miskevich grabbed him from behind and tried to wrestle him to the floor. Arnie staggered a few steps, then caught himself against a stack of boxes. With his forward motion stopped, he kicked back with his right foot. On the second try, he connected with Miskevich's knee, pushing it backward until it hyper-extended. The agent gasped and fell sideways as his leg collapsed under him.

Arnie grabbed the switchblade hunting knife he kept in a quick-release holster on his belt, hidden by the company vest. He snapped the blade out of the handle as his hand came forward. He knew Foraker would come at him again. The knife was sharp enough to cut through everything he was wearing.

Foraker charged. Arnie slapped the agent's right arm up with a circular sweep of his own left arm, then drove the blade across Foraker's stomach. It sliced into the jacket, deflected off something hard, and cut diagonally across his abdomen.

Foraker screamed as the blade tore through muscle and intestines. He doubled over and fell.

Miskevich drew his pistol as Arnie stumbled out of the way of the collapsing agent. Despite the pain in his knee, the shock of his partner's injury, and his awkward position, he fired twice. The first bullet caught Arnie in the shoulder and spun him around. The second tore through his ribcage, lungs, and heart.

Arnie staggered back against the wall, then slid to the floor as his knees buckled. Miskevich watched him for a moment, keeping his gun trained on him as best he could. When he was satisfied Arnie was no longer a threat, he holstered the weapon. "Agent down," he called out. He twisted around to crawl across the cramped space. He had a hurt partner to take care of.

* * *

"We have to die. It's God's plan," Baxter repeated. "That won't be a very popular idea. So many people have abandoned God in the last few months, what words do I have to convince them to give up what they think they've got now?"

"That never bothered Jesus," Reece noted. "He—"

"Don't compare me to Him," Baxter snapped.

"Dr. King didn't worry about what was popular."

"Don't compare me to him, either. That's another standard I can't meet." Baxter stood and walked away. He leaned sideways against the counter next to the foot of the table and refused to meet his friend's gaze. "They killed Dr. King and all he was asking for was for us to be treated like human beings."

"That's right," Reece said. "They killed Abraham Lincoln and Jesus Christ too. Each one went up against earthly powers and lost. But why should you, a man of God, be afraid of that? Martin Luther King wasn't afraid. Remember his last speech?"

"Of course. He talked about having been to the mountaintop, that he might not make it to the other side."

"He said something else too. I had to memorize that speech in school. He told the story of the Levite—a man from the tribe who served in God's temple!—who refused to stop to help the man who'd been attacked by thieves. The Levite asked, 'If I stop to help this man, what will happen to me?' But the Good Samaritan came along and asked, 'If I don't stop, what will happen to him?' He was the wounded man's salvation that day." Reece stepped in front of Baxter, his hands on his hips. "Are you another Levite? Are you going to turn your back on the wounded man? If you think I'm right, who's going to carry that message? The Black Ministers' Convocation elected you president because they thought you would lead them, didn't they? Will you? Were they wrong?"

"No!" Baxter said. "I mean… I don't want to seem boastful but—"

"That's right," Reece said. "You *are* a leader, and a good one. You're the one leader who understands what needs to happen and why. It's a hard message—my God, I can't imagine how hard—but we need someone to lead us out of this wilderness. Not just we blacks, not just we Christians, not just the poor, all of us. And I," he poked Baxter in the chest with his finger, "nominate you."

The minister took a step back. "You can't."

"I just did."

"*I* can't. I'm not Isaiah, saying, 'Here I am, send me.'"

"You just told me you could lead."

"Not like that." Baxter sighed. "I don't know. Leading a group of like-minded, God-fearing people—that's not so hard."

"Even counting Brother Elijah?" Reece winked when the minister looked up.

"All right, all right," Baxter laughed and held his hands up. "Most of the time, it's easy. But this is a lot different."

"And because it's different, because it's not easy, you're not willing to do it?" Reece's stare bored into his friend's eyes. "There's a crisis out there on the streets. Are you going to deny the most important thing you know and believe? Are you telling me that when you get up in the pulpit on Sunday and preach about the ultimate salvation and eternal life, what you're saying is just words? Where's your *faith*, preacher man?"

Baxter gasped and clenched his fists at his sides.

Reece grabbed him by the shoulders. "*You're* the man to bring us back to God, Will. We need you. We need you *now*."

Baxter met Reece's eyes for a moment, then looked away. "Laval, you've been getting me into trouble since we were little boys. What makes you think you can do it again and get away with it?"

Reece shrugged and grinned. "Just doing what I'm good at, that's all."

"No one's done this alone, not even Jesus Christ. Will you help me?"

"Yet in his hour of greatest need, Christ's human friends abandoned and betrayed him. Please, Will, don't put me in that position. You don't need me to be with you. You've got the greatest power in the universe on your side." The mortician watched as Baxter struggled with his uncertainty and fear. "You know He won't test you beyond what you can bear."

Baxter met Reece's eyes for a moment, then gazed at the body of the dead man on the table. Finally, he nodded. "The words of wise men are as goads."

The mortician wrapped his minister and friend in a tight embrace.

* * *

In the front of the store, Toby jumped when he heard the scream and the gunshots from the back. He turned away from the blonde, forgetting her as he started to run toward his boss' office. Before he could take a second step, however, the woman had his arm in a tight grip.

"Hold it," she said and spun him back around to her. She was holding up a badge and ID card. "Texas State Police. Stay right here." She used the badge holder to brush her hair back, revealing an earpiece. "Trouble in back. Shots fired. Someone's down."

She looked older, her eyes hard, her mouth a thin, pale-pink line. Her dimples had disappeared.

"Shirley," a man called from the back of the store. "Need help in here."

"On the way," she replied. "Don't move," she told Toby, letting go of his arm. As she ran to the curtain and shoved it open, Toby realized she was holding a gun. A big gun. He couldn't imagine where she'd been carrying it.

Seconds later, two men in police uniforms, their guns drawn, ran into the store and toward the back. An ambulance pulled up, followed by several more police cars, most of them unmarked, their lights flashing.

Wide-eyed, Toby watched the police and EMTs.

The blonde officer came back to him.

"What—"

She took his arm again and walked him to the side of the store. "We'd like to ask you a few questions, Mr. Cagle. Would that be okay?" Her bearing and her tone of voice suggested there was only one right answer.

* * *

By late afternoon SAFE-T was broadcasting its new message. In one video, a group of children were playing in a field of flowers on a sunny hillside. The narrator said, in voice-over, "The future for America's children is brighter than ever. Hundreds of deadly diseases have been wiped out. The promise of long and healthy lives, once just a dream, is becoming a reality."

The scene shifted to a frightened little girl in a hospital bed, surrounded by a tangle of tubes and wires. Mysterious machines surrounded her, beeping and flashing, with jagged lines crawling across their glowing displays. The narrator continued. "But the Eternity Plague did not cure every illness or heal every injury. Our children remain at risk." As the narrator spoke, the child and equipment dissolved into soft focus and a list of diseases scrolled across the screen; then everything faded to black.

The screen brightened to reveal dispirited, white-coated researchers sitting in a darkened medical lab, doing nothing, their centrifuges, rocking mixers, and analyzers still. "Meanwhile, thousands of doctors and scientists across the nation need new careers, new direction."

The camera zoomed in on the doorway into the lab. Sarah walked through the door into a spot of light and stopped. A caption appeared at the bottom of the screen, identifying her as she said, "Every day, thousands of children in America get sick, even die, from curable diseases. Others suffer preventable injuries. We can't wait for the government to act." She flicked on the lights. As the camera zoomed back, the scientists smiled and turned to their lab benches, their equipment running, beakers bubbling. "SAFE-T is putting our scientists and research labs back to work, matching them with our children's needs."

The image dissolved back to the children playing on the hillside while Sarah continued in voice-over. "It's their future. It's our future. Join us: we're making the future bright."

* * *

After he left the funeral home, Baxter drove to Raleigh's King Memorial Garden. He wasn't sure he was grateful the car had guided itself there because that had left him to deal with the hurricane of his thoughts and emotions. He was worried about Maureen, what she'd say, what he'd say to her. What he could say to anyone.

He lowered himself onto one of the concrete benches at the periphery of the circle in which the bronze statue of Dr. King stood, his hands frozen in mid-gesture, his robe rippling in the breeze.

He bowed his head in prayer, recalling the words from the first book of Samuel: "If He calls you, you shall say, 'Speak, Lord, your servant hears you,'" but all he heard was the chaotic roar of the traffic rushing by.

CHAPTER 11

IN MID-AUGUST, Janet's team received a small box from Peking University in Beijing, China. The box held only a small vial of pale green liquid stuffed into foam packing and a cryptic message: "We assay our wishes for your eternal health." The customs label listed the contents as *Ostrinia* spp. hemolymph extract.

Rumors were circulating on the Internet, vague hints that a lab at Peking University, headed by Dr. Yu Qilin, had tried to make an antidote to the Plague, was forced into human trials long before they were ready, and their test subjects, all prisoners, had died quick but horrible deaths. Photos and videos surfaced but their authenticity couldn't be proven. Personal and professional inquiries about the rumors were turned away, not always politely, or ignored. Dr. Yu, a well-known, respected, and formerly approachable scientist, went silent.

Janet asked around and discovered other labs working on the Eternity Plague viruses had received similar packages, all unsolicited. Some of the labs had destroyed the fluid, not wanting to take any chances, despite, or perhaps because of, its origin. Others, like Janet's, had set it aside.

"I've been thinking about that vial and the rest," Satya told Janet one day. "The Chinese are afraid of what will happen if the truth is known."

Janet leaned back against the work bench. "We've got enough to deal with. Even if the rumors are true, what could we do?"

"Someone took a big risk sending those packages, especially to us. Customs inspectors were bribed, I'm certain. The Chinese send people to jail, or worse, for revealing state secrets, and anything they think makes them look bad is made a state secret. Sometimes people don't know it's happened until there's a knock on the door late at night."

Janet crossed her arms over her chest. "And you think?"

"We owe it to them. Look." Satya touched the tips of her index fingers together. "One: *Ostrinia.* That's the species of the corn borer our key virus originally infected. Two." She touched middle fingertips. "Hemolymph extract. Insects have one fluid in place of blood and lymphatic, and that's how the virus would circulate in their bodies. Three, the note uses the words 'wishes for eternal health.' Coincidence? I say not. Four, the note says, 'We assay our wishes.' What if that isn't an accident of poor English but an indirect way to say, 'please analyze this?' Now add number five." She touched the tips of her thumbs together. "The rumors of a failed, deadly antidote. It all fits. They want the world to know what happened."

Janet watched Ellanna load a centrifuge. "Could be. But how did they manage to develop the antidote in secret in the first place? And so quickly? Why did they go straight to large-scale human trials?"

"We'll never know," Satya said. "Let's not waste time wondering. We need to know what's in that vial. There's a reason we got it and I don't like having mysterious compounds in my lab."

Janet chuckled but understood her lab manager's concern. "Yes, Boss. Can you do it without taking too much time away from everything else we have to do?"

Satya put on a hurt expression, then grinned at Janet's reaction. "Watch me."

* * *

Weeks of intense work over the summer by the entire SAFE-T staff, pairing up scientists who needed work with money looking for work to support, came together by the middle of August. Sarah went on the road. In one week, she opened a high-yield organic farming program at an agricultural college, announced a program to retrain cancer doctors and nurses into specialties that were still needed, and delivered redirected research grant money to half a dozen labs working on bacterial diseases.

She'd dreamed of changing the world when she was a teenager. Now she was doing it. Every criticism was an opportunity to change someone's mind, every skeptical question a chance to show how things could be better if people would just try instead of focusing on the negative.

When she arrived for the reopening of one lab, she was surrounded by animal rights activists. "You're paying these killers to torture innocent puppies and kittens!" a college-age woman shouted. Costumed protesters, pretending to be locked in fake devices and made up in moulage gore, whined and howled as if they were the injured animals. "Stop the torture! Stop the killing!" they chanted.

Sarah halted her escorts. Instead of trying to push through the protesters, she let the reporters at the event capture the street theater for a few moments. When things had gone on long enough, she straightened to her full height, picked her shortest opponent, and in a voice that would tolerate no argument, said, "Fact: there is *less* research using animals now than there was a year ago. This lab will develop better simulations. Then even fewer animals will be needed. Soon there won't be *any* research using animals."

The woman thrust her picket sign, which showed a graphic picture of a cat locked into some kind of apparatus, toward Sarah. "This is what you want," she shouted. "More of *this*."

"You're not helping people," Sarah countered. "There are still diseases to cure and injuries to heal. We'll save animals by saving people." She faced the cameras. "These people want to save animals more than people. Our work will do both. They whine and cry and put on their little passion plays but accomplish nothing. SAFE-T is making good things happen and is proud to be doing it. We're making the future bright for people *and* animals."

She turned and strode into the building to the cheers of her supporters.

* * *

The Monday after Labor Day, Ellanna stuck her head through the doorway into Janet's office. "Got your VR gear handy?"

Janet glanced up. "Why?" She opened a desk drawer and pulled out the heavy gray plastic glasses and silver sensor gloves.

"G and Satya got the stuff from China sequenced. It *is* an antidote… an attempt at one, anyway. They're looking at the transcription products now."

"Oh, great! That was quick." She followed Ellanna out of the office.

As the women entered the ninth floor virtual reality lab, Gerardo and Satya were standing in the middle of the open room, wearing their goggles and sensor gloves and gesturing in the air. By the time Janet got her own equipment on, the embedded computers had synchronized with the lab's VR system. A knobby red, white, and blue column spiraled up from the floor in front of her. "What's that?" she asked.

"Messenger RNA from one of the modified genes," Satya replied. "We've been trying to isolate the mutated active sites. Some of the genes overlap. That slowed us down."

"We caught a few breaks, though," Gerardo added. "They used the *vaccinia* virus: that was a big one. We must have gotten a half-dozen modified genes just because Satya knows so much about it." He put his arm around the small woman's shoulders and squeezed her.

She playfully shoved him away. "Oh, now. Maybe two or three," she said with an embarrassed smile. "I was lucky, that's all. This is the first mRNA."

"Lucky's good," Ellanna said. "We were lucky just to get this stuff."

"Have you heard the latest?" Gerardo asked. "Dr. Sayid said people in Dr. Yu's lab are being executed because it got out."

Ellanna gasped.

Satya pushed her goggles onto the top of her head. "Didn't I say that would happen?"

"Sayid wasn't sure it's true," Gerardo went on. "Anyway, it's stupid that they've clammed up. We should know what went wrong."

Satya said, "That's what *we* think, but not them. They're too ashamed of this failure and the fact that word got out. They hide their failures, not admit them."

"So now they've failed at that too," Ellanna said as she adjusted her goggles. "Rule number one when you find yourself in a hole: stop digging. Someone should tell them that."

Janet said, "Satya, let's see what you've got."

Her lab manager slid her goggles back over her eyes and pressed a virtual button. A second molecule—its double-lobe shape identifying it as a ribosome—floated into the display space, approaching the transcribed gene. As the mRNA got close, the colorful, lumpy lobes, stacked vertically, pulled away from each other, exposing a bright blue line of negative electrostatic charge at the bottom of the central cleft.

Satya magnified the display so everyone could get a closer look.

The long molecule bent until an end entered the slit between the ribosome's lobes. A deep red ridge of positive charge along the side of the mRNA facing the cleft brightened as it pushed into the ribosome's active site. The smaller supermolecule's free end twisted and writhed like a worm caught in a fish's mouth.

The molecules were locked together by their charges but not touching. Two long rows of tall, evenly spaced peaks emerged, one along the ridge, the other in the ribosome's cleft.

A flock of smaller molecules floated in, display tags identifying them as transfer RNAs. Their fronts looked like short sections of the exposed part of the mRNA but they carried other blobs—the amino acids that would line up to become a new protein.

"I can't see what's happening with the aminos," Ellanna said. "Something should be building up by now. Do we know what it's going to code for?"

"Not yet," Satya replied. "Let's take a closer look." She flew their viewpoint around the paired molecules so they could watch the bustling scene on the outside of the mRNA. Three-legged columns grew from its backbone, each topped with a socket or spike colored red or blue, depending on its electric charge. Amino acids floated in to rest on top of each spire. An enzyme caterpillared across the column tops, leaving behind complexes of blobs connecting the aminos.

"Okay, typical ligase enzyme binding," Janet said. "The end result's the key."

Satya pressed a button on her controller. The reaction raced to its end and the enzyme shot away. The new structure and the mRNA split apart like an opening zipper. The freed protein, a long, lumpy string at first, curled and twisted.

"That folding always fascinates me," Ellanna said. "Look how much it's changing."

Bands and blobs of red and blue shading flickered across the protein's surface as regions of electrical charge came and went. After a few minutes, the process slowed, then stopped. The protein, originally yards long in the simulation, had shrunk itself to a ball a foot across. Orange shading flashed around parts of the new structure.

"I wonder what's going to come of all that," Satya said.

As if it had heard her, the computer displayed a red ball in the air in front of the scientists. Then a starburst of other balls appeared, connected to the first one, followed by even more starbursts expanding from points on the first one. The entire display looked like a Fourth of July firework, except that nothing faded away. One chain of balls brightened, outlined in flashing red.

"Look at those cascades," Janet said, touching individual balls to call up more information. "Pyrogenic exotoxins, unknown variants of streptolysin O and S. But those are bacterial toxins, from… from…."

"*Streptococcus pyogenes*," Ellanna said. "Causes necrotizing fasciitis." She wiggled her goggles, as if they'd become uncomfortable. "That doesn't make any sense. The Chinese modified a virus, not a bacterium."

Gerardo moved data blocks around, spreading them out. "Here are promoters to superexpress genes. That would make things even worse." He stood, pondering the display with his hand on his chin. "That's strange."

Janet had pulled up her own virtual control panel and was searching the lab's databases. "Maybe it's not so crazy," she said after a minute. "G, you said they used the *vaccinia* virus to insert the changes into this virus' genome, right?"

Gerardo nodded.

"Here's a disease called progressive vaccinia. It presents a lot like necrotizing fasciitis. If someone reacts badly to a *vaccinia* injection, like against smallpox, necrotic tissue spreads around the injection site." She tapped a button and a picture of a victim appeared. Too-white skin surrounded a hand-sized red ring of exposed flesh on the man's arm and shoulder. The center of the ring was dead black. "It can progress to toxic shock. If that's what happened to those prisoners... that's awful."

Shivering, Ellanna took off her glasses and sat down in an office chair along the wall.

"What's the matter?" Satya asked.

"I knew a kid in high school who contracted fasciitis on his forearm," Ellanna said. "He almost died. They had to cut out some—no, they had to amputate below the elbow to save him. He said it smelled bad and hurt worse than anything." She leaned back in the chair, wiping at her eyes. "Those poor men."

Janet took off her goggles, folded them, and put them into a pocket of her lab coat. "So Dr. Yu's team was trying to create an antidote to the Plague. Instead, they made a killer. Why didn't they catch it *in vitro*? Or in animals, or like this?" She waved at the VR space. "They're supposed to be among the best in China."

"They were rushed," Gerardo said. "Must have been, like the rumors said."

"But that's stupid," Ellanna said, shifting in her chair. "Even though they know they're going to have a population crisis, and soon."

Satya pointed a finger at Ellanna. "That's why they rushed, you can be sure. India's worried too. I hear that from my old classmates back home."

"This whole thing started with just a few base pairs changed here and there," Gerardo said. "It would have been easy to miss if they were looking for bigger mutations. We just happened to pick this one to look at and saw that mutation, then you guys walked in."

"Professionals don't skip basic steps and rush right to a human trial," Janet said, her fists planted on her hips, "then have all their test subjects die and try to cover it up. It's like they set out to make a killer from the start."

"But if anyone creates an antidote, wouldn't that be the same thing?" Satya asked. "Slower, sure, but what else would an antidote to the Eternity Plague do but kill?"

"What?" Janet exclaimed.

Ellanna shook her head. "This from a woman who was blown up for being part of our lab."

Satya shrugged. "I'm Hindu." She gestured in the air, touching virtual buttons to save the sim, then shut it down. "It doesn't matter whether I die tomorrow or in 2,000 years: I'll live again." She pushed her goggles onto the top of her head. "The Great Goddess Devi will determine how enlightened I became in this life, then decide how I'll live my next one. I guess she's testing me."

"But what will you have to come back to?" Janet said. "The longer the Plague goes on, the longer we live, the more people there'll be. It's an exponential growth curve. We don't know the exponent but it doesn't matter. We can recycle and conserve all we want but it won't be enough. The more people there are, the worse it gets until everything collapses."

"So you think Mr. Wade is right," Satya said.

"There's a biological reason for death," Janet replied. "Don't you understand that?"

"More than one," Ellanna said, "but would you rather your mother was dead now?"

Janet spun on her friend. "What are you talking about?"

"Do *you* want to die? Do you want the people you love to die? Of course not. Neither do I." Ellanna watched her hands turn her goggles over and over in her lap. "Deep down, people still want to believe they're immortal, that 'happily ever after' is here, even with all the ways people keep finding to die since the Plague came." She looked up again. "Yu's team created something in secret and botched it, whatever their reason. If that was all you knew, if you didn't know what we know now, would you want anyone else to try?"

Gerardo said, "The killer vaccine story is all over the web, even if the details are all wrong. If we announce this, the shit'll really hit the fan."

Janet fished a pen from her coat pocket and patted it against her hand as she paced. "So... suppose we say nothing. When someone else figures out what the Chinese did, people will attack us for not stopping them. We don't want that. What if we publish but do nothing else? Maybe a few labs learn from our data, try their own formulations, fail the way Yu's team did, and we're all forced to stop. Then if Wade's right, the population explodes and billions die of war, starvation, whatever. That sucks. On the other hand, if someone does create an antidote that stops the Plague, everyone dies sooner or later. Everyone." She put the pen away and shoved her hands into her pockets. "Billions die or billions die. Great choices, huh?"

"We shouldn't kill each other," Satya said, "but you're saying we have to, that we don't have any choice."

"I'm *not* advocating murder!" Janet threw her hands in the air. "If you think I am, you shouldn't be here. What the hell else should we do? What *can* we do?"

The awkward silence grew between the four scientists. Satya stared at the floor. The lab computers' cooling fans whined and the air conditioning hissed.

"Maybe you could mitigate—" Gerardo said.

"Mitigate what?" Janet asked, holding out her hands to him. "People either live or they die. It's a binary choice. Could we try to figure out how to control something the way Sayid suggested: let people live a few hundred years, then fade into the sunset? Sure, we're smart enough to do that, not get it *almost* right and make everyone die horribly at ninety. Or 33. Or go sterile… in twenty years. We can't test for every possible outcome." She swept her arm around the room. "Not even with stuff like this or the help of every lab on the planet."

"'First, do no harm,'" Ellanna said. "But no matter whether we do something or nothing, everyone's harmed. It's just a question of when and how." She looked up. "If this is what it's like to play God…."

* * *

UNIVERSITY OF TEXAS – SOUTHWESTERN MEDICAL CENTER

Department of Genetics
Dr. Mohamed Sayid, Chair
6000 Harry Hines Blvd., Ste. 623
Dallas, TX 75235-5303

For Immediate Release

Dr. Janet Hogan, discoverer of the viral complex colloquially known as the Eternity Plague, and her research team, today announce an important new development in the understanding of this syndrome.

The team is able to confirm that a sample received from the Institute for Biomolecular Studies at Peking University in Beijing, China, represents an attempt to counteract the effects of the Eternity Plague. *In silico* studies, confirmed in animals, have proven that the compound, derived from a species of *vaccinia* virus, is uniformly fatal. One hundred percent of rats administered the compound succumbed within 48 hours. Modeling suggests human survivability would be approximately 7 days, plus or minus 2 days.

A full report is being published today at arXiv.org.

Due to continued security threats to Dr. Hogan and her team, all press inquiries must be directed through the UT-Southwestern public relations office.

* * *

The morning the announcement was released, Ellanna gave plastic face shields and rain ponchos to Janet, Satya, and Gerardo.

"What's this for?" Janet asked.

"Like G said, the shit's about to hit the fan," Ellanna replied. "Wouldn't want us to get our nice clothes all dirty."

Janet watched her friend's lopsided grin hold, then crumble. She wrapped Ellanna in a tight hug. "Crazy girl," she whispered. "What would I ever do without you?"

* * *

Reverend Baxter's initial attempts during the summer to spread the idea that death was necessary had been halting and largely ineffective. Although he prayed for strength, courage, and the voice to convince the doubters and disbelievers, the right words failed to come. The Black Ministers' Convocation found itself tied up in knots over how, or whether, to support such a message, even as many of the association's leaders accepted it intellectually.

On a mid-September Sunday, Baxter stepped to the pulpit as the last echoes of the choir's hymn were lost to the gusty rainstorm that rustled across the high, wood-beamed sanctuary roof and moaned in the pine trees outside. The lights over the choir dimmed as the spotlight for the pulpit brightened. Cameras at the back and side of the room swung to follow the minister while the woman carrying the hand-held camera paralleled him across the dais.

Once he reached the lectern, he looked out over the congregation. It was larger than it had been until recently. The web audiences had been growing too. His media advisor had encouraged him to release the text of his sermon early to generate more interest. *How much of that is spreading the Lord's Word and how much is just vanity?* he'd wondered, then chided himself. *The Word needs to be spread now more than ever.* He recognized several local reporters in the audience, as well as many who had come from farther away, including a prominent redhead.

He leaned forward as if to confront each worshipper face-to-face. "What are you afraid of?" he asked. The challenge echoed around the room. "What are *you* afraid of? I'm not talking about spiders and snakes. What makes your very soul tremble?

"Is it the awesome power of Almighty God? Is it His power to command forces so great that we are not even straws in the wind against them?" He looked up toward the ceiling as a gust shuddered against the building and thunder grumbled in the distance. "Thank you, Lord, for that gentle demonstration."

In the pews, members of the congregation glanced at each other and chuckled uneasily.

Baxter returned his attention to the audience. "Or do we fear the power of His wrath, the might of His anger against the wicked, or that we might be His next target? We know what happened when He turned that wrath against Sodom and Gomorrah. We know how He sent plague after plague against the Egyptians until Pharaoh relented and let the Israelites go. And yet—"

A thunderclap rumbled and boomed above the church.

"And yet, because we understand that God's mercy and love for each of us are the counterweights to His wrath and anger, and because we have accepted Jesus Christ as our Lord and Savior, we believe we will one day enter into the Kingdom of Heaven.

"So perhaps God's power over us is not what we fear *most.*"

He waited to let the idea sink in.

"Is it sin? We're born sinners, after all, born into a world of sin. The Apostle Paul said that sin was the natural state of his body, bringing him into captivity of the law of sin. Some of us work hard every day to prove that law is still on the books. We seek out sin, seek out the works of the Devil. We drink, use drugs, covet our neighbor's goods or spouse; we lie, we cheat… we kill. And that, Paul said, is the path to the worst possible fate: 'they that are in the flesh'—that is, those who give in to the law of sin—'cannot please God.'"

Hail drummed on the roof.

"Yet we are all forgiven for our sins." Baxter raised his voice so he could be heard over the hail. "If we confess our sins, wrote the Apostle John, God is faithful and just to forgive us. Jesus Himself chose death to atone for our sins. *Our* sins, the sins we would commit today, two thousand years after He was nailed to the cross."

"That's right," a man called out.

"Now, confession isn't enough. We must also repent. Jesus warned us, 'Except ye repent, ye shall all likewise perish.' If we confess and repent our sins, Jesus will welcome us into His loving arms... and into immortality."

As quickly as it started, the hailstorm was over and the sanctuary was almost silent.

"So we fear sin," Baxter said, lowering his voice. "The wages of sin *are* death, after all... but because we can recover from sin, it isn't what we fear most, either."

Again he paused, letting the silence build.

"Is it death we fear most then? In Psalm 55, King David said, 'The terrors of death are fallen upon me and horror hath overwhelmed me.' Today we say we are 'scared to death.'"

The minister wandered away from the pulpit, stroking his chin. "At first we thought—even I thought—this Eternity Plague had spared us, saved us from death. I thought the Plague was a miracle, a marvelous work and a wonder from God, a way for us to have more time to seek Him, to learn the Truth of His Word, to earn salvation through His only Son. I thought it would lead to a new age of enlightenment and spirituality and godliness, a new land of milk and honey. I even—" He looked down, an embarrassed smile on his face. "One day on the radio I heard an old song by a musical group called The Fifth Dimension. My momma played 'Aquarius' on the stereo when I was just a little boy. I remembered it and in a moment of weakness I started singing along: 'Harmony and understanding/sympathy and trust abounding.'" The church ensemble's pianist and guitarist picked up the tune. "'No more falsehoods or derisions—'" Baxter stopped and made a big show of turning to fix the musicians with a baleful glare. Members of the congregation tittered.

Thunder boomed above the church again.

"Yes, Lord!" he cried, whipping around to face his audience, his arms spread wide, face turned toward the ceiling. "I know I was wrong."

The congregation broke out in whoops of laughter.

"And I've gotten down on my knees every night and prayed for Your forgiveness." Baxter joined the laughter. "I have. Really…." He let the laughter die out and be replaced by the rushing sound of rain driving against the sanctuary's tall stained-glass windows.

"Yes, I was wrong." He paused to sweep his gaze across the congregation. "I was wrong about the Plague too. I've learned the hard way, as we all have, that the problem isn't that death no longer comes for us. It still does. Not as soon as it used to, not in all of the old ways. The problem is, too many of our brothers and sisters have decided to seek not salvation, but sin, not Christ, but cursed ways. They've decided to save Christ for later and live for today.

"Then, when death does come for them, when the Angel of Death is hovering over them, horror overwhelms them and they're afraid."

Baxter returned to the pulpit. "What do we fear about death? Do we fear the lake of fire, the eternal damnation that awaits the determined, unrepentant sinner? Do we fear that we haven't measured up to the standards God has set for us, that our faults and failings will outweigh our imperfect attempts to walk the path of righteousness? Do we fear that what we've been taught all these years is wrong, that there isn't anything to look forward to after death? Do we fear that our fate is already decided, determined by some fickle and unknowable set of secret rules?"

He shook his head. "I tell you now: fear not!" He held up the Bible that lay open on the lectern in front of him.

"This book—*the* Book—has the truth and the answers and the rules. Learn them, live them, and the Kingdom of Heaven *shall* be given unto you.

"On the other hand, if you believe the way to eternal life is through the Eternity Plague, if you believe these rules," he patted the Bible, "don't apply anymore, then you believe against God. If you do not just fear death, but refuse death, you turn against God and our Savior, Jesus Christ."

Another gust of wind buffeted the church, rattling the outer doors.

Baxter set the book back on the lectern. "Now, there are some very prominent people who want you to believe in the Eternity Plague instead of in Jesus. They claim peace and goodness will come from a set of mutated, deformed viruses. They don't say there'll be peace for a thousand years or that Christ will return to His earthly throne. They can't say that. Instead they say, 'Don't worry, be happy. Just wait a little while. All your problems will be solved. Eternity will be yours, right here on earth.'

"How can they promise that? Do they think that because they wear expensive suits, walk the halls of Congress, and lunch with movers and shakers, with today's Pilates and Pharisees, they have the power to make such promises?" He rolled his eyes. "Oh yes, Lord, I believe that. Just like I believe five tiny viruses—or five billion viruses—can replace the joy of Jesus Christ."

In a voice just above a whisper, he said, "Their promises are lies."

"Lies!" a woman shouted.

"Tell it!" a man called. "Tell it now!"

"There are other people who claim the Plague will ruin the environment and spread death and destruction around the world. Some even say that it must happen, because it's the only way to save humanity and the earth, as if they believe in the Book of Revelation. *I'll* tell you what Revelation says." He opened the Bible to a spot he'd tabbed the night before, then picked up the book. "Seven angels of the Lord, *each* with a vial of plague, cast their plagues on the earth, and when they were cast, there were thunders and lightnings and a great hail out of heaven, and those who perished were the ones bearing the mark of the Devil." He stabbed at the page with his finger. "*That's* just the beginning of the great destruction awaiting those who turn to Satan instead of Christ."

He set the Bible down and scanned the congregation. "Still others, we call them scientists, claim that these viruses are 'natural,' that they simply 'evolved,' and by some random quirk, by some accident, we're all going to live for a long time, if not forever. In our secular society, science holds a high place. But listen to the words of Isaiah, scientists: 'Thy knowledge has perverted thee. Therefore shall evil come upon thee.'

"I say to you, brothers and sisters, these scientists and these others who claim great powers for the Eternity Plague, or claim that science can undo this Satanic affliction, worship false gods.

"Before the coming of Christ, the kingdoms of Israel and Judah were destroyed because their leaders and people turned to false gods. Today our whole nation—indeed, our whole sinful world—is threatened with destruction because of those who would turn us to false gods again.

"Did the false god of evolution create these viruses? Will the false god of biology defeat them, or make them tame, the submicroscopic pets of a new, Christ-free age of man?"

Baxter chuckled. "As the Psalmist said, 'Such knowledge is too wonderful for me. I cannot attain unto it.'

"This idea that we can turn away from Jesus and turn instead to the false gods of our day, and with their help, avoid death, is worse than sinning. There is nothing more wicked than turning man and woman away from Christ."

The rain, which had been easing, picked up again, hissing against the windows.

"This is a sign of the coming of the Antichrist: 'For many deceivers are entered into the world,' wrote John, 'who confess not that Jesus Christ is come in the flesh. This is a deceiver and an antichrist.'" Baxter looked over the congregation and straight into the lens of the camera in front of him. "You know who those deceivers are. They walk the land, speak to us on the web and TV, try to draw us into their evil plans, make us believe that death is the ultimate evil.

"But when we accept Jesus Christ as our Savior, no Antichrist—no scientist, no lobbyist, no environmentalist, not even Satan himself—can win us over, no matter how hard they try.

Baxter straightened to his full height. "There is no reason to fear death. 'Who shall deliver me from the day of death?' God's holy Word has the answer: if Christ be in you, even if the body is dead, the Spirit *is* life. Paul wrote to the Romans, 'if we be dead *with* Christ, we shall also *live* with him. Christ being raised from the dead dieth no more; death hath no more dominion over him, he liveth unto God.'

"What is death for one whose savior is Jesus Christ? Nothing, I say, but the door into eternal life. *True* eternal life, not the false eternal life of the Eternity Plague.

"I will not be the fool who says to God, 'I know better than You how I should live my life, how long it should be, and how it should end… or not end.' No, no. As the Jewish heroine Judith told us, it's not for us to impose conditions on the Lord. He won't yield to threats or be bargained with like a mere man."

"No, He won't!" a woman shouted.

"If we refuse death, we refuse the crucible that is this life, that tests us, refines us, and prepares us for what's to come. Worse, if we refuse death, we refuse Christ.

"Brothers and sisters, do not reject your Lord and Savior Jesus Christ. Do not give in to the temptations of Satan and his minions. Do not give in to evil.

"Christ has a plan for each of us. That plan includes death in this world because death in this world is a step we must take on the path to eternal life. In fact, the Proverbs tell us, the righteous person has *hope* in his death.

"Accept Christ's plan for your life, your death, and your eternal life in God's holy spirit. Trust in His plan. Trust in the Lord with all your heart, and all your soul, and all your might. The day of your salvation, your birthday into true eternal life, is at hand.

"And let us say, amen."

As the congregation echoed his call, the storm eased outside, leaving only the mournful sound of the wind in the trees as a reminder of its passage.

* * *

Janet was sitting on her sofa with Michael that evening, watching a movie, when Lisa called her for comment. "So how does it feel to be an agent of the Antichrist?"

Half a dozen answers flitted through Janet's head but none felt right. She knew that whatever she said would spread around the world seconds after she'd said it. She wriggled closer to Michael, needing to know that somebody was on her side.

Sensing her mood, he put his arm around her shoulders.

Janet glanced up at him, then turned back to the phone. "I'm just trying to do what I think is right, what's best for everyone."

"Are you a Christian, Dr. Hogan?" Lisa asked.

"That's the way I was raised."

"So this must be pretty hard for you."

Janet turned, laying the side of her head on Michael's shoulder. "I've learned that no matter what I do, someone's going to hate it. I guess this week it's Reverend Baxter's turn."

CHAPTER 12

"SO REVEREND BAXTER WANTS TO KILL everyone off," Sarah said to Ken Bowersox the morning after the sermon. She turned away from the computer screen in her desktop. "Thank you, Clarissa, that's enough." Her digital assistant turned off the video.

Bowersox shifted in his seat on the other side of her desk. "That's not exactly—"

"Oh, I know." Sarah waved off his reply. "And he doesn't like lobbyists, either. Never mind that his Convocation has one here in DC." She grimaced. "'Pilates and Pharisees,' indeed. We need to respond."

"We can take another swipe at the Chinese while we're at it."

"Good: two at once. They both deserve it. The pairing's appropriate too." She thought of SAFE-T's communications director. "Ask Louis—"

"He's already got something mocked-up for you."

Sarah's eyebrows jumped. "He's good but—" She glanced at her clock. "It's not even ten."

Bowersox smiled. "We talked about it yesterday as soon as I heard about the sermon. I think you'll like what he's done."

After the draft video played, Sarah sat back in her chair, her fingers steepled in front of her mouth. "'Dying for a lie' is too harsh."

"A myth?"

"No, unproven belief, maybe. Well, tell Louis to dial it back. The rest is fine. The Chinese are murderers. We're not going to soft-pedal that."

"Done," Bowersox said. He tapped the screen on his tablet to send the notes. "One more thing: Congress."

Sarah leaned forward to rest her arms on the desktop. "Leenie told me."

"When?"

"Friday night."

"It's gotten worse." Bowersox set his tablet on the desk. "I heard this morning that your best buddy, Senator Kapel, and his friends in the House Caucus for Christ worked over the Sabbath...." He paused, waiting for Sarah to catch the irony.

She snorted.

"To put together legislation to sweep all funding for medical research—"

"*What?*"

He held up one hand to signal his boss to wait. "On the remaining diseases, the ones the Plague didn't cure."

"You're kidding."

"I wish I were. At least they're still going to allow—so far—research on wound healing, that sort of thing."

"Stem cells? Organ regrowth?"

"Not if it's needed because of 'sinful behavior.' I heard the working title for the bill is the Restoring Nature's

Excellent Works Act—the ReNEW Act. They can't use 'God' so they're using 'Nature.' Pretty clever, huh?"

Sarah gaped at him. "You've *got* to be… where do these people have their heads?"

"I never knew the view out of someone's belly-button would be so… so…."

"So… *new!*" Sarah rocked back in her chair, laughing and clapping. The more she thought about the image, the funnier it seemed. She pulled a tissue from a box in a desk drawer and wiped her eyes. "Whoo! That's really not funny."

"There's more," Bowersox said.

Sarah peered at him. "Do I dare ask what?"

"My source told me she thinks they'll get enough co-sponsors in both Houses to scare off a Presidential veto."

"Does Charlene know? Isn't she fighting it?" She wiped at a spot on her desk with the tissue. "I wonder why she hasn't asked me for help."

"We can't wait for her to ask. She can fight this tooth and nail but without help she's going to get steamrolled. She's trying to stop a tidal wave. Everyone else is looking for a surfboard."

Sarah leaned back in the chair again. The energy and excitement she'd felt just a few minutes earlier were draining out of her, replaced by a sucking emptiness. *Buck up, Sarah. You've been through this before. The tide's been in our favor the past few weeks but tides turn, don't they? They'll turn again but we don't know when. We've got to stop this, but how? How?*

* * *

Wade's office computer chimed that Monday too, announcing the arrival of a news story. *Area Minister*

Declares Eternal Earthly Life Sinful, the headline from the *Raleigh News & Observer* read. *Calls Eternity Plague Supporters Antichrists.* He skimmed the article, then watched the sermon. Before long, he was caught between a smile and a frown. *He called a lot of people antichrists. He thinks I'm his enemy but we have so much in common. Well, one thing, anyway. One very important thing. How's that saying go? "The enemy of my enemy is my friend?"* He leaned forward in his chair, resting his chin on the heels of his hands. *But what do you do when who's a friend and who's an enemy isn't clear-cut?* His leg bounced as he considered his options.

His phone chimed. "Lisa Lange from Global News dot com calling."

He glanced at it but didn't move.

A few seconds later, the phone announced again, "Lisa Lange from—"

"I heard you," Wade replied. "Find out what she wants." *As if I don't already know.* "Wait. Tell her if it's about Baxter's sermon, I'll call her back."

"Message relayed. She'll be waiting for your call."

"Thanks. I'm not available to any other reporters."

"I understand," the phone said and ended the conversation with a click.

Wade's leg bounced harder.

Half an hour later he phoned Lisa.

"Reverend Baxter called you, among others, an enemy of God," she said. "What's your response?"

Wade leaned closer to the webcam mounted in his desktop. "It's kind of funny, in a sad sort of way."

Lisa's eyebrows arched. "How so?"

"There's so much we agree on, so much that's so important—"

"More important than God?"

"Maybe not in his eyes, but we do agree about the need for everyone to die… eventually, of course."

Lisa angled her head so she was looking at him sideways. "But you've been saying—"

"That earth's human population should be smaller, yes, but not that it should happen catastrophically." He sat up straight. "Listen, Lisa, I don't care why Reverend Baxter thinks death is necessary. If he wants to say it's part of God's plan, that's fine with me. But if he's willing to treat me and EARTH and our position with just that much courtesy and respect, instead of calling us names, I'm willing to make common cause with him, as much as we can."

"That's very interesting," Lisa said.

"If you'd like to relay that offer to the good reverend," Wade said with a smile, *and I know you'll be all over it when I say,* "exclusively—"

Lisa's eyes widened just a little.

Gotcha. "I'd be willing to work with Dr. Baxter, and EARTH will work with the Black Ministers Convocation, to develop a joint position on this and a joint strategy for making it a reality."

"Unconditionally?"

Wade favored her with a wry smile. "It would be nice if he refrained from insulting us in the future."

"Do you think he'll accept?"

"Looks like you've got one more reason to interview him now," Wade said, and winked.

* * *

Lisa wasted no time contacting Baxter and was delighted when he agreed to an interview in his office. Although he greeted her and Oriel with the courtesy she'd come to expect from him, she noticed a change in his demeanor as they chatted while Oriel set up his equipment.

He's being much more careful about what he says, she thought. *Wonder if he suspects I'm recording already.* She was. *He's a lot more fidgety than I've seen him before.*

Once they took their places, sitting knee-to-knee among the light stands and cameras, Lisa tried to ease him into the conversation. "That was a very powerful sermon."

Baxter bowed slightly. "I can't take credit for the words."

"Or the special effects," she said, grinning.

"Certainly not those," he replied, with a small, awkward smile.

"The combination had quite an effect on the congregation, though. Everyone I talked to afterward thought God must have felt it was important to reinforce your message."

"The Lord knows all things," Baxter said, squeezing his hands together in his lap. "If He chooses to support this mere mortal, who am I to disagree?"

"Did He inspire your words too?"

"I pray daily for His guidance and support."

Not going to get any more out of that. "Was the public's response what you expected? How do you feel about it?"

Baxter took a deep breath and looked away. "One can anticipate a reaction, but until you experience it… let's just say I've spent a lot of time in prayer today."

"For?"

"Souls who are crying out for Jesus' healing touch."

Lisa regarded the minister for a moment. "Very gently put. I think Dr. Hogan may have experienced some of the same things a few months ago."

"I suppose that's true." He shifted in his chair.

"Would that make you reconsider calling her an antichrist then, or the servant of one?"

Baxter's eyes widened. "I—" He stared past Lisa's shoulder. When he met her gaze again, he said, "On a personal level, I take your point. But if a person chooses to follow a path that is not the path of righteousness but rather an unholy way, a way contrary to God's will, they shouldn't be surprised if they reap a whirlwind. If they are not too far gone into the Devil's hands, they retain their ability to return to their Redeemer and come back into the light."

"I asked Dr. Hogan last night if she was a Christian. She told me she was."

"Then her actions should be in accordance with her beliefs."

This is going to be so good, Lisa thought. "Along those lines, David Wade asked me to relay an offer to you."

Baxter frowned. "He couldn't contact me himself?"

Oh, he knew what he was doing. "He says you and he have enough in common, at least when it comes to the need for death to be a part of the human experience here on earth, that the two of you, and your respective organizations, should work together."

The minister took his time considering his response. "A strange offer made in a strange way," he said at last. "More than passing strange."

"The Lord working in mysterious ways?"

"Or the Devil in devious ones."

* * *

That evening, Sarah tapped her lips with her finger as Lisa's report ended. Deep in thought, she pushed her chair back from the home office desk in her northwest Washington, D.C. condo, and wandered to the kitchen. Automatic low-intensity lights highlighted door frames and the single step down in the hall as she neared them. After living there for ten years, she'd stopped seeing the safety features she'd once insisted on having put in.

She poured a glass of filtered water from the refrigerator and leaned against the rounded edge of the counter, sipping and pondering. *Religious conservatives have fought the Plague from the start. Baxter didn't at first, then changed his mind. He's gotten a lot of pushback but hasn't wavered. If the entire Black Ministers Convocation takes his position, we've got a problem. Now Wade wants to be his friend.* The corners of her mouth inched upward. *His friends aren't supporting him but some of the people he attacked are.* The faint crows' feet at the corners of her eyes deepened. *What a pickle you're in, Reverend Baxter. Time to make it worse.*

An idea bloomed as she sipped the water. *Oh, yes… right out of their own playbook.* She pushed off from the counter and strode back down the hall to the office, glass in hand.

Perched on the edge of the chair, she called Ken Bowersox at home. When he answered, she said, "Sorry to be calling you so late."

"This is payback for me calling Louis over the weekend, isn't it?" He smiled to make sure she knew he was kidding.

"Of course," she said, smiling in turn. She took one more sip from the glass and set it down. "Glad you got the message." She turned serious. "Have you seen Lisa Lange's latest?"

"Not yet."

"Watch it. We have to stop Baxter. He's standing firm against life. We need to remind him how many people favor it. He's vulnerable; you'll see it in the video."

Bowersox looked away from his phone, a thoughtful expression on his face.

"We're going to do what he and our dear friend Mr. Wade like to do," Sarah said, watching to see whether SAFE-T's co-founder was catching her drift.

"And that would be?"

She outlined her plans.

"We've got a few friends we can call on," he said.

"I want thousands of marchers, Kenneth. Thousands."

* * *

A few days later, the headline of another news item from Raleigh made Wade frown: *Activists to Protest Minister's Message. Thousands Expected for March and Rally.* He scanned the text, then watched the video.

Sarah and her friends think living long enough to create Hell on Earth is a good idea, he thought. *Mother Earth begs to differ. Baxter's going to need some support and we're the ones to give it, despite our differences with him.* His leg bounced as he leaned over his desk, considering his options: what to do, how to do it, who to focus on, who to invite to join in.

There were too many choices at first, too many variations and too many potential consequences to consider or try to foresee. He closed his eyes, forced himself to relax, to surf on the chaos of his turbulent thoughts, to let them coalesce, find their own form, a billion billion idea-atoms, unformed, partial, incomplete, flying around, slamming into each other, sometimes rebounding away, sometimes sticking together, sometimes being smashed apart until… until something created that unique isotope, that critical mass, that island of stability, and became that nucleus, that cell, that seed of a plan, that survived, that germinated… that bloomed.

He smiled.

He opened his eyes, pulled his computer closer, called up a certain list of friends, and began typing.

* * *

"Dr. Barnes," Wade said later that afternoon. "This is a pleasant surprise." A hutch filled with table service stood behind her on the screen of his phone. *Not calling from the lab.* He checked the time. *Four-thirty. Makes it six-thirty in Dallas.*

"Remember the last time you came to the lab?" Ellanna asked. "How you offered us a safe place to work?"

"Of course."

"Was that for all of us together or could…?" She couldn't get the rest of the question out.

"If you think you need to…." *She looks so stressed. Better find out what's going on.* "Maybe you should start at the beginning."

Ellanna took a shaky breath. "Janet's my best friend—besides Gar, my boyfriend, I mean."

Wade waited.

"I don't… I can't…." She swallowed. "I'm sorry. I shouldn't have called."

"No, that's all right," Wade said, trying to keep her on the line. "I can see how hard this is for you. Take your time." He let the silence stretch, then asked, "Are you still getting threats?"

Ellanna bit her lip, nodded. "We're getting used to them, I guess."

"But nothing's been carried out." *Wonder if she's heard about Sarah's march. That shouldn't be bothering her.*

"They don't tell us much," she said, grimacing. "The protective detail, I mean."

A black man about her age pulled up a chair close to hers and put his arm around her shoulders. She glanced at him and smiled.

"I take it that's Gar," Wade said.

"Gar Waverly. Good to meet you, Mr. Wade."

"So, were the two of you considering moving to Portland?"

"I feel so guilty for even making this call," Ellanna said, glancing at Wade's image on her phone, then looking away.

"She feels like she'd be abandoning Janet if she left," Gar said.

"Gar!" Ellanna protested.

"You do, Babe. It's all you've been talking about for days."

"I'm sorry, Mr. Wade," Ellanna said, shooting an angry glance at her boyfriend. "I shouldn't have bothered you." She stabbed a button on the phone and hung up.

Wade sat back in his office chair. *Okay, don't want to drive a wedge between them… or make it worse, hurt Jan. She wants to do what's right.*

He waited a minute, then called Ellanna back. When she answered, he said, "We can set things up so you're still working together."

"I know." She was standing now but Wade couldn't tell where in the house.

That's not what she wants? He switched the display from his phone to his desktop screen.

"Tell him the rest, Babe," Gar said from somewhere outside Wade's field of view. "You're going to have to sooner or later."

Tell me what? He watched her struggle. *Does she think Sarah's going to do a protest march at their lab? Is she afraid of that?*

"She wants… I mean, I think she wants…." The video image shook as she heaved a big sigh. "She's talking about making an antidote—"

"That's great!" Wade exclaimed. When he saw Ellanna's hurt expression, said, "I mean, okay, that's interesting, but I can see that you've got a problem with it."

"We can't!" She remembered who she was talking to. "I know you want us to make something right now, but we can't. It's so dangerous. We don't know enough. Look what happened in China. I'm sure they thought the changes they made were minor and wouldn't affect much but they were wrong. The body's so complex. We can't just guess. It's people's lives. And it's morality. I mean, is there a right way to kill people? That's what we're talking about."

Jan cares about people too, Wade thought, *but I'm sure she understands the bigger problem too, the earth's problem. This is about more than just people.* "So what can I do? I don't think I'm the right person to help you."

"I know, but I don't know who else to turn to."

"Why not talk with your boss, Dr.—"

"Sayid? No, he'd… no. Just no." She sat down on a sofa and the picture on Wade's screen steadied. "I want to keep studying the viruses. It's so important. But if Janet wants to make an antidote now, I can't be a part of that." She shrugged. "Not yet. Maybe not ever. Would you let me just keep doing the basic work that has to be done?"

No, Wade thought. *No, we can't wait. I'd love to have her here but if not she isn't willing to do what's necessary. But… maybe I could string her along for a while, see what develops. Get her to bring Janet here, even. They know what went wrong. They could save the earth, and humanity too. It's worth a try.* "Let me talk with my staff, see what we might be able to do."

CHAPTER 13

BAXTER HAD EXPECTED THE RESPONSE to his sermon to be negative, both in Raleigh and beyond. He explained over and over that he was not advocating a return to the bad old days of sickness, disease, and suffering, and that he had not given in to or been bought off by those who wanted to keep blacks or all minorities or the poor down. He quoted Scripture to justify his case. He talked until he was hoarse. He prayed for those who suggested he should lead by example and die first. He prayed even more for those who offered to help him be that leader.

The Raleigh police and North Carolina Highway Patrol began protecting the minister and his church, which stood across the street from the old state capitol building. Every visitor was screened by a series of metal and explosives detectors. Not all made it through.

Baxter wasn't surprised when the police chief called to tell him about Sarah's march, planned for two Sundays away, which would end with a rally next to his church. He added them to his prayer list.

"We ought to plan for trouble, Reverend," Chief Samuel Goree said. "I'm not too worried about the right-to-lifers—they'll be noisy but peaceful, probably. It's the others they'll attract. They'll cause trouble… at least, some of them will."

"I put my trust in the Lord, Chief—and in your officers too," Baxter said. "God has guided their hands so far."

"And let's pray He continues," Goree said, "but you should have services on Saturday. If they get as many people as their permit allows, the Capitol grounds won't hold them all."

"That's wise, Chief," Baxter said with a nod. "Thank you."

* * *

Not quite two weeks later, the Sunday morning weather was the kind the Chamber of Commerce would brag about: cool autumn air with just a hint of a breeze, clear skies, and bright sunshine.

Sarah buzzed around the Peace College campus north of downtown Raleigh, meeting the leaders of the groups that had come to support her. She spoke with Chief Goree, who would guide them from the women's college, around the state government complex, and up the hill to the old capitol. The night before, she'd looked over the covered stage on the corner of the grounds where she and others would speak. She'd gone back earlier this morning to check the sound system.

Buses were pulling into the unloading area along Halifax Street. Men and women were climbing out, pulling signs and banners from the luggage compartments. Many looked tired, as if they'd been riding all night, but as they mixed with those who had already arrived, they lit up with renewed energy. There were accents from the deep south all the way up the east coast to New York and as far west as her native Chicago, many voices saying the same things: "never done this before," "so excited," "life is so important."

They'll still be unloading by the time we start, Sarah thought. Her body thrummed with the crowd's energy, the exhaustion from the weeks of intensive planning now forgotten.

* * *

Lisa tried to follow Sarah for a while, but on her short legs she couldn't keep up with the lobbyist's long strides. She and Oriel fell back on basic techniques, grabbing ordinary people, asking them to describe their feelings, to say why their group had come from so far away, to "give our viewers a sense" of how important the day was. Surprised and delighted to be interviewed, they chattered and gushed. Oriel kept careful track of their time to make sure they'd be at the front of the march before it began.

* * *

A mile to the south, on the other side of the low hill crowned by the Capitol, another, much smaller group was forming at the Raleigh Convention Center. Rather than rushing around, Wade was busy on his phone checking on last-second details.

EARTH's North Carolina chapters had called out their members and friends from the entire region, but few were nearby. Most of those were young, dressed in the latest rebellious fashions—the men in their 1950s-style throwback suits, the women in bobby-soxer skirts, mocking unthinking conformity. But there were a few others, dressed in black coats, wide-brimmed hats, scarves, and heavy boots, sprinkled like peppercorns through the crowd. Wade had gotten reports of more like them from his other teams.

I don't like this, he thought. None of the locals knew the ones in black. Hoping his people could keep them under control wasn't a plan he could count on. *And if they don't….* He looked up the hill at downtown and took a deep, slow breath.

He checked the time and the video feed on his phone. *Almost ten.* The other march was about to start. His teams were going to wait a little longer. The lifers had farther to go but most important, he wanted them to fill the park around the Capitol and be facing the video screens or the platform, absorbed in the organizers' speeches. *They won't hear us coming,* he thought. *When we show up, they'll get distracted, worried. Then things will get interesting.*

* * *

The local EARTH chapter had invited Antonio Corolli to cover their "disruption action." He noted that Wade was a little surprised to see him there. He noted too, the environmentalist had made it clear he wasn't in the mood for an interview and wouldn't be drawn into a conversation.

Corolli picked a few people to interview. Some of them turned out to be lucid and thoughtful. He left them as soon as he could, searching for the wilder ones, the ones who seemed to be right on the edge. *This can't be all there are,* the reporter thought as he watched the small knots of people milling around the parking lot. *He wouldn't have come all this way for just this handful.* He checked the map of the city center on his phone. *Bet he's got little groups scattered all over.* He noted the time. *No chance to try to find them.*

* * *

Baxter sat with Maureen Sams in the front pew of his church. They were alone in the sanctuary. Bird songs and the occasional rush of a passing car accentuated the stillness of the great room. She'd turned toward his usual chair up on the dais, beside the altar, when they'd walked in hand-in-hand. "No," was all he'd said. *I don't belong there.*

He'd moved the services to the day before to keep his congregation out of danger and asked the members to stay away, stay safe, and pray for everyone concerned. Now the building was all but deserted. A few policemen remained on guard. He could have gone back into his office to watch Sarah's group come up the hill but there wasn't any reason to. The office phones were set to reject all calls to keep them from ringing. His personal phone was inside his jacket, turned off.

He wanted peace. A peaceful demonstration outside, peace in his own heart. Peace, and the courage to act, to stand up, to speak out, if necessary. A pilgrim, he sat in the sanctuary with Maureen at his side and prayed.

* * *

Sarah hurried to the south end of the Peace College campus and gathered her leaders together as ten o'clock neared. Chief Goree went over the rules with them one more time and reminded them that space in the park around the Capitol building was limited. "If you've got too many people for the park, there are parking lots they can use or they can stay on the sidewalks or in Bicentennial Plaza behind the stage. We don't want them blocking the streets."

"That's fine," Sarah said.

Some of the groups wanted to pray before the march began. Sarah stepped back and let one of their leaders conduct the prayer over a bullhorn.

Oriel held his camera as high as he could above the praying group. Standing at a respectful distance, Lisa said, "The energy in the crowd, the electricity, is palpable. The people here know this is an important day, maybe a pivotal one, in the history of the Eternity Plague. They're ready to make history."

Up the hill, a bell chimed the hour.

Sarah placed herself in the middle of the front row, along with the other leaders, carrying a wide banner that read *Life Is Precious, Death Is Unjust* as the crowd moved forward. A tall, haughty black man dressed in a silver, black, and white robe and matching round hat eased into place next to Sarah.

"I'm afraid I don't know you," she said.

"I am Brother Elijah," he proclaimed, "a close friend and confidant of Reverend Baxter. I'm sure you won't mind my joining your quest to convince my misguided but well-meaning brother to mend his ways. I could offer a few words of wisdom from the stage at the proper time—"

Who let him *in?* Sarah thought. "I'm afraid everything has been scheduled and the seats reserved."

"I see," Brother Elijah said with a solemn nod. "Well, I remain at your service."

Sarah busied herself by leading a chant. "What do we want?"

"Life for all!"

"When do we want it?"

"For*ev*er!"

The march swept around the government complex, led by police on motorcycles and reporters from around the world, past the white legislative building with its turquoise pagoda roofs, and up into Capitol Square. Helpers took the banner to hang it from the front of the raised platform. Sarah and the others climbed the stairs at its side to their seats while the chanting, clapping, singing crowd flowed past the stage. A large, custard-yellow church stood to Sarah's right. *Will Baxter come out?* she wondered. *Will Baxter, come out! Ha! Have to use that.*

The protesters filled the square, then the parking lots, then the sidewalks, the plaza, and the streets, but there were more coming. Sarah waited as long as she could, then stood from her front row folding chair and turned on her microphone.

* * *

Wade checked the time again, then glanced at Lisa's webcast. The lifers' crowd was big and disorganized and had overwhelmed the cops. *Perfect,* he thought.

He called his local EARTH leader to his side and activated the video conference with the other teams scattered around the city's center. "Remember the plan," he said. "Infiltrate the other group. Everyone stays cool until I give the signal. We're here to disrupt their little party, then deliver our own message. Got it?" He scanned the tiny faces of men and women on the screen, watching heads nod. "Be disciplined. Don't get too eager. Take

EARTH Action at the right time. We'll start in five minutes."

* * *

Randy Grant, Corolli's cameraman, scanned the knot of people around Wade as the reporter announced, "This group is energized but focused. They know this could be a pivotal day in the history of the Eternity Plague. They're ready to make history."

* * *

Minutes later, Wade strode across the parking lot toward Wilmington Street. Corolli and Grant hurried to get ahead of him. The protesters clustered together and at Wade's signal, started up the hill. A few peered down each cross street at the buildings beyond as they walked.

Wade kept checking his phone. People had overfilled the square. *Good. Easier for us to filter in, stay inconspicuous, but make people nervous at the same time.* He showed the display to those around him. As they got closer, they could hear the speeches—*the screeches,* he thought—channeling down the street from the PA system.

The group crossed Morgan Street, entered the square, and spread out. Wade and a few others pushed north. One of his assistants handed him a wireless microphone.

"You got it," Wade said.

The young man grinned. "Told you not to worry about it."

"And they—"

"Don't have a clue. Think it's broken, back at the shop."

Wade clapped the man on the shoulder and worked his way through the crowd, cutting across the lawn and sidewalks toward the far corner.

The marchers from Sarah's group were looking around, uncertain how to react to the strangely-dressed newcomers spreading among them.

* * *

Corolli found a place to stand along Morgan Street on the south side of the park, with the Capitol behind him. Sarah was speaking, her voice booming from the huge speakers set up next to the giant video screens around the square.

"It's absolutely deafening here," he shouted into his microphone. Grant was standing on a bench, holding his camera high to sweep the crowd. "Pure pandemonium. The square is already full and now the EARTHers are coming in. They're planning on disrupting this rally, but with so many people here, just one spark…."

* * *

Sarah was winding up her speech, reaching her rhetorical climax. The on-stage camera operator zoomed in on her, setting the close-up projected on the video screens. "Every human life is precious," she proclaimed. "And every moment of human life is precious. Every moment of human life is a gift from our creator, and yet…." She waited while the audience cheered and clapped. "And yet, a minister, a servant of God and a leader among African American ministers across the nation, doesn't think so. The pastor of that church right there," she pointed to the yellow building to her right, "says it's our obligation to die."

Some in the crowd booed.

"How can he say that? How *can* he say that?" Waiting while the applause died down, she glanced at a young aide who was standing at the top of the stairs leading up to the stage. He nodded when their eyes met. "Now, I have learned, from a very reliable source, that Reverend Baxter is in that church. I'm pretty sure he can hear us. Will he come out and explain himself to us? Will he explain how a religious man can say such things? Will Baxter come out?" She paused to let the idea percolate. "Will Baxter, come out!" she called. "Will Baxter, come out!"

Her supporters picked up the chant, repeating it over and over.

* * *

From their perch on the west portico of the Capitol, Oriel panned to the front of the church as Lisa shouted into her microphone, "This could be it, the moment we've been waiting for. Reverend Baxter challenged Sarah Green-Dale and the life movement. Now she's thrown it back in his face. Was Sarah right? Is he in the church? If he is, what will he do?"

* * *

Baxter and Maureen had moved to the back of the sanctuary, then into the foyer beyond it so they could hear despite the echoes that hammered around the large room. *They must have the volume turned up to 20,* he thought. He laughed and shook his head when the chanting started.

Maureen took his hand, a worried look on her face.

"I'll bet her publicist worked overtime to come up with that line," he said.

"Now, Will, that's not—"

"I know." He looked out the small windows. *I just wish Laval was here.* He sighed. *No, he was right. This is my cross. Jesus told his disciples not to worry about what they would say when they preached His gospel, that God would speak through them.* He clasped her hands in his, kissed her fingers, then bowed his head so his forehead touched hers. *Lord, if it be Thy will, speak through me now.*

He turned, pushed the panic bar, and opened the heavy wooden outer door.

* * *

The chant Sarah was leading surprised Wade as he neared her stage.

"That's pretty funny," the young man walking with him said, leaning in so he could be heard. "Think he'll come out?"

"She's blowing smoke," Wade replied. "He's miles away."

The chant faded suddenly and people in the square pointed toward the church. A door facing the street had opened and a black man had walked out onto the steps.

"Who's that?" Wade's assistant asked, pointing at the nearest video screen.

"I'll be damned," Wade said. "That's him. That's Baxter. Either he's got balls the size of cantaloupes or a brain made of one. Tell our people to get ready. Things are changing fast."

* * *

By the time Baxter reached the bottom of the stairs, the protesters on the sidewalk in front of the church had turned to see what the others were pointing at. They stepped back, opening a path for him to the stage. He kept his head up, shoulders back, eyes toward the platform. He expected to be shouted at, maybe worse, but the people around him were silent, not sure how to respond. Some, he could see, were angry, even fearful, but he held to his faith, to his belief that he would be protected if that was what he deserved, and the aura he projected held back the protesters.

A police officer came over and guided him to an opening in the orange mesh fence that surrounded the stage. A sound like fallen leaves blowing in the autumn wind hissed through the crowd as he climbed the steps. A woman at the top held out a microphone. He took it from her and she walked away without a word.

Sarah stood at the front center of the stage. She didn't move or speak, but waited for Baxter to come to her.

Two can play this game, he thought. He stopped and turned on his mike.

"Good morning, Mrs. Green-Dale," he said as the camera operator framed him in medium close-up. "Thank you for bringing so many of your friends to Raleigh." He turned to the dignitaries seated on the stage. "And good morning, Mayor Jeffries. Good to see you." Baxter hesitated when he spotted Brother Elijah standing behind an empty chair in the back row. His lips curled into a tiny smile before he faced Sarah again. "I didn't think so many would come here just to listen to me but since you asked me to speak, I'd be happy to share a few words with you."

"That would be wonderful, Reverend Baxter," Sarah said. "We are all very interested to hear you explain how it can possibly be moral to force people to die. As a Christian and an American, how can you deny anyone the right to life, which the Constitution and the Bible guarantee? How can you force anyone back to the sickness and suffering that used to be the fate of so many? And how can you deny anyone eternal life here on Earth, which these miracle viruses have granted?"

"Amen," Brother Elijah called.

The audience applauded and some chanted, "Right to life, right to life…."

Baxter turned his back on the dignitaries, waited for those in front of him to quiet, then smiled. "So many questions at once. It's good to know you seek the truth."

An uneasy rustle of whispered conversations rippled through the crowd.

He walked toward the center of the platform. "As a Christian, *I* certainly do not have the power to grant or deny anyone eternal life. Only God the Father and Jesus Christ, His only Son, have that power. As the president of a convocation of ministers of many faiths, I know they all deal with the issues of life and death. But they all believe the power of decision lies with their god, not," he half-glanced toward the seats behind him, "with their earthly ministers.

"Here's another truth, and I know you know it too: the Eternity Plague does not guarantee us eternal life on Earth. It does *not*. Not long ago, a young man died in my arms. He'd been shot in the head in a drive-by shooting." Baxter paused, his lips pinched. "The Plague didn't save him.

"The Plague viruses are an abomination against nature and against God, whether they were made by Satan directly or by man working under the Evil One's guidance. We mere humans may believe we can long delay the day God will call us home with our medicines and our safety devices." He lowered his voice. "But for each of us, the day will come when God's merciful messenger, the Angel of Death, will reach out for us. Then we will die, with the chance to be reborn into true eternal life. As the Bible teaches us, the righteous have hope in their death, but we must needs die."

Another voice boomed over the crowd, "And sooner is better than later. Better death in peace than life in misery."

Startled, Baxter paused.

Sarah leaned from side to side and craned her neck, trying to identify who had spoken.

"Down here," Wade said. "Right in front of you."

Sarah and Baxter looked down, spotting him standing against the orange fencing.

"What are you doing here?" Sarah demanded.

"Let me up on stage and I'll tell you."

People cheered from scattered spots around the square as they watched the screens.

"You know, the Reverend's right," Wade said. "It is our duty to die. If he wants to sell that as the door to salvation, that's his business." He looked onto the stage, found the camera that was tracking him, and said, "For those of you who don't know me, my name is David Wade. My group's called Earth Action: Return To Harmony. I'm here to save the earth, this place we're living on now—from people like her." He pointed at Sarah.

"Go away!" Sarah shouted. "You don't belong here."

"You let the preacher come up. No, you *demanded* he come up, so you could attack him. Are you afraid of me?

There's only two of us—the reverend and me—and thousands of you."

Wade's supporters were chanting, "Let him up! Let him up!" The people around him, however, blocked his way. Some shouted or cursed at him.

"Listen to what these nice folks are saying," Wade said and held the mike out toward them, broadcasting their curses over the square. Police officers struggled toward him, intent on keeping him from being attacked while they figured out what else to do.

"Brothers, sisters, stop," Baxter called out. "That's not the way. Let him come up here. There's no reason to be afraid of him." *Dearest God in heaven, guide me.*

"No," Brother Elijah proclaimed as he trotted down the risers. "Satan's feet shall not tread on this sacred altar." He stationed himself at the head of the stairs, his feet planted, arms across his chest, head held high.

Sarah turned off her mike and called to Chief Goree, standing on the ground near the front corner of the stage, "Can't you do something?"

The chief was busy on his walkie-talkie. He listened for a moment, then looked up. "Bring him over here," he shouted to the officers who had reached Wade.

When the environmentalist reached him, Goree said, "You're not going to cause trouble."

"Look," Wade replied, his microphone broadcasting the conversation, "the Reverend wants me up on stage. Green-Dale wanted him up there. It'll be better if I'm up there." He headed for the stairs Baxter had climbed earlier without waiting for an answer.

The minister walked up behind Brother Elijah and put a hand on his shoulder as if to talk with him. As the preacher turned, Wade sprinted onto the stage. Baxter followed him without a word, leaving Brother Elijah glaring at his back.

"Now then, Mrs. Used-to-be-Green-but-now-it's-a-polluted-Dale," Wade said as he strode out to stage-center, "how do you think you're going to feed all the billions you want to save? They'll need someplace to live and grow their food. There's only so much farm land available." He turned toward the minister. "Will Reverend Baxter have to do the loaves and fishes thing every day? Even Jesus only did it twice. Where's their clean water going to come from when they're all pissing in it? How are you going to make electricity when there aren't any more back yards for the NIMBYs to defend against power plants? Put a windmill on every tenement block?

"There's famine in Africa and Asia again. It'll be in South America soon. Think that doesn't matter? Wait 'til the resource wars start."

People near the stage shouted, "Get him off!" "He's a nutball!" "Shut up, asshole!"

"There's one solution," Wade said, ignoring them. "The Plague has to be stopped. We have to start dying again. It doesn't have to be today or tomorrow, and not all at once. But we can't wait a thousand years for your miracle cures, Sarah. 'The land shall be desolate and waste,' right reverend?"

Baxter was careful not to react.

"That's what'll happen if people don't die," Wade said. "We need to clean up the mess we've made and vaccinate the world against this Plague." He faced the crowd, raised his fist, and shouted, "Defend the earth!"

There was a loud bang to Wade's left. A cloud of smoke appeared near an access road that led to the Capitol building. He ducked and exclaimed, "What the hell?"

People tried to get away from the explosion but too many were packed too close together for anyone to move easily, or at all. Other explosions and clouds of smoke erupted and the mob surged back and forth. Those closest to the edges fled down the streets around the square. Strings of firecrackers went off, sounding like rapid-fire gunshots, creating more panic.

* * *

As Oriel scanned the turbulent mob from their perch above it, Lisa shouted, "It's complete chaos in the square. There's panic everywhere. This was supposed to be a peaceful event, a celebration. Now it's mayhem and confusion."

* * *

"The counter-protesters are cheering," Corolli reported from a spot at the southwest corner of the park, "while everyone else is trying to get out. I knew there would be trouble. The police are overwhelmed. Who will be held responsible?"

* * *

The police tried to keep everyone away from the stage but some pushed down the fencing and hid under the platform while others streamed past it.

Brother Elijah charged Wade, who dropped his mike and dashed down the steps, cursing.

Chief Goree and a group of officers surrounded Baxter, Sarah, the mayor, and the others, and hustled them down the steps. "Get them over to the church!" the chief shouted.

* * *

The black-clad anarchists and other troublemakers who had joined the EARTH protesters streamed out in two directions. One mob headed south down the mall, the other north into the Bicentennial Plaza and the government center beyond, breaking windows and setting fires as they went. The scattered and overwhelmed police charged after them but the rioters slipped down side streets and circled back toward the Capitol to do more damage.

* * *

The crowd around Corolli and Grant churned like water tumbling through rapids.

Some of the protesters were putting on tight-fitting swimmer's goggles and cloth masks.

The cameraman noticed. "You see that?"

"Yeah. Follow them."

They turned into the mall and merged with the compressed flow of rioters. Large planters full of trees and flowers channeled most of the whooping, shouting people onto the sidewalk but they spread out after the planters ended. The screaming and shouting got louder and mixed with the crash of plate glass windows breaking and the whoomp of small explosions.

"Firebombs—there!" Corolli shouted in Grant's ear, pointing over his shoulder.

Then metallic thunks and ominous hisses joined the mix. "Tear gas!" Corolli shouted. "Go! That way!" He pointed down the hill toward the police lines.

They were caught in a standing wave of humanity between the protesters running into the mall and others trying to get away from the gas. They pushed sideways, trying to get up against a building that wasn't burning. They succeeded but another cloud of gas and smoke poured over them. Choking, their eyes and noses running uncontrollably, they staggered up the hill toward the capitol, then headed east for Wilmington Street, Wade's original route.

Finding themselves in relatively clear air once they turned the corner, they stopped and sagged against the building, panting. "Shit," Grant gasped. He leaned over and blew his nose onto the sidewalk. "That was too much fun."

"We've got to find a way back in," Corolli said.

"What about that guy… Wade?"

"Screw him," Corolli said. "The riot's the story now."

* * *

Lisa and Oriel left the balcony, raced across the interior of the Capitol building and down the marble stairs to the first floor. The Highway Patrol officer guarding it tried to stop them as they ran for the exit. "You shouldn't—" she called as they dashed past. The rest of her words were lost to the noise outside.

"Which way?" Oriel shouted as they crossed the short outer entry.

Lisa stopped to look around the grounds. They were on the wrong side, away from the stage by Baxter's church. "That way," she said, pointing north. "Back to the college."

They both coughed as they looped around the building, heading for the route Sarah's marchers had followed. Lisa glanced over her shoulder, then stopped.

"Hey!" Oriel danced around her, trying not to knock her over. "What?" He followed Lisa's gaze. A white cloud was billowing from the Fayetteville Street Mall. "Tear gas," he said, and coughed. "Go there?"

"Unh-uh. Got to find Sarah."

* * *

The old buildings, packed close together in the compact city center, many restored with wood interiors, were ripe for a cataclysm. Fire crews from all over the city responded but struggled to get through the crowds fleeing down the streets. Only the sprinkler systems SAFE-T had forced cities to require kept the flames in check until the firefighters arrived.

* * *

Wade swung around the back of the stage and worked his way against the flow of panicked protesters toward the far side. As he did, he glanced back and caught a glimpse of Brother Elijah's bright clothes as the frantic crowd swept the preacher along with them.

Within minutes, the sounds of the throng around him faded as the square emptied, replaced by the noise of the chaos farther down the hill toward the state government complex. The silence was eerie. His nose tingled and his eyes felt gritty from the drifting tear gas.

He walked around to the front of the stage. A cluster of sobbing women were huddled behind the banner that still hung across the front. One of them asked, "Is it safe? Can we come out now?"

He looked across the square toward the mall and the clouds of smoke flowing up from it. "Better stay here."

Baxter's church caught his attention and he headed for it, his hands in his pockets. His mind had calmed down enough that he could start thinking about how he and EARTH were going to respond. *We'll get blamed, of course. We'll deny responsibility… blame the damage on outsiders, and on Sarah, for coming here in the first place. Have to find some way to make amends, anyway. But that's all tactics. Big picture, what have we achieved?* He stopped on the sidewalk across the street from the church and scuffed at a small pile of sand there with his shoe. *Too soon to tell. Maybe not much. Guess I should go apologize to Baxter.*

He crossed the street and trotted up the stairs the minister had walked down minutes earlier.

* * *

Sarah was sitting in a chair in the safety of Baxter's office, rocking and crying from the tear gas and her own anger and frustration. "This is *your* fault," she hissed.

"You chose to come here," the minister snapped. "If you hadn't come, those crazies wouldn't have followed you. Now we both look like fools."

A Raleigh police officer knocked on the open door. When the minister looked up, the officer said, "Sir, there's someone here to see you."

Puzzled, Baxter frowned. The frown deepened when Wade stepped into the room.

"*You!*" Sarah growled.

* * *

The next morning, Wade and Sarah appeared at a hastily arranged press conference at City Hall. Mayor Jeffries, Chief Goree, and Fire Department Chief D'Quan Harrison, all looking grim and angry, flanked them. Lisa was in the front row of reporters.

Wade ended his statement by saying, "I understand that passions run high when it comes to the Eternity Plague. All of us who lead organizations involved in this matter must be sure our followers behave responsibly, even as we disagree.

"I acknowledge that EARTH must do a better job of controlling those who take part in our public actions." He paused to look at each video camera. "So must all the others.

"For our part, the Board of Directors of Earth Action: Return To Harmony met in emergency session last night, and agreed to lead by example. We will begin a ninety-day fundraising campaign to help the City of Raleigh defray the clean-up costs and repair the damage done in yesterday's riot. We hope SAFE-T and its followers will join us in this effort."

Sarah stared straight ahead, her face a mask.

Lisa turned, caught Oriel's eye, and raised a quizzical eyebrow. "Hush money?" she mouthed.

He shrugged.

* * *

That afternoon, Antonio Corolli called Janet at her lab.

"I'm sure you saw the press conference this morning," he said. "What did you think of it? Who's to blame for the riot? Does that give you any second thoughts about your work? Was it right to tell the world about the Eternity Plague in the first place?"

Janet waved her hands in front of the camera on her computer's screen. "Wait, wait, wait. I can't answer all of those at once."

"Were you wrong to announce the discovery of the Eternity Plague?" Corolli asked. "Do you feel any responsibility for what happened in Raleigh yesterday?"

"I... no," Janet said, hands clenched into fists out of the camera's view. "I can't be responsible for every stupid thing somebody does and then blames on the viruses we discovered."

The reporter's voice became ominous. "My sources tell me your lab might be the next target of David Wade and his mobs."

Janet closed her eyes. *He wouldn't. They wouldn't.* Her mind went cold. *Would they?*

CHAPTER 14

BACK IN HER WASHINGTON OFFICE the afternoon of the press conference, Sarah stalked back and forth, seething. Ken Bowersox sat at the end of the sofa farthest from her desk, where Gayle Forrester usually sat, while Sarah raged.

"First he blows up our rally!" she spat. "Then his goons tear up the town, then he backs *me* into a corner by promising to buy off the city! He offered them a bribe, in public, and they took it! And he blackmailed us into doing the same thing!" She shook her fists. "I *hate* David Wade! Arrogant… scheming… murderous… *bastard!*"

She stomped over to stand so close to Bowersox that she was almost on his feet and stabbed a finger in his face. "And you'd god*damn* well better hate him too!"

He didn't flinch.

"You'd better—" She stared down at him, chest heaving.

"You'd better calm down," he said. He held up a hand to stop her objection, then stood, forcing her to step back. "Yes, you're right. You got fucked and you didn't get kissed. That doesn't mean you were wrong."

Sarah spun away from him. "Except in the eyes of the press and the public."

"You sure?"

"Yes."

With a small smile, he watched her jaw muscles work. "I'm not."

"Really." Scorn coated the word like spilled crude oil.

Bowersox eased past the coffee table and walked behind Sarah's desk. "Clarissa," he said to her electronic assistant, "bring up that news summary I asked you to put together, please."

Sarah peered at him, suspicious.

"Here it is, Mr. Bowersox," the computer replied.

He scanned the display, moving charts around on the desktop screen with his hands. "Even better," he said, mostly to himself. He looked up at Sarah. "Come see."

She walked over to stand beside him, cold waves of doubt radiating from her.

"Gayle would appreciate this analysis," he said.

Sarah snorted.

"So let's see: news reports about the riot are running ten-to-one unfavorable. I'm surprised they're not higher. Social media 80-to-1 against. That's a big hit, even if people are split on whether to support you or him and Baxter on the issues. You're still ahead there 65 to 35 but they've been closing on you."

Sarah's expression softened, but only a little.

Bowersox slid some graphs out of the way and moved others in front of his boss. "Here's where you're falling short. People like the fact that Wade's not exactly taking the blame for the riot but is trying to make things better. They don't like the way you played Great Stone Face this morning. They understand why you're angry and they agree, but look at this." He pointed at a graph. "Almost 80 percent want you—want us—to do something to help Raleigh too."

Sarah said through clenched teeth, "I won't let that—"

"No, you won't," Bowersox said. "Think *ju jitsu*, not *kung fu*. Use his energy against him, rather than taking him on directly, *mano a mano*."

The displays blinked from time to time as they updated with new numbers. Sarah asked while she watched, "How do you propose we do that?"

Bowersox waved at the desktop. "Part of it's right here: that's a thirty point gap in favor of life. We need to widen it again. Push life and health in the here and now while Wade's on the defensive. He turned to face Sarah. "And, we have a secret weapon."

"Ohhh?"

"Who knows more about the Eternity Plague than anyone else?"

She frowned. "How's—"

"Who best knows the viruses' strengths and limitations, and so will best know what needs to be done for us to reach our goals?"

Sarah gazed out her office window, one hand holding her elbow, the other hand holding her chin. "Has she—"

"Taken a position on how to respond to the viruses?"

Sarah nodded.

"She didn't appreciate Reverend Baxter calling her an antichrist."

"So she could use some support… or encouragement."

"That idea-flower starting to open up?" Bowersox asked with a sly smile.

Sarah smiled slightly. "Starting to."

* * *

A week later, Janet was fidgeting in a makeup chair in a corner of the Dallas virtual reality lab as she prepared for Lisa's joint interview with her and Sarah. She tried to ignore the other women. Their obvious ease with interviews, their casual self-confidence made her muscles knot with tension. *I'm no good at this,* she thought. *I hate being interviewed. Nothing good ever comes of it.* The transmitter box for her wireless earpiece and microphone dug into the small of her back. *Just get it done, will you?* she thought at the guy fussing over her makeup. *What's taking him so long? Hasn't he got the bull's-eye on my forehead right yet?*

Sarah, sitting in the makeup chair next to Janet's, had been all but gushing since she'd walked into the lab, chattering about her last visit, just after the bombing, a visit Janet hardly remembered. The other makeup tech finished with Sarah and crossed the room to give Lisa a last-second touch-up. Sarah flashed Janet a big smile, making her wonder again, *What's she up to? She's got to have an agenda, doing this instead of a one-on-one. Is Lisa in on it? Bet she is. Why did I let Sayid talk me into this?* She forced herself to unclench her fists and keep her nails from digging into her palms more than they already had.

"There," her makeup tech said with one last fluffing-up pat at the bottom of her hair. "You're all set."

"Three minutes," Oriel said. "Let's get everyone in place, please."

Janet's stomach growled and churned. It was almost seven p.m., the beginning of prime time. She'd been hungry but was too nervous to eat before she came up to the lab. Now she wished she'd forced herself to have something. *I'll be okay once it starts,* she told herself, hoping it would be true this time.

She glanced at Michael, Ellanna, and Gerardo. Her lab partners had come up early to prepare the simulations of the Chinese vaccine's reaction products. Now they were standing behind the bank of equipment that integrated Oriel's webcast gear with the lab's VR system.

Ellanna had been losing her sparkle since they'd talked about creating an antidote but she winked at Janet. Gerardo flashed a thumbs-up sign. Michael mouthed, "Love you." With a grateful smile, Janet eased through the equipment to her seat at a plastic table covered with a white cloth.

There were glasses of water and pairs of silver mesh gloves at all three places, and VR goggles at two of them. Janet grabbed her glass to wash out the glue that filled her mouth. Lisa's and Sarah's goggles and gloves were loaners from the lab. "My goggles," she gasped, realizing she'd left them by the makeup chair.

"Two minutes," Oriel said. He asked Gerardo to get the goggles, then settled into his seat and brought the portable studio lights up to full brightness. After a quick check of each woman's microphone, he said, "We're ready, LA."

Gerardo hustled around the control console and light stands, being careful to not trip over their legs. He sneaked Janet's goggles to her as Oriel counted down from thirty seconds.

When he reached five, the monitor screen in front of them filled with the Global News logo. The webcast director said, "Cue Lisa… now," in their earpieces and the logo was replaced by a medium close-up of Lisa, the surface model of a very large molecule in the background.

Why didn't El tell me what they picked? Janet wondered. *She had time.*

Lisa said, "The strange saga of the Eternity Plague continues to take ever more startling twists and turns. Two months ago, word leaked out that the Chinese government had tested a vaccine against the Plague. Reports said it quickly killed everyone who received it. Then there were rumors that samples had been smuggled to the West. Weeks later, Dr. Janet Hogan, the discoverer of the Plague, announced that she and her team had unlocked the mysteries of that deadly potion. Their discoveries were rushed on-line by *Science* magazine.

"Since then, the controversy over whether or how to respond to the Plague has become more intense, culminating in the riot in Raleigh a week ago last Sunday.

"Today, in the very laboratory where the research team did their ground-breaking—or perhaps I should say, code-breaking—work, Dr. Hogan is here to explain it."

Janet stared at the camera pointed at her.

"And joining us is Sarah Green-Dale, a long-time advocate for the Plague who opposes any kind of vaccine." Even seated, Sarah towered over Lisa.

The reporter turned to Janet. "Dr. Hogan, in layman's terms, doesn't what went wrong in China illustrate just how dangerous it is to try to stop the Plague?"

Janet took a deep breath. "We believe the vaccine made the test subjects' bodies create a protein that caused major tissue necrosis, leading to toxic shock and systemic organ failure."

Ellanna waved to catch Janet's eye, then pointed and mouthed the name of a protein.

Janet glanced at the monitor, then pointed behind her in the general direction of the simulated molecule. "That's what you see behind us. Once the condition became severe, it may have been irreversible. Their only chance would have been significant intervention."

"Like what?"

"Surgery to excise the dying flesh, maybe even amputation. Maybe organ transplants."

Lisa looked horrified.

"But even that might not have saved them. New lesions could have developed and the process started all over again."

"'Could have?' You're not sure?" Lisa asked, her expression hardening.

Janet spread her hands. "Without access to the bodies, or more information from China, we can't be sure. There might have been other problems as well. Let me show you what we've learned." *Maybe I can control this—for once.* She slipped her goggles on, then grabbed her gloves and stood up. Lisa copied her while Sarah fumbled with the goggles. As Janet walked into the VR space with Lisa, she noted the other virtual molecules, as big as beach balls, that hadn't been visible on the monitor. *Perfect. Thanks, El.*

Sarah got her goggles and gloves on and rose to join the other women.

"How could the scientists have made something so dangerous?" Lisa asked, trying to figure out where to stand. "Were they incompetent?" She squeezed through the space between two of the virtual molecules floating in the air and, without thinking, raised her hands to push them aside. "Oh! I can feel them," she said.

Janet pointed to a spot at her right side. "Stand over here, Lisa." A control panel appeared in front of her. She pushed a series of buttons and the molecules shrank to the size of basketballs. "The lead researcher, Dr. Yu, is highly respected."

"Then how could he have made such a major blunder?" Lisa asked as she edged around Janet's panel, trying to look like she did it every day.

"People who know Dr. Yu say he's very careful." Janet bit her lip, thinking, then pressed another series of buttons. "Our best guess is that they were forced to test on human subjects too soon." Clouds of orange fog pulsated on some of the multicolored globes. "These molecules are the reaction products."

"What are those blinking things?"

"The harmful mutations. Here, let me give you a better view." She turned some of them so the clouds faced Oriel's cameras.

Lisa turned to Sarah. "You think the idea of a vaccine is just wrong."

Sarah pushed through the row of molecules. The images bounced away as she reached them, then drifted back into place. "What we need are *real* vaccines, ones that cure or prevent disease. My organization, SAFE-T, is now the largest private supporter of research and development on them." She gestured at the displays around her. "Since the Eternity Plague isn't a disease, what the Chinese created isn't a vaccine, it's a poison, a venom."

"A venom, Dr. Hogan?"

Janet scratched her cheek. "One of the ways venoms kill is via toxic shock. That's a pretty good description of what the Chinese made." She noticed Ellanna clap her hands over her mouth, her eyes wide, and wondered why.

"I know your heart's in the right place, Janet," Sarah said, stepping in front of Lisa to take Janet's hands. "You're a doctor. You want to heal people. I'm sure you didn't think it was a mistake to study this venom. But by publishing the technical details about it, the genie's out of the bottle. Now anyone with a decent biology lab and the right training can make it. No one should be doing that, here or anywhere, intentionally or by accident." Sarah's eyes held Janet's through the goggles' lenses. "That's why I'm here: to ask you—to beg you if I have to—to come back to that mission of healing, to return to your true calling. I thought—I truly thought—I had your agreement to work with me the last time I came to see you."

Janet swallowed. *Did I agree to something then?*

Behind Oriel's equipment, Ellanna and Gerardo exchanged worried looks.

"You and your team have done some truly remarkable work," Sarah said, "even if I don't agree with it. How long did it take you to decode this awful thing?"

"Two weeks, more or less." *I don't like where this is going.*

"Two weeks. A month ago we had no idea anyone would change viral DNA this way. Now we've got all of this." She swept her arm toward the virtual molecules floating in front of the women. "Imagine what you could do if you were working for the benefit of us all. Just by coming over to the side of life, you'd have access to all the funding you need and—"

"We're fine now," Janet said.

"Or staff. We know of dozens of eminent scientists who would love to join your lab."

"I don't—"

"You could even start your own company." Sarah turned and held her hands out in front of her, spreading them as if she was unrolling a banner. "You could call it 'Hogan Life Sciences.'" She turned back to Janet. "Wouldn't that be wonderful?"

Janet blinked, not knowing what to say.

"There are so many rewards for serving life, Janet. Just think: how many Nobel Prizes have been given for death research, and how many for helping people live longer, healthier lives?"

Janet looked away.

"You'd be respected, famous, a celebrity."

Janet laughed. "Like I am already, with twenty-four hour body guards and death threats and car bombs? Being famous hasn't been a lot of fun."

"But don't you understand?" Sarah said. "When people see how much good you'd be doing for them, how many problems you and your teams would be solving, all those threats would stop. You shouldn't be afraid of success."

"Success?" Janet said. "I can't meet all those expectations. I'm not Schweitzer, Salk, Sabin, and Collins and Venter all wrapped up in one. Plus Gandhi and Mandela and Mother Teresa."

Lisa had slipped around behind Janet. When she took one of the virtual molecules and held it in front of her, Janet jumped. *Oh, God!* she thought. *I forgot about Lisa.*

Before Sarah could respond, Lisa asked, "Ms. Green-Dale, whether Dr. Hogan agrees to your proposals or not, doesn't she have a point? How would anyone solve all the problems so many people see coming?"

"Some of those people are terrorists," Sarah said. "All they're doing is spreading fear. Rather than work with legitimate, honest scientists like this team, they want to kill them. They haven't proposed a single life-affirming solution, not even to the problems they're trying to terrify us with. Not one." She brightened. "Meanwhile, *we're* working to ensure the right science and technologies are ready to prevent those things from ever happening. SAFE-T has matched scientists to new areas of research.

If they need training, we're helping them get it. Why, Janet could even provide some of that training." She smiled at the scientist.

"But will science and technology alone be the answer?" Lisa asked.

"Absolutely not," Janet said, trying to regain some semblance of control of the conversation. "Science doesn't work the way Sarah thinks. The remaining problems are hard, even after what the viruses have done. Biotech and the life sciences can't fix everything."

"You're so right," Sarah said, squeezing Janet's arm. "While we need Dr. Hogan and her team to lead the life science effort, social changes are important too. That's why we're building support for them, as well."

"Social change is something I wanted to ask you about," Lisa said, but first she turned to Janet, holding out the virtual molecule. "What can I—"

"Just let go," Janet said. "It'll stay where you put it."

Lisa released the molecule as if she expected it to fall to the floor, but it hung in the air, spinning slowly. She watched it for a moment, then pushed past it. Walking back to the table, she asked Sarah, "Haven't SAFE-T and groups allied with you, been advocating homosexual relations in place of heterosexual ones? It's no secret you have a special relationship with Senator Charlene Hamilton."

Startled, Sarah managed to smile her standard television smile as she followed Lisa. "SAFE-T has always advocated safe sex practices for everyone. It's better to prevent disease than to treat it, whether that disease is natural or man-made," she looked back at Janet. "After all, both diseases *and* poisons kill."

Ignoring Sarah's jibe, Janet froze all the simulated molecules in place, then followed the other women. *She wants to hijack us.* She pulled off her goggles. *Plenty of people to work on other cures. If we don't cure the Plague, or mitigate it.... No. I can't walk away.* She slid into her seat at the table. *If I don't go along, she'll keep pushing.*

"But wouldn't homosexuality solve a lot of the population growth problem?" Lisa pressed. "With so many STDs gone, some groups say it means sex without fear."

"SAFE-T isn't one of them," Sarah said. She took her goggles off and ran her fingers through her hair. "We all know the only absolutely safe form of sex is no sex. We're not advocating that, either. You're both young and attractive. I'm sure you know how hard it is to be abstinent." She winked at Lisa.

Janet thought, *Wade too. All of them. How long?*

"So what about unwanted pregnancies?" Lisa asked, not missing a beat. "Won't they add to an already exploding birth rate?"

Who else? Baxter? Yeah.

"Beyond health issues, we let others speak in that debate," Sarah said.

Lisa.

"What about that, Dr. Hogan?" the reporter asked. "Doesn't abortion come back on the table?"

"What? Oh, I—" A memory of Janet's college friend Vanessa, how she'd cried after she'd gotten her abortion flickered through mind her. "I have enough to deal with without taking that on too."

"But won't some people demand that we bring abortion back, say we have to make it legal again?" Lisa noticed Janet wasn't wearing her goggles and slipped her own off.

Oh, God, not that too. "I don't think we want to follow China's 'one right child' policy, if that's what you mean."

"And we won't if SAFE-T has anything to say about it," Sarah said. "That's every bit as much murder as this venom they created. Condemning innocent babies *or* innocent adults to certain death is utterly immoral. Dr. Hogan should be working on curing what the viruses didn't, not on deadly poisons. After all, her Hippocratic Oath says, 'first, do no harm.'"

Lisa slid her chair back so she could look at Janet and Sarah, a perplexed and worried expression on her face. "So we're in an impossible situation: abortion is unacceptable, contraception or other forms of birth control probably aren't enough and some groups oppose them anyway, homosexuality isn't a realistic alternative for everyone, and a vaccine is too risky or even immoral, as you called it, Sarah. Where does that leave us? Dr. Hogan?"

Janet picked up her goggles and turned them over in her fingers, stalling for time. She glanced at Satya, who'd slipped in sometime during the interview, then at Michael, Ellanna, and Gerardo, hoping for their support. "A year ago," she said, choosing her words with great care, "millions of people were dying every day and we accepted it. It was natural. The eternity viruses changed that. What's happening now is *un*natural, even though it's the result of natural processes. We can't foresee the consequences of that, much less control them."

"*I* can," Sarah said. "You want us to go back to pain and suffering and undeserved death."

"Pain and suffering haven't gone away," Janet said. "I don't want to see them come back, either—"

"So stop them. You can."

Janet opened and closed the earpieces of her goggles. "Sarah, the work you're sponsoring is great, but—"

"But?" Sarah said. "It's vital! There's no 'but.'"

Janet put the goggles on the table, then picked them up again. "A few weeks ago, right in this room, we were talking about what we should do, about all the reasons—moral, biological, and practical—why death is necessary. It's not an easy subject."

"Genocide shouldn't be," Sarah said.

Janet refused to look her way. "Since we determined what the Chinese vaccine did—"

"It murdered people."

"We've learned enough that we think we can split the difference between what you want and what others—"

"Like Wade? Like Baxter?"

Janet nodded without realizing she had. "What others want. We don't have the exact pathway mapped yet—"

"And you never will!" Sarah exclaimed, rising to her feet.

Oh, no! Janet pushed her chair back to get farther from Sarah.

Lisa jumped up and grabbed Sarah's arm, while saying, "Wait, wait, wait. What do you mean, Dr. Hogan?"

"You know what she means!" Sarah said. "She wants to kill us."

"You mean," Lisa asked, her head twisted around so she could look at Janet, "despite what you learned about the Chinese vaccine, you still think you should make one? Even after people tried to kill you just for discovering the Plague?"

"Why are you picking on me?" Janet said. "I'm not a terrorist. I'm not trying to frighten people with horror stories."

"Is that what you think Sarah's doing?"

"When she's not making impossible promises."

"At least I have the courage to try to help people," Sarah said, looking over Lisa at Janet. "You will never carry out your threat, Dr. Hogan. You'd better understand that."

"It's not a threat," Janet said.

"Remember what happened to me in Raleigh? What happened to you? Think about that. You said fame wasn't any fun. How do you think infamy is going to feel?" Sarah stabbed a finger at Janet. "I will not let you murder me, Dr. Hogan. Not now, not a hundred years from now, not ever!"

* * *

Even from his office phone screen, Ken Bowersox could see Sarah quivering with glee. Before the webcast had finished he'd known she'd call as soon as she could. He could tell from the darkness and moving lights behind her she was in her car, on her way back to her hotel.

Gloating, she asked, "Wasn't *that*, just what the doctor ordered—no pun intended?"

He gazed at her. *Need to cool her down so she doesn't get carried away.* "Don't you think you came on a bit strong at the end?"

"Oh, no," Sarah said. "She dug that hole all by herself. All I did was roll the stone over it. That interview's going viral right this instant."

"I wouldn't be doing a victory dance just yet."

"And why not? Hogan thought she was going to be some kind of sick hero—"

"She did nothing—"

"Announcing she's going to murder every one of us, without the slightest bit of pity or remorse. She's a psychopath, a Hitler with boobs."

"Sarah!"

Sarah pushed her hair behind her ears. "She won't get away with it now. Her funding's going to get pulled, they'll fire her, she's—"

Bowersox decided he'd heard enough. "Sarah, shut up."

"*What* did you say?"

"I said shut up. You're *being* an ass and you've got your head up your ass as well."

Sarah gasped.

"Don't you dare hang up on me," he ordered as he saw her look for the phone button on the steering wheel.

"Don't *you* dare talk to me like that!" she said but pulled her hand back.

"I'll talk to you any way I need to," he said, "and you'll listen."

Lips pinched, Sarah stared daggers at her business partner. He stared back, drawing the silence out.

"What?" she said finally.

Bowersox remained silent.

"All right, what?"

"You ready to listen now?"

"I haven't heard anything yet."

He saw her glance out the windshield.

"And you'd better hurry. I'm back at the hotel."

In the background he could see parked cars sliding slowly past. "Okay, so you think you've won."

"I'm so *glad* you could tell."

"Sarah…."

She favored him with a humorless smile.

"You think this gets you over Raleigh." He held up a hand to forestall her reply. "Maybe it did with some people, but by coming on so hard you've alienated others. We've got to keep our heads on straight."

"What do you mean? Mine is!"

"Victories come and go, just like defeats do. You made some important points tonight. Points you were *right* about. Points some people care about and agree with. If you get overconfident now and do something rash, you'll throw it all away."

Sarah looked away from the camera mounted in the dashboard. She leaned to her right and reached for something.

"What are you doing?" Bowersox asked.

"Reading my messages," she said. "I've got… the count just passed a hundred. They're…," she paused to scan one, "saying I'm right, that I did to Janet what Wade did to me." She smiled at him. "My flower's bloomed and it smells so sweet."

He shook his head. "We're running instant polls. So is Global News. Others are too. They're not showing anything like that." He could see Sarah wasn't listening. "You know you need to know what the real trends are, not—"

Sarah was still looking at the car's center console screen, not at him, her face colored an eerie combination of blue from the screen and orange from the hotel's security lighting.

Reading other messages, the ones that say what she wants them to. He sighed. *I told her to stay cool. Lisa set her up and she walked right into the trap. I should've expected she'd do that.*

Sarah kept reading messages. The car had parked itself in the hotel lot. Bowersox watched a family of four walk by behind it, not even noticing her.

One more try. "Let's sleep on this, Sarah, get some good data in, so we can make *good* decisions, not hasty ones."

She said nothing.

"Sarah, did you hear me?" His phone screen blanked, then displayed, "Call ended." "Okay," he said to his empty office. "Time to call in the big guns." *And if that doesn't work, Sarah can just screw the rest of this up by herself.* "Phone, call Charlene Hamilton."

* * *

Dr. Sayid met the scientists in the hall outside the VR lab after the interview. "Let's go down to your lab."

When they walked in, they spotted six long-neck bottles of Lone Star beer chilling in ice-filled plastic bowls that were usually reserved for cooling biological samples. Puzzled, Janet looked at Sayid.

"I thought you'd be thirsty after being under those hot studio lights," he said.

"Damn right," Gerardo said, pulling a bottle out of the nearest bowl. "And I wasn't even in the line of fire." He twisted off the cap and took a long swallow.

Janet collapsed into the nearest chair. "God, I screwed that up." She picked up a pen from the desk next to the chair and started clicking the top button. Ellanna rolled another chair over and sat beside her.

"You did your best," Michael said. He pulled a bottle from the ice and held it out to her.

She shook her head.

"That demo was brilliant," he went on. "Really effective. You said the right things and—"

"No, I didn't. I caved. I failed. Sarah ran over me like a semi running over a possum." She slapped one palm across the other. "Splat."

Sayid took a long pull from his beer, then hitched himself up onto a lab stool. "Maybe that's not such a bad thing."

"Thanks!" Janet said. "I feel so much better."

Sayid held out his hands. "Wait, wait. I said that badly."

"You sure did," Ellanna said.

"What I *meant* was that by Sarah appearing to have won—"

"She didn't?" Janet asked.

"The attention shifts to her," Sayid said. "The pressure's on her to deliver, instead of you."

Michael leaned back against a lab bench. "So these guys can work on the antidote, like they've been talking about, under the radar." He sipped his beer. "Winning by losing."

Sayid pointed his bottle at Michael. "Exactly right."

"I don't know," Janet said, putting the pen down. "If we try to make an antidote, word'll get out. It always does. Then we'll—I'll—have to face Sarah and whatever wild claims she'll come up with. Or Lisa. She'll never go away."

"But someone will try to make one," Satya said. "We all know it. What if, a year from now, they come out with an antidote and promise it works right, but nobody's seen their tests or their results, or replicated them? Would you take it? Even if their motives were as pure as pure? Even if we're right and Dr. Yu's lab was rushed, would *you* trust them?"

"We can't work in secret," Janet said. "It's unethical and—"

"We couldn't do it anyway," Gerardo said, "even if we wanted to."

"Worse," Ellanna said, "what if somebody just releases something, doesn't tell anyone, and hopes it works? Or makes a mass-murder weapon? What if nobody knows until it's too late?"

"We'll have to make sure that doesn't happen," Sayid said. He took a pull from his bottle. "That won't be easy in some places—"

"More like impossible," Ellanna said. "If just one lab doesn't go along… or, what if everyone does, all the testing goes okay, but then some people still refuse to take the antidote?" She put her hands to her cheeks. "And I know just who would—besides Sarah."

"Who?" Janet asked. "Oooh, Brother Elijah."

"I don't want to face him again," Ellanna said. "And if *he* gets a following, this whole thing goes from impossible to impossible squared."

Satya said, "But if Wade's right and people start fighting over it—"

"Impossible cubed!" Ellanna rocked back and forth in her chair, laughing crazily.

The lab became silent. The lights seemed unnaturally bright to Janet, like a giant spotlight shining down on them through the ceiling. She ran her hands through her hair. "I wonder whether anyone will remember that we know why the Chinese failed. If they talk about that, maybe they'll talk about what's right too, what they think we should do."

"Yeah, sure," Ellanna said to herself.

Janet glanced at her, worried.

"You got that 'talk about' part right," Gerardo said, looking at his phone's screen. "They're doing it so much now my phone can't keep up. Look." He held the screen out so they could see messages replacing each other in a blur.

Ellanna looked up. "Opinions and assholes."

"What?"

Ellanna waved her hand at Gerardo's phone. "Everybody's got 'em. No rule says either one has to be informed."

"We can't let anyone do it the wrong way again," Janet said, picking up the pen and rattling it between her thumb and index finger. "We *can't*." She laughed. "We *could* do like Sarah suggested, become like the big overseers of everybody else's work—"

"That's it!" Ellanna shouted, leaping from her chair and thrusting her hands high in the air. "Thank you, Jesus!" she called, her head tipped back. "*That's* the answer—we'll play pretend!" She looked around wildly at her colleagues. "It's brilliant! We'll pretend to solve a problem that can't be solved. Let Wade and Baxter think we're doing what they want while telling Sarah she's got all the time she needs to be a hero 'cause the problem's so complex. Then, if someone fucks up, *they* can take the heat. We'll just tell 'em what they did wrong."

"That's not—" Janet said.

Ellanna grabbed Janet's shoulders and locked eyes with her. "It's a great plan." She waved a hand at the lab's walls. "Think those crazies out there will let you get away with it? Oh, no. You know what we'll get? More death threats, more car bombs. Somebody's going to get past our security again one of these days. Which one of us is going to win *that* lottery, huh? How many more times do *you* want to get blown up?"

"They won't...."

Ellanna staggered away, her head lolling, arms straight out in front of her. "Look at me, I'm a zombie. Dead on my feet but happy to be here. Go ahead, shoot me again. It doesn't hurt anymore."

She stopped, facing them from the far side of the room, near the door into the hall. "I'm all right," she sniggered. "It's okay. I'm just going to go home and tell Garvin I need to get knee-walking, commode-hugging, totally shit-faced drunk. Then tomorrow—" Her voice quavered. "Tomorrow I'll be back to normal. Hung over but the same old Ellanna you know and love."

Janet ran to hug her best friend tight. "I'm afraid too, El," she whispered. "More than you or Sayid or Michael can ever know. I've thought about this a lot. Prayed about it, even." She choked on a laugh, then sniffled. "Haven't done *that* in a long time." She pulled back and took Ellanna's hands. "You're right: we can't just tell people what they did wrong."

Ellanna gave her a long, searching look.

"I know," Janet said. "If we make an antidote and it works right, we'll all die. If we don't, or we get it wrong, we'll all die. Just because we're trying, or people think we're trying, we could die. No matter what we do, something or nothing, it's just a matter of when and how." She eased a hand free to wipe away a tear. "I can't stand it. I don't *want* to play God. But I can't stand by and do nothing, either, knowing the potential consequences." She shrugged. "It's a bad answer but it's the best one there is, as far as I can tell. Maybe we can just make things normal again."

"Sure," Ellanna said, poking an index finger into the tube made by her other hand. "Good genie. Nice genie. Back in the bottle, now."

Janet spun and stalked away, then turned back. "Remember how one of my profs at Stanford called me a bulldog… and how you told me you were bulldog-loyal to your friends?"

Ellanna nodded, her chin and lips quivering.

"It's okay," Janet said softly. "You don't have to stay. If you're too scared, go. I've told you you could." She looked over at Satya and Gerardo. "You too."

Satya squinted at Janet. "After what they just did to you, you're…."

Janet walked over to the bowl of beer bottles, pulled one part-way out, then slid it back into the ice. "Yeah," she said, still pondering the bottle. She turned to Satya. "Yeah. If you think I'm crazy, you're probably right." She yanked the bottle out of the ice, twisted the cap off, and drank. "I hate being embarrassed, even if it's my own fault."

Gerardo stuffed his hands into his jeans pockets and stared at his shoes. "I'll stay," he said. "It isn't right to walk away and make other folks do this. We know the risks."

"And we've always known the Eternity Plague didn't make people immortal," Satya said as she walked over to stand beside him. "Do we risk dying to keep terrible things from happening? We have to, I think. It's the right choice."

Janet set the bottle down on the counter and looked back at Ellanna. "See?" she said, pulling down on her cheeks. "Bulldogs, just like you and me."

CHAPTER 15

THE FUROR THE INTERVIEW had caused had died down a month later. A hazy early November Texas dawn filled the windows beyond the lab benches with soft pink light as Ellanna entered.

Gerardo looked up, then did a double-take. "Um, good morning," he said.

"Better close that mouth, G," Ellanna said, laughing. "You're gonna catch something." She crossed the lab to her desk, her half-inch thick Afro rusty orange rather than its usual black.

"That's a… ah, different look. Not one we usually see around here."

Ellanna rested her hand on a cocked hip. "And where, exactly, do we see this look?"

"I knew that was wrong as soon as I said it." He shook his head. "It's too early. Since my foot's already in my mouth, wig or bottle?"

"Bottle. I hate it." She headed for the anteroom in front of Janet's office. "Coffee brewing?"

"Waiting for you to pour."

The pot rattled as she pulled it out of the coffee maker. Gerardo called back to her, "I've got last night's gene-chip run results when you're ready."

"Good," she said as she returned to the workroom. "Let's see."

When Janet arrived a few minutes later, the first thing she had to do was warm her hands over Ellanna's hair. "Not going to need a campfire, are you?"

"I can light Garvin's fire without one," Ellanna replied, grinning. "And without this." She pointed at her hair.

"Has he seen it yet?"

"Nope. Couldn't tell him. Security, y'know." She winked.

"You sure won't need to pack any orange clothing to keep hunters from shooting at you," Janet said.

"Oh, you stop! It wasn't my idea."

Janet pulled up a lab stool, perched on it, and gave Ellanna's arm a quick squeeze. "I'm glad you're getting away for a while." Half-serious, she shook her finger at her friend. "Just don't screw it up for the rest of us."

"I promise," Ellanna said, crossing her heart. "Thanks for letting me go."

"So you're going camping?" Gerardo asked. "This time of year?"

"Portland first, then up into the Cascades. I'm so ready to get away from this craziness."

"Won't it be cold?"

"For somebody from Laredo like you, yeah. We'll be fine. I used to go up there every year from Stanford. I've still got my flannel shirts, down vest, hiking boots."

"So you're going to live in a tent and eat berries and like that?"

"No, silly! There's this cute little bed-and-breakfast in Rhododendron—"

"C'mon."

"It's true! It's on Mount Hood between Zigzag and Government Camp—"

Gerardo laughed. "You're making that up."

"It's true, G," Janet said. "I've stayed there too. Your Sophia would love it."

He loaded the sample vials he'd been filling into a centrifuge. "She won't leave Texas. She didn't even want to go to New Orleans for Mardi Gras."

"I can understand that," Janet said. "Once was fun but I don't need to go back."

"You all packed?" Gerardo asked.

Ellanna slid a set of Petri dishes into a metal rack. "I won't pack until tonight. Otherwise I'll try to take everything in the apartment and Gar'll whine the entire trip 'cause I'll make him carry my bags. If I wait till the last minute, I pack light and then I'm so exhausted I sleep like a baby."

Gerardo chuckled. "Yeah, 'pack light.' Four bags instead of five?"

Ellanna swatted him. "Better watch it, mister. It could get pretty hot in here."

Gerardo danced away, whooping. "You're right. Your hair might set me on fire!"

"What about your security thingy?" Janet asked. She fingered the little plastic box that hung around her neck.

"Not taking it," Ellanna said. She turned and walked to the windows. Her chin quivered.

"But—" Janet took Ellanna's arm again. "What's wrong?"

Ellanna took a slow, shuddering breath. "I'm… we're not going on vacation." She glanced at Janet, then looked away. "I'm not coming back. I gave Sayid my notice a couple weeks ago. I asked him to let me tell you." She wiped at her mouth. "Then I couldn't do it. Made up the vacation story instead."

Janet gaped at her friend. "El, *why?*"

"Guess I'm not the bulldog I thought I was," she said, her voice quavering. "Got kicked once too often. My little tail's between my legs. I don't want any more of this."

Gerardo took her other arm for a moment, then let go, unsure what to do with his hands. "What are you going to do?"

"Got a job with Wade. He's been talking to me for months… since the bombing. He offered me this crazy salary but I told him I didn't care about that, I just wanted to disappear, get out of the crosshairs. He promised he could keep it quiet. Me working there, I mean. He got Garvin a job too."

"So the B&B?" Janet asked.

"Oh, we're going. They found a condo for us up there… in Portland. No names on the contract. They'll pack us out, move everything. We'll come off the mountain and move right in."

"Wow," Gerardo said.

"Yeah," Ellanna said, glancing at each of them. "I guess. They're giving this runaway doggie a special cage at the back of the shelter with a golden water bowl. Whoopee." She turned and hugged Janet as tight as she could. "I'm sorry," she whispered.

* * *

"You weren't kidding when you said this place was secure," Ellanna said two weeks later as she stepped through an unmarked, biometrics-protected door at the end of an empty corridor in the basement of EARTH's headquarters building with David Wade. The opening door had broken an air-tight seal with a sound like fabric tearing. The outer door, marked *Employees Only*, had required their iris scans and voice- and fingerprints.

Wade had pointed out the closed-circuit cameras which fed face-recognition software, and the ducts that drew air through breath- and body-scent scanners. "Even a highly visible organization like EARTH sometimes needs a place to do quiet work," he said.

Ellanna scanned the room. To relieve its crypt-like feeling, two large datawall screens in video mode displayed mountain scenes. A Stellar's jay swooped through one of the images as she watched, its screeching punctuating the low rush of air through the pines coming from the screens' speakers. Two work benches defined the arms of a U extending fifteen feet out from one wall. There was more work space along the wall at the base of the U. When she opened the cabinets above and below the work surfaces, she saw they were well stocked with glassware, stands, electronic equipment, and boxes of supplies. There were spigots for oxygen, distilled water, and gas for Bunsen burners along the walls and inside protected risers on the benches. There were computer terminals every few feet.

She walked around the first bench and into the U. Beyond the second bench there was a vented workspace for protecting samples from contamination. Refrigerators and freezers lined the other wall.

"We're fully connected into the data cloud," Wade said, "and capable of complete anonymity if you want to keep an inquiry private. The human, mouse, rat, and pig genomes are on the lab's server in case of a connection failure. So are those other databases you asked for. If you need anything else, let me know. We're adding an account for you on our v-Mouse site license. That should be done in a few days."

"This is impressive," Ellanna said. She spun slowly where she stood, her arms spread wide. "My own lab." She stopped and faced Wade. "VR?"

"Coming. Not here yet."

"Staff?"

"None for now. Think about it: if somebody works for you, they'll tell their friends and family who they work for, and before you know it...."

Ellanna hugged herself. "Yeah. Back to the way things were in Dallas."

* * *

"Thanks for talking with me, Dr. Hogan," Lisa said. "I know I'm not your favorite person."

You have no idea, Janet thought, keeping her expression neutral. She glanced to her right as Gerardo set a tray of analysis chips on the work bench next to her. "It's all right. I don't have much time, though." *And even if I did,* she thought, *I wouldn't spend it with you.*

"I was wondering if I could ask Dr. Barnes a few questions."

"She's… not back yet." Janet swallowed, wondering how long she was going to be able to keep putting Lisa off. "Why can't I help you?"

"You've been telling me she was on vacation for three weeks, now. Isn't that a long time for her to be away from your lab?"

"It was approved." Janet crossed her arms over her chest. "Why does that matter to you?"

"My sources tell me Dr. Barnes isn't on vacation anymore, if she ever was. Would you care to comment on that?"

Stunned, Janet stared at Lisa for a second, then said in a tight voice, "No, as a matter of fact, I wouldn't." A centrifuge to her right chimed. Even though Satya was the one using it, Janet took the opportunity to cut the interview short. "I'm sorry, Lisa. I'm very busy."

"Is it because you're short-handed now, with Dr. Barnes gone?"

"I have to go." Janet reached up to touch the screen and break off the call.

"Where has Dr. Barnes—"

Janet stabbed the button. "Why don't you just use your sources to find out?" she said after the screen blanked.

* * *

Ellanna strolled into the break room next to the lab. Another datawall was a blank patch of white against the pale green wall. She pulled out one of the chairs from the small table and sat down. Wade joined her, waiting as she picked up the remote for the display, turned on the scenic views, and scrolled through several before selecting a rugged coastline. Breakers crashed on the rocky shore. She turned the volume almost all the way down, then turned to face her new boss.

"It's time we got specific about what I'm going to be doing here," she said. "I didn't care before, but now...."

"I'm surprised it's taken you so long to ask." He gazed at her for a moment. "That says a lot, doesn't it?" When she said nothing, he held out his hand for the remote. "Let me show you."

He turned off the coastline scene and called up a file of photos and charts. "We humans have become an invasive species," he said as he flipped through the images. "We didn't mean to. We didn't even have the concept for a long time. Now that we do and now that we are, we can't do anything about it: too many competing interests. Religions say, 'Thou shalt not kill,' governments see more people as a way to more power, businesses want to make and sell more things to more consumers to make more money, and on and on. We've had some successes in holding things back—recycling, renewable energy." He looked away from the screen. "Then the Eternity Plague viruses came along, or somebody made them."

Ellanna shifted in her chair.

"I know, you don't believe that. Maybe they didn't intend… well, it doesn't matter. They're here, they're everywhere, and we're all in trouble." He set the remote on the table and looked at Ellanna. "I need your help. The whole world does."

"To?"

Wade stood and walked to the small counter where a microwave oven sat next to a sink. He opened one of the overhead cabinets, took out a water glass, and filled it. "That's the hard part," he said. "I don't know. That's why I hired you, to figure it out. People can't live forever, that much is clear."

"But they don't…."

"And the viruses won't make them." He tipped his glass toward her. "No argument there. But what they *do* is bad enough. How do we stop that? Where are the viruses most vulnerable to disruption? Where's the best place—or even just a good-enough place—to break their chain, so to speak?"

Ellanna put her face in her hands. "It's not that easy." After a minute, she looked up. "You've got to understand: the more we study the viruses, the more complicated everything gets. You can't just turn on some little microRNA, have it interfere with some protein, and *voilá*, everything's all better. When people like you started pushing for a cure, the pressure—and the threats—came back worse than ever. Then Janet decided to do what you want and things got even worse. That's what I had to get away from."

"I understand that," he said, turning to lean against the counter. "I understand complexity too. I may not have all the advanced degrees you do but I've been in this business a long time. There are more interconnections in the body of Mother Earth than there are in the human body." He sipped from the glass, then pushed away from the counter and ambled across the room's open space, sipping the water as he did. "That's where you biologists are making your biggest mistake," he said, pointing at her. "You're trying to understand everything first. We don't have to do that. Name me one disease that medical science understands completely. You can't." He set the glass down on the table Ellanna was sitting at and leaned on the back of the chair across from her. "And yet, every day doctors cure people suffering from any one of hundreds of different diseases, maybe thousands. We've eliminated polio, malaria, smallpox. The Eternity viruses wiped out dozens more and they didn't understand squat. Still don't."

"They can't," Ellanna said, leaning back in her chair, an annoyed look on her face.

"Of course not. Look, the Chinese tried something. It didn't work. You know what they did and why they failed."

Ellanna's mouth went dry. She tried to swallow but couldn't. "You don't want me to—"

"Do what they did?" Wade stood straight again. "No, but they were trying to think outside the box and—"

"No they weren't!" Ellanna exclaimed. "They were…." She paused to consider what she'd just realized. "What they were trying was very conventional. Maybe that's why they screwed up so badly: they got overconfident."

Wade stroked his chin with his fingers. "I'm glad you caught that. That's why I want you to be creative. Get out of the rut everyone else is in. We can't keep on fiddling around with this while the whole earth, not just Rome, gets ready to burn."

"By myself."

"You've got access to the entire data cloud."

"I can't be anonymous. Nobody'll talk to me if they don't know who I am. Once they know, they'll want to know where I am and who I'm working for. Once they know that—"

"Okay. I understand. We'll figure something out. In the meantime, I want you to look for a way to attack the problem. We have to do it soon. " Wade glanced at his watch. "I have to go. I'll check back with you later this week to see what you've come up with. And I'll get my tech folks working on your problem." He poured the remaining water down the drain then stepped back to the table. Ellanna stood as he approached. "I'm glad you're working for me, Dr. Barnes," he said, shaking her hand. "I know you can do this."

Ellanna remained standing until she heard the lab door seal itself shut behind Wade. The walls of the room seemed to close in on her. "Out of one frying pan…," she said, rubbing her hands on her jeans.

* * *

Janet called Ellanna at her new condo later that evening. "Guess who called today? Lisa."

"What'd she want this time?"

"To know where you were." Janet's expression reinforced her worried tone of voice. "Said she'd found out from 'sources' that you'd left."

Ellanna bit her lip She looked up at Garvin, who'd proposed while they were in the mountains. He joined her on the couch when he saw the look on her face. "What sources?" she asked.

"Didn't say. Almost no one here knows—Satya, G, me, Sayid. Maybe someone in personnel." Janet rubbed her hands together. "That's probably who."

"If she was telling the truth." Ellanna pulled Garvin closer to her. "Maybe it was just a guess to see how you'd react."

Janet grimaced. "I don't know. She's so good at getting people to talk." She looked away from the screen for a moment. "Michael says you'd better tell Wade."

"What can he do?"

"You'd better find out. He said he'd protect you, didn't he?"

Ellanna shrugged. "Not really. Just said he'd keep the fact he'd hired me a secret."

Janet's lips formed a thin, tight line. "He knew what might happen when he hired you. If you're that important to him, he'd better take care of you—both of you."

Ellanna looked at Garvin, who hugged her and said, "We'll be all right."

* * *

Later that week, the workstation nearest Ellanna chimed and announced, "David Wade approaching." The screen showed him striding down the hall toward the lab's inner door. Ellanna touched the Admit button on the display and the door unlocked before her boss reached it.

"Thanks," he said as he entered. "What have you come up with? Too early to have a protocol, I presume." He climbed onto the tall lab stool next to Ellanna's.

"I have something I need to ask you first," she said.

"The VR system will be here next week, if that's what you're wondering about. Tuesday okay for them to install it?"

"Yeah but that's not—"

Wade looked puzzled. "What else do you need?"

Ellanna put her hands on her thighs. "For you to stop interrupting me! This is important."

"What's the matter?"

"Lisa Lange called Janet on Monday. Said she knew I'd left UT-Southwestern."

Wade frowned. "That didn't come from us. But you knew it would come out eventually."

"We were getting death threats," Ellanna said, holding out her hands to him. "Janet got blown up. I came here to get away from all that. I just want to do my work and be left alone. Once the media finds out I'm here, you'll get all the crap we were getting in Dallas." She got off the stool and walked out into the open space between the lab door and the work benches.

Wade turned in his seat to follow her.

"I don't want to move again," she said. "Where would I go? What about Garvin?"

"Okay, okay," Wade said, reaching out to her. "Remember who you're working for. EARTH is the biggest, most powerful environmental group around. That means we've got lots of enemies. We get threats all the time. We know how to do security. We've done things you don't even know about just to protect you."

"Like what?"

"Have any of your electronic addresses changed?"

"No…."

"We worked out with the university a way to make it look like you're still there."

"But what if there's a protest, or a riot, outside?"

"We lock down the building," he said, drawing a box in the air with his hands. "We can stay inside for days if we have to, not that we ever have."

"I can't. There's only one way out and no place to sleep."

"There are Murphy beds in the break room."

Ellanna's eyebrows arched with surprise.

"Let me show you." Wade led her into the side room and pulled the small table and chairs away from the datawall. He touched a button Ellanna hadn't noticed before and a seam appeared near the top of the wall. A section of the wall arced down. Legs folded out and the datawall turned off as it angled toward the floor. "There's another one on the other side and you can partition the room off for privacy. Now you know why we put a full-size refrigerator in here, not just a cube." He opened its door. "Looks like you should do a little shopping."

Ellanna folded her arms across her chest. "So what else don't I know about this place?"

"Come up with a plan for disabling the viruses," Wade said with a secretive smile, "and I'll show you."

After he left, Ellanna returned to her stool in the lab. The forest scene on the datawall wasn't soothing. *What have I gotten myself into?*

* * *

Even with every screen set to show some outdoor scene at full size, Ellanna never lost the sense of being in the basement. She missed the constant interaction of working with Janet, Gerardo, Satya, even Dr. Sayid, but at the same time she relished her freedom from the threats and outside pressure. Garvin worked for EARTH a few floors above her, so they had lunch together almost every day, even though that meant he had to come down to the lab. She wanted to sample the many restaurants within easy walking distance of EARTH's headquarters, but with Lisa's reports all over the web, she didn't dare take the risk of being recognized.

Getting researchers at other labs to talk with her had been even more difficult than she'd expected. On every video call, they would ask where she was, having heard the rumors she wasn't in Janet's lab anymore, and invariably there were frowns and awkward silences when she told them, "I'm still at UT-Southwestern, doing independent research, *so far as you know*."

True to Wade's word, the installation team showed up the following week to put in her virtual reality system. To her delight, it was a top-of-the-line model, complete with the newest capabilities, including collaborative VR, which would let her work with similarly-equipped labs around to world. She couldn't help grinning when she posed for the system's cameras as they recorded her avatar image. She wondered, though, whether there was a hidden message when she discovered the system also came with workout programs featuring virtual personal trainers.

But all the latest gizmos and high-tech toys could give her only limited help with her central problem: what she was going to do. Every time she thought she'd come up with a new and clever idea, she'd discover someone else was already doing it or had done it. Wade was more persistent and insistent than Janet or Sayid had ever been. He contacted her every day, his impatience clear.

When he came down to the lab one afternoon, he kept the pressure on. "I'm investing a lot of money in you. I expect to see results."

She forced herself to walk away from him, out into the center of the U. "You have to understand," she said, then stopped, not liking how quavery and emotional her voice sounded. *Calm down,* she told herself. "You called us an invasive species. You don't want to create something that would be like spraying everyone with weed killer. If you want an answer—a real answer, not a tragic mistake—you have to give me time. Rush me and you're playing Russian Roulette."

"So how much time do you need?" Wade asked, leaning against the work surface of the lab bench. "A year? Five? Ten? Over 150 million babies will be born this year. Only a few million people will die from accidents, wars, and the diseases the Plague doesn't cure. The delta gets bigger every year. Speed matters. The longer we wait, the worse the problem gets. But you're right, I'm not asking you to create RoundUp for Kids. I'm not crazy."

"Just—" Ellanna crossed one arm over her stomach and rested her chin on her other hand. "Think about this," she said after a few moments. "You know how the Chinese antidote killed? It created a bacterial toxin. Bacterial, not viral."

Wade frowned. "So?"

"If I rush, or get rushed, I could create something without realizing it that would make your friend Sarah's dreams come true. Something that would kill off the bad bacteria that are still around, make immortality more possible, not less." She favored Wade with a wry smile. "It could happen."

Wade gazed at Ellanna for a minute. "That's very interesting," he said at last. He pulled out his phone, and worked on the screen. He pointed his phone at one of the lab's computers. "You'll find that interesting too, I think. It's a press release I can have sent out at any time." He slipped the phone back into his pocket, strode past her out of the U, and left the lab.

After the door squished shut, Ellanna hurried to the computer to read the message. It was undated, but the first line read, *Earth Action: Return To Harmony is pleased to announce the hiring of Dr. Ellanna Barnes.*

* * *

The next day, Ellanna decided to look for a way to convince Wade she was doing what he wanted while she stalled for time. The lists of genes and regulatory segments on the chromosomes, proteins, and other reaction products the viruses affected had grown into the thousands since Janet's team had begun working. Now, with more and more labs joining the effort, the list was growing exponentially. Each change affected something: made more or less of a protein, for example, caused it to be made at a different time, or even changed its exact chemical makeup from what had been normal before the Plague struck. Following each sequence of reactions, some hundreds of steps long and often branching into alternative paths took a lot of computer and personal time. Worse, the reaction paths didn't just branch, they interconnected too. Ellanna knew there would be no silver bullet. Wade's expectations weighed heavier and heavier on her.

Her phone chimed from the break room. She rubbed her face and pushed her chair away from the desk. *Needed a break, anyway.* She stood, stretched with a loud groan, then picked up her empty soda can and wandered into the other room to see what news the phone had found.

Still thinking about her work, she poked the *View report* link before she'd registered what the summary said. She fidgeted as the Global News site loaded and the lead-in advertisement played. The story opened with Lisa standing in front of the giant globe in EARTH's headquarters' plaza, two floors above her lab, while people walked past.

"This is Lisa Lange in Portland, Oregon. Dr. Ellanna Barnes, a member of the team that discovered the Eternity Plague, has been missing from the University of Texas Southwestern Medical Center in Dallas for weeks. There are new tenants in her former condominium and she hasn't been seen on the campus. Her parents, coworkers, and former department head, Dr. Mohamed Sayid, have ignored my repeated requests for information."

"That's because they know better than to say anything to you," Ellanna said, her free hand on her hip.

"As I've been reporting," Lisa said, "sources inside UT-Southwestern say Dr. Barnes has, in fact, left. Now, those and other sources suggest she may be working for Earth Action: Return To Harmony, or EARTH, the world's preeminent environmental advocacy group."

Ellanna bit her lip. *Good thing I'm driving to work, not taking the Maxx,* she thought. *But if she ever stakes out the parking garage entrance….*

Lisa continued. "Given that the woman who discovered the viruses, Dr. Janet Hogan has advocated creating an antidote, it makes sense that Dr. Barnes would come to work for EARTH." The report showed a snippet of video from Lisa's interview with Janet and Sarah. "Yet David Wade, EARTH's president, has also refused to comment."

Old video showed Wade shaking his head.

"Environmentalists everywhere are demanding the Eternity viruses be stopped. But why do it in secret? Perhaps Dr. Barnes felt things were moving too slowly. But if so, why would she sneak away from the Texas lab? If she wanted to escape the visibility that came with working there, why move to one of the most visible organizations in the country?

"The Eternity Plague represents either the greatest health crisis or the greatest opportunity the world has ever known, depending on who you ask. Ellanna Barnes' mysterious disappearance raises disturbing questions that demand honest answers. I intend to get them.

"Reporting from Portland, I'm Lisa Lange."

"There's no mystery at all, Lisa," Ellanna said as she stabbed the button on the screen to close the video. "Just look in a mirror. Think about what you're doing to us." She stared at the phone for a few minutes, her mind a jumble of thoughts and emotions, before she set the little yellow box on the table.

The underground room was cool, which Ellanna liked, but it had just gotten colder. She went to the closet and took out a gray cardigan sweater, buttoning it up as she returned. She sank into one of the chairs. The datawall was blank. She reached for the remote but pulled her arm back, leaving the wall off. The computer out in the lab beeped from time to time.

A teardrop formed at the corner of her eye. "I won't cry," she said through clenched teeth as she wiped it away. "I'm done crying." She took a slow, deep breath. "No more. Maybe I'm not a bulldog but maybe I can be an alligator, with a mean bite and a thick hide."

She was reaching for the phone when its screen lit and it played Janet's ring tone. "How did you know I was thinking of you?" she asked with forced cheerfulness when her friend's image filled the screen.

"A little red-headed weasel told me," Janet replied. "You saw her latest?"

"Yeah." Ellanna smiled a little at the description. "She sure is full of herself." She popped out the phone's legs so it could stand on the table.

Wrinkles formed on Janet's forehead and around her eyes and mouth. "You okay?"

"I don't know," Ellanna said, her eyes closed.

"Wade seen it yet?"

"I'll hear about it when he does."

"And Baxter's still pushing…."

Ellanna sat up. "Guess he thinks God's got something up His sleeve. We just have to wait for Jesus or someone to ride out of the sky and deliver us from evil."

"Let's just hope it's not the Four Horsemen of the Apocalypse," Janet said, running her fingers through her hair.

"Amen to that." Ellanna leaned back in her seat. "Funny, he hasn't mentioned them."

"He couldn't," Janet said with a wry grin, "or he'd be agreeing with your boss."

"Can't do that, 'specially since Wade wants me to do it the scientific way."

Janet chuckled, then turned serious. "You getting any help?"

"Wade won't hire anyone. Says he's protecting me. He's right, I guess, but… thank Sayid for me for getting a few labs to talk with me. That helps. And I've got Garvin. And you."

"What if you do come up with something?" Janet asked. "Will he let you publish it or make you keep it a secret?"

Ellanna looked down and ran her fingers along the crease on her pants leg. "You're asking questions I don't know the answers to."

"Sorry. Been hanging around certain people too long."

Ellanna wagged a finger at the screen. "You need to pick better friends."

"I've got great friends, the best. Even you." She winked. "*Especially* you. I've just got lousy enemies, that's all."

"Me too," Ellanna said. "Old Chinese proverb: choose your enemies wisely, because they're the people you'll become most like."

"As if we had a choice," Janet said, grimacing. A loud beeping sounded from the lab. "What's that?"

Ellanna glanced toward the break room door. "Right on cue. I'd better go see what he wants."

"Be careful, El."

"Dr. Barnes!" Wade barked.

"You too," Ellanna said, and punched off. "In here," she called as she stood. *Here it comes.*

Wade strode into the break room and marched up to Ellanna, stopping when he was nose-to-nose with her. "Do you want to explain how your friend Miss Lange found out you're here?"

Ellanna swallowed but didn't back away. "That's funny," she said, "I was going to ask you the same thing. You had the press release ready."

"Don't get smart with me."

"Don't get stupid with *me*, Mr. Wade. Who wanted to come here to get *away* from the spotlight? It wasn't you: you live in the spotlight. Nobody I talked to at UT-Southwestern, besides Dr. Sayid and Janet's team, knew I was coming here, and they're smart enough to keep their mouths shut. Lisa said as much. You, on the other hand," she put a finger against his sternum, "just might have a reason for wanting it known that I'm here."

Wade shoved her hand away. "I've kept my promise," he growled.

"Really?" Ellanna spun on her heel and walked a few steps away, keeping her back to him. "Then I can't imagine how she figured it out." She crossed her arms over her chest.

Wade rubbed his forehead with his fingers. "The press has a short attention span," he said, keeping his voice under tight control. "We can stonewall them."

Ellanna shook her head. "You don't know Lisa Lange the way I do. She won't give up. She's…." *A bulldog, just like Janet,* she realized. Her insides turned cold. "She'll do whatever it takes to find me. All she has to do is catch me driving in or out of the garage." She paused for a few beats to let that sink in. "Maybe I should wear a wig and a fake moustache. What do you think?" She turned to face him.

"Don't be a smartass," Wade said his face red, hands clenching and unclenching.

That's enough. "There's got to be a way to solve this."

"Like?" His gaze flicked around the room.

"I can… I don't have to work here all the time. There's a lot I can do without being in the lab if I've got the right software and a good link to the data cloud. I don't need the VR all the time. When I need it, I can come in."

Wade pressed his lips together.

"Lisa doesn't know where I live," Ellanna said. "I can work from home. Just until this blows over. We'll still be in touch."

Calming down, Wade shoved his hands in his pants pockets. "I want you here."

"But—"

"I want you here. End of discussion."

Ellanna walked back to her boss. "Mr. Wade, I… look, I'm not going to argue with you about stopping the Plague, assuming it can be stopped. Let's say it can. Then there's the whole issue of how to spread whatever someone comes up with, assuming it's… it doesn't do what the Chinese antidote did. There'll be resistance. You know who's going to lead it too."

Reluctantly, Wade nodded.

"This is a wonderful lab, it really is, even if I don't need everything it can do right now. But please understand this." She met and held his eyes. "If Lisa finds me here, I will have to leave. I can't take what happened to Janet and the others. I can't take any more death threats. And if the Texas Rangers couldn't protect Janet and Satya, there's nothing you can do."

"You don't know what we can do," Wade said, with a small, grim smile. "You'll just have to trust that we have a lot of tools we can use. I'm going to send your fiancé down. You two talk it over." He strode out of the break room, with Ellanna following. When he got to the door, he pointed at the floor as he said, "Just understand this, Dr. Barnes. You're staying here."

Garvin came down to the lab a few minutes later. "What's this about Wade wanting me to talk with you?"

he asked as the inner door shut behind him with its usual squish and click.

Ellanna took his hand and led him to a pair of chairs next to her work desk. After she'd described her encounter with their boss, he was quiet for a long time before asking, "Where would you—we—go? What would you do?"

Ellanna shrugged. "I don't know. We could get me pregnant and I could be a stay-at-home mom. I don't care if I never see the inside of a lab again."

Garvin slid his chair close to hers, put his arm around her shoulders, and looked into her eyes. "You're serious about that, aren't you?"

Ellanna shifted so she could lean against him and hold his free hand. "I'm a scared little puppy dog." She was silent for a minute, then said, "I thought instead of being a bulldog, I could be an alligator, with a thick skin and all, y'know?" She looked up at him.

He smiled, encouraging her.

She looked away. "But they shoot 'gators, don't they?"

* * *

The next morning, Sarah agreed to an interview with Lisa on Ellanna's apparent disappearance. She got ready in SAFE-T's studio while Lisa and Oriel returned to the front of EARTH's headquarters building.

Lisa's first question was, "Ms. Green-Dale, what do you think of the reports that Dr. Barnes has left Texas to work for Earth Action: Return To Harmony here in Portland?"

"It's an absolutely terrifying development," Sarah said. "Think about it: David Wade and EARTH want to decimate the human population. There have been rumors for years that his organization has ties to some kind of shadowy eco-terror group. EARTH is infamous for its disruptive and destructive protests. Dr. Barnes knows how and why the Chinese poison—their so-called antidote—killed. What better—I mean—what worse combination can there possibly be?"

"But to be fair," Lisa said, "no one's seen Dr. Barnes here."

"That's true, and I'm not one to condone conspiracy theories, but they've been awfully coy with the media, haven't they? If she's not working for them, they should just come out and say so. If she is, why all the secrecy? It breeds so much suspicion."

"Suppose we take at face value," Lisa said, "the Dallas team's comments that they didn't want to reproduce the Chinese antidote, just understand it so no one else would make the same mistakes. Wouldn't an organization like EARTH hire someone like Dr. Barnes to help them create a safer antidote?"

Sarah put her hands against her cheeks. "I can't believe you said that, Lisa. There is no such thing as a safe antidote to the Eternity Plague, which, by the way, we should be calling the Eternity Present. It's a gift, not a plague. Remember what any antidote will do if it works 'right.'" She made quote marks in the air with her fingers. "It will kill you, me, and everyone else in the world. Everyone. It would be mass murder, the worst genocide ever."

* * *

One-hundred-fifty feet from where Lisa was standing, Ellanna closed the phone's video window. Sarah's face blinked out but her voice seemed to echo around the lab.

Ellanna leaned on her forearms over the work desk, her head bowed. “That’s it,” she said. “I’m not a mass murderer.”

CHAPTER 16

ELLANNA STAYED HUNCHED over her desk for a while, staring at the desktop, her breathing even and slow. *I'm done,* she thought. *No more responsibilities. Not to EARTH, not to Janet or Sayid or anyone back in Dallas, not to the Eternity Plague, not to anyone besides Gar and me.* Earlier in the morning she'd put a view of a river valley up on the datawall. The river was wide. Tall and steep walls hugged its banks. A bridge arched over it in the distance. *Wonder if that's the Rubicon.* Cars and trucks drove along the highway next to the river. A barge eased into view, working against the current.

Ellanna imagined putting her cares onto the barge so it could carry them away. It seemed to work. A kind of peace settled over her. "I'd forgotten what it's like to feel like this," she said to the empty lab. "It's been so long…." Her stomach growled. She chuckled and patted it. "Freedom makes you hungry, doesn't it?"

She'd expected Wade to make some kind of appearance that morning but he never did.

At 11:30, she called her fiancé. "Ready for lunch?" When he asked for 15 minutes, she agreed and said, "Meet me in the lobby." She met his puzzled expression with an air-kiss and clicked off before he could ask if she was crazy. When he called back, she let the phone ring.

He was still confused twenty minutes later, but Ellanna first put a finger to his lips, then kissed him. "Shoot," she said as they passed EARTH's emblem in the plaza. "Lisa's not here."

Garvin looked at her sidelong but said nothing.

As they walked to a Chinese restaurant a few blocks away, a cool, humid wind gusted down the city streets and clouds like puffy gray sponges hurried overhead. Ellanna asked the hostess for a table by the windows facing the street.

Garvin couldn't take it any longer. "What's going on?" he demanded after they'd brought their trays back to the table.

She sipped her hot and sour soup, then told him. "They can play their little reindeer games without me. Forever if they want. This little 'gator's going to swim away, find a nice, sunny bank, and snooze."

"What do you think Wade's going to do?" he asked as he dipped a crab roll into a little bowl of hot mustard sauce.

"Don't use too much," she said, then leaned forward to whisper, "Do you think I fucking care?"

Back in the lab, she hand-wrote a resignation letter, then sent an e-mail to Janet, but set the software to deliver it the next morning. She spent the rest of the afternoon writing up what she'd learned during her research. She printed a copy, which she left with the resignation letter, and e-mailed delayed-delivery copies to Janet, Sayid, and a few other colleagues. She spent the last half-hour at the computer, planning routes to the bed and breakfast they'd stayed at on Mt. Hood, the lab in Dallas, her parents' home in Atlanta, Garvin's mother's home in Houston, and to Seattle and St. Louis. The last thing she did was make sure the computer's history cache had recorded all of that work and wouldn't delete it when she shut it down.

By the time she and Garvin drove out of the parking garage to go home, the rain that had been threatening at noon had arrived. After they finished dinner, she had him load and run the dishwasher while she disappeared into the bedroom. When he joined her a few minutes later, she was laying out clothes on the bed.

"When do you want to leave?" he asked.

"As soon as we're packed."

"Tonight? In this rain?"

Ellanna pulled a handful of his shirts on hangers out of the closet and handed them to him. "It's time. Pick the ones you want."

He took the shirts. "Will you at least tell me where we're going?"

"Away," she said, rubbing his arm. "That's all I know."

While she put their few houseplants out on the back patio so they wouldn't dry out before they were found, Garvin brewed a Thermos of coffee. They pulled out of the driveway at ten o'clock and headed west toward the Willamette River.

Once they cleared Portland's western suburbs on the Sunset Highway, Ellanna punched at the buttons controlling the car's entertainment and information system while she tried to drive through the heavy rain.

"What are you doing?" Garvin asked.

"Turning off the tracker," she said. "Don't want anyone following us."

"It'll just turn on again next time we start the car. And that's not what you turned off."

Ellanna shot him an angry glance. "You do it then."

"It's all right, Babe," he said, stroking her cheek with the back of a finger. "Just drive."

A few miles later, she guided the car through the sweeping turn onto the Wilson River Highway. Ten miles beyond the overpass, they left the last of the farmland behind and climbed into the mountains. The trees pressed close to the roadway, swaying in the wind and throwing additional splatters of water onto the car. Ellanna hunched over the wheel, trying to see beyond her headlights and the washed out head-up display in front of her.

The highway twisted and curled through the narrow river valley. The trees sometimes gave way to a clearing or the river came so close to the road they could catch a glimpse of the water. A nerve-wracking hour later, they cleared the canyon and eased through more farmland before reaching Tillamook.

"Why don't we stop here?" Garvin suggested.

Ellanna guided the car into a gas station. "I thought this place was on the coast." She reached behind his seat and pulled out the Thermos. "Want some?" she asked as she poured.

Garvin took a deep breath, savoring the smell. "How much longer are you going to go?"

"Just to the coast," she said, handing him the cup. Holding the Thermos between her legs, she tapped at the navigation display screen. "Okay, it's not too far." A few minutes later they were headed west again, through the coastal forest.

* * *

The little hotel in Oceanside looked like it was at least fifty years old, its siding showing the wear of years, even under the orange glow of the street lights. The night clerk looked at least as old and worn, her dingy blonde hair forced into a rough bun behind a lined and tired face.

Ellanna hesitated when she spotted the security cameras behind the registration desk but pressed forward, thinking, *First, they have to look for us out here. By then we'll be long gone.*

She signed them in as Trenicia and Collier Starling. When she told the clerk they'd pay in cash, the woman said, "I don't think we can—"

"Yes, you can," Ellanna snapped, her expression cutting off any argument.

They took a room on the back side of the hotel, facing the water. Despite the building's shabby appearance, the door and windows sealed well, blocking out most of the roar and thunder of the wind and waves. Garvin had just set down their overnight bags when Ellanna grabbed his hand and pulled him back toward the door. "C'mon," she said.

"What?"

"Just come."

A short, weathered staircase led from the hotel's back balcony to a path through high grass to the beach. The rain had stopped for the moment but the fierce wind drove high-tide waves far across the tidal flats, leaving just a narrow strip of sand.

"What are you doing?" Garvin shouted against the wind as Ellanna led him down the stairs by the hand.

"I want to stand next to freedom," she replied. "Just for a little while."

"The surf's real high."

Ellanna pulled her fiancé close. "You'll keep me safe."

"This is close enough for me." He yawned.

"But not for me." She kissed him on the cheek, then dashed down the path.

"Jesus, woman," Garvin said under his breath. He pulled his black rain slicker tighter around himself and followed her down to the beach. The small slope was enough to cut off most of the lights from the town above and the spray from the waves diffused what light did make it down. By the time he reached the shore, he had lost sight of his lover. He stepped out onto the open ground, looked around, and shouted, "La-na! La-na!" The roaring wind and surf shredded his cry and snatched it away.

Ellanna tackled him from behind, shouted, "Boo!" and raced off down the beach. He stumbled after her, staggering across the uneven surface he could only half-see, and caught up with her a hundred feet later.

With a wild grin, she wrapped her arms tight around his waist and kept walking crabwise on the wet sand, right at the water's edge. Over the noise of the storm, they never heard the incoming big wave. It slammed into them hip-high. Already off balance, Ellanna went down with a shriek, pulling Garvin with her. Before they could regain their feet, a second, bigger wave tumbled them apart.

"Garv—!" Ellanna screamed, the second half of his name cut off as her head went under water. She thrashed around, trying to figure out which way the surface or the ground were, but the turbulent water gave her no chance. *Oh God oh God oh God—Garvin!* The cold, the dark, and the terrible need to breathe made her flail even more. She found nothing but water.

Garvin was luckier for a moment. The swirl popped his head above the surface. He gulped a deep breath and shouted, "Lana!" as he tried to tread water. He thought he heard something off to his left. He took another breath and dove, but the undertow caught him and he too, became disoriented. Fighting his panic, he swam hard for where he prayed Ellanna was.

The third wave, the biggest of the set, surged in, lifting them both high above the sea floor, then slamming them down. By the time Ellanna's hand brushed the sand, she was too cold, too disoriented, and too terrified to react. The backflow churned her and her fiancé out into the cold, dark depths.

* * *

"Phone, call Ellanna," Janet gasped the next morning even before she finished reading her friend's e-mail. She checked the time as it dialed. It was early in Portland, two hours earlier than Dallas, but she knew Ellanna would be awake.

The call went to voice mail. Janet left a hurried message: "Got your e-mail. Call me." She sent a text message and dashed up to Dr. Sayid's office. Thinking Ellanna might have been in the shower, they decided to wait twenty minutes, then call again. While they waited, Janet checked Ellanna's social media sites. There was nothing new.

The second phone call got the same result.

"What do we do now?" Janet asked, rattling a pen between her thumb and forefinger.

Sayid scratched at his short grey hair. "Not much we can do. Maybe she just turned her phone off."

"No way," Janet said. "She'd know I'd call as soon as I saw that message. Wait: Garvin." She dialed his number. "Voice mail," she said to Sayid a moment later, then,

"Garvin, it's Janet. Have El call me, please. 'Bye." She ended the call, sent him a text, set her phone on her boss' desk, and rattled the pen again.

Sayid thought for a minute. "Call Wade," he said. "Might as well if you're that worried."

Janet snatched up her phone and in seconds was talking to EARTH headquarters' answering service. "Yes, he knows me. I discovered the Eternity viruses. It's urgent… okay, I'll wait." She glanced at Sayid, then picked up the pen and tapped it against her knee.

Wade's face appeared on the screen. "Good morning, Dr. Hogan. Why do I have—"

"Have you checked your e-mail?"

"It's 6:30 in the morning."

Janet could see he hadn't shaved yet. "Something's wrong. Did you know Ellanna resigned last night?"

"What do you mean, resigned?"

"She sent Dr. Sayid and me some notes saying she'd quit and everything we'd need was in the lab. I just called her and her boyfriend, got their voice mails. Texted them; no reply. There's nothing on their social sites."

Wade's eyes narrowed. "And that's not like her," he said, scratching at his beard.

"I'm worried."

"All right," he said. "I'll check and call you back."

* * *

After he hung up, Wade set his phone on the kitchen table and stared at it. *She said she'd leave. I didn't think she was that serious. Didn't do anything else to pressure her after… ohhh, that Green-Dale interview.* He hurried into the bathroom to shave.

As he left his loft apartment, he called Lew Crandall. "Meet me at the basement lab. As soon as you can."

Fifteen minutes later he was clattering down the stairs from the headquarters lobby, heading for the lab entrance. His calls to Ellanna and her fiancé as he trotted the half-mile to the building hadn't been answered.

The lab was dark as he entered. When the lights came on, he spotted the pile of papers on the work desk. He was reading the resignation letter when the security system announced Crandall's arrival. Wade showed him the letter and told him what had happened.

"Find anything else?" Crandall asked.

"I just got here," Wade said, looking around. "I'll check the break room. You see if there's anything on the computer."

"I'll need her accesses," Crandall said as he pulled out the chair.

"Use mine," Wade said, easing his assistant aside. A few seconds later, he said, "Okay. Go."

When Wade returned from the break room, Crandall was hunched over the screen. "Got something," he said, glancing at his boss. "Maybe." He ran his finger down the screen as Wade came to look over his shoulder. "Bunch of map accesses." He selected one, then frowned. The line on the map ended at a small town. "On Mount Hood?"

"Sure," Wade said. "She and her guy went up there for a couple weeks before they came to work for us. Maybe that's where they went." He reached over Crandall's shoulder to tap the icon at the end of the line. "Call that B&B."

"Wait a second," Crandall said. He activated the datawall and put the map on it. "There's five, six others."

"That's… it's like she's laying false trails," Wade said as he scanned the list. "No way to know which one's right."

Crandall leaned back in the chair, stroking his beard. "If any of them are."

Wade shoved his hands into his pockets. "I don't want to get the police involved."

"Okay," Crandall said, "maybe we could ping their phones, or their car's emergency locator."

"Can you do that?" Wade asked, looking down at the younger man.

"*I* can't," he said as he swiveled his chair around. "But I know people who can. All I need are their phone numbers and the car's VIN."

"I've got the phone numbers," Wade said. "Security's got the vehicle ID. Here." He pulled out his phone and read off the numbers. "I'm going upstairs. Let me know what you find out."

Twenty minutes later, Crandall called Wade in his office. "I don't like this," he said. "The car's at a hotel lot in Oceanside."

Surprised, Wade said, "That's interesting. What don't you like?"

"The phones are both miles away, off shore. Weak signals."

"On a boat?"

Crandall shook his head. "They're a half mile apart… reporting elevations below sea level."

"Below—" Wade blanched, then frowned. "You'd better get out there and find out what's going on."

"On my way," Crandall said as he stood up.

"Quietly, Lew."

"Yes, Sir."

* * *

Late on Friday, Wade's phone burbled to get his attention, then said, "Urgent q-encrypted message from Lew Crandall. Will you accept?"

Quantum encryption, Wade thought, his lips forming a flat line. *This isn't good.* "Accept."

Instead of text or audio, the message was a slideshow of five photographs. The first was a car. The next was two phones, one light yellow, one gray, their batteries removed and placed next to them. The third and fourth were of bloated, decomposing faces revealed by the open zippers of body bags. The last was a sheet of paper bearing one handwritten word: "Instructions?"

Wade stopped the slideshow before it could repeat. He drummed his fingers on the top of his desk, thinking hard. *It would have been better if he hadn't found the bodies. Fuck. Now what?*

His computer chimed. "Ten minutes until your morning staff meeting."

"Thanks." *Jesus… what do I…? Fuck. Fuck fuck fuck. No time.* He took a deep breath. *Okay. Calm down. Think.* Think! *Worst thing we can do is try to cover this up. Body bags! Jesus! What was he thinking?* His leg bounced as he considered his options.

"Gaia," he said to his computer, "tell the staff I'll be a few minutes late."

"Yes, Mr. Wade."

He picked up the phone and placed a q-encrypted call to Crandall. "Body bags?" he demanded when the man answered.

"Well, you… didn't want anyone to know about her," Crandall said.

"Jesus, Lew," Wade said, his head in his hands.

"I didn't know what else—"

"I know. Okay, are the bodies together?"

"Almost a mile apart. We're lucky it's a pretty remote area."

Wade groaned. "Where are they? Still on the beach?"

"No, they're hidden."

Wade winced and rubbed his forehead with his fingers. *Stupid stupid stupid.* "Can you get them back to where you found them?"

"Not without being seen."

Wade thought for a long moment. "Okay, here's what you're going to do. Early tomorrow, before sunup, put them back where you found them, near the high-water line. Cover up all the signs you left moving the bodies. Get rid of the goddamn body bags. Then, at dawn, call the cops from where you just found one of them while out jogging. Make sense?"

"I can make it work," Crandall said.

"You'd better," Wade said, and ended the call. He stayed in his chair, his leg still bouncing. *That gives us a day to come up with something.* Another thought made him slump backward. *What am I going to tell Janet?*

* * *

An excited crowd of reporters and camera operators were milling around in EARTH's lobby at one o'clock the next afternoon. When Wade walked out of the elevator, they rushed him, shouting questions.

"Wait, wait," he said, holding up his hands. "We're not doing this here. Come with me."

"Where are we going, Mr. Wade?" Lisa called.

He just waved for the gaggle to follow him. They surged along behind, thrusting their microphones at him, asking questions, but once they entered the stairwell, the echoes forced them to stop. As they passed through the door into the hall leading to the lab, which was being held open by an EARTH staffer, the videographers pointed their cameras this way and that, capturing whatever they could of the security cameras and sensors. Still quiet as they entered the lab, the reporters fanned out into a quarter circle facing the work desk and the nearer arm of the U.

"A secret lab," Lisa said.

"That's right," Wade said. "This is where Dr. Ellanna Barnes was working before her tragic and untimely death." He pulled his tablet computer from his jacket pocket. "I have a statement to read, and then I'll answer your questions. There'll be time for you to get video of the lab afterwards."

His voice quavered as he read the words he and his public relations staff had worked on for hours the day before. "In the end," he concluded, "the pressure became too much for her. She left a note for me, and for her former colleagues in Texas, in which she said she couldn't take being accused of doing something—mass murder—that she was never going to do. What she wanted to do here was to keep on working to understand the Eternity viruses. She felt that had become impossible and was compelled to leave.

"We don't know why she and her fiancé went to Oceanside, where they were headed, or what they intended to do. We don't know—" He swallowed hard, then swallowed again. "We don't know why or how they drowned. We do know the surf was high that—Monday—night.

"What I do know is that the world has lost two fine people, and an exceptional scientist in Ellanna Barnes.

We have taken a terrible step backward this week in our efforts to end the scourge of the Eternity Plague, all because some people refuse to accept the natural path of life or respect and care for humanity's only home, this planet earth." He looked up from the tablet. "Questions?"

"So you're denying Dr. Barnes was working on some kind of antidote, like the Chinese one?" Lisa asked.

"She made it very clear very early in our discussions that she would not do that."

"How do you expect us to believe you?" another reporter asked.

Wade picked up a manila folder from the work desk. "We are about to release electronic copies of these papers," he said, holding the file up so everyone could see it. "These are Dr. Barnes' notes on the work she did here, so you'll be able to see for yourselves. We will also be releasing a copy of the e-mail she sent me and her colleagues in Texas, her—" He stopped to swallow again. "Her final words to us."

* * *

Later that afternoon, Janet and Michael watched Lisa, standing in the plaza in front of EARTH's headquarters, holding up her own tablet. "My study of these documents," Lisa said, "does not support David Wade's assertion that Dr. Ellanna Barnes was only studying how the Eternity viruses work. Independent scientists I've spoken with today confirm my assessment."

Janet sat hunched over, her face in her hands, her shoulders shaking. Michael picked up the remote and muted the screen.

"Why am I still doing this?" she asked.

Her boyfriend rubbed her back and shoulders with his free hand. "You knew something like this was going to happen to all of us one day, didn't you?"

Janet sat up and glared at him, her red eyes wide, her mouth an O of horror and hurt. She jumped from the sofa with a howl, ran to their bedroom, and slammed the door behind her.

Michael looked down the hall and sighed. "Guess *that* was the wrong thing to say."

* * *

Wade directed EARTH's staff to cooperate fully with the police investigation that followed the discovery of Ellanna's and Garvin's bodies, but the records of two phone calls never made it into the investigators' hands. When the medical examiner was done with the autopsies and the bodies were ready to be taken home, Wade accompanied them to Dallas for a memorial service before Ellanna's body was to go on to Atlanta.

Even set at an angle on the small stage in the Simmons Research Building's auditorium, the closed caskets dominated it and forced the lectern to be squeezed into a corner. The dead's friends and coworkers filled most of the lower section of the room. Reporters and cameras lined up along the aisle that separated the lower and upper sections. When Wade tried to sit next to Janet, she gave him a hurt look, then got up and moved to the other side of her boyfriend. Wade busied himself reading the program.

After the service, the mourners went to the cafeteria for refreshments while the reporters were escorted out and the caskets moved back to their hearses. Dr. Sayid, Janet and the remaining members of her team, along with

Garvin's former boss and coworkers went through the ritual of the receiving line, accepting the hugs, handshakes, and inadequate words of condolence they were offered. Wade stood to one side, sipping a plastic cup of punch, waiting for the other guests to go through the line, before joining the last stragglers.

When he reached Janet, he held his arms out to offer her a hug. After an awkward moment, she accepted it but pulled away as soon as she could.

"I wish there was something I could say," he said.

"You can't," Janet said, not looking at him. "I mean, it's not your fault that… that she went to Portland. Maybe if I'd—"

"Please, Janet," Wade said, "don't beat yourself up over this. We make the decisions we have to make, that's all."

Sayid turned from talking with another guest to face the two of them, and Michael also came over, carrying a cup of water for Janet.

She took the cup and sipped, then said, "Or feel forced to make."

"What do you mean?" Wade asked.

"You know very well what I mean," she said, anger smoldering in her eyes as she looked him in the face for the first time. "El and I talked every day, sometimes more than once a day. I know what you were doing."

"I was giving her everything she asked for," he protested. "All the equipment, all the privacy, all the security—"

"And all the pressure she could stand, and then some."

"I didn't push her over the edge," Wade said, his hands on his hips. "Sarah—"

"No, but you took her there and showed her the view," Janet snarled. "Couldn't you see how close she was, how the ground was crumbling under her feet? She told you… she *told* you what was happening. Didn't you listen?" Her hand was shaking so hard the water slopped out of the cup. She switched it to her other hand and wiped the wet one on her skirt. "Didn't you care?"

"Of course I did," Wade said. "Of course I cared. Just as I care about you now." He reached out to hold her arm but she turned away. "I never wanted her to be hurt. I don't want to hurt you… your feelings, either."

Janet gaped at him. "Don't want to hurt my feelings? *My* feelings? One of my very best friends is dead because she worked for you and you say you don't want to hurt my feelings? Part of my heart's been ripped out and you come here to say you *care* about me?"

"I—"

"If you really cared—"

Michael took her arm. "Not so loud, sweetie."

She scorched him with her eyes, then glanced around the cafeteria at all the people being careful not to look their way. In a lower voice, she said, "I'll tell you what you can do if you care about me, Mr. Wade. You can go right back to Portland, go down into that dungeon of a lab you gave Ellanna, and *rot* there." She spun and stormed out of the room, heading for the elevators.

Michael glanced at Wade, then followed.

After the elevator doors had closed behind them, Sayid asked, "Are you still planning to go to Atlanta?"

Wade nodded, his gaze still on the elevator lobby.

"Then if you care for Dr. Hogan as much as you say you do—and as much as we do here—I suggest you stay as far away from her as possible."

* * *

Ellanna's funeral was an awkward affair for everyone except Ellanna herself. Her family didn't know quite how to respond to Wade's presence, whether to shun him as her murderer, accept him as a fellow mourner, or do something else. He tried to assure them that he shared their grief but everywhere he went, the press was on his heels, pointing cameras, microphones, and smart phones at him, shouting questions, demanding answers. No matter what he tried, he couldn't stop being the center of attention, something this time he desperately did not want.

Janet found herself in the same predicament, even being accused of somehow being responsible for Ellanna's death. Despite her own grief and anger, she felt a twinge of sympathy and compassion for Wade, seeing him forced to run the same gauntlet but without the support she was getting from Michael, Satya, Gerardo, Sayid, and her parents, who had driven down to Atlanta from their home in Raleigh.

During the funeral service, Wade and Janet sat a few places apart in the same pew behind Ellanna's family. He kept glancing at her but she refused to look his way. He caught her eye at the cemetery and mouthed, "I'm sorry."

She held his gaze for a moment, then turned to lean against her boyfriend.

* * *

Wade got away from Atlanta as soon as he could, catching a late-afternoon flight to Raleigh. The next morning he met with Revered Baxter, seeking to build the partnership against the effects of the Eternity Plague he'd wanted from the start. In the end, though, their differences were too great to bridge, at least in one meeting.

Baxter ended their discussion with a warning. "If you and Dr. Hogan continue to push some cure that will kill us all, no matter how natural you claim it will be, my people will fear it and fight it. I've got a good idea who's going to lead that resistance. You've encountered him once. I know him very well. A lot of people discount him as a self-promoting publicity hound. I know better. He's a force, and he's going to use your own tactics against you."

Wade's next stop was Sarah's office in Washington, D.C. He hadn't expected she would agree to see him after the riot two months before. When she did, he used the train ride from Raleigh to prepare himself for whatever she might throw at him. He had a gambit to play and hoped it would surprise her: an offer to merge, or at least coordinate their research efforts. Ellanna had made him understand that stopping the Plague wasn't going to happen quickly, no matter how much he wanted it. He hoped to convince Sarah it was going to take more time than she wanted to find the cures she desired. He went over and over his arguments, searching for the words and ideas that would penetrate her resistance. He had one other angle to try too.

The reception he got at SAFE-T's headquarters was frigid. After sparring with Sarah for several minutes, he brought up what had happened to Ellanna. "Dr. Barnes left a note that repeated what she'd been telling me since she'd arrived in Portland: if the pressure got to be too much, she'd walk away from the research she'd done for me, what she'd done in Texas, everything. It did, she did, and it killed her."

"Which would have never happened if you hadn't lured her away."

So much for her caring for others, Wade thought, then made his offer to work together.

Sarah snorted a laugh. "You've been smoking some of the finest buds of Mother Earth's special flora, Mr. Wade." She held her hands together, fingers pointed upward. "I like to say that when an opportunity to do good comes along, it's like a flower opening up." She spread her fingers out, then snapped them down into fists. "This flower doesn't deserve to get out of its bud… and it never will."

Well, that's that, he thought as he rode the elevator down to the building's lobby. *My path's clear now: find a way for Janet to succeed.*

* * *

Lisa had been shadowing Wade, beginning at the memorial service in Dallas.

When Oriel asked at the funeral why she wasn't running with the pack of reporters who were dogging his footsteps, she replied, "Honey and vinegar. Those guys are making nothing but enemies."

Her philosophy worked. First she scored an exclusive interview with Ellanna's parents. Then she followed Wade to Raleigh and Washington, where she cadged quick interviews with Baxter and Sarah and a phone call with the environmentalist himself.

While he was catching up on other business in his hotel room that evening, she reported from the lobby below, "David Wade's high-stakes gambles to patch up relations with Reverend Baxter and Sarah Green-Dale have failed. Humanity's search for a proper response to the Eternity Plague is as muddled as ever." As she spoke, Oriel placed pictures of Wade and Baxter to Lisa's left on the screen, and Sarah to her right, leaving one corner empty.

"All eyes turn back to Janet Hogan," Lisa said. Janet's image filled the center of the screen while Lisa's slid into the previously-empty slot and the other three heads turned as if to look at the scientist. "Can she even go on, or does the tragic death of her colleague and confidante, someone so close to her heart, spell the end of her quest for an antidote? The citizens of the entire world hold their collective breath, waiting to learn whether they'll live or how they will die."

* * *

The next morning, Brother Elijah released a video. "Brothers and sisters," he proclaimed as he stood in front of a slowly changing montage of joyous faces, "it is time for us to raise our voices in praise of life, the life the Eternity Present has brought us, and in defiance of the death the harbingers of hate and the ombudsmen of oppression would force on us all.

"We shall not thrust our heads into the guillotine of guilt. We shall not be forced across the Bridge of Sighs into the dungeons of death and the gardens of graves.

"No! Today is the day we lift our voices in everlasting songs of praise and support for those in this world who believe in the sanctity of life and are working for its preservation. Today is the day we lift our voices in songs of holy righteousness to bring back onto the road of glory those who have strayed from its straight ways.

"Today, brothers and sisters—today we go in peace and joyfulness to build chains of love around the workplaces of those who cherish life, and chains of loving correction around the workplaces of those who need correcting. Come with me today to do our sacred work."

Within hours, his followers had surrounded SAFE-T's and EARTH's headquarters buildings. Brother Elijah himself was at Baxter's church.

* * *

Janet was perched on a lab stool, just finishing loading some sample trays before she headed to lunch with Michael when an alarm tone sounded over the PA system. "This is campus security. The North Campus is locked down. A protest has formed on the grounds, all exits are blocked, and no one is being allowed in or out. Remain inside and do not try to leave. This is campus security. The North Campus is locked down."

Shocked, Janet stared through the space under the overhead cabinets at Satya. "Did you hear anything about this?"

"No, nothing." She opened her news browser. "Here it is, of course," she said as Janet joined her. "Top of the queue. You're the target. They want you to stop."

"Figures, especially after what Lisa said last night." She walked to the windows and looked down at the lines of people that stretched around the building and out of sight. Some of the protesters had joined arms and swayed back and forth. Others clapped and sang. *Maybe,* she thought. *Maybe.* She turned and strode toward the anteroom outside her office, taking off her lab coat as she did.

Frowning, Satya called after her, "Where are you going?"

"Out."

* * *

Mohamed Sayid found Janet sitting bundled up in her winter coat in the Simmons Building's cafeteria twenty minutes later. The room was noisy and crowded but no one came near her. She looked up as he settled onto the plastic chair next to hers. "What are you doing down here?"

For a while she said nothing, just stared at the brown stumps of the now-dormant perennial plants in the barren garden beyond the windows. Sunlight filtering through thin, high clouds added no warmth. At last she said, "I had this idea that I could talk the protesters into going away and leaving us alone." She glanced at Sayid, who raised a quizzical eyebrow. "Bright, huh? The guards are smarter than I thought: they wouldn't let me out."

"They'll surprise you that way sometimes," he said with a wry smile.

Janet studied her boss, the lines on his face, the bags under his eyes, the way his skin sagged more than it used to. "I'm beginning to understand what Ellanna felt. It's never going to end, is it?"

He reached over to take her hand. "We need you, Janet."

"I wonder," she said.

CHAPTER 17

LISA AND ORIEL DECIDED TO RETURN to Raleigh from Washington, D.C., as soon as they heard of Brother Elijah's plans. The protest at Baxter's church was the most interesting one they could get to quickly.

When they arrived, the first layer of the human chain had already formed and a second one was taking shape. The men and women in the chain had linked their arms and were singing "We Shall Not Be Moved." Brother Elijah was striding along Salisbury and Edenton Streets, the north and east sides of the church, shouting directions and encouragement, leading an occasional song, and ensuring he remained the focus of attention of the reporters who were covering the event. Lisa and Oriel worked their way through the crowd so she could ask, "You called this a 'chain of correction.' If Reverend Baxter is your target, what are you trying to correct?"

"It's a chain of *loving* correction," Brother Elijah said. "We Christians can love a sinner while we hate the sin he or she commits."

"So what's the sin you're trying to lovingly correct?"

The preacher looked past Lisa to a group of women who were standing on the sidewalk, uncertain about what to do. "Around the corner, sisters," he called, pointing down the street. "Join the chain there." He turned back to Lisa. "I apologize. This is a very dynamic demonstration of love, as you can see."

"The sin?" Lisa prompted, shouting to be heard over the singing behind Brother Elijah.

"My brother-in-Christ, Reverend Baxter, despite his frequent denials, is placing himself in league with the very people he has condemned from the pulpit, those who would strike us down as if they were the Angel of Death. It is not the place of any mere mortal to do the work of the Lord's holy angels. It is beyond the sin of hubris to even suggest that anyone can."

"But I was in the congregation when Reverend Baxter called scientists, I take it that's who you're referring to—"

"Among others."

"He called them antichrists. How does that square with your accusation that—?"

A young man rushed up to them. "Brother Elijah," he said, panting, "Reverend Baxter is on the front steps of the church. He wants to see you."

"Thank you," the preacher said. "Come along, Miss…?"

"Lange. Lisa Lange."

"Miss Lange, and you'll have the answer to your question in full." He turned and strode toward the front of the church with Lisa, Oriel, and the rest of the reporters trailing behind. "Let the Red Sea of Love part," he called out as they approached the point in the chain where he wanted to pass through. The protesters opened a path.

When they reached the stairs leading up to the landing facing the State Capitol Square, Lisa and a few others tried to follow Brother Elijah up to get close.

Baxter motioned for them to move back. "I'd like a private word with my Brother, if you don't mind."

Lisa and the others backed down and arrayed themselves below the landing. Oriel pointed his camera at the men and turned the microphone's gain up. Lisa pulled her link box from the back of her waistband to make sure she could hear through her earpiece whatever the mike picked up.

Baxter turned Brother Elijah so their backs were to the people below them. "What in God's name do you think you're doing, Jeffrey?" he whispered.

Brother Elijah jerked back.

Lisa caught Oriel's eye and mouthed, "Jeffrey?"

He raised an eyebrow and shrugged. There was a rustle among the other reporters who had also heard Baxter's question.

"Don't call me that," Brother Elijah whispered, then turned so his profile was visible to some of the reporters. In a louder voice he said, "Brother William, I am—we, all the brothers and sisters you see around this edifice—are calling on you to renounce and reject and put away any and all connections you have now, may have had in the past, or might have in the future, with those who oppose God's will or seek to usurp His power. We are calling on you to repudiate the pagans who worship the Earth Mother and the heathens who would tie mankind's fate to the contents of a test tube."

"Again?" Baxter demanded. "*Again?* And how many times more, my Brother? Who do you think you are, Balaam's ass, who would turn me, being blind to the Lord, away from sin?"

"Will you smite me, three times, as Balaam did?"

Trembling, his fists at his sides, Baxter glared into Brother Elijah's eyes. "Just as when we were boys and you deserved it," he whispered through clenched teeth, his lips barely moving. Louder, he said, "It is not me who's been doing the smiting, Brother. Nor should I be the target of your blows. My eyes are open to the directions of the Lord, and my ears to Jesus' words of love."

"Then you join me in decrying the evil work of Dr. Hogan and the other scientists around the world who seek to count the number of our days in the atoms of our bodies, rather than letting the Lord measure that length?"

"*I*, join *you*?" Baxter said, struggling to keep his temper in check. "No, it's time *you* joined *me* in refusing to die by lethal injection."

"Amen!" Brother Elijah shouted, turning to face the reporters below and raising his arms above his head. "Amen! Our work here is done!" He trotted down the stairs crying, "Hallelujah! Rejoice! Sing hallelujah!"

Most of the reporters hurried to follow the preacher. Oriel started to, also, but Lisa stopped him. "Get a shot of Baxter. I've never seen murder in the eyes of a real minister."

Oriel pointed the camera back up to the landing and zoomed in on Baxter's face. "There's got to be something to him calling Brother Elijah Jeffrey," he said

"Yeah... what *was* that about?"

* * *

Early the next morning, Janet checked her rear-view mirrors for what felt like the thousandth time. She'd been on the run for just a couple of hours but it seemed like forever—and like ten seconds. She expected the red and blue lights of a police cruiser to explode in her mirrors any minute and end her crazy, desperate escapade.

She'd hatched the scheme one night after being invited to a small meeting on possible Plague vaccines at the Centers for Disease Control in Atlanta.

"Going to visit your folks while you're there?" Michael had asked as he flipped a salmon fillet over on Janet's grill.

"As if I could get away," she'd replied.

Now she was driving her father's old Dodge away from Atlanta as fast as she dared. She'd gotten to Atlanta a day ahead of schedule, but instead of having a pre-meeting conference as she'd told Sayid she would, she'd dropped her bags at her hotel and taken its shuttle bus back to the airport to catch a flight to Raleigh.

At the Raleigh-Durham airport, her parents were full of curiosity about why she wanted to take the old car to Atlanta but all she'd say was, "You'll see."

"The gas tank's full," Robert Hogan said as they stood in the parking lot next to the car. "Plenty to get you down there but you'll need to fill up before you come back. Remember, the cruise control just controls your speed. It doesn't drive for you like modern cars do."

Janet hugged him. "I remember." She let him go so she could hug her mother. "I promise I'll be careful."

"Please do," Janice said.

Janet wondered just how careful she was being now, alone, driving a gasoline-powered, candy-apple green antique car, before dawn, just over the Georgia/North Carolina line. She pulled up to an intersection and checked the directions she'd written out longhand. To her right, the December sky was pink above the mountains, fading to lavender and navy higher up. She let a semi pass, then turned onto the highway, heading east.

As she accelerated away from the intersection, she sipped the energy drink she'd brought along, grimacing at its sour tang. *I used to like this stuff,* she thought. *So much has changed.*

She marveled at how easy it had been to get away from the hotel. Her presence had been a secret, her tickets purchased under a different name and special arrangements made to get her through security at the airport. She had a morning workout routine at home, so every day during the conference she'd gotten up early and carried a big sports bag down to the fitness center. No one from her protective detail went with her. They watched her on the hotel's security system instead. *Thank God they got complacent.*

Almost no one else would be in the neighborhood of her parents' cabin in the Blue Ridge Mountains south of Blowing Rock this time of year. Most of the cabins were rentals or second homes for people from Charlotte, Raleigh, or even Atlanta, and with Thanksgiving behind them, the last tourists and summer residents would be long gone.

Janet checked the car's clock. *I'll be there by ten.*

She'd loved the cabin ever since her parents bought it: the rustic furniture, the exposed wood ceiling and log walls that glowed in the sun or by lamplight, the deck that looked out across the valley, her cozy bedroom in the basement, decorated with her mother's and local artisans' craft work. It was her family's refuge from Raleigh's summer heat and humidity.

The rising sun did little to lift her spirits. The bare elms and oaks ghosting among the pines and spruces reminded her of too much: the dead, the living, and the new undead among the living—the old, the crippled, the frail, awaiting some kind of resurrection. She shivered and tried to focus on the winding road. *How did it come to this?* she asked herself. *Why can't I handle this, stand up to the threats, finish the work? I've never given up before.* "People haven't wanted to kill you before, either," she said, answering herself. *But….* She drummed on the steering wheel with her fingers. "Oh, let it *go*, Janet. It's done. It's over."

Another nagging worry struggled to the surface of her consciousness. She reached over to the passenger seat, opened her purse, and felt around inside. Her phone was there, the battery and memory card pulled out so she couldn't be traced. Her fingers found the pinecone-shaped plastic fob that held the keys to the cabin and her father's tool shed. Knowing she had the keys did nothing to ease her real concern: *Did Michael find my note? Did he call? Did Daddy understand the message? What if he didn't?*

"'Foofy Wock, us'ns, 10th.' Michael, please say it just that way. Luv U w/L my ♥. J."

During their first trip to the cabin, in a fit of little-girl silliness, Janet and her sister Chris had renamed the town of Blowing Rock "Foofy Wock." Family trips to the mountains had become "Us'ns goin' to Foofy Wock." Even her father still said that.

Janet wriggled in the seat. *Can't call. Don't dare. Just have to wait.*

* * *

The gray gravel driveway from the road to the cabin was empty as Janet drove up the hill. She stopped short of the house, gauging the size of the shed at the far edge of the lawn. She decided it was too small to hold the Dodge, and pulled up to the front steps.

She locked the cabin door behind her, hiked her overstuffed gym bag onto her shoulder, and hurried down the carpeted steps to her room. Unpacking took just seconds and then she stood in front of the antique bureau, wondering what to do next. She laughed and shook her head. "Smart girl, aren't you?" she asked her reflection in the oval, oak-framed mirror. "All you thought about was getting away."

The sound of tires on the gravel outside sent her flying up the stairs to peek around the edge of the closed living room curtains. Leaning against the log wall, biting her lip, she watched her father walk cautiously up the steps onto the porch. She slipped past the arm of the loveseat that rested under the window as his key rattled in the lock.

Robert Hogan opened the door a little, stuck his head in to look around. "Janet?" he called.

"Hi, Daddy," she said. She didn't remember crossing the room or noticing when her mother joined their tearful hug.

* * *

"Won't this be one of the first places they look?" Janice Hogan chided as they sat at the kitchen table after lunch.

"No."

"Somebody will."

"Why?" Janet asked, sipping her mug of tea. "Who'd you tell?"

"Nobody," her mother protested. "Your father wouldn't let me. He told Mrs. Saunders we were just going away for a while. She'll figure it out, though; she's always been so nosy."

Janet tore open a packet of sweetener and poured it into her cup. "Nobody'll come," she said as she stirred. "Maybe they think I'm somewhere else."

Janice peered at her daughter, who wouldn't meet her eyes. "Well, what if they do?"

"I'll stay out of sight. You won't know anything and you'll be worried sick. Daddy too."

"What if someone calls?"

Janet shrugged. "I won't answer the phone."

"*Your* phone, Janet."

Janet patted the pockets of her jeans. "Gee, I must have lost it somewhere."

"What about—"

Janet fixed her mother with a hard stare. "The fewer questions you ask, the less you'll have to forget later." Her anger crumbled. "Momma, please, I'm exhausted. I'm scared. Everybody wants me to find the perfect miracle solution. There isn't one but nobody wants to hear that. My best friend and her boyfriend are dead. Michael does the best he can but he doesn't know what I need. You're all I have left." *And that's never been much.*

Janice stood and walked around the table to her daughter, leaned over and wrapped her in an embrace. "You know we'll never let you down," she said. "How could we? We're so proud of you. You've been so brave, despite everything. And after your viruses cured me—"

Janet flew out of her chair and her mother's arms. "They're not my viruses!" she shouted from beyond the table. "It's not my plague. I didn't make them. I... we... all we did was discover them, figure out how they work."

"But—"

"That's all I ever hear: it's *my* plague, it's *my* fault. That's why they tried to kill Satya and me. They killed Ellanna. I'm sure they did. Don't you pin it all on me too." Janet ran out of the kitchen, down the stairs, and slammed the bedroom door.

Janice stood, forlorn, in the kitchen, staring toward her daughter's room. "Oh, Janet," she whispered. "Oh, my baby."

* * *

"So after nearly a week of fruitless searching, the Cascade Range seems to have swallowed up Dr. Hogan, the other half of the Eternity Plague team, and with her America's best chance at finally understanding—and curing—this worldwide pandemic.

"Reporting from Zigzag, Oregon, I'm Lisa Lange."

Lisa sat in the back seat of the car, staring at her computer screen, thinking. She decided she'd done all she could do with the report, closed it, and sent it to her editor in Los Angeles.

"Done?" Oriel asked from the front seat.

"Another one in the can. Jesus, I wish we could find a different angle. We're following the pack."

Oriel shifted to look at her, hooking his arm over the back of the driver's seat. "So why aren't you following your own instincts? Did you believe the note they found in the hotel?"

The status bar on the screen finished growing. The computer chimed and the display cleared. Lisa watched a search and rescue team climb out of their truck and amble into the convenience store. "Sure," she said, "it made sense. They had both vacationed here. Then Wade confirmed he'd found a map leading up here on Barnes' computer in that secret lab, even if it was a false trail. They were best friends, not just coworkers. You could see it." She pointed at Oriel. "Even *you* could see it."

"Thanks," he said, laughing.

"I'm serious. You did see it. You caught it in your shots." Lisa turned off the computer and stuffed it back into its case.

"But to wait this long after Barnes' death?"

Lisa zipped the case closed. "Maybe it just took that long for the pressure to get to her. Her boyfriend said she loved it up here."

"You don't believe it was suicide, though." Oriel watched the traffic passing the small strip mall they were parked in front of, then turned back to Lisa. "Here's a thought. Where did you go after you got back from that bad time in Laos?"

Lisa straightened from putting the case on the floor and looked sideways at Oriel. "LA."

"After LA."

Lisa thought for a minute, then grinned. "Ohhh." She leaned forward between the seats and kissed him on the cheek. "I knew I kept working with you for a reason." Oriel turned around and started the car as she climbed out of the back. "We've got a plane to catch," she said as she settled into the front passenger seat.

"The car won't let me drive until you fasten your seatbelt."

Grumbling, Lisa snapped the catch into place. Oriel eased out of the parking lot, heading back to Portland on Highway 26.

* * *

As they flew toward Raleigh, Lisa and Oriel searched for the clues they'd missed before.

"Here's something," he said, pointing to the screen on the seatback in front of him. "Hogan's folks left town the day she disappeared. Didn't say where they were going." He glanced at Lisa. "Wild goose chase?"

She rubbed the side of her chin with her thumb. "Somebody's got to know where they went. We ask enough people, we'll find out. Just have to dig harder than anyone else."

"Maybe they're hiding at Baxter's church."

Lisa laughed. "That would be pretty clever." She typed on the keyboard built into her seat tray, scanned her screen, surfed through a few pages. "He's saying the usual stuff—praying for her, Jesus is looking out for her." She shaded her eyes with her hand and scanned the seats around her as if she were Jesus. "Nope, not here."

Oriel looked at her out of the corners of his eyes. "You're very bad," he said, chuckling. "As a good Catholic, I should be offended."

Lisa whistled. "'Good Catholic.' You're going to hell for that one. One way, non-stop, express service." She turned serious and began surfing again. "What's Janet's best friend Sarah saying?" A moment later she nudged her partner. "Check this out: 'While we hope Dr. Hogan will be found soon, this search wouldn't have been necessary if she'd been carrying the proper equipment, as prescribed by SAFE-T. No one, not even Dr. Hogan, can count on the Eternity Viruses to protect them from every threat or bad decision.' Mee-yow." She poured the last of the Jack Daniels from the service bottle over the ice in her glass and took a sip.

"And she should know," Oriel said.

Lisa sputtered, choked, and waved her free hand in front of her face. Oriel handed her a napkin as she coughed. "Whiskey up the nose," she gasped, wiping away tears. "Not good."

"SAFE-T couldn't protect you, either. They can't do anything right."

* * *

"Thank you, Dr. Sayid. I'll be in touch." Wade stabbed at the screen of his phone to end the call and resumed pacing across his office.

"Nothing new?" Lew Crandall asked from his seat next to the coffee table.

"Not a damn thing." Wade shoved the phone into his pants pocket. "There's more snow coming tonight. If she's up on Hood and wanted to get lost, she's—" He swallowed. "She's probably lost for good."

Crandall turned his chair so he could look out the office windows while Wade paced. After several minutes, he said, "Y'know, there's a reporter we haven't heard anything from lately."

Wade grunted. "So?"

"Lisa Lange. Think that might mean something?"

Wade stopped pacing and faced the younger man. "It might," he said. "It just might." He pulled out his phone and tapped at the screen, then frowned. "That's odd."

"What?"

"She's gone totally silent: no posts anywhere since Tuesday." He tapped at the screen some more. "Nothing on Global News about her, either."

It was Crandall's turn to frown. "Huh. Unless…." He had his phone out too, and was working at it. "Unless she's on some secret mission, got some idea she doesn't want any other reporter to guess at and beat her to."

"She'd do that?"

Surprised. Crandall looked up at his boss.

"Oh, yes, she would," Wade said.

They both laughed.

"So, can we find her anyway?" Wade asked. "Can *you?*"

"Son of a—" Crandall said. "Sneaky bitch. Turned off her locator." He looked up at Wade. "Yeah, she's chasing something."

Wade started pacing again. "So, how can we… airline tickets?"

Crandall squinted at his phone. "Could be traveling under an alias, or—"

"What about her camera guy? What was his name? Funny one. Orville? No. *Shit!*"

"C'mon, c'mon," Crandall said to his phone. "Okay, who's Lisa Lange's cameraman?"

"Please wait," the phone replied. "Lisa Lange's videographer is Oriel Salvador."

"Yes!" Crandall said. "Where is he now?"

"Checking… Raleigh, North Carolina." The phone displayed a map showing his location.

Crandall glanced up at Wade, who was looking over his shoulder.

"Of course," Wade breathed. "Of course. And he's going to lead us to Janet."

* * *

A week without the pressures of the lab, the protests, news reports, phone calls, or threats was what Janet needed most. She missed Ellanna, missed her work, missed Gerardo and Satya and Michael, even Dr. Sayid. Just not enough to go back to Texas.

She'd made a couple of brief calls on a phone her father had purchased in Boone, the nearest city. "I'm all right," she'd told Michael and Dr. Sayid. "I'm safe. Don't worry. Don't try to find me. Don't call back. Please don't tell anyone you've heard from me."

She was sitting against the headboard of her bed, propped up on pillows, her mind wandering as she thumbed through the copy of *Cosmopolitan* her mother had downloaded onto her tablet. *We were just doctors and lab techs, doing what we always do—trying to fix something that was broken, do what was right. Didn't think about how anyone else would react.* She flipped the off-white box onto the flower-garden quilt. *Sarah says she's doing what's right. So do Baxter and the others... and whatever I'm doing is wrong. It's not fair.*

She slid down until she was flat on the bed and stared at the ceiling. Their second summer at the cabin, when Janet was nine, her father had sanded the ceiling and painted it sky blue so her mother could airbrush on clouds that looked like animals. She smiled. *Life was so simple then. Her smile became lopsided, sardonic. Sayid would say, 'Life's not fair. Quit wasting your time whining about it.' If only.* She pulled her knees up and rattled her thumb and forefinger against her right thigh. *El ran away, tried to hide, and....* Her insides crinkled up. She gritted her teeth against the tears that wanted to come. *I got away this time, but... where else could I go? How? Daddy's car would be so easy to spot.*

A faint sound from outside made her sit up and listen hard. At first, she couldn't hear anything over the sounds of the football game her father was watching upstairs. Then there were the thumps of car doors closing.

Janet's pulse surged. They hadn't had any visitors, even though her parents had friends in the area, permanent residents. *Maybe Momma saw someone when she was shopping. She'd invite them over, never thinking about what that means.* She got up and shut the bedroom door.

The doorbell rang. She could hear her mother talking to someone. She couldn't make out the words, even with her ear against the door, but her mother's tone of voice confirmed it was someone she knew. *Okay, but this stays shut.*

A few minutes later, lounging on the bed again, she heard footsteps on the stairs. *It's all right,* she told herself. Her room wasn't in a direct line of sight with the steps, so if her mother was bringing friends down to the game room, away from the TV, they wouldn't notice anything.

The soft tap at the door made Janet jump so hard she knocked the tablet onto the floor.

"Janet?" her mother called.

The door opened a little before she could answer and her mother peeked in. "There are some people here to see you. You know them. I hope it's okay."

The bright light shining in the short hall, and the glimpse of red hair, told Janet all she needed to know. She got off the bed. "Mother," she said, her voice low and tight, "come inside and shut the door."

Her mother said, "Just a minute," to the people in the hall, then slipped into the room.

"Shut the door."

"What?"

Janet noticed a black ball at her mother's collar. "What are you wearing?"

Janice looked down. "Just an old blouse."

Janet slammed the door closed behind her mother, then felt across the small of her back. Finding what she expected, she wrenched the older woman around, unclipped the transmitter from her belt, turned it off, and disconnected the mike from the black plastic box. She yanked the microphone wire out of her mother's blouse, threw the mike and transmitter into the trash took her arm, marched her into the walk-in closet, and shut the door behind them.

"What the hell did you think you were doing, letting them in?" she hissed, backing her mother against the wall. "*They're* the people I've been trying to get away from! *They're* the reason I've been getting death threats! *They're* the reason Ellanna's dead. What part of 'You don't know where I am' didn't you understand? Do you have any idea what you've just done?"

"I... but... they're such nice people," Janice said, cowering before her daughter's fury. "They were so nice to Robert and me."

"They're *paid* to be nice, Mother," Janet said, her forehead and nose against her mother's. "It's an act. It's a *lie*. They just used you to find me." Hot, angry, betrayed tears flowed as she realized what she'd just said, what had just happened, how her world was collapsing around her again. "It's all over," she whispered.

"Oh, sweetie, no," Janice said, wiping the tears from her daughter's cheeks. "I'll tell them you can't see them now. They could come back tomorrow and—"

Janet turned away. "You still don't understand. You never did. " She faced her mother again. "It doesn't matter. They've found me. And you, and Daddy. Know what'll happen next?"

"No?"

"There'll be satellite trucks all up and down the street tomorrow. The sheriff's department will have to be up here, all around the yard, all around the neighborhood, to keep the crazy people away. There aren't enough cops in the whole county to do that.

"Your life will never be the same. The calls will start, the threats. They'll be after you: 'Where is she? Have you spoken with her? When is she coming back?' They'll never stop, Momma. Never."

"Lisa?"

"Lisa, other reporters, the wackos. All of them."

Janet watched her mother search her eyes, knowing she was hoping for even the slightest bit of reassurance, of comfort, but finding only haunted bitterness and resignation.

"I'm sorry," Janice whispered.

"Not as sorry as you're going to be," Janet replied. Ignoring the hurt look on her mother's face, she pushed her hands into her jeans pockets and hugged her arms against her sides. "I tried to protect you from all this," she said. "I guess that was a mistake. I suppose I can ask them to sit on the story for a few days."

Janice sniffled. "Will they?"

"Maybe. They won't want to, but it's my only chance."

* * *

Lew Crandall caught Wade at home as he was making lunch. "Found her," he said over the phone. A map appeared on Wade's screen.

The environmentalist peered at it, then at the small image of Crandall in the corner. "Who?"

"Who would I be calling you about on a Saturday?"

Frowning, Wade expanded the map to see more of the area around the pointer Crandall had sent. "Blowing Rock, North Carolina?"

"It checks out," Crandall said. "Her father owns it. He's there. Mother too."

A smile spread across Wade's face. "Fantastic work, Lew. Get me tickets."

* * *

The women returned to the bedroom and Janet handed her mother a couple of tissues from the box on the nightstand. After Janice had blown her nose, Janet pulled her close and whispered, "Find out if they're broadcasting. I won't talk to them if they are." She pulled back, met and held her mother's eyes. "If anything's going out of the house, no interview. Understand?"

"I'll try."

"No, Mother. No 'try.' You failed me once. You can't do it again."

Janice took a deep breath and squared her shoulders. "I… okay."

Janet went into the bathroom after her mother left. She washed her face and brushed her hair. All the old feelings were back, the tension in her stomach, the tight shoulders, the headache. She looked at herself in the mirror. The bags under her eyes were gone but not the worry lines. *Should I color my hair before I leave? Does it matter?* She closed her eyes, leaned on the counter, and took a long, slow breath. *God, I wish I knew.* She stood there, practicing the breathing techniques her yoga master had taught her to find the calm she needed. *Okay.*

She left the bathroom, picked up the tablet, and checked the Global News site to see if Lisa was webcasting, no matter what she had told her mother.

There was another timid tap on the door. "They're waiting for you, Sweetie. Lisa says they're not live right now."

"Thanks," Janet called. There wasn't anything on the site. *This is too big a story—they wouldn't hide it. She's not lying… for now.* She smoothed her shirt, gave herself one last look in the bureau mirror. *No make-up. Fine, let them see what this has done to me.* She opened the door and stepped into the hall.

"If there's anything—"

"Go upstairs."

"But—"

"Please, just go." Janet ached at her mother's expression as she turned and walked away. *It has to be this way, Momma.*

She stepped back into the room, pulled the equipment her mother had worn out of the waste basket, then strode through the hallway to the game room. Oriel was waiting with another wireless mike in his hands. Janet tossed him the other mike and box. "I'm not wearing that. No interview."

They'd set up the room for a two-shot: two cameras, opposing chairs (one from Chris' bedroom, Janet noted), lights. She stopped before she got to the empty chair, amazed at how fast they'd done it.

Lisa stood up. "Dr. Hogan, why did you run away?" Oriel held up a third camera to record this part of the conversation. A small boom mike jutted from above the lens.

"What lies did you tell my mother?"

"Why did you leave that note saying you'd gone to Oregon? Did you want people to think you were going to commit suicide in the mountains?"

The question hurt but Janet pushed the pain down. "Do you know how many more lives you've just ruined by coming here? Do you care?" She fought to remain calm, knowing Lisa wanted her to get emotional, to scream at her. "Who's going to pay for the 24-hour security my parents are going to need now? *They* sure can't afford it. Do you have any idea what it's like to get death threats all the time?"

"Actually, I do," Lisa said. "Look, this isn't getting us anywhere. What do you want?"

"I want to go back to what I was doing before this all happened. I want the threats and the protests and the craziness to stop." She held her hands out to Lisa, palms up. "I'm just a scientist. I don't want to be famous. I don't want to be hated, either."

Lisa grinned. "Kind of like Greta Garbo, huh? 'I *vahnt* to be *ah-loon*.'"

"I'm not like you. I didn't ask for this." She took a deep breath. "How did you find me?"

"Wasn't hard," Lisa said with a shrug. "You made yourself a story when you ran away. We did a few interviews, a little research. " She glanced up and to the left, toward the front of the cabin. "Oriel recognized your father's car in the driveway. That sealed it. Now I've got you and I'm not letting you get away without talking to me."

"I'm talking now. Isn't that enough?"

"If you'll sit down." Lisa pointed to the chair opposite hers.

"You'll just go off and put it on the web as soon as we're done. I need some time."

"Time for what?"

"To get away."

Lisa snorted. “Be serious. You’re too famous. There’s nowhere you can go. Besides, I can’t sit on a story forever. It doesn’t matter if we interview you first. If someone else finds you and broadcasts first, I lose. My competition’s back in Raleigh, hot on my tail. I’m *not* going to let him get this story. If he does, you’ll lose too.”

Janet hung her head. “I’ve already lost. Again.”

Lisa watched the scientist, calculating how hard she could push, how much she could risk. “What do you really want, Janet?”

Janet leaned on the back of the chair. “I told you.”

“So you’ve given up on curing the Plague?”

“I can’t… I… I don’t know. No.”

Lisa walked around the chairs to stand next to Janet and put her hand on her arm. Oriel shifted to keep them both in the video frame. “You can’t cure the Plague,” Lisa said gently, “or do whatever you want to do with it if you keep running.”

She’ll never quit, Janet thought, *still looking down. I could quit… call Sayid, tell him I’m done, but it wouldn’t matter. Momma was right: it is my Plague… in two ways. But I don’t know how to cure either one.* She swallowed, nodded once.

Upstairs, the crowd at the football game roared.

“How much time do you want?” Lisa asked.

“A day. We’ll do the interview tomorrow.”

“And then?”

Janet shrugged. “I hear Portland’s pretty dreary this time of year.”

CHAPTER 18

LISA PICKED JANET UP at ten the next morning. She'd reserved a suite at her hotel in Boone for the interview and gone to the cabin while Oriel was setting up the room. Wearing a microphone, and with a couple of small spycams placed on the rear-view mirror and on the dashboard near her passenger, she hoped to get some additional tidbits while she tried to put Janet at ease.

"Would you believe, I've never been here before?" Lisa said as she guided the car down Blowing Rock Road into town.

"Lots of people haven't," Janet said, trying to say as little as possible without being rude.

"Been coming here for a long time?"

Janet stared straight ahead. "Didn't you find that out when you were tracking me down?"

"I'm not your enemy, Dr. Hogan," Lisa said. "Is that what you think I am?"

Janet glanced at Lisa. Their eyes met for a second, then Lisa had to return her attention to her driving.

"You're always stalking me."

"Staying in touch with you is my job," Lisa replied as she turned right onto King Street. "That's all I'm doing. Like it or not, you're one of the most famous—and most important—people in the world, so if I have to track you to the corners of the earth, that's what I'll do. It's not personal."

Janet said nothing while Lisa turned in at the hotel parking lot and parked the car. After she shut off the engine, Janet said, "It's very personal on my side of the camera. I hope one day you'll understand that."

* * *

Senator Charlene Hamilton sat back in the big leather chair behind her desk in the Russell Senate Office Building and pushed her hair behind one ear. "I guess I must be slow," she said to Sarah, who sat in an armchair on the other side of the desk, "but how is getting Dr. Hogan's public funding cut off going to help when she's disappeared?"

Roger Dale nodded his agreement from his seat next to the desk.

Sarah copied Hamilton's gesture. *I explained this to you last night,* she thought. *Just tell Roger to go along.* "Because, there's still a research team in Dallas and they're still working. That has to stop."

Roger said, "Even though the majority of their funding is coming from private sources?" He consulted his tablet. "Some of the same sources that are supporting SAFE-T's research?"

Sarah's hands clenched. "We've told them playing both sides of the street is unacceptable."

Hamilton shrugged. "They're hedging their bets. What if they decide to cut *you* off?"

"They won't if you introduce the bill we've drafted for you, making antidote research illegal."

"I take it you've done that for the parliaments of every other nation with a serious biotech program and the U.N. too," Roger said.

"We have the moral high ground," Sarah said to the senator, ignoring him, "or we will have if you'll lead Congress and the White House there."

"It's not that simple, and you know it." She got up and walked around the desk to lean against its front. "Let's say I went ahead and introduced the bill. Let's say I got lots of co-sponsors in the House and Senate. Before it ever got to a vote, even in its first subcommittee, there'd be a huge fight over it—"

"You're not afraid of that all of a sudden," Sarah said.

"Of course not," Hamilton snapped, "but I also pick my fights. Don't forget, I represent the Great State of Vermont, home of the *Green* Mountains. You're not the only constituent I represent." She leaned forward to squeeze Sarah's hand. "Even if you are an important one." She pursed her lips at her lover, then pushed off the desk to return to her seat. "But I'm up for reelection next year and you're not a voter there."

Roger said, "Even if the bill passed and the President signed it, I can see a First Amendment challenge."

Sarah picked at the fabric of her skirt. "Kenneth said the same thing. They're… it's all hypothetical. We have a Plan B."

"You didn't mention that last night," Hamilton said, steepling her fingers in front of her chin.

"Someone was trying to distract me," Sarah said, a small smile sneaking onto her face.

"Someday someone's going to learn she can't be all business all the time," Hamilton said, with a small smile of her own.

"Good luck with that," Roger noted.

Sarah shot him a sharp glance, then returned her attention to the senator. "So, Plan B: I go to the International Criminal Court and file genocide charges against a few of the major players, and maybe a government or two."

"Sarah!" Hamilton exclaimed.

Roger studied the surface of his tablet. "You've never been one for half-measures, have you?"

"Not when it comes to protecting people from evil," Sarah said, leaning towards him.

"Even when…."

"What? Say it."

Roger glanced at his boss, who was keeping her expression neutral. "Just don't let your passions cloud your judgment, Sarah. This is too important."

Sarah reached down to snatch her purse from the floor by her chair. "It certainly is," she said as she stood up. "I'm glad you see things my way."

After the office door thumped shut behind her, Roger turned to the senator. "The bill have a chance?"

Hamilton shrugged. "By the time it got to a vote, it might not matter. Sarah's not the only one with strong opinions… and ideas to match." She ran her fingers back and forth along the edge of the desk. "I can stand the heat. The question is whether it's worth drawing it."

"Drawing more of it, you mean."

"She'll get over it."

"Don't be too sure, Boss." He closed the cover over his computer and left the office.

* * *

"It is not at all a contradiction," Reverend Baxter said to the reporters seated in the pews of the sanctuary, "to call for Dr. Hogan to come out of hiding." The minister himself was in a chair that had been brought down from the dais to the same level as the pews. Video cameras on tripods crowded the center aisle and perched in the rows of seats behind the reporters.

"Even after you've been so critical of her and her work?" one of the reporters asked.

"That's right, Reverend," Antonio Corolli chimed in. "You called her the Antichrist."

"*An* antichrist," Baxter said, correcting him. "And as such, the thought of her working in secret should concern us all. Such work should be brought into the light, where it can be seen for what it is, not allowed to fester in the darkness."

"So you don't believe what her note said, that she didn't want to be associated with the Plague anymore?"

Baxter shrugged. "It's possible, I suppose, but as long as people like you can't investigate what she's doing, or measure the veracity of her words, her words alone leave room for doubt."

"Reverend," Corolli said, "there have been rumors that this is all some kind of cover-up, and that Dr. Hogan is actually taking refuge right here in this building. What's the truth about that?"

"That's ridiculous," Baxter said. "I'm surprised you'd take such a statement seriously."

"So you're denying that she is here now, ever has been, or might be in the future."

"I can't imagine why or how she would ever come here… or why she would ever want to."

* * *

"That's odd," Lisa said as she drove Janet back to the cabin after the interview.

Janet had been staring out the side window, trying to have as little to do with Lisa as she could. The interview had been tense and combative, forty-five minutes of one-word answers to a barrage of questions about Janet's plans, desires, and fears.

Lisa felt the weight of the opportunity the interview presented and how it could vault her into the class of elite reporters. *I must have seemed like a medieval inquisitor,* she thought. *Tough. Be evasive and uncooperative, chicky, and you're waving red flags in front of me, telling me you've got secrets, and if you've got 'em, I want 'em.*

But Lisa felt she had failed, that she hadn't been able to pry open the clamshell that Janet was fighting with everything she had to keep shut around her. The interview had been the worst one of her career, far more frustrating than all the ones she'd done with lying, sleazy, brutal dictators, revolutionaries, perverts, and schemers.

I'll get something, she thought. *I'll piece together what I got today and what happened yesterday at the cabin. Just can't let it be a piece of shit.*

Then she'd noticed the truck from a TV station, its body covered in garish commercial artwork, following her and Janet up the hill as they drove out of Boone. "Satellite truck," she said. "Behind us. Second one I've seen."

Janet sat up and looked out the back window.

"Recognize it?" Lisa asked.

"They're from Charlotte." Janet turned to Lisa. "Turn around. Please."

The reporter glanced right and caught the hunted-deer look on Janet's face. One of the microcams still in the car was in position to capture the image and a little tremor of excitement tingled through her.

Janet grabbed Lisa's arm. "Turn around," she begged. "I can't go up there."

Lisa spotted a side street coming up on their right. She braked, signaled, and turned onto it. The TV truck continued up the hill. Lisa pulled onto the road's narrow shoulder and stopped. "Your parents are up there," she said. "Alone."

Janet slumped back into the seat. "I know."

Lisa watched the tumult of emotions play across Janet's face, knowing she was getting something from behind the mask.

"After you left the cabin," Janet said, "who did you talk to? Who did you tell you'd found me? What did you report?"

"Nothing," Lisa said. "I talked to Phil, my boss in LA, but that was it."

"What about your—"

"Oriel?"

Janet nodded.

"He didn't talk to anyone. He knows how to keep a secret. So does Phil, especially from the competition. In fact, I didn't even use my phone to call him, I used Oriel's. I've turned off everything that would let anyone locate me."

Lisa could see Janet evaluating whether or not to believe her.

In a very small voice, Janet asked, "Did he?"

"Why sure," Lisa said, then hesitated. "At least, I think…." She caught a glimpse of another satellite truck heading for the cabin on the road behind them. "Shit!"

she exclaimed. She pounded the steering wheel with her fists. "Shit! Shit! Shit!"

Janet gaped at her.

"You're right," Lisa said, "we can't go back up there." The morsel of satisfaction she'd just tasted turned to poison and flowed out of her like a sudden burst of diarrhea. "Stupid mistake! *Stupid!*" She put her hands over her face. "Goddammit! I'm fucked." She pulled her hands away to look at Janet, who was staring wide-eyed at Lisa's outburst. "*We're* fucked. You too."

Janet bit her lip, then reached over to Lisa. "What do you mean? How?"

"Remember yesterday, how I warned you if you ran away again you'd better hope I was the first one to find you?"

"Yeah?"

"We both just got our wishes." She slammed the car's gear selector into Drive and wrenched the wheel to turn the car around. "Merry *freaking* Christmas."

* * *

David Wade was also manually driving his rental car, heading toward the Hogan's cabin. He'd slept as best he could on the overnight flights from Portland to Atlanta, but having to change planes in Chicago had ruined the quality of what little sleep he'd gotten. He'd let the car drive itself most of the way from Atlanta but had been too keyed up to get any more sleep. As he'd approached Blowing Rock, he'd taken manual control to try to help himself settle down and focus on what he needed to do and say once he found Janet. *The most important day of my life and I'm going into it on nothing but adrenaline,* he thought, worried. *A couple more miles to go.*

Up ahead was a brightly-colored panel truck with a satellite dish on the top. It was laboring to climb the hill and he caught up to it in minutes, swearing as he did. *They found her!*

A car sped past, going the other way. Wade noted the red-headed female driver and her brunette passenger. "Hey!" *Was it?* He replayed the flash memory of the two faces, then slammed on the brakes. Despite being in the middle of a blind left-hand curve, he swerved onto the shoulder and slewed the car around to head back down the hill, ignoring the car's warnings about the unsafe and illegal maneuvers he was pulling.

"Forget it," he told the car. "This is an emergency. No, don't call 911. Phone, call Lew Crandall."

"Lew," he shouted when his assistant answered, "where's that… that Salvador guy?"

"Right now?"

"Yes, right now."

"Uhh, hang on."

Wade half-watched Crandall on the screen as he continued driving down the hill.

"Some hotel in Boone. Here."

A map and location appeared on the screen.

"Navigation," Wade ordered, "take me there."

"Course set," the car replied. "Driving."

"What's up?" Crandall asked.

"We weren't the only smart ones," Wade said. "Hope we're the quickest."

* * *

Wade pounded on the door of Lisa's hotel suite with his fist. "Miss Lange," he called. "It's David Wade. I know who's with you... besides Mr. Salvador."

Inside, Lisa and Oriel were sitting on the living room couch, Janet in an arm chair. They'd all jumped when Wade knocked.

"I'm alone," Wade said, "but that won't last long."

He waited. When nothing happened, he added, "We need to talk. You need to talk with me."

Lisa pointed toward the back part of the suite where the bedrooms were. "Go there," she whispered to Janet.

As the scientist hurried away, Lisa said, "See if he *is* alone."

Oriel went to the door and checked the security screen mounted in it. He turned back to Lisa and mouthed, "Seems to be."

"Okay,"

Keeping the security chain in place, Oriel opened the door. "Who's with you?"

"Nobody," the environmentalist replied. "Let me in. Quick. You don't want me seen here, either."

Oriel let him in and locked the door.

The environmentalist strode into the room and looked around. "Where's Janet?"

"What makes you think she's here?" Lisa asked.

"I saw her in the car with you. Coming down from her folks' place." He glanced around the room. "Now you've both got a problem. She doesn't want to face more reporters and you don't want your competitors to see her." He pointed at Lisa's and Oriel's computers on the coffee table. "You need to be the first with the interview and you're running out of time."

He smiled at Lisa's stone face, then took a step toward the rear of the suite. When Oriel moved to block him, he stopped and faced Lisa again. "That's all the confirmation I needed."

Lisa crossed her arms over her chest. "What do you want?"

"To help you... and Janet." He stepped around the coffee table to sit next to Lisa on the sofa.

She shifted to watch him. "I'll bet."

"And myself," Wade added. "Of course."

Oriel sat in the armchair. His eyes met Lisa's for a moment. He asked Wade, "Care to share with us how you plan to do that?"

"Depends on whether you're willing to keep my part quiet or not."

Lisa stared past Wade, her lips pursed, her fingers tapping the arm of the couch. When she refocused on him, she said, "Why don't you tell us how you plan to help us first?"

"Easy: you want to scoop your competition." He waved his hand at the computers on the table. "You were getting ready to do that. But once that report goes out, then what? Everyone will know where Janet is."

"Not necessarily," Lisa said. "Even if they do, so what?"

"Wouldn't you like to have continuing, exclusive access to her?"

Lisa rested her chin on her thumb, her fingers curled in front of her mouth. She squinted at Oriel, who responded with raised eyebrows. "You can do that?" she asked Wade.

"I think so," he said with a small smile. "But not here. And Janet needs to have a say in the decision."

"That would be nice, for a change," Janet said as she walked into the living room.

Wade slid toward Lisa on the sofa to make room for Janet, but she shook her head when he looked up at her. "Where would we go?" she asked.

"West," Wade said. "I know some places."

"To Portland?" Lisa asked.

Janet groaned.

"Somebody's going to wonder if you're involved again," Lisa went on, "and where you are right now."

"Another reason to move fast, so I'm not gone long."

"There aren't many places we can drive to fast," Oriel noted.

Wade's face scrunched up as he thought. "Louisville should be enough. We could charter a jet, fly the rest of the way."

"But I don't have any clothes," Janet objected, "or money, or make-up. Momma and Daddy are probably sick with worry. What do we tell them?" She shoved her hands into her jeans pockets. "It can't be much. Momma can't keep a secret… can she, Lisa?"

"That's a good point," Lisa said, ignoring Janet's jibe.

"You can go shopping if you're someplace no one expects you to be," Wade said.

"Yeah," Janet said, "like here."

"Get back," Lisa sang to herself. "Get back. Get back to where you once belonged." When Wade and Janet looked at her, puzzled, she said, "The Beatles, 19, uh, 72, I think. Old songs—hobby of mine."

Oriel slid forward on his chair so he could close his computer. "Whatever we're going to do, we need to get going."

"Yeah," Lisa said. She pointed at the other computer on the table. "Give me that," she said to Wade.

Oriel said, "While you were gone, I saw where somebody asked Reverend Baxter if Dr. Hogan was hiding at his church. He said no, of course. Getting a plane's going to take some time. Do you think—"

Lisa looked at Wade. "That would be crazy. Maybe crazy enough to work." She folded the computer's cover closed. "But I can't ask him."

Wade looked up at Janet, who laughed. "I can just see him inviting me to come on down."

"It *is* a nice bit of misdirection, though," Lisa said, smiling at her partner. "I kind of like it."

"That's what I get for hanging around with someone—I won't name any names—for so long," he said.

"You're learning," Lisa said with a wink. "At long last."

"Let's go pack while Mr. Wade makes his phone call," Oriel said as the environmentalist pulled out his phone.

"C'mon," Lisa said to Janet. "You can help me."

Janet tried on some of Lisa's clothes but they didn't fit well. Oriel offered Janet a cap to hide her hair. They stacked the equipment boxes and luggage in the living room while Wade was on the phone.

Oriel did a quick reconnaissance trip to their car, and when it appeared no one had found them yet, he and Lisa loaded it as fast as they could.

Wade was waiting when they got back from the last trip. "Baxter won't do it, but he called in a favor from some friends in Winston-Salem. They'll put us up for a few nights."

"Know how to get there?" Lisa asked.

Wade held up his phone.

"Unh-uh," Lisa said. "Think: how'd you find us?"

Wade grimaced.

"Disable your phone." She turned to Oriel. "Yours too."

"Cars' nav systems can be tracked," he replied.

"Shit." Lisa stamped her foot. "Can't be helped. Let's go."

CHAPTER 19

THEY WERE HURRYING down the hotel hallway toward the exit when Lisa stopped. "Wait," she said, "I've got a better idea."

"It's all arranged," Wade said. "We can't change now."

"Yes we can," Lisa said. "We have to." She pointed at Oriel. "You need to stay."

"What?" he said. "Why?"

"You're our decoy. Listen: this whole thing's gone to shit because your phone was still live." She grabbed his arm as he started to object. "I'm not blaming you. I screwed up too. Now we take advantage of that. You stay with your stuff. We leave. Last you saw me, I was taking Janet home. You don't know where I've gone. My phone's dead or something. You can't trace me." She turned to Wade. "Anyone seen you?"

He shrugged. "I don't think so."

"Good. We go with you, Janet and me. I take some camera equipment and the video so I can file my report from an undisclosed location."

"I don't see how that helps anything," Janet said.

Lisa held up a finger. "One, if no one knows Mr. Wade's here, no one will think to track his phone or his car. That makes it safer for us to get to Winston-Salem. Two, once we get there, we can get you some of your stuff, especially if, three, Oriel tells my competition he thinks we're headed somewhere else." She looked at Oriel. "You can come up with something." She turned back to Wade. "Meanwhile, four, you have more freedom to work on getting all of us out of here."

Wade rubbed his chin. "Might work."

"It's also one less person our hosts have to put up," Lisa said. "They'll appreciate that."

"How do we get back together?" Oriel asked.

"I'll get word to you somehow," Lisa said, "maybe through Phil."

"I don't know," Oriel said.

"One car's easier to hide too. If they haven't done it already, someone will find out what ours is. If it's still here with you—"

"It's another false lead. Okay, I get it. Let's get my stuff."

* * *

Janet lay in the back seat of Wade's car until they were well out of Boone on their way to Winston-Salem. Lisa tucked her hair up under the cap Oriel had given Janet and stayed scrunched down in the seat.

"Momma's going to be beside herself," Janet said.

"That's good," Lisa said. When Janet gasped, she turned around to look between the seats. "I don't mean it's 'good' good, I mean it's good for us. Reporters are suckers for worried mamas. If she cries, even better. Lets us give our viewers that vicarious sorrow."

"That's mean, Lisa," Janet said.

Lisa raised her hand. "Guilty as charged. It's one of the ways we get viewers."

"That's very cynical." Janet sat up.

"That it is," Lisa said, facing forward again.

"And if you have the chance, you'll do it again."

"Welcome to my world."

* * *

Terrell and LaWanna Collins' modest split-level home sat in the middle of the block on a residential street close to the Wake Forest University campus. Terrell, an associate professor at the Divinity School, helped Wade unload the car while LaWanna took Lisa and Janet downstairs to the guest bedrooms in the basement.

"Don't you have any other clothes?" she asked when Janet didn't put anything in her room.

Janet picked at her blouse. "I didn't expect to be coming here. It's all… somewhere else."

"You're about my size," LaWanna said. "I'll get you something." She checked the time on the clock-radio. "You must be starving."

"It's been a long day," Janet said.

* * *

"You're sure you don't want something?" Robert Hogan said to Watauga County Deputy Sheriff Louie Blake. He held up a small can of chicken noodle soup. "We've got plenty."

"I'm fine, Sir," Blake replied, sitting at the kitchen table in the cabin. "Take care of the missus."

"If she'll eat. When she gets upset like this—" Hogan's phone rang. He shoved the soup cans into the microwave and slammed the door so he could grab the phone. The name and number on the caller ID made him frown.

"What's the matter?" Blake asked.

Hogan held up the phone. "I don't know him."

Blake stood. "Answer. I'll listen with you."

Hogan accepted the call and nearly dropped the phone when Lisa's face appeared on the screen. "Where's Janet?" he said.

She held up one finger. "Is anyone with you? Any reporters?"

Hogan glanced at Blake, who shook his head. "No," Hogan said. He glanced at the deputy again, then repeated, "No. Where's—"

"Just a second," Lisa said. The image on the phone jumped wildly, then Janet appeared.

"Oh, Janet," her father gasped. His knees went weak and he grabbed the counter to keep from falling. Blake took his arm to support him. "Oh, baby."

"Hi, Daddy," Janet said, struggling to keep a tremulous smile on her face. "We gotta stop having calls like this, huh?"

"It's all right, Sweetie," Hogan said, laughing with relief. "You're okay?"

Blake caught his eye and whispered, "Where is she?"

"I'm… I'm fine. I'm with Lisa. Well, you could see that. We're okay. We're safe."

"Where are you? What happened? You know your Momma's worried sick."

Janet smiled sadly at him. "I know. I'm sorry. We were coming back and saw the TV trucks and… we couldn't stay. We're—" She glanced off screen. "We're not in

Boone anymore. That's all I want to say. Don't trace the phone number, please."

"What about your clothes and things?"

"We'll figure out a way for me to get them," Janet said. "Don't worry."

"It's hard to do anything else!"

Janet sniffled. "I know. I'm sorry." She looked off screen again.

Hogan heard voices in the background, a woman's and a man's.

"Lisa says you should go home tomorrow," Janet said after a minute. "Someone will meet you along the way."

Her father frowned. "Are you sure?"

"And don't tell the police," Janet said. "The reporters will follow them."

"But—"

"I'm *fine*, Daddy. I'm safe. Truly. It's okay."

Hogan gave his daughter a long, appraising look. "All right, Sweetheart. I'll tell Momma."

After Hogan hung up, Blake reached for the phone. "What was that number?"

"You heard her," Hogan replied, putting the phone in his pocket. "Don't trace the call."

"This is a possible kidnapping, Mr. Hogan," Blake growled. "You don't want her found?"

Hogan drew himself up to his full height. "I know my daughter," he said. "I know what I saw. Wherever she is, she's okay."

"Obstructing a police investigation is a bad idea, Sir."

Hogan turned and pointed toward the cabin's front door. "See that door, Deputy?" The officer nodded. "Don't let it hit your ass on the way out."

Blake took his hat from the table. "Even if you don't want your daughter found, Sir, there are people who do. Think about that."

"I have, Deputy. I surely have."

* * *

The next morning, Lisa called again, using LaWanna's phone, to tell Robert Hogan how to deflect reporters' questions after the news surfaced that Janet had called him. She also told him where Wade would meet him to pick up Janet's bags.

Lisa had found the interviews with Oriel too, once reporters turned their attention to him. He'd denied knowing where she was. She snuck him a quick message of thanks. "He's so good," she told Janet with a grin.

Wade returned just before lunch with Janet's bag and a tentative plan for flying them out of Winston-Salem in a couple of days.

* * *

"Hey, look at this," Lisa said after lunch. She and Janet had linked their computers to the Collins' home network. She motioned for Janet to come over to where she was sitting. "India's just announced a vaccine trial. Another failure."

Janet leaned over Lisa's shoulder to read through the article, then watched the video it linked to. "Doesn't tell me much," she said. "Mind if I try a few sites?"

Lisa handed her the computer. "Be my guest."

Twenty minutes later, Janet sat back, a hand cupping her chin, eyes squinting.

Lisa waited as patiently as she could. Janet had jumped from page to page and site to site so fast the reporter couldn't keep track of what she was looking at, much less figure out what she was looking for. She didn't seem to have found it.

Janet stood suddenly and brought her computer next to Lisa's. "Think I've got something," she said. She pulled up file after file. Some held rows of colored letters, others had diagrams full of curlicues, circles, partial circles, and bars, or tangles of ribbons and lines. "Wish I had VR."

Watching Janet work—first on one computer, then the other, then comparing the two—Lisa was struck by how different their worlds, their outlooks, even their priorities were. *Politics I understand. Refugee camps, rebel hideouts. A year ago I was in Somalia, hating the conditions, the reasons the refugees and the aid workers were there, wishing I was somewhere else. I hated it but I understood it.* She looked at the display Janet had left on her computer while she worked on her own. *That might be some kind of weird art for all I know.* She'd visited dozens of labs since she started covering the Plague, but stayed only long enough to do the interviews. She'd never been employed by a lab. *Is this what it's like* every *day? My brain hurts just watching.*

Chasing around the country since Janet had disappeared had given her time to think about what had happened since the Plague had hit and to marvel at how little so many things had changed. Now, as if this was yet another high-profile kidnapping, the news sites were full of speculation about where she and Janet were. Some of them were getting closer than she liked. *At least we're the top story—but for how long? If I don't get my story out at the right moment, something else could come up and it'll be like we never existed.*

Lisa got up and paced the length of the room, her head down, hands in her pockets. *The viruses changed the world so much. "The Eternity Plague" was just a catchy phrase. Who could have known it would have the effects it's had? Or lead to this?* She looked at Janet. *There she is, doing her scientist thing, working like a mad little beaver. What good will it do*—can *it do?*

The room was silent except for the occasional faint thumping of Janet's fingers on the screens as she worked, but the feeling of time passing and opportunity threatening to slip away from Lisa filled all the empty spaces. *What would she have done if she'd just run away again? Maybe it's her good luck that I'm here. God, I hope so.*

Lisa sighed and returned to her own computer, which Janet seemed to be done with.

"Wait," the scientist said. "Don't."

"What?"

"Give me a minute."

Janet seemed to be on to something, so Lisa stifled her impatience and sat back again to wait. After a minute stretched to five, then ten, her patience ran out. She got up and wandered around the room, looking at the photos on the wall, trying to come up with a story for each one. *This is worse than when the Laotian rebels had me. I was completely isolated then. There was nothing to do but wait. Now I can watch and listen while she works but I can't do a damn thing.*

"Ahhh," Janet said.

Lisa thought she was going to get an explanation but instead there was another round of tapping and linking, and switching back and forth between computers. She returned to her chair, leaned over the table, and angled her body so she would be in Janet's peripheral vision. She drummed her fingers on the table.

Lost in her research, Janet had forgotten Lisa existed. Finally, the scientist sat up from her crouch over the computers. She stared at the wall beyond them, then said to herself, "That explains it." She stood and stretched, letting out a big groan. As her hands flopped down to her sides, she looked around. "Oh, there you are."

"Yeah, I just got back. Went for a jog in the park, then stopped at the convenience store on the corner on the way back."

Janet was taken in for a second by Lisa's deadpan delivery. When she realized she was being kidded, her shoulders slumped. "I'm sorry. I didn't realize I was taking so long. Was it—" She looked at the clock on the computer. "Oh my gosh, Lisa! I *am* sorry."

"Well, reporters get good at waiting. Now, give it up. What'd you find out?"

Janet hesitated, then made a decision. "First, I know why the Indians failed. They thought if they could better control the expression of p53, Puma, and mTORC1 to influence their autophagic and apoptotic process activation —"

Lisa waved her hands. "Stop, stop, stop. I'm lost already. Does it help us?"

"It might." Janet rattled her right thumb and fingers against her thigh, then leaned close to Lisa. "They came so close. The mistake they made was so subtle I'm sure they had no idea they'd made it. The answer's so simple. I could—" Lisa's expression made her pull herself up short. "You know what Wade wants me to do?"

"Make a vaccine. He said that a long time ago."

"Yeah. He hasn't come right out and said so but what he wants is something like the Chinese vaccine that killed everybody who got it within a month."

"Are you sure? He's been consistent about having changed his mind."

Janet took a deep, shuddering breath. "Remember who worked for him before? Ellanna, from my lab. Now he's after me. He could have hired anyone he wanted to, but he didn't."

A puzzle piece clicked into place in Lisa's head. "Oh. You going to do it?"

Janet balled her fists on her hips and cocked her head. "How stupid do I look?"

Lisa was going to object again, but stopped.

"That's where you come in," Janet said.

Janet's sudden attitude change had Lisa's full attention. "Oh? How?"

"It's time for you to file your interview with me."

"Now you *want* me to?"

Janet's lips curled into an ironic smile. "Not really, but now you can add that I know about the Indian antidote and why it failed."

"And how to make it work."

"Absolutely not," Janet said. "I'll tell you this. The Indians and the Chinese made the same kind of mistake: they tried to fix everything all at once."

"So when you said a few months back that you were going to stop the Plague—"

"I was making the same mistake." Janet rubbed her arms as if she were cold. "I was overconfident. The problem's too big, too hard, given how little we know. I *think* I know how to change *one* thing the viruses do, but I need to test the hypothesis. I could be wrong."

"Given everything you've been through, I can almost see you wanting to be wrong."

"It doesn't matter whether I'm technically right or wrong anymore. I'll always be wrong in someone's eyes. The only way out… you were right. Running away won't solve anything. I'm not sure I want to go back to Dallas, either, though."

"So you're willing to go with Wade, then?"

Janet's eyes bugged. "God, no! Not… not to where Ellanna worked. I told you, I know what he was pushing her to do."

"Isn't that just what you've figured out, though?"

Janet got up and paced around the small room. "How can I make you understand?" she asked, half to herself.

"You want to have your cake and eat it too," Lisa snapped. "You want to solve the problem but not have to deal with the consequences, especially in the short term."

"That's not true!"

Lisa stood to face her. "Like hell it's not. And I've been goddamned nice to you. I felt sorry for you because of the way you've been treated. Well, the poor, little naïve waif act isn't going to cut it anymore. You know too much for that to be credible. And now I know," she held up her hands to stop Janet's objection, "that you *think* you know how to end the Plague. It's my job to report that and let the chips fall. It's your job to deal with it."

"You can't!"

Lisa picked up her computer. "Want to watch me?"

Janet snatched her tablet and ran out of the room.

* * *

Janet had just finished sending a hurried e-mail to Dr. Sayid when Terrell Collins knocked on her bedroom door and walked in, with Lisa on his heels, her expression grim. He got right to the point. "I'm going to have to ask all of you to leave, Dr. Hogan."

Janet gasped. "Why?"

"You heard the doorbell a few minutes ago?"

"Yeah."

"That was someone you and Miss Lange know, a Mr. Corolla?"

"Corolli," Lisa corrected. "Son of a bitch—oh, sorry," she put her hand on Collins' arm, "found us. Thought he had, anyway."

"How?" Janet asked.

"He said Reverend Baxter had told him you were here."

"Lying sack of—" Lisa stopped herself and glanced apologetically at her host. "He *is* lying. He's fishing. That's the way he works. Sometimes he gets lucky."

You know all about that, don't you? Janet thought.

Collins said, "I told him you weren't here, but I'm not a good liar."

"And he spotted it right away," Lisa said, fuming. "Dammit! Now we're trapped here."

"Where's Wade?" Janet asked.

"Oh, ffff—fudge," Lisa said. "If Corolli sees him, we're totally screwed."

Wade joined them. "I don't think he did, but Lisa's right. We won't be able to fly out, now."

"Why not?" Janet asked.

"Pilot has to file a flight plan," Wade said. "It's public information. Anyone can get it if they know how, right, Lisa?"

She grimaced.

Collins said, "Well, I'm sorry, but you can't stay here. I've seen what's happened to people when Miss Lange's colleagues descend on them. I'm not going to play Pharaoh to your Moses."

"But where can we go?" Janet asked.

"I'm afraid I can't tell you that."

CHAPTER 20

"OH KENNETH, GOOD," Sarah said as Ken Bowersox walked into her office. "I was just about to buzz you." She synced a set of files from the screen embedded in her desk to her tablet computer, then slid the center desk drawer open and dropped in a pen and notepad.

Bowersox checked the display on his phone. "Senator Hamilton called while you were doing that interview and—"

"I'm going back to my condo to get some things." She shut the desk and tablet down. "You'll be in charge while I'm gone."

"She's called a—"

"If I hurry, I can catch the 4:30 train to Norfolk, then transfer to one going to Raleigh at 6:15." She folded the small computer closed.

"But Senator Hamilton—"

"Call and tell her I won't be able to have dinner tonight. I know I promised but this is too important." She slid the device into its pouch in her black leather tote bag.

Bowersox strode to the side of her desk. "Sarah! Are you listening to me?"

Sarah slung her purse over her shoulder and walked around the desk, pulling the tote with her. "I may not be back until next week. I've got a room at the—oh!" She stopped, blinking in surprise when she realized Bowersox was standing in her way. "What?"

"I said, Senator Hamilton wants you to come up to Capitol Hill for a short-notice meeting of her subcommittee. It starts in an hour."

"But—"

"Why are you going to Raleigh all of a sudden? There's big news on the Plague. Lisa Lange's found Dr. Hogan and says she's found a cure. Hamilton wants to hear from experts. " He folded his arms across his chest. "You need to be there."

"That's where they are!"

"Nobody besides Lange knows where they are and she didn't say."

"*I* know. They're with Baxter. He's the perfect cover. He's been on their side all along."

"After what he's called her?" Bowersox sniffed the air. "If I didn't know you so well, I'd say you've been smoking something."

Sarah tapped her temple with a finger. "Intuition. That's why it's right."

"Intuition, my ass. Even if you're right, what the hell are you going to do down there?"

Sarah grimaced at him, as if she was having to explain something to a stubborn child. "We can't let these death-mongers have all the publicity. I… SAFE-T has to stand up to them, show everyone there's another way. If I'm up here when Hogan surfaces, what'll happen to the fire-proofing bill, the truck safety regs, and everything else we've been working on? They'll get buried. I have to be where the attention is."

"You could...." Bowersox sighed. "No, you won't. All right. I suppose I can stand in for you, even though the senator herself called to ask for you *by name.* Even though she wants *you* to be the lead witness." He leaned closer to Sarah. "I suppose I can take the hits when I explain that your *intuition* has told you where Hogan is, and it's more important for you to get your face in front of the cameras as soon as she appears. I've been your spear-catcher before."

Sarah gaped at her deputy. She lowered her gaze to his chest as she weighed her desires. *I've just got to get down there.* A piece of fuzz from his sweater was clinging to the front of his shirt. She picked it off and put it in the pocket of her skirt. *But Leenie's giving me a chance I haven't had in months. She knows how important that is to me.* She put the tote bag back on her desk. "You're right. I'm sorry." She smiled at him. "Tell me what I need to know for the hearing." *I'll catch the 8:30 train instead.*

* * *

"Okay, thanks, Lew." Wade ended the call. "That was my assistant, Lew Crandall," he said as he pulled a slice of pizza out of the delivery box.

Lisa poured him a glass of soda and slid it across the kitchen table to him.

"The bad news is we can't fly out of here tonight or tomorrow. Charter company doesn't have a crew." He took a bite of the pizza and chewed. "The good news is Lew found a company at Raleigh-Durham International that can go in the morning. He got us hotel rooms nearby. If we leave the hotel early, before seven, there's a good chance no one will find us."

Lisa wiped her hands and lips. "I need to tell Oriel."

"There's no rush," Wade said. "He'll have plenty of time to get you in the morning."

Lisa froze, her finger about to touch her phone's screen. "We're going with you."

Wade swallowed a mouthful of soda. "Unh-uh. This is just Janet and me."

"Wait a minute," Janet said.

"Yeah, wait a damn minute," Lisa added. "You're not stealing her away from me. Just because you were clever enough to catch our screw-up doesn't give you the right to screw me again. This is the biggest story of my career and I'm not losing it."

Wade took another bite of the pizza and savored it. "I don't see that you've got much choice, Lisa," he said, smirking.

Lisa's mouth pinched into an angry pucker, then relaxed. She touched the phone's screen, then announced in her reporter's voice, "This is Lisa Lange reporting from Winston-Salem, North Carolina. I'm staying at a safe house with David Wade and Dr. Janet Hogan. Mr. Wade plans to fly out of Raleigh tomorrow morning to a location he has refused to reveal, taking Dr. Hogan with him.

"Dr. Hogan, are you going willingly with Mr. Wade, knowing that he wants you to produce an antidote to the Eternity Plague in secret?" She held the phone toward Janet to record her answer. When Janet hesitated, Lisa pulled the phone back to ask, "Have you even agreed to his demand that you go with him?"

"That's enough!" Wade snapped. "I'm not kidnapping her."

"That's what you say," Lisa said with a cold smile. "It may not be what I say. Or suggest. I can be very persuasive without—"

"You—"

"Wouldn't think twice," Lisa said. She touched the screen as if she were stopping the recording. "I've got you by the balls, and we both know it." She picked up her glass and took a slow drink, her gaze never leaving Wade's. "The good news, and don't misinterpret this, is that while I do, I can also do something that should make you very happy."

Wade squinted at Lisa. "Like what?"

The reporter set her phone down so she could hold her pizza slice with both hands. "Mmm," she said around a mouthful, "yummy." She put the slice back on her plate, wiped her hands, and leaned forward. "You have a PR problem, Mr. Wade... have had since Day One. You want to kill people."

"No I—"

Lisa waved him to silence. "Yes, you do. That's what people think, anyway, and with good reason. Baxter's got the same problem." She tipped her head to the right. "So does Dr. Janet. Sarah's played your game, put you in the position of defending the indefensible."

"But—"

"Get a clue, Mr. Wade. People don't give a flying flip about protecting the earth if they're not going to be around to see the result. *That's* your problem."

Wade crossed his arms over his chest. "And you're going to give me that help. What do I have to do, hire you away from GlobalNews the way I hired away Dr. Barnes?"

"No, Lisa," Janet gasped.

Lisa sat back and smiled. "Nope," she said, "just take Oriel and me with you. Let us report on your and Janet's work. Exclusively. No one else gets access."

"For how long?" Wade asked.

Lisa looked at Janet. "How long do you think you'll need?"

Janet grimaced. "I don't know. It depends on a lot of things."

"I can't work with that," Wade said.

Lisa gazed across the kitchen. A Bible quote was stuck to the refrigerator door. *But if we hope for what we see not, then do we with patience wait for it. —Romans 8:25* "We can talk about that down the line."

Wade turned his plate back and forth. "I'll have to approve what you report."

"No."

Wade stared at her. Her expression didn't change.

Janet looked back and forth at them as the silence stretched. "Don't I get a vote?"

"You have another plan?" Lisa replied.

"No…."

"What's your decision, Mr. Wade?" Lisa said. "The night's not getting any younger and my pizza's getting cold."

Wade stood and shoved his chair against the table. "You can have it for breakfast on the plane."

* * *

An hour later, Janet held her gym bag across the basement hall, blocking Lisa's path as they got ready to leave. "I don't like the decisions you're making for me, or how you're making them."

"I'm not surprised," Lisa said, setting her own bag down. "I don't like it, either. I'm playing your game, helping you 'run, run, run, runaway.' Jefferson Starship, 1978."

Exasperated, Janet sighed.

"Look, I'm buying you time. I'm not sure why, but I am. Maybe I'm feeling protective, and not just of my story, which I damn sure am protecting. But like I told you before, you need to face up to your situation and take charge of it, as much as you can."

"Like maybe discovering my idea was wrong, and it won't work, so he lets me go? Until I discover I was wrong about being wrong?"

A sly smile crept across Lisa's face. "Like maybe."

"That would cut your big story short, though."

Lisa patted her on the arm. "Not your problem."

* * *

"Turn around, turn around, turn around!" Lisa exclaimed. "Don't go in!"

"What?" Wade asked. He stopped the car just short of the entrance to the parking lot of the hotel where Lew had made reservations. The rotating beacon at the Raleigh-Durham airport, half a mile north of them, swept a beam of green light across the tops of the pine trees surrounding the hotel.

"Klieg lights," Lisa said, peering through the darkness. "In the lobby. Someone's there."

Wade glanced at the rear-view mirror. Another car was approaching but it eased around them. "Anybody you know?"

"Can't tell," Lisa said. "Wait." She fished her phone out of her purse, pointed its camera lens at the hotel entrance, and zoomed in... and swore.

"Who is it?" Janet asked.

"How does he do it?" Lisa asked herself. Louder, she said, "We can't stay. It's Corolli. *Son* of a—"

Wade worked the car's heater controls. "We don't have to go in through the front. Lew can meet us at a side door."

"What's he look like?"

"Six-footer, red beard."

Lisa handed the phone to Wade. "Take a look."

It was Wade's turn to swear.

"He's got to be the luckiest—" Lisa fumed.

Janet had scooted around on the back seat to look over Wade's shoulder at the screen. "How would he know?"

Lisa glanced back at her. "Who, Corolli? To talk to Lew?"

"He's wearing one of our company shirts," Wade said. "Reporter sees it, wonders why someone's wearing it here, figures it's worth asking a few questions. Lew's not that experienced dealing with the press. Reporter senses it, asks more questions. Right, Lisa?"

"Bingo," Lisa said. "B-i-fucking-n-g-o. I swear he's the luckiest reporter I've ever met."

Another car swung around them. "I can't keep blocking traffic like this," Wade said. He gave Lisa's phone back to her, took manual control of the car, and eased forward until they were out of sight of the hotel entrance. Then he pulled to the side of the road.

"Is there a problem, Mr. Wade?" the car's computer asked. "Your destination is 43 yards behind you."

"Just a temporary stop," he replied. "What do you suggest we do?" he asked the women. He looked back at Janet. "Go to your parents' place?"

"No way," she said.

"It's probably staked out," Lisa added.

Janet slumped against the back of her seat. "Why can't they leave them alone?"

White lights exploded behind them, overlaid with flashing red and blue ones.

Wade jumped. "What the—"

Lisa glanced back. "Police. Now we're toast."

"They're going to arrest us?" Janet said.

"No," Lisa said, "but as soon as they check IDs, somebody'll catch it off the web. Dammit!" She pounded the seat with her fists.

After checking their IDs, the officer stood by the car, watching his phone for a few minutes, then rapped on Wade's window. "Seems there's lots of folks looking for all y'all," he said, "but there's no call for me to take you in. Mr. Wade, you need to stop blocking the roadway and move along. Find yourselves a place to stay tonight, all right? Good place back there." He pointed toward the hotel behind them.

"We, ah… yes, Sir, we'll do that," Wade said. As he eased away, he asked, "Ideas?"

"We can't stay anywhere near here," Lisa said.

"So we're back to the one place we've been avoiding," Janet said. "Baxter's church."

Lisa laughed.

Wade shook his head.

"What?" Janet demanded. "You got any better ideas?"

"'I can't imagine why she would ever come here,'" Lisa said, pitching her voice as low as she could, trying to imitate the minister, "'or why she would ever want to.'"

She chuckled. "Guess you don't need much imagination to be a preacher."

"You might be surprised," Janet huffed.

"Interstate's up ahead," Wade said, pointing at the overpass. "What's the name of his church?"

"Christian Covenant," Lisa said.

"Navigation," Wade said, "take us there."

"Maybe you should give him a call, let him know we're coming," Lisa said. "It would really suck if we got there and couldn't get in. I need to call Oriel." She looked back at Janet, who was staring out the window, her chin in her hand. "Having second thoughts?"

"Me?" Janet replied, meeting Lisa's gaze. "Never."

* * *

The antique clock standing in the corner of Senator Charlene Hamilton's office softly chimed nine p.m. The rest of the office suite was quiet as she and Sarah settled into chairs on opposite sides of Hamilton's desk. The senator had asked Sarah to come back to the office and sent her remaining staff home after the subcommittee hearing.

Hamilton flicked the remote control at the large screen on the wall. It switched from the coverage of the reports that Janet Hogan had been sighted in Raleigh to its default display of photos of the Senator with other dignitaries and constituents. The only sounds in the room were the ticking of the clock and someone walking down the marble hall outside the suite, whistling. Turning to Sarah, who sat across the desk from her, she said, "Think they'll run the rabbit to ground this time?"

"It's not my fault," Sarah said, knowing that wasn't much of an answer. She forced herself not to fidget.

She'd missed the 8:30 train. There was one more going out. She needed to be in Raleigh more than ever.

"It was your idea to have that little rally down there. Things have gone to hell since."

"They wouldn't have if you'd done what I told you!" Sarah snapped. "But instead, you listened to the people who were going to profit if things got worse. Now they have and it isn't what you expected and you're looking for a scapegoat." She leaned forward and stabbed the desk with her finger. "I will not take the fall for your bad decisions!"

"I'm not asking you to take a fall—"

"You wouldn't *ask*."

Hamilton glared at Sarah, who glared back. The senator slumped in her leather chair and steepled her fingers in front of her face. "Look, people aren't buying what you're selling anymore." She held up her hand to stop Sarah's protest. "I know, I know... they expected the moon and the stars but instead they've gotten the same old crap. They see trouble here, there, and everywhere and believe everything the scare-mongers say. They want somebody to do something about it *now*, not fifty years from now." She paused, debating whether to reveal what she knew. "People are starting to panic... and not the ones you might expect."

Sarah fidgeted, wishing Hamilton would get to the point. "Okay, who? Panic how?"

"Some of our friends—academics, think-tankers, staffers here on the Hill—are saying we ought to focus on our own interests and let the rest of the world fend for itself. 'Fortress America, like we really mean it,' one of them said to me."

"That's mad," Sarah said. "It's suicidal. It can't work! It *won't* work."

Hamilton recited a list of names. "Tell them. I have. They know how to spin it and put Joe Sixpack in their pockets—" She snapped her fingers. "Like *that*." She put her hand over her heart and looked toward the ceiling. "We're protecting the right-thinking people. God's on our side." She returned her gaze to Sarah. "It's already happening in Europe. Xenophobia's got a long history over there. They're even better at it than we are."

"But…."

Hamilton rested her forearms on the desktop and leaned forward over them. "Nobody's worried about not living forever anymore, Sarah. They're worried about not living past next week."

Sarah looked down at her lap, watched her hands clasp and unclasp as if they were under someone else's control. "Well, that just proves my point. People don't want to die. And they don't have to." She looked up again, met Hamilton's gaze. "SAFE-T's agile. I can shift our focus. We can do diplomacy, food security. The environmental threats are just wild stories."

The senator pulled back into her chair again. "That doesn't explain why Wade hired that other scientist and is chasing Hogan now... has her, I guess."

"We can't give up now, Leenie. We can't. He's wrong. They're all wrong. We have to be the voices of reason and hope."

Hamilton got up, walked around the desk, and reached out to take Sarah's hands. When she had them, she stepped back, pulling her lover up into an embrace. "Squeekie," she whispered into Sarah's hair, "it isn't working. What you want is a utopia. It's impossible. We don't know how to live that way." She hugged Sarah for a few moments longer, rocking her.

"We can learn," Sarah said into her shoulder.

"At what cost?" She pulled back to hold Sarah's hands. "How many will have to die to learn those lessons, Miz SAFE-T?"

"No," Sarah whispered. "Nobody."

Hamilton watched Sarah's eyes lose focus, as if she was mentally leaving the room. "It's time to face the real world," the senator said.

She's wrong, Sarah thought. *They always say that. Anything worth doing is hard. Maybe this is too hard for them, but not for me. I'm right… I'm right and they're wrong.* Aloud, she declared, "No. I can't let it go. It's going to take leadership. I can do that."

"You're not a leader if nobody's following you."

Sarah pulled her hands from Hamilton's and bent to pick up her purse. "If you're not willing to follow me, don't." She straightened up. "I'll find my followers. It's wrong to die. People understand that." She slung her purse over her shoulder. "And now, if you'll excuse me, I have a train to catch."

"Sarah!"

The door thumped shut.

Hamilton sagged against the front of her desk. "Please don't do something stupid, Sweetheart," she whispered.

* * *

"I know women who don't take that long in a fitting room," Maureen Sams said, teasing Will Baxter as he emerged, carrying three pairs of dress pants. Then she noticed the puzzled and unhappy expression on his face. "What's wrong?"

They were in a menswear store in Raleigh's North Hills Mall, taking advantage of a rare night off to do some shopping.

"You wouldn't believe the call I got while I was in there," Baxter said. He put a pair of navy pants back on the rack, then turned toward the cash register. "It was Wade."

Maureen's eyebrows arched. "Oh?"

"He's in town, with that reporter, Miss Lange." He handed the pants to the cashier and pointed his phone at the register to pay for the purchase. "And Dr. Hogan."

"I heard they found her."

"Thank you," Baxter said as he accepted the bag holding the pants. He waited until they were leaving to store to go on. "They want to come hide at the church."

"What? Where are they?"

"On their way from the airport," he said through gritted teeth.

Maureen took his hand. "What are you going to do? Are they in trouble?"

"They seem to think so. Wade looked upset. Angry. No, frustrated. But not in any physical danger."

The doors leading to the parking lot were just ahead. "Shouldn't we hurry?" Maureen asked.

Baxter opened one of the inner doors for her. "I'll call the guard detail from the car."

"And then go down to see them."

The minister opened the outer door, trying to read Maureen's expression as he did. "They asked for my help," he said, trying not to sound like he was pleading for her approval.

"I'm going with you."

"Maureen…."

She stopped at the edge of the sidewalk. Baxter stopped with her. "*Doctor* Baxter," she said, smiling to take the sting out of her words, "Doctor Sams feels compelled to help too, even while she, like her dearest friend, has her doubts about the wisdom of doing so."

Baxter gazed into her eyes for a moment, then leaned in to kiss her. "'Thy rod and thy staff,' to say nothing of my love and my Lord, 'they comfort me.'"

* * *

Janet watched Raleigh flow past her as the car headed east on I-40 toward downtown. Even at night the route was familiar, one she'd ridden or driven dozens, even hundreds of times before. Lisa and Wade were talking strategy in the front seat.

Wonder if she's recording all that, Janet mused. *Like she did with me back in Boone.* She'd caught Lisa doing it when something she'd said in the car showed up in one of her reports. She'd challenged Lisa on it and gotten a shrug and a "What did you expect?" in return.

The car passed the exit she'd have taken to go to her parents' house. The word "house" pulled her up short. *House, not home. Where is home, now? My condo's just a place. So is Michael's. Do I feel home—safe—when he holds me?* An ache of guilt and sadness throbbed in her chest when the answer wasn't an instant yes.

An odd thought struck her as she watched Wade and Lisa argue. *I haven't driven since I got to the cabin, what, ten days ago? It's always been someone else driving me… in more ways than one. I've just been a means to someone else's end.*

She considered what she'd been through and the people she'd encountered since the spring, Wade and Lisa in particular. *If I wasn't here, they wouldn't be here, doing what they're doing.* The irony of her situation left her numb. *Everybody has a stake in what happens to me, but I'm just a marionette in a mad outdoor theater in the middle of a storm. They pull on strings, thinking they have control, but they don't.*

I don't, either. She laughed to herself at the bitter truth. *Never did.* Her heartache turned to anger. *Because….*

The car slowed as it reached the South Saunders Street exit and pulled off.

Because I never tried to take control… not really. Because I let other people push me around, make the decisions for me. She recalled how she'd sent word to Sayid about what she'd discovered just the day before. How she'd snuck it to him, afraid. *Afraid of what, Janet?* She rubbed her hand on her pants, then rattled her thumb and fingers against her leg. *Of everything, wasn't it? Of dying, of living, of being wrong… of being right.*

Downtown Raleigh's skyscrapers loomed ahead of them. The church stood just beyond, hidden by the buildings and the rising ground.

Janet closed her eyes. Ellanna's words came back to her: "I'm just a scared little puppy dog." She sighed. *I was too, El. I was. And I'm tired of it. Sick and tired.* She chuckled mirthlessly. *That's something else the viruses don't cure.*

No more. No… god… damn… more.

I just have to figure out how. She chuckled again. *Yeah, no problem. Piece of cake.*

The traffic light ahead changed from yellow to red.

Sure.

CHAPTER 21

THE CHURCH PARKING LOT WAS ALL BUT EMPTY as Wade pulled in. Half a dozen cars sat in the row under the trees along the street at the south side but none in any of the four ministers' slots near the building's entrance. A few subdued lights glowed in windows of the office complex above the rear of the lot. Brighter ones shone through the glass doors of the entrances, signs of the security teams that still patrolled the building twenty-four hours a day.

"Is anyone here?" Janet asked.

"Baxter said he'd call ahead," Wade replied. "Security system's probably ID'd Lisa and me already."

They parked near the doors, got out, and unloaded the car. Wind swirled around the rectangular lot, surrounded on two sides by the sanctuary and the two-story office complex. Janet shivered and paused to zip up her coat. "Brr."

"Yeah," Lisa said. "Never thought I'd miss Somalia." She held out one of her bags. "Mr. Wade, can you carry this? I'm running out of hands."

"Sure."

"I've got a free hand too," Janet said.

Lisa passed her the video camera case. "Careful with this. It's not heavy but it's expensive."

"Good," Wade said, "we can do this in one trip. Let's get inside."

"Which door?" Lisa wondered. "Did Baxter say?"

"Let's try that one," Wade said, nodding toward the entrance to the offices.

As they tottered toward the door, headlights swept across them as a car turned into the lot.

Wade looked back. "Ah, good. That's Dr. Baxter. Let's wait."

Janet set the camera case down. Lisa did the same with one of her bags.

The car raced across the lot, heading right for them. As it got closer, Lisa was the first to see that the two men in the front seat were white. Then she recognized the passenger. "Oh, shit!" she exclaimed, fumbling for the handles of the bag she'd set down. "It's Corolli!"

A second car turned into the lot as if it was chasing the reporter's.

"Come on," Wade said. "Let's get inside."

The three grabbed their bags and hustled toward the doors as fast as their loads would allow. Wade reached the entrance first and yanked at a handle.

The door was locked.

Behind them, car doors thumped shut.

Wade tried the second door. It was locked too.

A bright light flared.

"Damn it," Lisa swore, recognizing the color of a video camera's klieg light. "Which way?"

"Over there," Wade said, pointing to his right.

They staggered that way.

"Dr. Hogan," Corolli shouted. "Why are you back in… hey!"

The second car screeched to a stop between the reporter and Randy Grant, his cameraman, and their quarry. As the driver got out, Corolli spun around the car and took off after Janet again, Grant on his heels.

"Dr. Hogan!" he shouted again. "What are you running away from? Why have you been hiding?"

Wade caught Lisa's eye. "Go on," he said to Janet, pushing her between them. He and Lisa turned to face their pursuers. He dropped his bags and grabbed Corolli as he tried to get past. Lisa did the same to block Grant.

"Leave her alone!" Wade shouted. He held only Corolli's jacket sleeve and the reporter was trying to shake free.

Lisa hugged Grant and tried to shove him away from the building while he tried to keep his balance and point the camera at Janet or Wade and Corolli. Dressed in winter coats, he and Lisa looked like circus bears stumbling through an awkward dance.

Lew Crandall, the driver of the second car, ran up to grab Corolli from behind.

"The door's locked," Janet called. She pounded on the metal frame. "Let us in!"

"I'm broadcasting live from the Christian Covenant Church in Raleigh," Corolli shouted, "where Dr. Janet Hogan is trying to hide. She's being protected by—"

"You bastard," Lisa shouted. "You're not taking her from me." She grabbed for the back of the video camera and the cables and antenna mounted there. Grant spun away and Lisa fell hard.

"Got him, Lew?" Wade asked.

"Yeah," Crandall grunted. "I think."

Corolli continued. "I'm being accosted by David Wade, President of Earth Action: Return To Harmony, who needs to follow his own advice. Why won't you let me talk to her? Has she already made some secret potion for you that's going to kill all of us?"

Gritting his teeth to keep from cursing, Wade grabbed at Corolli's microphone. The reporter waved it around to keep it out of Wade's hands.

Janet glanced over her shoulder, then cupped her hands against the glass to block the outside light so she could see inside. When she couldn't see anyone, she continued to bang on the door with her fists.

Lisa got to her feet and ran after Grant again before he could get close to Janet.

As Crandall and Wade wrestled Corolli out into the lot, two police cars turned in, their lights flashing. One blasted a couple of whoops from its siren to catch the attention of the people in the lot. A third vehicle followed them in.

Sergeant Sherinne Standing Eagle took a moment to assess the situation as she got out of her patrol car. She looked over at Officer Tad Corey as he got out of his. "You take those two," she ordered, pointing at Lisa and Grant. "I'll take these guys."

"Got 'em," Corey said and ran toward his targets.

"Hold up, now," Standing Eagle called toward Wade, Corolli, and Crandall. "Y'all hold up now."

"Dearest Lord," Baxter said as he pulled up behind the cruisers. "What now?"

"What a mess," Maureen said, shielding her eyes against the flashing lights.

* * *

Brother Elijah had been following the reports of Janet Hogan's whereabouts with great interest from his private apartment at his church. When his computer picked up Corolli's excited live reporting as he approached Baxter's church, his interest grew even more. He made a cup of coffee, then sat on his sofa to follow the events. His phone chirped every few seconds as his followers posted messages, many asking what they should do.

Nothing yet, he wrote back. *Be patient.*

When Corolli arrived at the church and cornered Janet and the others, he reached for the phone again, then stopped. "Wait," he told himself. "Wait. Good things come to those who wait."

* * *

Furious at the way the situation was unfolding, Janet turned her back on Grant and Lisa and stood still. She could see most of what was going on behind her in the reflections on the glass doors. She allowed herself a small smile when the police officer took Lisa's side and pushed the man with the camera away.

Lisa came to stand behind her, cursing under her breath. "Freaking great security Baxter's got. Real pros."

Meanwhile, Grant turned back to cover the struggle between Corolli, Wade, Crandall, and the other cop.

"Officer, these men are assaulting me," Corolli said. "They're keeping me from doing my job, as protected by the First Amendment of the Constitution. Are you going to protect my rights and stop them?"

Standing Eagle said, "All of you are going to stop right where you are and answer *my* questions."

Before she could ask, Baxter tapped her on the arm. "Let me help you, Sergeant."

"Sir, if you'll just… oh, hello, Dr. Baxter."

Corolli said, "Reverend Baxter, are these people under—"

Crandall grabbed at the reporter's microphone.

"Freeze, both of you," Standing Eagle ordered. "Either one of you act up again and Officer Corey and I will cuff both of you."

"But—" Corolli said.

"Shut it!" Standing Eagle snapped, then turned to Baxter. "What's going on here, Reverend?"

Grant moved around to get a good shot of Baxter and the officer.

"God*dammit*," Lisa fumed. "He's still getting all the good stuff. Where the hell's Oriel?"

"There's a camera right here, Lisa," Janet said, "and I'd appreciate it if you'd stop swearing."

Lisa turned, with head bowed, and squeezed Janet's shoulders. "Sorry," she said, "you're right—twice." She pulled out her phone, dialed, and pinned it between her ear and shoulder with her head as she knelt to open the camera case. "Trish, hey, it's Lisa," she said into the phone. "I need a sat-link… yeah, hold on a second."

Janet turned a little to watch Lisa link the phone, camera, and microphone together.

"I owe you one," Lisa said as she stood up and put the camera on her shoulder. "Okay, go," she said to the woman on the phone.

"I don't know this man," Baxter was saying to Standing Eagle, pointing at Crandall.

"He works for me," Wade said. "I'm—"

"I recognize you, sir," the sergeant said. "You were here in October."

"So you know what kind of person he is," Corolli said. "Reverend Baxter, why are you—"

Crandall grabbed at the reporter's mike again.

"Corey!" Standing Eagle said. She wrestled Crandall away and had him handcuffed before he realized what was happening. Corey did the same to Corolli. The officers placed the men in separate patrol cars.

As soon as she was connected into GlobalNews' network, Lisa provided her own commentary on the scene in front of her.

Standing Eagle returned to Baxter, straightening her jacket. "Okay, Reverend, can I get an explanation now?"

"Mr. Wade called me about an hour ago and asked for shelter for the night for himself, Dr. Hogan—"

"Who's that?"

Baxter pointed at Janet. "That's her, with Miss Lange."

"The one with the camera?"

Wade nodded.

"And you agreed?"

Baxter took a deep breath. "Reluctantly."

The sergeant regarded him for a moment. "Are you still willing to take them in?"

"We didn't expect… them," Wade said, glancing at the patrol car Corolli was sitting in.

"Reverend?" Standing Eagle asked again.

"I'd like Lew to come with us," Wade said.

Baxter looked up at the dark sky. "All right. Those four."

* * *

Brother Elijah picked up his phone and began typing, then stopped. *What shall I call this?* His fingers tapped against the side of the phone's case. *What am I wrapping you in, Brother Will? A chain? Arms? How do I get you to repent of your evil… and all that you've done to me these many years?*

He typed, *The woman Brother Will is shielding has listened once again to the Snake and eaten of the forbidden fruit of the Tree of Knowledge. Shall our Brother once again be the son of Cain? No! Let the Army of the Righteous gather at the temple to drive away evil and return our Brother to fealty to the Holy Word.*

Despite the hour, a crowd soon formed outside Baxter's church. Corolli and Grant were there as it did, having been released once Baxter and the others were inside.

"You thinking what I'm thinking?" Grant asked.

Hands in his pockets, the reporter scanned the scene in front of him. "Should be an interesting night."

* * *

Sarah was so eager to get off the train that she was standing at the doors, her suitcases behind her, before it had even pulled in to the station in Raleigh. When she'd boarded in Washington, she was angry and frustrated at Charlene's lack of support and the crazy things she'd said. She napped most of the way to Norfolk on the express, letting her subconscious work.

As she changed trains, she caught bits and pieces of a report from Raleigh on the screens scattered around the station. Her train was waiting at the platform. She hurried to get on board so she could catch up on the news. It told her just what she needed to know. *It's perfect,* she thought. *Like a flower opening up, revealing the beauty inside.*

In Raleigh, she ran through the nearly empty building and out to her rental car, threw her bags into the back seat, and climbed in.

"Good evening, Mrs. Green-Dale," the car's navigation system said. "I have the directions to your hotel. Shall we go?"

"No, abort," Sarah said. "Take me to the Christian Covenant Church downtown."

The computer hesitated. "I'm getting reports of police activity there."

"I know, I know. Override. I accept responsibility. Take me there."

"Very well. I'm ready."

She had to park in a public lot a block from the church. A crowd was gathering. The bright spotlight of a video camera shone in the distance. A large white truck rolled by and disappeared around the corner. *Raleigh Police Department Mobile Emergency Response Center* was painted in gold-trimmed black letters on the side. Sarah followed it, a vague memory of a parking lot entrance there tickling her brain.

That must be it, she thought when she rounded the corner and saw an even larger gathering of people bathed in bright lights. *How are people getting so close?*

An officer stopped her as she tried to slip under the yellow police tape that was stretched across the parking lot entrance. "Sorry, Ma'am," he said, "you can't go any farther."

"Oh, that's all right," Sarah said, favoring him with her best grandmotherly smile. She peered around him, straining to get a better view. "I'm just looking to see if Antonio is still in there. He was, earlier."

"Who, Ma'am?"

"Antonio Corolli. He's interviewed me before." She smiled at the officer again.

He touched the button on his headset mike. "Who should I say is looking for him?"

A few minutes later, Corolli and Grant hurried toward Sarah. "What brings you down here so late at night, Ms.

Green-Dale?" the reporter asked once Grant was in position to record the conversation.

"Earlier this evening I was a witness at Senator Hamilton's subcommittee hearing on Dr. Hogan's reappearance," Sarah said. "The senators, of course, were very concerned about what she's been doing, and now the situation is even more dire. I want Mr. Wade and Reverend Baxter to know that there are people who believe in life and want to protect and defend it."

"Does that include Dr. Hogan's life?" Corolli asked. "After all, you oppose her efforts to create an antidote."

"Of course," Sarah said, her eyes wide with surprise. "I don't believe anyone should die, not even Mr. Wade or Dr. Hogan. I'm sure there are many positive ways for them to contribute to a safer future, if only they would."

"And there are thousands of brothers and sisters here who believe just as you do," a deep male voice to Sarah's right added.

"That's certainly heartening," Sarah said as she turned toward the voice. "And I'm sure… oh, you're—"

"Brother Elijah. I'm sure you remember me from a few months ago."

"Why, yes." *All too well,* she thought. *You horned in on the rally. Now I can turn the tables.*

"Excuse me, folks," the police officer said. "I need you to move aside, please. Need to let someone through." He put a hand on Corolli's arm.

Behind them, the crowd parted as a car eased up to the police tape. The officer lifted it so the car could pass under. "Thank y'all," he said to Sarah and the others.

"Who was that, Officer?" Corolli asked.

"I don't know, Sir." He touched his earpiece. "They told me to let him through."

"I know," Grant whispered to Corolli. "Tell you later."

* * *

Lisa recorded Oriel's arrival from a darkened office next to Baxter's second-floor conference room, which overlooked the parking lot. She noted Sarah's surprise and displeasure when Brother Elijah had arrived seconds before. *That could make things interesting, but I'm stuck in here! Okay, calm down. You can't be everywhere at once.*

She got the GlobalNews studio reporter who was covering the story to take over so she could help her partner bring their bags in.

She met Oriel in the hall and hugged him. "I'm glad you're here. It's been hard doing both our jobs."

"I thought you were the 'talent' on this team," he teased.

"Quit," she said, swatting him on the arm. "You know better. There more stuff to bring in?"

"One bag. Where's our story?"

Lisa hooked her thumb at a closed door. "Having a private powwow. Kicked me out so the bad guys won't know what they're planning. You see who was at the police line?"

Oriel squinted, recalling. "Corolli. I didn't see who he was with."

"Sarah and her best buddy, Brother Elijah."

"You gonna let him have that?"

Lisa looked sideways at him. "And give up *this* story? What do *you* think?"

"I am *not* going to do that and that's final!" Janet shouted from behind the door.

Lisa turned to Oriel, her eyebrows raised. His expression matched hers. She sidled toward the door. "Maybe I should just—"

The door opened and Janet stormed out, almost knocking Lisa over. "Once you figure out what 'no' means, we can talk some more... *maybe*," Janet said over her shoulder. "Sorry, Lisa," she added as she stomped down the hall.

"Janet, wait," Maureen Sams called as she left the room and hurried after the scientist.

Lisa swallowed a curse with a pinch-lipped nod. "Wish I'd caught *that*," she whispered to Oriel. "Here." She handed him the camera. "Time to get back to work."

* * *

Sarah took Brother Elijah's arm and pulled him along the side of the church until they were out of earshot of Corolli and the other reporters who were gathering at the parking lot entrance. "Let's get one thing clear," she said to the preacher. "You are *not* in charge here."

Amused, he said, "I didn't realize you had a hand in calling all these people out."

"That doesn't matter," Sarah snapped. "I won't lose control of a crowd again. We can't have another riot."

Brother Elijah surveyed the people milling around them. "Well said, Sister Sarah. What's your plan?"

Sarah realized the plan she'd worked out on the trip down from Washington had been blown apart by the flash mob. *Or has it?* She smiled to herself. *No, it just got better.* "Here's what we'll do."

She was about to lay out her plan when a man in mismatched camouflage clothes strolled by, a black-handled pistol riding in a holster strapped to his thigh.

Brother Elijah spotted him too. "Brother," he said. He reached out to the man and when he stopped, the preacher pointed at the weapon. "That isn't necessary here."

"I got a right to carry it," the man said, eyeing Brother Elijah with suspicion.

"Yes, you do, you do," the preacher said, "but I wouldn't want the guardians of the temple to misunderstand your intentions. We're assembling peacefully here."

"Damn right," the man said, and walked off.

The preacher turned back to Sarah. Seeing her surprised expression, he said, "I take it you don't leave Washington very often."

Sarah collected herself. "I don't associate with those people. I presume he's part of your crowd?"

"I have no control over whom the Lord sends to answer my call."

Sarah looked at the people milling around on the street. "They need something to do, a focus. We can't... can you get them to make one of those human chains again?"

"Certainly." He took out his phone. "What else do you want them to do?" He started typing.

Sarah found herself bumping up against the limits of her plans. Too much was uncertain. "Just seal the place off," she said, temporizing. "Peacefully, of course."

"Of course." He finished typing.

A chorus of chirps, chimes, and other tones broke out around them. People checked their phones, then looked around and began linking arms and forming lines.

"Good," Sarah said. "Make sure they go all the way around."

* * *

Janet slowed but didn't stop, even when Maureen caught up to her.

Lisa and Oriel followed, keeping a discreet distance. Oriel turned up the gain on his camera's and Lisa's microphones to catch the women's conversation.

The doctor took Janet's arm and pulled her to a stop when they reached the T intersection at the end of the hall. "Didn't you say you were through running?"

Janet spun back on her, her face red, then white with fury.

Maureen took her other arm. "Don't get mad at me." She met her angry glare with a gentle gaze. "It's time to put away wrath."

Janet's hard breathing slowed.

"And take off those running shoes," Maureen added with a soft smile.

Janet leaned back against the wall. A picture of Jesus at prayer in a garden was hanging behind Maureen. Janet gazed at it for a moment, then closed her eyes and willed herself to relax. "I'm so tired of being told what to do. Go here, no there. Do this, no that." She drew a long, slow breath, then let it out. "I don't like confrontation. It's not professional. It's not me." She opened her eyes. "It got so bad that Ellanna ran away. I was mad at her for doing it. Then I reached my breaking point and I ran too." She reached up, took Maureen's hands, and tried to return the smile. "I told myself it was time to take control but it's hard to break a bad habit."

"Time to break it. Give it a good kick."

Janet pushed off from the wall. "Like this?" She turned and did an awkward imitation of the Rockettes. "One-two-three-kick?"

"Only for you, dear," Maureen said with a laugh. "These old bones won't do that anymore, even with the viruses' help."

"I'd probably pull something too."

"So now?"

Janet looked past the doctor's shoulder at the picture.

Maureen glanced back, then looked at Janet. "Jesus—"

"Jesus knew what was to come when he accepted his burden. Me?" She looked to her right, spotted Lisa, and started. "Do you really need to be here?"

"We're not broadcasting," Lisa said. "And yes, we do. This is a historic moment."

Janet regarded the reporter for a moment. "Historical, hysterical... I'm not sure which anymore."

"So what happened in there?" Lisa asked.

Janet hooked her arm around Maureen's and turned her back toward the office they'd come from. "Doesn't matter. Forget the past. Time to make the future." She marched off, pulling Maureen with her.

Lisa and Oriel backed up ahead of them. "What are you going to do?"

Janet smiled. "You'll see."

When they got to the office, Baxter, Wade, and Crandall were watching Corolli's broadcast. As the flash mob milled around behind him, Sarah and Brother Elijah were visible in the corner of the screen, apparently arguing.

"Well," Janet said, "look who joined the party."

The men turned to her, surprised by her happy tone.

"Your best friends," she said.

Wade glanced back at the screen. "I wouldn't—"

"Reverend Baxter," Janet said, "why don't you invite them to join us?"

"What?" Baxter exclaimed.

"Janet, are you—?" Wade asked.

"Corolli too," Janet said.

Lisa glared at her.

Janet crossed her arms over her chest. "It's time to settle this.

CHAPTER 22

BROTHER ELIJAH HAD JUST RETURNED to Sarah to report the human chain was complete when she noticed a bearded man talking to Corolli. The reporter pointed at her, and the man strode over. He looked anything but happy.

"You Sarah?" he asked when he reached her.

"Sarah Green-Dale," she said, reaching out to shake hands. "President of Save—"

"That's Brother Elijah?"

Sarah pulled back her hand. "Yes, it is."

"Dr. Hogan wants to see you," Lew Crandall said. He turned without waiting for an answer.

Sarah looked at Brother Elijah.

The preacher smiled. "Mysterious are the ways of the Lord."

When they reached the police line, an officer raised the tape for them. "You too?" Sarah said as Corolli and Grant joined them.

Corolli announced to his audience, "One can only guess why Dr. Hogan, the discoverer of the Eternity

Plague, wants two of its staunchest opponents to meet with her. In a few minutes, we'll find out."

* * *

Crandall led the four into Baxter's conference room. Corolli kept providing a running commentary that Sarah tried to shut out.

Lisa was standing against the wall overlooking the parking lot, also reporting. She glanced to her left as the newcomers walked in, then turned back to Oriel, making sure her rival saw that she was ignoring him.

Janet sat at the head of the table, tapping a thin red plastic coffee stirring stick against the palm of her hand. She put the stick down, looked at the back of her hand, and scratched at a brown patch of rough skin.

Lines of people, visible through the room's big windows, were swaying back and forth beyond the police line at the parking lot entrance.

"You should close the blinds," Sarah said, waving a hand toward the windows. "People have guns out there."

Baxter stood.

"Leave them," Janet said.

"Sister Sarah speaks wisdom," Brother Elijah said. "I myself am somewhat concerned for our safety in these circumstances."

"God defends the righteous," Baxter snapped. "*Brother.*"

Raleigh Police Chief Goree, looking tired after a long day, had joined the gathering while Crandall had been fetching Sarah and the others. "It wouldn't be—"

"Leave them," Janet ordered.

Baxter, Goree, and Wade exchanged uncomfortable glances.

"Sarah, sit there." Janet indicated a seat at the table. "Brother Elijah, sit next to her." She looked around. "Hmm, we didn't set this up for a press conference. Lisa, you and Corolli come up front." She pointed to the sides of the room.

Lisa took a look out the window, then moved up to stand between the window frames. Corolli took up a position opposite her.

"Okay." Janet slapped her palms on the table, pushed herself up, stepped around the chair, and pushed it in. She picked up the little plastic stick, toyed with it for a moment, then tossed it onto the table. She flashed back to the first press conference, not even a year before. *How nervous I was then. How naïve. How little I knew.* She smiled at the thought, then lost the smile. *How little I still know.*

"I have an announcement to make," she said. "Maybe more than one. Just like the first time, when Lisa christened the Eternity Plague, the whole world's going to hear this one."

The faces in front of her were expectant but worried, the camera lenses, round voids.

In for a penny, again, Janet thought. *Keep this up and I could be rich.* She scratched at the back of her hand. "I'm going back to Dallas… back to work. It's a risk, I know—"

"Jan, you don't have to," Wade said.

"I am *not* going to elope with you," she snapped.

Oriel swung his camera around in time to catch Wade's shock and embarrassment.

"I don't care how much you—" She stopped herself. *Don't humiliate him.* "I'm not going to work in secret. There's too much at stake. I've had to think about those stakes over the past few months.

"Brother Elijah, back in the spring, when my best friend Ellanna—" A tremor ran through her body and tightened her throat. She stopped for a moment. "When Ellanna went to Reverend Baxter's convention to tell those people what we knew, you ripped her up—"

"I only wanted to raise—"

"You ripped her up! You have no idea how much you hurt her… unfairly. Maybe that's why, or the start of why she isn't here today." Janet took a moment to compose herself again. "But you did force us to start thinking more about consequences. Other people did too."

She stepped away from the table to look out the window at the parking lot and the people beyond. "I wondered," she said, "why every living thing dies. A mayfly lives a day, a bristlecone pine a thousand years, but everything dies. I know I'm not the first person to wonder why.

"As a scientist, I could talk about how death is built into the genes of every living thing, from bacteria to blue whales, how we're not born to die, exactly, but even though our genes have mechanisms that kill off damaged or malfunctioning or just old cells, eventually something fails to repair damage well enough or fast enough and the body dies.

"Or I could talk about evolution and the death of the individual as a way to ensure the survival of the species." She paused. "I could do that, but I won't."

She turned away from the window and walked around the table to put her hand on Wade's shoulder. "If I were an environmentalist like Mr. Wade, I could talk about ecosystems and overpopulation and carrying capacity, about producing food and drinkable water and processing waste, about pollution and preservation and restoration." She paused again. "But I'm not, so I won't."

She strolled around the table until she was next to Sarah, who inched away from her. "If I was a safety advocate like Ms. Green-Dale, I could talk about accidents and carelessness, about greed and malfeasance, about laws and regulations and enforcement, about protecting people from each other and themselves." She regarded Sarah for a moment with a neutral expression. "Again, I'm not, so I won't."

She took a few steps to the left so she was next to Brother Elijah. "If I were a religious person like Brother Elijah or Reverend Baxter, I could talk about faith and fate, about God's plans for us, and the Devil's, about sin and salvation, about earthly life and eternal life. I could talk about those things too, but I won't do that, either."

She returned to the head of the table. "I won't because by themselves, each of those conversations is necessary but not sufficient. They're incomplete. Science can explain some of the mechanics of how death occurs but only now is getting an idea of the biology of why. Religion offers explanations for why we die, but for people like me, those explanations don't satisfy." She glanced at Baxter to gauge his reaction. He didn't seem upset. "I want to know the why behind the why, and to me, saying, 'It's God's plan' is saying, 'I don't know. Stop asking questions.' Meanwhile, advocates place blame on people but refuse to accept the randomness of natural phenomena. The solutions they try to impose are never quite good enough or complete enough... and never will be.

"So despite our best efforts to prevent it or explain it or make it palatable, death still comes for every living thing. The Eternity Viruses didn't change that, much as some of us might wish they had. What they *have* done is leave us confused, upset and afraid, wondering what's next."

She shoved her hands in her pockets and gazed at the top of the table for a moment. "I can't tell you what's going to happen next. If that's what you were hoping for, I'm going to disappoint you. I know a tiny little bit, but not a lot. I suspect a little more."

She looked up again. "I know we don't know how to live forever. Our minds aren't built for it. Our institutions aren't, either. What does 'forever' mean, anyway? A thousand years? A million? A billion? No, much, much longer than that. So much that we can't grasp it.

"Even if we could grasp it, we couldn't do it. Astronomers say the universe will eventually dissolve into isolated atoms so far apart and so cold they can't interact. Some religions say the universe will end with God's final judgment. Maybe *some*thing of us will survive that day, but it won't be our physical bodies and it won't be here on earth."

"Amen," Baxter said.

Janet scanned the people seated at the table, stopping at Sarah as she continued. "Whether either of those ideas is right, or something else is, I don't know, but I know this: living forever on earth in our current bodies is a pipe-dream, a fantasy, and acting as if we can or even should is a waste of time." She stabbed the back of the chair with her finger as she said, "It. Won't. Happen.

"I *suspect* something else: that in the end, all of what we're doing now won't matter. Reverend Baxter and Brother Elijah may not believe in evolution but I *know* it's at work right now. I *know* the Eternity Viruses are changing, mutating. Right now. Viruses are never static, they're changing all the time. We've been so caught up in what they did a year ago that no one's been watching to see how they're changing. What are they doing to us *now* that we don't know about? This?" She held up her hand to show everyone the discolored patch. "I'd like to think it's just a stress reaction, but it doesn't look like any I've seen before."

Maureen Sams shook her head, a worried look on her face. Wade leaned forward.

"How can we find out what's happening to the viruses? They're all changing in different ways. Some of those mutations will survive, many won't. What will those surviving effects be? Will we be able to tell the difference between a bad change and a good one? Will we find out before it's too late? Look at how we've struggled with what the viruses have already done, and many of us think those changes were good."

Janet took a deep breath, held it, and let it out. "So, like I said at the start, I'm going back to Dallas, where I can do what I'm pretty sure I can do: restart the aging process. I'm going to do it in public, so everyone can see what I do every step of the way."

"You can't!" Sarah exclaimed.

"Sister Janet—" Brother Elijah said.

"I must," Janet said, cutting him off. "I must, even knowing that because the viruses are changing and we don't know how, in the end what I do might not matter. If they surprise us again, all bets are off.

"Ellanna… I miss her so much. I wish she'd learned what I understand now. I wish she'd lived to learn this, to see past the threats and the riots and the pressure. But maybe that's the meaning of her death. Maybe it happened so I could learn from it." She paused and looked down, her chin quivering. She wiped at her eyes. "What a horrible, wonderful gift. One life—no, two; Garvin's, also—lost so the rest of us could see our way to better lives. I don't mean to blaspheme, Reverend Baxter, but isn't that why Jesus died too?" She turned to Sarah. "And see, Sarah, not all deaths are bad."

She looked around the table, a fragile smile on her face. "So that's what I'm going to do. I'm not trying to save the earth, or humanity, or anyone's soul. I'm just going to do what I think is best given what I know. I'm just me, just one person. I don't know everything. I can't do everything. You can do things too." She paused to look at Sarah and her smile strengthened. "Sarah, you've invited me to work with you, even demanded that I do."

Sarah blinked, surprised by this sudden change of direction. "It's—"

"Time we started talking about working together… all of us. We don't have to be enemies. Maybe sharing our ideas and our resources *would* be a good idea." A big yawn surprised her and the people around the table laughed. Some yawned too, or stretched. "It's been a really long day," Janet said. "Let's all get some rest… the people outside too."

Sarah and Brother Elijah exchanged glances. "We'll talk about it," Sarah said.

* * *

The room was silent for a few heartbeats after Janet finished, then everyone was talking at once, but to each other, not to her. It was as if she'd disappeared. Surprised, amused, and a little bit hurt, Janet sat down, put her chin in her hands, and watched.

Lisa and Corolli were interviewing the people nearest to them. Chief Goree and Maureen Sams had their heads together at the far end of the table.

Janet turned to look out the windows, half-expecting to see a mob surging across the parking lot toward the building. Instead, the lot was as empty as it had been earlier, a few cars scattered around the edges.

Funny, Janet thought, *first I'm the center of attention, and then, just like that,* she mentally snapped her fingers, *I'm invisible. Again. I ought to enjoy it while I can.*

The hubbub in the room died down a little and Janet turned back to see Corolli and his cameraman hustling out the door. Sarah and Brother Elijah were gone.

Chief Goree pulled out a chair and sat next to Janet. "How do you plan to get back home?"

Janet caught Wade's eye and he came over.

Lisa was interviewing Baxter.

"Let's go into the office," Janet said, standing. Once inside, she turned on the lights and Wade closed the door behind them. "Mr. Wade has a chartered jet ready for us." She glanced at him. "If he's willing, we can still use it."

"Whatever you need," Wade said, a bit too eagerly.

Janet almost snapped at him, then pulled herself up short. "Thank you." She turned to the police chief. "Big question is how we get to the airport, especially if the crowd's still here."

"You're staying here tonight?"

Janet and Wade exchanged glances. "So far as we know," she said.

"Helicopter?" Wade asked.

Goree grimaced and walked over to the office window. "It's big enough," he said, looking at the parking lot, "but I don't think my pilots would like how enclosed it is: trees on two sides, the church on the other two." He came back to them. "Our SWAT team has a Stryker we could use."

"What's that?" Janet asked.

"Armored vehicle. Army used to use them."

"Like a tank?"

Goree chuckled. "I don't dare give my cops a gun that big. But seriously, no, it's this big eight-wheeled box. Seats eight. Armor plates all over." He held up his phone. "Here's a picture."

Janet looked at it and grimaced. "No. I'm not hiding in that."

"Jan—" Wade said.

"No." She put her hand on his arm. "I'm glad you still care, but the truth is, my lab knows what I know. If…," she took a breath. "If I don't get back there for some reason, it won't matter. They know what to do."

"So what do you want to do?" the Chief asked.

"David's got a car. Can you give us an escort?"

The Chief looked thoughtful. "Ten o'clock."

"We'll be ready," Wade said.

* * *

Despite Corolli's efforts to get them to talk, Sarah and Brother Elijah said nothing to him, demanding instead time for private discussion.

Once they were out in the parking lot, Sarah said, "Now the whole world knows her plans."

"Do you accept them? Will you accept her offer?"

"She—" Sarah stopped, her hands in her coat pockets, and watched the protesters on the street. "I'll bet she thought she was pretty clever, trying to pull that switcheroo on me."

"With the whole world watching."

Sarah grunted and continued staring at the people beyond the police lines. "And yet… it seemed like she understands me. Like she wants me to go on." She glanced at Brother Elijah, then looked away. "A long time ago, a friend of mine died in a horrible accident. I never understood why. I made it my goal to see that no one would ever die again the way Charlie did. Maybe… maybe that wasn't why he died that day. Maybe there was another reason." She was silent for a long time before turning to her companion. "You?"

"The devil speaks honeyed words with a silver-gilt tongue," he said, and walked away.

* * *

Lisa and Oriel followed Baxter and Maureen into the office after Chief Goree left. Oriel was holding the camera by its handle rather than up in front of his eye.

Janet flopped down onto the sofa. "What, no more interviews?"

Lisa yawned. "I'm *done.* I'm toast." She sank onto the other end of the sofa.

Maureen came over to sit between them and took Janet's hand. She looked at the brown patch for a moment, then pulled a tube from her purse. "Let's at least put some lotion on that," she said, "and have your physician look at it when you get home."

Janet closed her eyes as Maureen spread the cream. "Yes, Doctor," she murmured, smiling. "Oh," she added, yawning, "I'm dead."

"Janet…," Wade said.

She opened her eyes. "Figuratively." She peered at him. "You superstitious?"

He looked away. "I just don't like you talking like that."

"I've got some people setting up cots downstairs," Baxter said. "One room for the men, another for the ladies. I hope that'll be all right."

"Wonderful," Janet said. "We'll sleep like the… like babies. And then in our own beds tomorrow." She yawned again. "I can't wait." She struggled to her feet, stretched, and walked over to Baxter to give him a hug. "Thank you for helping on such short notice." She hesitated, then added, "I hope you don't think I'm such an evil person now."

The minister regarded her for a moment. "Christ's love and charity are not reserved for those who are without sin. I'm just trying to follow his example."

* * *

"Hey," Lisa said to Janet a few minutes later, as they were clunking down the metal staircase toward the basement. "Hang on a second."

Janet stopped and turned. "What?"

"I want to tell you something you'll never hear me say in front of a camera."

Janet cocked her head. "Oh?"

Lisa took her arm and guided her down the stairs to the next landing. "You know why I've been chasing you so hard all these months?"

"You've told me: what I discovered, your shot at your big break."

Lisa stopped. Janet stopped with her and was puzzled by how the reporter looked up and down the stairwell before she said anything. "That's part of it, but not all. Want to know the rest?"

Janet put a hand on her hip. "I'm not sure I do."

"Yes, you do," Lisa said. "I know you do." She scanned the stairs again. "From the first press conference, I could see that you and your team were in over your heads. The story was too big for you. You were naïfs and you were going to get eaten up."

"And you wanted to see us fail," Janet said. "You're a real bitch, Lisa."

"Yes, I am. I was going to chronicle every mistake, every failure on your way to collapse, not to mention all the unrealistic hopes and dreams of all those people who didn't understand what was really happening. I wasn't there for your meltdown, when it finally happened, but I got the aftermath."

"I don't need to listen to this," Janet said, and turned to continue down the stairs.

Lisa grabbed her arm and yanked her back. "Yes, you do. In Boone, I figured you were done. Then you showed me something. And then a little more. And then tonight, you blew the roof off."

"Yeah?" Janet asked, not believing her.

"Oh, yeah. I should have sensed it during that dust-up with Sarah in your lab. Maybe I did and that kept me coming back too. Anyway, you know what you did tonight?"

Janet crossed her arms over her chest.

"You told all those self-righteous so-and-sos they had their heads up their collective ass and you were going to do what you thought was right and you didn't care who didn't like it. You know the risks and you accepted them." Lisa stopped to take a breath and grinned. "Girl, you got a pair hangin'."

Janet looked down at her chest. "I've got a what?"

Lisa's grin widened. "You've got more balls than ninety-nine-point-nine percent of the men I've known."

Janet snorted and looked away.

"And you know what else?"

"I'm afraid to ask."

"I can't wait to tell the world about what you do next."

Janet looked at Lisa for a long time. "So I'm stuck with you?"

"Sing this with me," Lisa said. "Yes it's true." She pointed at Janet. "Your turn. Same line."

Dubiously, Janet echoed her. "Yes it's true."

"I'm so happy to be stuck with you." Lisa paused. "Huey Lewis and the News, 1986."

Janet rolled her eyes. "You are so full of shit."

"Unh-uh," Lisa said. "Look here." She pointed to her own eyes. "Green, not brown."

Laughing, Janet headed down the stairs. "I'm going to bed."

CHAPTER 23

THE NEXT MORNING, Janet was sitting at a plastic folding table in the big room next to the church kitchen when Lisa walked in and sat down across from her. Janet sprinkled pepper on her over-easy eggs, then broke the yoke of one with the corner of a slice of toast. "What's up?"

"Crowd outside's gotten bigger," Lisa said. "Men-folk are planning our getaway upstairs."

Janet swallowed a mouthful of eggs. "How come you're down here?"

"I'm on a break. Oriel's with Wade and the police chief. They don't want me there so I won't give anything away." She shifted in the chair. "I know when to keep quiet, but fine. They would have told me a bullshit plan anyway, then changed to their real route at the last second."

Janet peered at Lisa over her coffee cup. "They'd lie to you?"

"It's called tactical deception." Lisa shrugged. "Same thing as I did with Oriel, what, yesterday? Day before? I forget. Anyway, it's an old game and given the circumstances, I'd have gone along. My butt's on the line too." She reached out and took Janet's hand. "That rash, or whatever it is, has gotten worse, hasn't it?"

Janet looked at the back of her hand and nodded.

"Hurt?"

"Itches sometimes. My fingers are stiff." She met Lisa's eyes. "Yes, I'm going to see my doctor when I get home."

"Don't wait." Lisa chewed on her lip, then winked at Janet. "I spent a long time developing this story. I don't want to lose it just when it's getting good."

* * *

Sarah returned to the church at 7:30. After Janet's announcement, she'd watched Brother Elijah's flash mob for a while. The late hour had taken its toll and the crowd had dwindled, although those who remained were the most agitated. She'd gone to her hotel and gotten some sleep, taking the risk nothing would happen during the early morning hours.

When she got back to the car after her nap, the navigation system warned her that driving with so little rest could be unsafe. "I know it is!" she snapped. "Let's go." Nevertheless, she let the car drive itself while she contacted Brother Elijah.

She handed him a cup of coffee when she found him. His face was puffy and his eyes were red. "You stayed here all night?"

"Someone had to provide leadership here." He tore open a packet of sweetener with his teeth and poured the powder into the cup. "I thank you for this. The night has been chilly."

Sarah scanned the parking lot. "When did all those vehicles arrive?" The matte-black, eight-wheeled Stryker hulked toward the back of the lot. The command post stood to one side, with an ambulance, other large trucks, and patrol cars parked in neat rows beside it.

"The Legion brought its war horses…." The preacher paused to check the time. "About an hour ago. It would seem they fear for the life of the Queen of Death."

Sarah looked at the vehicles again, then at the people on the sidewalks around the church. "What are you going to do?"

"The Lord has not spoken to me yet," Brother Elijah said. He sipped the coffee. "He will."

Sarah put herself in front of the preacher. "No violence, understand me? No violence."

Brother Elijah held his ground. "So your newfound sympathy for this minion of Satan tells you that you shall not oppose evil wherever it appears?"

Sarah's eyes narrowed. "I choose my battles. The time, the place, the weapons. Sometimes it's better to let one's opponent seem to escape so they can enter a better trap." She turned to look at the parking lot again. "I realized this morning when I got up that the deaths of her friend and mine have different meanings. I have to honor mine."

"Speak plainly, Sister. What do you mean?"

"How does that saying go, to everything there's a time…?"

"Ecclesiastes: To every thing there is a season, and a time and a purpose under heaven."

"There's still time to achieve our purpose."

* * *

A little later, a truck loaded with metal barricades pulled into the parking lot and workers set them up along both sides of Hillsborough Street on the south side of the church. Raleigh police officers moved the crowd behind the fences so the street would be clear. Traffic along Hillsborough, and McDowell and Dawson Streets west of the church, was directed away.

As ten o'clock neared, the Stryker and some of the other vehicles moved into position, forming two columns pointed toward the narrow exit of the lot onto Hillsborough. An officer moved Wade's car, then Lisa's, into the gap between the lines.

At Brother Elijah's call, the people in the crowd flowed around to the south and west sides of the church, packing into the narrow spaces under the trees behind the barricades and filling the large lot on the west side. Uniformed and plain-clothes officers filtered through the crowd and escorted away anyone they thought might cause trouble.

Sarah and Brother Elijah found themselves caught in a tunnel of barricades that was closed off at the lot's exit onto Hillsborough Street. The police let Corolli and Grant and the other reporting teams into the lot but kept them close to the fences. News drone helicopters hovered overhead, the humming of their blades filling the space with noise.

"We should be over there," Sarah fussed, pointing down the street.

"This might be the best spot," Brother Elijah replied. "Just because the Legion is pointed at that exit doesn't mean they'll use it." He craned his neck to look at the lot's other entrance. "They have room to turn and run rather than face the righteous."

"I still don't like it," Sarah said. "I feel trapped."

* * *

Inside the church, Lisa and Oriel followed the preparations the police, Wade, Janet, Baxter, and the others were making. She and GlobalNews had agreed not to reveal when the convoy would leave or what route it would take. When Chief Goree had asked her not to, she'd grinned and said, "Remember, Oriel and I are going to be in there with you. We've gotten pretty attached to our skins over the years."

At 9:45, officers loaded the travelers' bags into their cars.

At 9:50, the chief told them, "We'll escort you to your cars at nine-fifty-nine and thirty seconds." He checked the time. "The engines will be running and the doors open. All you have to do is get in and buckle up. We'll roll as soon as you have." He turned to Lisa and Oriel. "I don't want you holding things up getting sexy shots. Speed matters."

"Roll her window down," Oriel said. "I'll hand her the camera, then get in."

"Too slow," Goree said. "Get in, *then* hand her the camera."

Oriel shrugged. "It's your show."

The chief turned to Janet, Wade, and Crandall. "We have body armor if you want it."

"Didn't help me last time," Janet said. "It'll just slow us down."

"What about you two?"

The men exchanged glances. "We'll do what Janet does," Wade said.

Goree looked at them, then turned to Sergeant Standing Eagle. "Walls of shields, Sergeant."

"Yes, Chief," she said and headed out the office door.

He checked the time again. "Run to the rest room if you need to. We'll move out in five."

Baxter stepped forward. "Let us gather for a moment of prayer." He held out his hands and Janet, Maureen, Oriel, and Chief Goree joined the circle. "You too," Baxter said to Wade, Lisa, and Crandall, smiling. "It won't hurt."

Lisa joined next to Janet. Not wanting to be left out, Wade did the same on Janet's left.

When Baxter finished, Goree said, "Time to go." He led them out of the office and down halls and stairs to the entrance behind the line of vehicles. Teams of officers with riot shields stood outside on either side of the double doors.

"I've only got two teams, Chief," Standing Eagle said. "Do we make two trips?"

"Everyone at once," Goree replied. "Miss Lange, get close behind Miss Hogan. You two gentlemen, behind Mr. Wade." He turned to the sergeant. "Ready?"

Standing Eagle opened the door in front of Janet and held it. "Form up," she ordered the officers. When they were in place, she opened the other door. "Go," she said over her shoulder.

* * *

"Here they come," Sarah said from her spot behind the barricades, watching Corolli's webcast on her phone.

Brother Elijah glanced that way then turned his attention to the lead vehicles and the crowd. "A mechanical Moses to part this sea, but this time it's the Egyptians fleeing."

* * *

Lisa reestablished her webcast link as she rushed to her car. "Gary," she shouted into her microphone, calling for the webcast's director in LA, Gary Fain. "Can you hear me?"

"Yes, Lisa," he said in her earbud, "we're with you. You're live."

A howl of protest rose from the crowd on the street beyond them as it became aware of what was happening.

"We're moving," Lisa said. She grunted as she threw herself into her seat and slammed the door. "Thanks," she said to Oriel as he handed her the camera. She pointed it forward as Janet, Wade, and Crandall got into their car.

"I hear you, Lisa," Fain said. "Okay, okay, we're getting video now."

"I can hear the crowd screaming at us," Lisa said, "even over the roar of the engines of the big vehicles in front of us. They don't like that we're leaving. Are there people in the street too?"

"No," Fain said, "it's clear."

"Okay, wish us luck."

* * *

Janet slammed her door closed and fumbled with her seat belt.

"Nervous?" Wade asked.

Janet snorted a laugh, then looked around. "Wish I'd had a chance to pee."

"Me too," he said with an embarrassed grin. He reached over to squeeze her hand. "We'll be okay. After we get through the first few blocks—"

"Go," Crandall said from the back seat. The police vehicles around them were moving.

Wade dropped the car into gear and eased ahead. As they got to the exit, the police cars on either side squeezed in close.

Janet gasped. "Be careful." Something thumped onto the top of the car and she squeaked.

Then they were out onto the street and turning right. Ahead, on their left as they turned, they got their first view of the crowd. Janet sucked in a breath through her teeth.

The patrol car on that side pulled into position and cut off the view.

* * *

Oriel squeezed his car through the narrow exit behind Janet's.

"Someone just threw a rock at Dr. Hogan's car," Lisa reported. "Did you see it? It hit the top. They're okay. The crowd is loud, angry. Lots of police, but are there enough?"

Oriel set their car in position right behind Janet's.

The convoy eased forward at first to make sure the trailing vehicles weren't left behind. Once they were all out on Hillsborough Street, they picked up speed, passing the church's office complex and coming abreast of the west lot.

"Okay, looks good," Lisa said. "Big crowd in the parking lot on the west side of the church. No one in the street. Convoy's starting to turn."

* * *

Antonio Corolli found Sarah and Brother Elijah as soon as the convoy had passed. "Ms. Green-Dale, isn't Dr. Hogan's escape a defeat for you? What are you going to do about her promise to bring back aging? Doesn't that really mean she's going to bring back death?"

Sarah watched the last vehicles inch down the street. "She *claims* she knows what to do." She turned back to Corolli. "But her own words may come back to haunt her."

"How do you mean?"

"She said the body is tremendously complicated. She may be wrong about what she thinks she knows."

"I'm sure she is," Brother Elijah put in. "The Lord will not allow evil to triumph. This may not be the End of Days, but it can be the end of ways… her ways."

"But Ms. Green-Dale," Corolli pressed, "what can you do to ensure that Brother Elijah is right?"

"There are ways," Sarah said grimly. "This isn't over."

"Protests like these? Riots?"

Sarah watched the convoy turn the corner but said nothing.

* * *

"I guess it's a good thing I sent all my notes back to the lab," Janet said, looking out her window at the people behind the barricades. "Wonder how they're doing."

"You could check," Wade said as he turned right onto McDowell St.

"I'll do it later." She looked outside again. "So many people." The police car had fallen back a little, its driver, Officer Corey, in line with the back seat.

"Just a few more blocks," Wade said, "and we'll—"

There was a sharp cracking sound to his right and something warm and wet splattered his face. He looked right and had just enough time to be shocked at what he saw before a second bullet crashed through the broken window, deflected off his cheekbone, and sent shards of bone and metal through his right eye socket and into his brain.

"Mister—" Lew Crandall shrieked. He lunged forward, only to be stopped by his seat belt.

Wade slumped back to his left, his left hand pulling the steering wheel around and drifting the car into the cruiser on that side. The officer driving it was caught by surprise and steered away from the collision. Wade's car, accelerating under the pressure of his foot on the gas pedal, crossed the remaining traffic lanes and plowed into the crowd on the sidewalk.

Meanwhile, Corey had seen Janet's window shattered by the bullets and the spray of blood inside the car. "Shots fired, shots fired!" he screamed on his radio as he followed the car. "Protectees hit!"

To his right, the people nearest the shooter were screaming in panic and trying to get away but were blocked by those behind them. As the panic spread, the compression wave of terrified people finally cleared the back of the crowd and they fled in chaos through the big parking lot and in both directions along the street.

* * *

From her position behind Janet's car, Lisa's camera caught in full detail the blood and flesh from Janet's head spattering Wade's face, then his head snapping back as the second bullet hit it.

"Oh, my God!" Lisa screamed. "They're hit! They're shot! Oh, my God, Gary, they've been shot!"

Oriel tried to follow the car as it drifted into the crowd.

"It's going to crash!" Lisa exclaimed. "Stop it, oh, please stop it! Oh, no. Oh, no."

Oriel was forced to stop as the police cars around them cut him off. As soon as they stopped, Lisa was surging out of the door, camera in hand. "She's been shot, Gary, they both have! I saw the blood. I don't know if I want to show this. I—"

An officer cut her off. "Stay back, Ma'am. Don't go any closer."

"But I'm—"

"No, Ma'am. Stay here. Let the EMTs get in."

Behind her, an ambulance chirped its siren a few times, then pulled to a stop. The driver hopped out and ran to the back to get more gear while the EMT ran to the crash scene.

Oriel made it to Lisa's side and gently took the camera from her. She glanced at him, then back at the crash scene, and took his arm. "C'mon," she said, and pulled him around the ambulance. "Gary, the car went into the crowd. We're moving around to see if we can learn any more… okay… okay… yes, there. There. I can see people down, others trying to help. Police. There's just one medic, doing triage, I guess... okay... okay... there's another." She tried to look at Janet but Oriel kept blocking her way. She got the message.

A black woman dashed past her.

"I'm a doctor," Maureen Sams called as a police officer tried to intercept her. "What do you need?" she asked the EMT who was checking the people in front of the car.

"In there," he said, pointing at Janet.

"Gloves?"

"Right here," the ambulance driver said, holding out a box.

"Ma'am," the police officer next to Lisa said, "I need you two to move back, please."

"Yeah, okay." Lisa glanced behind her and guided Oriel toward the far sidewalk. "Gary," she said, "they're setting up the perimeter now. Oh, here's Reverend Baxter."

One of the officers intercepted him as he hurried past Lisa. "Sir, stay back please."

"I'm a minister," Baxter said. "Someone may need me in there."

"Get back, sir," the policeman replied. "Give the EMTs room."

Oriel zoomed in on the minister's horrified and heart-broken expression as he nodded and backed up.

* * *

Twelve hundred miles away in Dallas, Satya was the last person into the lab, arriving just after nine a.m. Central Time.

"Any news about Janet?" Gerardo asked, looking up from the light transmission microscope he was working at.

"I didn't watch on the way in. Want to check?"

"I don't know," he said as she walked behind him to her desk. "I'm too nervous. I'm glad she's coming home."

She set her purse down, then returned to him and put her hand on his shoulder. "Me too." She pointed at the Petri dish on the microscope's platform. "Anything new?"

"Take a look."

Satya peered into a second set of eyepieces, offset to Gerardo's right, and adjusted the focus. She examined the image for a long time. Most of the cells in the culture were in their usual disordered array, their walls showing as sharp black lines. But a few were fuzzy, blurry.

"Let me look there," she said, moving toward Gerardo's seat.

He slid off the stool to give her room.

She turned a knob to move the microscope platform up and down. Different layers of the culture slid in and out of focus. Some of the cells' nuclei were also irregular and fuzzy, not their usual tight black circles.

Gerardo stood beside Satya as she worked.

She pulled away from the eyepiece and turned to him. "Do you think…?"

"Apoptosis? From what Janet said, dying cells are the first things we should see."

* * *

Sarah and Brother Elijah struggled through the mass of people streaming away from the crash scene and those standing in shock along the sidewalk. Sarah spotted Corolli and slipped up to tap him on the shoulder.

Still talking, he turned. "I've just found Sarah Green-Dale again," he announced. "Ms. Green-Dale, what does this crash mean for your work? David Wade and Dr. Hogan were in that car. If they're dead, which I should add, we don't know at this point, will that mean you'll be able to keep a vaccine against the Plague from being developed?"

Sarah stopped hearing Corolli or the babble of the other chattering reporters when he said, "if they're dead."

She stared at the car. Paramedics and police officers were clustered around the front and the passenger compartment. A tall man with a red beard, clearly in shock, stood off to one side, talking to an officer.

"Ms. Green-Dale?"

"If they're…." Sarah took a deep breath. "Our work will continue, of course, no matter… no matter… it shouldn't have come to this."

Reverend Baxter, Lisa, Oriel, and other reporting teams gathered around them. "Brother Elijah," Lisa said, gesturing at the wrecked car, "gunshots were fired through that window. Can you consider this justified in any way?"

"I am, just as my Lord and Savior Jesus Christ was, a man of peace, and a believer in life eternal. I do not, and never have, advocated death for anyone." He looked straight at Baxter. "Unlike some men of the cloth."

"How dare you?" Baxter demanded, his whole body shaking with fury. "How dare you, Jeffrey?"

"I am—"

"Jeffrey Elijah Baxter, my little brother," the minister growled. "And you've been jealous of me since we were boys. And now you'd inflict this outrage on the dead? What demon has your tongue?" He pointed down the street, away from the crash scene. "Go! Get thee gone! You desecrate this place with your presence."

"I? Desecrate?" The preacher pushed past the people around Baxter to stand nose-to-nose with him. "That which you wished for, which you called for, has come in the most heinous form. Do you rejoice now, in the victory of the Lord God over one you labeled a servant of Satan?"

Baxter raised a clenched fist. "I should thrash you the way Daddy did when the Devil got in you."

Sarah pushed between them and shoved them apart. "No!" she cried. "No. There's been enough tragedy here."

Brother Elijah glared at Baxter for a long moment. "The Lord have mercy on your soul," he said through gritted teeth, and stalked off.

* * *

Ten minutes after the crash, the police moved the growing crowd away from the center of the parking lot. "Helicopters coming in," one said. "Give them room to land."

Another ten minutes later, after the first two helicopters and a trio of ambulances had left, the area became almost silent, the open spaces absorbing what little noise there was. The cross streets were empty. Investigators worked the scene. Markers tented the two shell casings on the sidewalk. A photographer and a videographer collected images. Spectators spoke in whispers.

Lisa found herself repeating things she'd already said until a police spokesman assembled the reporters to give them an update: there had been two fatalities, one male, one female, but he wasn't going to identify them or speculate on how they'd died. He confirmed that an investigation into all aspects of the incident would be conducted. The Raleigh PD would be asking all of the news agencies and the public for their help with eyewitness accounts and for copies of any still or video images they had. He didn't know when more information would be available.

Lisa went through the motions of recording and reporting what he'd said. Her mind kept flashing back to what she'd seen in those first awful seconds. Every replay went through her mind slower and slower.

"We'll come back to LA in thirty seconds," Gary Fain said in Lisa's ear. "Ronnie, you'll pick up with your guests."

Grateful for the change, Lisa wrapped up what had happened. She could feel herself coming apart. With six seconds to go before the shift, she said, "Now we'll return to our studio in Los Angeles. Reporting live from Raleigh, North Carolina, I'm Lisa Lange." She continued to stare into the lens of Oriel's camera until she heard the director guiding the studio program, then took a step toward Oriel. "Put the camera down," she said, her voice husky.

Puzzled, he set it on the ground.

Without realizing she was doing it, Lisa ran the last few steps and buried her face in his chest, sobbing.

He wrapped his arms around her, then knelt with her as her knees buckled. "It's all right," he said, stroking her hair, not knowing what else to say. "It's all right."

The other reporters and camera operators crowded around them, elbowing each other for room, holding microphones out to capture what they said.

"No, it's not," she said, shaking her head against him. "It won't ever be."

Will Baxter had been standing behind Oriel, for the moment not being interviewed, watching the police working around the crash scene. His face lined with sadness, he knelt and embraced Lisa and Oriel. "Let the Lord be your strength," he whispered.

"She's dead, she's dead," Lisa moaned.

"We don't know that," Baxter said. "Whoever perished, being innocent? As I have come to know Dr.

Hogan, I have learned she was innocent of evil. The Lord will bind her up. He will comfort you in your sorrow."

"No. No."

* * *

The helicopter thrummed northeastward, heading for the WakeMed hospital complex. Inside, the flight nurse kept close watch on the woman's vital signs. They were weak but holding steady. The trauma to the front of her head was severe, but not as bad as he'd first expected: lots of blood, of course, and bone loss, but from what he could see, the brain damage didn't seem too bad. She was lucky. Maybe. Brain injuries could be deceiving.

He knew she was the doc who'd been at the center of the whole mess. He wanted to do as much for her as he could, but someone else would have to deal with the brain damage, if he could keep her alive just a little longer.

Since he had a minute, he turned his attention to her hands, wanting to get her mittens off. "That's odd," he said, frowning, when he discovered the brown coating wasn't cloth but something on her skin.

"Two minutes out," the pilot said over the intercom. "Trauma team's ready. Telemetry's good. Video's good."

"Let me talk to them," the nurse said.

* * *

Mohamed Sayid ran into the lab. "Turn on the news!" he shouted. "Janet's—"

Satya grabbed him as he ran past toward her computer. "Look," she said, pulling him toward the microscope's eyepiece. "She was right. The clues she sent, they're working. The cells are dying."

“It’s working?” Sayid whispered. He hung his head, tears flowing. “Oh, Janet.”

Which Anguish was the utterest — then —
To perish, or to live?

Emily Dickinson, from "'Twas like a Maelstrom"

# # #

ACKNOWLEDGMENTS

SO MANY PEOPLE CONTRIBUTED to the development and growth of this story I know I won't be able to name all of them. So if you did and your name doesn't appear below, please know that your ideas and inputs were appreciated.

I'll start at the beginning, with Dr. Steve Garrison, of the English Department at the University of Central Oklahoma (UCO), whose "Writing the Novel" classes forced me to write the first draft of what would become my Master's Degree thesis (draft 3 of what you've just read). Dr. Christopher (Kit) Givan was instrumental in convincing me to come to UCO in the first place, and Drs. John Springer and Pamela Washington completed the book's thesis committee with Dr. Garrison. Novelist and writer-in-residence John Domini allowed me to keep working forward while the rest of his class labored over their first chapters. Then there were all of my classmates and the members of the Broncho Writers Workshop (yes, that's the correct spelling; for some reason, UCO's mascots are the Bronchos, not Broncos): Kevin Adkisson, J.C. Mahan, The Kimmy, Marty Branstead, and the rest.

Dr. Michael Kyba kindly allowed me to spend a couple days in his lab at the University of Texas—Southwestern Medical Center in Dallas, which my cousin Debra Clamp arranged.

In Arizona, the members of the Cochise Writers Group get the thank-yous, especially Cappy Hanson, Debrah Strait, Steve Smith, Annette Cafazza, Priscilla Stone, Bob Patten, Terry Frederick, and others who have come and gone. Then there are my beta readers, Tami

Balser, Susan Trombley, and Ted Mouras in Arizona, and John (Dallas) Kennedy.

Arizona funeral director Pamela Woolard was kind enough to give me a sanity-check (and a thumbs-up!) on the scene in Laval Reece's preparation room and Sierra Vista Police Department Sergeant John Kosmider provided hints on SWAT team tactics and procedures which, unfortunately, ended up on the cutting room floor when I rewrote the last 100 pages.

Mr. Russell Rian, the Public Relations Manager for the University of Texas Southwestern Medical Center, and Ms. Nimisha Savani, UT-Southwestern's Vice President for Communications, Marketing, and Public Affairs, gave their approval for me to use UT-Southwestern's name in the story. Heather Monackey of the WakeMed Health & Hospitals system's Public Relations Department gave her approval for me to use WakeMed's name.

Jeanne Cadeau did the copy editing. Harvey Stanbrough did the content editing and provided advice and guidance on self-publishing. Damon Za did the cover art. Brian Schade took the back cover photo. Thank you, one and all.

Oh, there's one more: my mother Mary, to whom this book is dedicated, for her unfailing support, even if it came in the form of asking, a few months before she died, "Are you *ever* going to finish that thing?" That was when I told her I was going to dedicate the book to her and, oh yes, I was going to finish it. And now I have.

ABOUT THE AUTHOR

Ross B. Lampert has been in love with both science and words—and hence science fiction and fantasy—since at least third grade, when he wrote a one-act SF play based on the Mercury space flights. After detours through public school, college, and the Air Force, he returned to writing full time in, appropriately enough, 2001. Today he blogs, writes occasional op-ed pieces, newspaper articles, training material, and short stories, and crafts novels in southeastern Arizona.

THANK YOU AND PLEASE

Thank you for reading The Eternity Plague. I hope you enjoyed it, or it engaged you, challenged you, or at least made you think. Now I'd like to ask you to do one of the following things. I'd appreciate it if you left a review wherever you bought the book, on Goodreads or any other readers' web site, on any social media platform you use, or on my web site (where you can also sign up for my occasional newsletter). Or tell one friend about the book. Just one! I'll think you're wonderful if you do.

CONNECT WITH ME ONLINE

Web site: http://www.rossblampert.com
Twitter: http://www.twitter.com/#!/Ross_B_Lampert
Facebook: https://www.facebook.com/rblampert
LinkedIn: http://www.linkedin.com/in/rblampert
Google Plus: http://google.com/+RossLampert
Goodreads: https://www.goodreads.com/user/show/1132463-ross-lampert